THE WALLED CITY

By the same Author

*

THE FLAME TREES OF THIKA
(MEMORIES OF AN AFRICAN CHILDHOOD)
THE MOTTLED LIZARD
LOVE AMONG THE DAUGHTERS
WHITE MAN'S COUNTRY
(LORD DELAMERE AND THE MAKING OF KENYA)
EAST AFRICA
(COMMONWEALTH IN PICTURES)
RACE AND POLITICS IN KENYA
(WITH MARGERY PERHAM)
THE SORCERER'S APPRENTICE
(A JOURNEY THROUGH EAST AFRICA)
FOUR GUINEAS
A NEW EARTH
FORKS AND HOPE
BACK STREET NEW WORLDS
(A LOOK AT IMMIGRANTS IN BRITAIN)
BRAVE NEW VICTUALS
(AN INQUIRY INTO MODERN FOOD PRODUCTION)
THEIR SHINING ELDORADO
(A JOURNEY THROUGH AUSTRALIA)

NOVELS

DEATH OF AN ARYAN
MURDER ON SAFARI
MURDER AT GOVERNMENT HOUSE
RED STRANGERS
(A STORY OF KENYA)
THE WALLED CITY
I DON'T MIND IF I DO
A THING TO LOVE
RED ROCK WILDERNESS
THE MERRY HIPPO
A MAN FROM NOWHERE

The Walled City

A Novel by

Elspeth Huxley

1973

Chatto and Windus

London

PUBLISHED BY
Chatto & Windus Ltd
42 William IV Street
London WC2N 4DF

*

Clarke, Irwin & Co. Ltd.
Toronto

First published 1948
Second Impression 1973

ISBN 0 7011 2003 7

© Elspeth Huxley 1948

Printed in Great Britain by
Redwood Press Limited
Trowbridge, Wiltshire

Prologue

1942

I

A SILVER-HAIRED man with a fresh complexion and incisive features sat looking at *Punch* in front of a coal fire burning comfortably in the grate. The January afternoon was raw and the sky glum, and a cold wind cut down St. James's, plucking at the hats and skirts of people hurrying past the club windows. Inside it was warm and cosy, but neither this elderly man stretching out his damp shoes towards the fire, nor any of his fellow-members, felt at ease. The news was as bad as the weather, without either the virtue of being seasonable or the hope of early improvement. It was not pleasant to sit by and watch an empire to which your life had been devoted coming to pieces in front of your eyes.

A newcomer entered the room and joined the man by the fireside, plumping himself down in a chair opposite with a little nod and turning his attention to an evening paper. He was a short, stout man with a reddish face and white eyebrows, nearly bald, and wearing a slightly pugnacious expression. Sir Bertrand Hockling, the man already by the fireside, did not remember his name or his occupation, and knew him only to nod to and exchange a greeting.

"News is none too good," the newcomer said.

"Rotten."

"Never say die, you know. Look at Dunkirk. They're bound to start off with a few successes—value of surprise, and all that—but they'll never get us out of the East."

Sir Bertrand Hockling grunted. The subject was such a distasteful one that he had no wish to pursue it. A number of men who had been his colleagues—younger, it was true, but men he had liked and respected—were at the moment trapped in various embattled outposts of the empire, about to be submerged under an advancing tide of Asiatic invasion.

The stout man had gone back to his paper and now seemed excited by its contents.

"By George, have you seen this?" he exclaimed. "This is more like it! A slap in the face for those yellow swine—refusal to capitulate. A real fighting answer, the voice of old England at last!"

Sir Bertrand looked up, mildly surprised. "A refusal to capitulate? That sounds more like the voice of King Canute than of old England."

The stout man read aloud from the newspaper. " 'Sir Frederick Begg, the Governor and Commander-in-Chief, has returned a stirring refusal to the enemy's surrender ultimatum.' Sir Frederick Begg—ever heard of him? Of course, you were in the colonies too, I believe."

"Freddy Begg? Yes, I know him well. An excellent fellow in every way, but not one I should expect to find snorting defiance in the path of Goliath with his little sling and pebbles. May I see your paper?"

"I'll read it to you." The stout man was delighted to have an audience. "This man Begg must be a true fighter—one of the old type that made the empire. Listen to this."

He continued to read aloud a special correspondent's message. At this time, outlying pockets of British resistance in the Far East, lightly garrisoned and defenceless before the upsurge of Asiatic militarism, were falling one by one like apples from a gale-tossed tree. Now a small but strategically important island was invested, and the British public, for so long quite unaware of its existence, awoke to find it being snatched from them and glumly awaited its inevitable surrender.

The Governor's rejection of the enemy's ultimatum was therefore electrifying. Here at last was a man determined to go down fighting in the old tradition, his colours fluttering from the masthead to the end. Although it was clear to the crudest strategist that his action could not possibly postpone disaster for so much as a week, let alone avert it, the Governor's brave defiance stirred the hearts of all who read his message and enabled them to hold their heads a little higher and to walk out a little faster, their resolution reinforced.

The message itself was clear, bold, and in style somewhat Churchillian. It concluded: 'The Union Jack which flies over the fort will never be hauled down by my orders, or by the orders of any officer under my command. If the valour of our soldiers and the fortitude of our civilians should fail, in face of overwhelming odds, to prevent its seizure by blood-stained and guilty hands, rest assured that for every man struck down, a hundred will rise in his place to avenge him, and that, in God's good time, this flag, symbol of justice and freedom, will fly again over a liberated island.'

Sir Bertrand Hockling, sitting up in his easy chair and looking openly incredulous, exclaimed:

"Well, I never would have thought it of Freddy!"

But the hand in which his companion held the paper was shaking, his pink face glistened with emotion.

"Magnificent! Absolutely splendid! If we'd had more of that spirit before, and less safety first and umbrellas, we'd never have found ourselves in this mess." Only a long training in the decorum of club and city checked his impulse to wave the newspaper over his head.

"Do you know what I think, sir? I think that message should be circulated to every school in the country, and the schoolchildren made to get it by heart."

"H'm." Sir Bertrand Hockling sounded dubious. "If you feel so strongly about it, why not write to the *Times*?"

The stout man stared at him at first with surprise, then with mounting enthusiasm.

"That's not a bad idea. In fact, quite a practical notion. Yes, I believe I will."

Still gripping his paper, he hurried off to the writing-room to carry out his intention.

Once more alone, Sir Bertrand Hockling stared into the fire with lines of perplexity marking his handsome ivory forehead. It was a small point, perhaps a trivial one, but he felt that his old friend and junior, Sir Frederick Begg, had acted out of character. An excellent civil servant, an able and conscientious administrator, fair-minded, hard-working, modest, shrewd—he had many virtues, but not, one would have thought, the qualities to prompt a rather theatrical last-ditch defiance of the enemy, a somewhat highfalutin' profession of patriotic faith—and, one might add, an unsuspected turn of prose style. On the contrary, Freddy belonged to the modern school that thought in terms of child welfare and workmen's compensation rather than of flags and bayonets.

Sir Bertrand Hockling sighed and, glancing at his watch, rose to keep an appointment. It all went to show that you never could tell!

Nevertheless this little inconsistency chafed his mind like a pebble in a shoe. Several days later, back in his country home, he mentioned the puzzle to his wife, who had known well both the Beggs and, if the truth were to be told (which it was not, for she was a discreet woman) had never greatly cared for either. But she was getting old, and was not much interested.

"I don't suppose he wrote the message himself," she suggested. "Perhaps his private secretary . . ."

"Perhaps," her husband agreed, but without conviction, for he had had several private secretaries in his time, and none who had seemed in the least likely to write stirring messages about blood-stained hands and symbols of justice. His wife added dryly:

"Unfortunately it has not intimidated the enemy." For news had just come through on the wireless that this imperial outpost had fallen like the rest, and a long silence had swallowed up the Governor and his staff and the island's garrison. "I hope Lady Begg is safe, and the two girls."

"I hope so, too. Now if *she* had written the message, I shouldn't have been surprised. A remarkable woman, that. She's been the making of Freddy Begg."

"I seem to have heard that remark before."

His wife's tone was a little tart, and Sir Bertrand Hockling smiled. Women, he remembered, had never much cared for Armorel Begg. Well, whatever the faults of either—and he did not believe that these had been very black—they were paying for them now.

He opened his copy of the *Times* and saw that the stout pink-faced man had got his letter in. It urged that every school-child in Britain should learn by heart the inspiring and defiant message of one of England's finest sons.

II

The short conference was over. The General and the Rear-Admiral and their staff officers had gone, and at last the Governor was alone. His respite would be short. Someone would hurry in with a message, or to report the latest movements of the enemy, or with news of panic in the town; some snap decision would have to be taken, some preparation made for the approaching end. For he knew now—the General had made it perfectly plain —that they were without hope. The convoy of reinforcements that he had felt certain would somehow arrive, the fleets of bombers that would pulverize an encircling enemy, even the ships that would appear to take off the beleaguered garrison—all these, he knew now, were not to be. Isolated and abandoned, they could only await their destiny.

And now the final decision rested with him. It was a dreadful responsibility—appalling. He sat at his desk, a smallish man with glasses, in appearance preoccupied but nondescript, his hair thinning on top of a rather large head and his pale face lined with fatigue. Government House stood on a hill above the sea, and from its high windows he could watch the busy traffic of the harbour, the big liners and the tiny sampans and ketches, coming and going like toy vessels on a smooth blue pond. At this distance the crowded squalor of the town was hidden and the tall stone buildings, the banks and offices that British enterprise had planted there, stood out bravely, sparkling in the bright sunshine. Behind the town a range of wooded hills rose steeply and from among the trees the clean-looking white houses of the merchants, Asiatic and European, gleamed as brightly as daisies in a meadow. All looked prosperous and serene; impossible to imagine the yellow armies that crouched just beyond the hills, the black war-ships that blockaded the harbour, the bombers that might at any moment come with bellies full of fire and destruction.

As he gazed out of the window, the Governor grew more than ever appalled at the weight of his responsibility for the lives of all these defenceless people, for the continued existence, even, of this great and once thriving city. The enemy's ultimatum demanded unconditional surrender; two hours were left before it expired. The question of whether or not to accept it was a question of whether or not effective resistance could be offered—a matter for the Service commanders. The Governor's dilemma arose from the fact that these commanders had disagreed.

The General's view had been pessimistic. With the forces at his disposal he could delay the enemy for perhaps four days, perhaps less—certainly not for more. In those four days the town would be bombed and set alight and thousands of civilians would perish and most of his own small force of soldiers would die. In war it was sometimes necessary, he had said, to make great sacrifices in order to gain time or to inflict critical losses on the enemy. In this case the time gained could be put to no good purpose and the losses likely to be inflicted were of no account. In such a predicament resistance was useless, surrender the abhorrent but humane course.

The Rear-Admiral had disagreed. No local commander, he had said, was in a position to know whether a delay of even four days would so throw out the enemy's time-table as to allow advantage to be gained in some other field. It might be that by tying up the enemy's forces even for that short time, the passage of convoys now steaming to the relief of the main naval base would be eased. There was also the question of morale. The meek surrender of British outposts at the mere threat of battle, besides being in itself ignominious, would so lower British prestige throughout the East as to render hopeless the task of those attempting to rally Asiatic resistance to the invader. Such chicken-hearted conduct (the Rear-Admiral had exclaimed, striking the table) would delight our enemies and appal our friends. And, finally, his simple orders were to resist the enemy. Better men than he had gone down fighting, and unless those orders were countermanded, he and the forces under him would obey them to the end.

And so, faced by this divided counsel, Sir Frederick Begg, titular Commander-in-Chief of the armed forces, must decide. As a civilian, it seemed to him that his first duty was to the civilians he governed—the hundreds of thousands of defenceless, peaceable, unoffending Asiatics who looked to his Government for protection and succour. It was true that they had shown very little gratitude for all that had been done for them—the peace, the prosperity, the trade, justice, a sewage system, hospitals, water supplies, schools. If, at a word from him, the colony became a battlefield, it was certain that they would display (if possible) even less. Bombs would rain down on them, their flimsy city would go up in flames; starvation, cholera, typhus, all the horrors of urban paralysis, would follow. The Admiral's argument about morale was a cogent one but, as Governor responsible for all these inoffensive people, he conceived it his duty to place the safety of their lives and property above the upholding of British prestige.

And yet he hesitated, and his mind slid round the central question like water dividing before a rock. Trivialities quite unworthy of attention at such a moment crowded in: whether he would be allowed to take into captivity the medicines he used against acidity and piles, how to dispose most mercifully of his Persian cats. Impatiently, he tried to shake off such old-maidish worries, but they kept returning, and in a way there was comfort in their very limitations.

For all his working life had been spent as a link in a chain. He had never known a time when he had not been grappled to a

strong link above him. He had always known that, provided he
himself did nothing rash, he would be sustained, just as he would
always support his dependant juniors. When faced with some
uncertainty he had always been able to refer it back to his seniors
and await instructions, and every time he had climbed up a little
further there had still been a link above him to take the strain.

And now, after nearly thirty years of a linked existence, the
chain had snapped and he was left dangling in the air. Whatever
might happen to him in the grim future that lay just ahead, no
shock could exceed that which he had felt when a white-faced
private secretary had come into his office carrying a handful of
undispatched cables to tell him that communications with
Downing Street had been severed.

And he had not even the comfort of his wife's presence at his
side. Her photograph stood on the desk—a dark, handsome
woman, her face perhaps a shade cadaverous with its high cheekbones and large, deepset eyes. A face of character: and Sir
Frederick sighed. Had she been here, she would have known
what to do. All his life he had counted on her shrewd, cool
judgment; but of course he was thankful that she had got away in
time. By now, he hoped, she was well on the way to Australia,
with their elder daughter and the two Sealyhams. Whatever
might become of him, they would be safe, and Armorel could be
trusted to take good care of the girls.

Sir Frederick sighed again. He had seen next to nothing of his
daughters during their childhood, and Lavinia had been with
them now for only a few months. He had hoped, they had all
hoped, for a long-delayed spell of real family life. And how
Lavinia had enjoyed herself! You could not call her a beauty,
but she was a fine, healthy, wholesome girl who enjoyed whatever
came her way—picnics in the hills, early-morning rides on the
racecourse, balls at Government House.

As these trifling recollections skimmed like shadows through
his aching and bedevilled head, Sir Frederick frowned, for even
these thoughts carried a sting, all the more piercing for being so
irrational. How could it matter, at a time like this, whom Lavinia
had chosen to dance with and to ask to tennis parties! Yet he
recalled his own uneasiness when he had shaken hands with a
young subaltern just out from home whose face, although vaguely
familiar, was impossible to place. And he remembered the shock
it had given him later when, in answer to his question, Lavinia
had said:

"That tall, fair boy with the attractive smile? Oh, yes, he said his father used to know you, years ago. Robin Gresham is the name."

At first he could not believe that Gresham's son could be so old; but of course, his own daughter was grown up. Time, with malevolent magic, turned babes in arms into men and women almost while your back was turned. And he could see the likeness then: a hint of the father's imperious, self-confident manner. But it was rather his mother that the boy's face recalled. He had her fresh colouring and corn-tinted hair, her warm smile and, in some degree, the masculine counterpart of her beauty.

Sir Frederick had been strangely disturbed by the boy's appearance. It was not the summoning up of distasteful recollections that had upset him so much as a curious and almost crack-brained fancy that Robert Gresham had returned, through his son, to demand some form of reparation.

Of course, it was utterly ridiculous. To begin with there could be no question of reparation where there had been no injury. He had been more than fair to Gresham, he had erred, if at all, on the side of leniency and consideration. No, the man had nothing to complain about: and even had that not been so, the idea of a kind of delayed-action, third-party, long-distance retaliation was fanciful in a positively morbid way. The strain of Sir Frederick's position, the worry and anxiety, must be telling on his mind. What a time for childish fantasies, when the world's very foundations were falling apart!

Rising impatiently to his feet, he walked over to the window, pulled off his spectacles, wiped them with his handkerchief and laid them aside. They left a mark across the bridge of a rather fleshy nose; his pale eyes, no longer sheltered by lenses, looked defenceless and tired. If indeed Gresham could seek revenge for imaginary grievances, he thought bitterly, the man would be satisfied now. Failure and irresponsibility had won him freedom, success and a devotion to duty had carried his rival to the verge of an internment camp. A queer world, and no mistake! It was hard to see any justice in it, any sign of rewarded virtue or punished sin; bombs, like rain, fell on just and unjust without discrimination, everything was fortuitous and blind, and now a lifetime of hard work honestly performed in the service of his country was to be requited by ignominy, suffering and perhaps an exile's unhonoured grave.

Justice, thought Sir Frederick, would have been better served if Robert Gresham had stood now in his place, gazing down over the harbour, faced with his terrible decision and his dreadful fate. Which choice would Gresham have made? The question was no sooner posed than answered. Gresham, with his love of the fine gesture, his weakness for the panache, would have chosen resistance, without a thought for all those helpless humble people below. This notion strengthened his own resolution, for if Gresham would have followed an opposite course, the way he had chosen must surely be wise.

The time had come when he could delay no longer his unpleasant duty. Turning from the window, he sat down again at his desk and began to draft a message of capitulation. He had done no more than write a few words and scratch them out again when he was disturbed by the sound of distant thuds, followed by the rattling of his windows. He frowned: demolitions should not have started until his decision had been made known to the Service commanders. More explosions sounded, and now he could hear the high whine of aeroplanes. Going again to the window, he was amazed to see several columns of smoke ballooning up from the town and, high above it, perhaps a dozen aircraft flying in close formation. No doubt about it, the city was being bombed.

Sir Frederick was shaken with sudden indignation and a rising anger. He glanced at his watch: an hour and three-quarters to go before the ultimatum expired.

Near the harbour, a dense bank of smoke proclaimed the birth of fire. Without warning, in the midst of a truce, they were bombing unmercifully a defenceless city! How could you hope for honourable terms from such murderous monsters, or treat as equals with such barbarians? Sir Frederick's face was burning, his hands were clenched, he itched to dash on to the lawn and seize a rifle from the sentry and empty its magazine into the sky.

A more practical means of retaliation was in his power. Striding back to his desk, he lifted the telephone receiver and asked for military headquarters.

"I shall reject the ultimatum. Dispose your forces accordingly; we must fight it out to the end."

For the next hour his office was full of people coming and going, and military dispatch riders tore up and down the hill. Then the turmoil began to subside. Once his order had gone out, its execution was in other hands. The private secretary staggered out of the room with armfuls of files from the secret safe and stuffed them into the incinerator; clouds of smoke arising from a bonfire at the back soon marked, as it were, the colony's funeral pyre.

Now that the Governor's impulse had spent itself, he was again assailed by doubts. Scarcely ever before in his life had he acted in hot blood; now he condemned his action as intemperate folly. He knew in his heart that his lonely decision had been too hard and too momentous to reach by the mere weighing of pros and cons; this had been a fence that he must rush or baulk. But he was surprised at his own decision. In hot blood or in cold, his temperament inclined him towards the path of caution. It was almost as if his mind, for a moment thrown off its balance, had been seized upon and propelled by some alien force towards a verdict foreign to its nature: as if some other will, more positive than his own, had taken charge and used his mind as an instrument to work its purpose.

Once again, fantastic notions were attacking him: that was the measure of his mental exhaustion! And now, horrified by his own decision, he was afraid to reverse it. His face sweating, his hand unsteady, he sat down to his final task—the drafting of his reply to the ultimatum.

He read through the completed message without satisfaction. Clear enough, couched in the familiar words of memorandum and minute, he felt it to be colourless and even pompous, to lack conviction. Not that the occasion should be regarded as one for the display of prose style, but such a message needed to express something of the spirit of defiance that must animate the fighting man. Perhaps, then, a fighting man should be called upon to express this spirit? Should he ask the General, or, better still, the Rear-Admiral? But they would be too busy, their staff officers no less so. All at once a strange thought came into his mind. His daughter's dancing partner, Robin Gresham—he was young, a soldier, and if he followed his father he would be full of fine phrases and glib with the pen. There was no time to look further; if this young man could be found, he must tackle the job.

A little later Robin Gresham stood at attention beside the great man's desk. His surprise at the summons was not lessened when the Governor, in a rather halting and diffident manner, inquired whether he had any facility with the pen.

Round-eyed, and clearly thinking that the old boy had gone crazy, the subaltern answered:

"Well, sir, I don't know—I was going to be a journalist if it hadn't been for the war."

Sir Frederick was relieved. He explained what he wanted, and the young man seemed to understand.

"You mean, the Guards die but they never surrender—that sort of thing?" He had an engagingly frank expression, now rather amused, with the fresh pink-and-white complexion of healthy youth and fine blue eyes that, with a stab of memory, brought his mother's image to Sir Frederick's mind.

"I'll do my best, sir; but I'm no Churchill, I'm afraid."

Once more the Governor, standing at the window, gazed down at the roofs below. Half a dozen fires were burning and one at least seemed to have taken hold. He was too far away to see the firemen struggling with their hopeless task, the panic-stricken crowds running before the flames, the twisted buildings, the broken bodies. He looked at his watch. Twenty minutes to go! Then, he supposed, the bombing would start in earnest. He began to feel sick, conscious of a pain in the pit of his stomach. What madness had possessed him to sign his own death-warrant, and that of all these innocent people! It was not fair to confront him with such a responsibility. It was not fair to have sent him to this far corner of Asia and to leave him there to perish—a baby thrown out to the wolves. He turned from the window resolved to accept the ultimatum while there was still time. But Robin Gresham, who had been scribbling furiously, looked up with a flushed face and said:

"It's finished, sir. It's not as—well, as terse as I should like, but it socks the yellow-bellies straight between the eyes."

Sitting bolt upright, he read his composition rapidly in clear, melodious tones that exactly recalled the voice of his father. Sir Frederick listened with a growing sense of unreality. Of what use were these fine and empty phrases! Like the sting of a gadfly, they would serve only to anger without injuring the enemy. But now a kind of fatalism had seized hold of him, and he listened stolidly until the end.

". . . rest assured that for every man struck down, a hundred will arise in his place to avenge him, and that in due course this flag, symbol of justice and truth—no, I think freedom's better— will fly again over a liberated island."

The author paused for praise, but Sir Frederick could only ask:
"You really believe that?"

"Believe what, sir? That we shall get the place back? Oh, yes, eventually. We've been caught with our pants down at the moment, but you know what it is—every battle except the last.

(Wouldn't it be a nice change to win the first battle, just for once?) You know, I don't like that phrase 'in due course'. Sounds too official, don't you think, sir?"

"Does that condemn it? Perhaps. I feel that some reference to a higher power . . ."

"Right, sir!" Robin Gresham scored out the offending words. "You're dead right. Churchill always brings that in. How about: 'and that, in God's good time, this flag, symbol of justice——'"

"Admirable."

The door opened and a colonel and a captain came in, saluted, and introduced themselves as the officers detailed to carry the message to the wireless station. Outside, Sir Frederick saw a military car drawn up with a driver waiting at the wheel. To his dismay, one of his cats approached and rubbed itself with sensuous enjoyment against a tyre.

With a frown he signed the message, face to face with the realization that he had not yet decided what was to happen to the cats.

PART ONE

Chapter One

1929

SUNLIGHT flooding through a high-vaulted doorway was subdued by the red walls of the audience chamber to a temperate complexion, as if to show respect to the ruler who occupied a high-backed chair in the centre of the room. He sat bolt upright, his hands resting lightly on his knees, his white robes lying about him in heavy folds. Of the flesh, only slender coppery hands and bearded face were visible, and only the dark eyes moved a little in a carven visage.

The man who sat opposite lounged in an easier position, stretching long trousered legs; but in build they were not unlike. Both were tall and slender with strong, bony features and both were bearded, but one, bare-headed and blue-eyed, wore the light tailored suit of the European and the other the heavy turban, embroidered shawls and stiff hand-woven robes of the Moslem chieftain. Before them, on an ancient folding bridge-table, its green baize worn and stained, stood two small coffee cups.

They had dealt amicably with crops, rains, a cattle epidemic, the defalcations of a village headman and the workings of a new system of tax assessment. The Englishman, Robert Gresham, had one more subject to raise, and he paused to consider how it might be insinuated into the conversation. It was, of course, the most awkward, since he had left it to the last; and one, moreover, he had raised several times before, to be met with that polite agreement on the need and suave postponement of the event which he knew to be the equivalent of a refusal.

The Emir drank his coffee, wiped his mouth on the back of his hand and said in his own language:

"You will remember that we have talked before of a matter for which the Government shows particular concern. I mean the opening of a school for girls."

Gresham was startled. He had never before known the Emir to introduce a troublesome subject of his own accord. Showing

1

no sign, he drained his coffee cup and understood, before he had put it down, that the Emir had hit upon a plan which would meet the letter of the Government's demand without actually introducing the disruptive force of education among the young women of his state.

"I remember very well," he replied. "I know that your highness does not wish to see your province lag behind others, and incur the odium of a backward state. Knowing this, I have not ventured to press the matter lately, for I was confident that you were applying your mind to a search for the correct course of action. I am happy, and in no way surprised, to learn that you have been successful."

The Emir's face flickered; it might have been a smile.

"You are right in supposing that I had not put the matter aside," he answered gravely. "Although we Moslem rulers may seem to some but ignorant and stupid old men, we, too, perceive that the changes which are coming to our country must infect the young women as well as the young men. The female child of a sweeper must learn many facts and, indeed, languages of which I, the ruler of a kingdom, am ignorant."

Gresham leant forward in his chair as if to speak, but checked himself, and gazed instead into the sun-flooded yard through the open doorway. Several figures lay like sacks under the shade of a mango tree, insensible; two palace guards stood half asleep on their feet, like horses, moving now and again to shake off an overconfident fly; an assortment of individuals, robed and turbaned, crouched on their heels in the red dust, scratching their lousebites pensively and spitting now and then. Some would await an audience all day, ducking their foreheads to the dust like courting cock-birds should the Emir pass their way.

Gresham knew that nothing he could say would convert the Emir, or any other devout Moslem, to the cause of women's education. Moslem teaching and custom and the practice of fourteen centuries stood in the way. He knew also that Moslem tradition was like a precipice which you must ascend inch by inch; rush forward, and the whole weight of prejudice and resentment would come toppling down.

"Your highness understands as well as the Government," he said, "that education will consume this country like a grass fire. It will start here and there, with small fires—a lot of smoke and little flame: those are the village schools. Soon these will join up, fanned by the winds of change, and the flame will gallop from border to border. Old trees and dry grass will fall before it; behind, fresh young grass and strong young trees will arise. Perhaps you may wish that this fire had never been kindled, but you are too late. It is already burning and you cannot put it out. All you can now attempt is to control its direction."

The Emir clapped his hands and a boy appeared, curtsied to the ground and went out for more coffee. Gresham saw that the Emir was pleased with the conversation.

"You have such grass fires," he asked, "in England?"

"Very seldom. Our fires occur mostly in towns, among houses."

"But your houses have many floors, one on top of the other?"

"Most of them have."

"Then how can those on the top escape the fire?"

Gresham launched into a description of fire engines. When he explained the use of extending ladders his hearer expressed the keenest delight.

"I must have such an engine with a jointed ladder here," he exclaimed. "I will instruct my Superintendent of Works."

"But you have no high buildings."

"True; those we can build later."

"In order to set them on fire?"

"Our houses do not burn," the Emir rejoined with finality.

The small boy carried in the coffee on a wicker tray, and each drank his sweetened mouthful. Gresham knew by now that the Emir had solved the girls' school question in a way which he found particularly satisfactory and which, therefore, would be correspondingly ill-received by the Secretariat. He had a great respect for the old man—not so old, perhaps, as his robes and his dignity made him appear. At least he was young enough to add continually to his already ample harem; it was said (though no one really knew) that his children numbered over fifty head.

The Emir, for his part, rather enjoyed these talks. As in all his relations with British officials, it was a battle of wits, and Gresham's wits were the keenest of any he had yet encountered among the younger men. Apart from that he liked three things about Gresham: he was a good horseman; he never shouted, bullied or lost his temper; and he did not insist on introducing his wife. The Emir had no great liking for any Europeans, but above all he could not stand their strident, indecent women. A touch of the theatrical about Gresham perhaps attracted him too; a quality which had led the European to pick the best horses and to ride them sometimes on the native high-cantled saddle, with leather stirrups and embroidered cloths; and to have as his companion, at one time, a tame cheetah trotting at his heels. He liked Gresham, and so far as was prudent (which was not very far) he trusted him; but he moved cautiously nevertheless. The Emir's spies in the provincial office had reported several remarks of the Resident's, and at least one letter from headquarters, which seemed to show that Gresham did not stand any too well with his superiors. It would be a waste of time to show favours to a man whose star was likely to wane.

Gresham ventured to bring the Emir back to the point.

"Ah yes, the school for girls," he said, as if he had forgotten all about it. "You know I am always anxious to please the Government, and in this case I have decided myself to set the example. I shall open a school in my own compound and my own daughters shall attend."

Gresham was dumbfounded. For three years the Emir had stubbornly resisted a steady pressure from headquarters. Both men had known that sooner or later he would have to give way. But Gresham had foreseen a reluctant agreement to open a small bush school in some remote village where the girls would neither desire nor profit from the schooling, and where resentful fathers would so harry and obstruct the teacher that the school's prospect of survival would be slight.

Besides, he knew that the Emir had good reasons for his reluctance to countenance a school. Although his rule was in theory absolute, in practice he could not govern without the support of the leading families of his kingdom: the landowners, the high officials and chiefs. Recently his introduction, at the Government's behest, of certain tax reforms which mulcted the richer individuals of his kingdom had strained to the utmost their loyalty to, or perhaps acquiescence in, his authority; and he had powerful enemies whom he could not afford to flout. In fact Gresham had sympathized a good deal with his attitude towards the girls' school; the time was impolitic to make further innovations which would offer disgruntled elders an opportunity to accuse the Emir of allying himself with infidels to betray the teachings of the Prophet and the customs of the faithful.

Yet here was the Emir proposing openly to defy orthodox opinion and to start the hated school in his own quarters, to expose his own daughters to the alien contamination.

A bold stroke! Gresham looked across at the Emir with renewed admiration. Here was a man who could use his fine
intelligence and deft fingers to pinch out the poison from the root
of a snake's fang.

"You are silent," the Emir remarked. "Do you not like my
plan?"

"I was silent from surprise," Gresham said frankly. "I had not
ventured to hope that the first girls' school to be started here
would find such distinguished patronage. You have, I suppose,
considered the matter of finding a teacher worthy of such
responsibilities? The Department of Education——"

The Emir lifted a thin hand, loaded with rings, in a dignified
and imperative gesture.

"I have made arrangements. A *malam* of unblemished reputation and great learning will give instruction. A thorough knowledge of the word of God is, of course, the foundation of all
wisdom."

Gresham's admiration mounted. Of course the old fox had
outwitted his masters once again. A school as the Government
had wanted it, at large (as it were) in some village, might fail
once or twice, but the more it failed the more the Government
would be provoked into seeing it established. At that game the
Emir was bound eventually to lose. But at this game he could
not be faulted. He would play literally on his own ground, in his
women's quarters—forbidden to males. By sacrificing a morsel
of orthodoxy to allow the ingress of one impeccable, and doubtless
very ancient, scribe, he would ensure the perpetual exclusion of
all inspectors or agents. What went on behind the walls of his
compound would be nobody's business but his own. It was a
master stroke; and everyone in the palace precincts and the
Native Administration offices would savour the joke.

"It is very gratifying," he remarked, a trifly sourly, "that your
highness proposes to give the lead. But there is one objection. A
school in your own quarters will be confined to your own daughters. That hardly seems fair. We do not want to have it said that
the blessings of education are hoarded by a miserly ruler for his
own family and not shared among the common people."

"That also has occurred to me," the Emir replied, "and I shall
guard against it. First of all, I shall invite some of my officials
and the members of my Council to send their daughters to this
school. And then we shall regard it as an experiment. If the girls
benefit from their education—and of this I am far from con-

vinced—and if their fathers are satisfied, I shall establish another
school for daughters of craftsmen and traders in the town."

"And who is to be the judge of that success? Your highness
will of course be ready to accept the opinion of earnest Europeans
whose whole life has been devoted to a study of teaching."

"I am a man," the Emir said kindly, "who has always welcomed
the advice which, indeed, I am bound by treaty to accept, unless
it should conflict with a law we both acknowledge to be higher.
As for the school, by starting it in my own quarters I shall put
down the prejudice and dislike which would certainly destroy it,
were such a new and unpopular institution to be introduced into
one of my villages. You surely agree that the common people
will accept a new idea only from the hands of a trusted ruler.
Even your own women, I have been told, model their style of
dress on that of her Majesty the Queen."

Gresham knew that further talk would be a waste of energy.
He would need time to think out his next move: and meanwhile,
the Emir's decision could be presented on paper in a form pleasing to the Secretariat. He took his leave and walked through the
courtyards of the palace to the main gate where his pony waited,
hanging its head under the thin shade of a half-grown tamarisk
tree.

Chapter Two

BEYOND the crumbling earth walls of the city you could
canter for miles over the flat open grassland, peppered with
trees and scarred with cultivation; but inside the walls a pony
had to pick its way. Small children played in the dust, flocks of
brown hairy sheep pattered along the streets and blue-robed men
on donkeys trotted by. All was activity and bustle. At the open
dyeing-pits in the centre of the town the dyers dipped long strips
of cloth into a viscous liquid; others, their bodies naked save for
a loin-cloth, dripping with sweat and spray, poured water from
big gourds to refill the pits. The sour smell of fermenting indigo
mingled with the stench of numerous ponds covered with green
slime, and with the sweet, dry odour of sunbaked dust churned
by the feet of innumerable men and beasts.

Once outside the palace courtyards, Gresham looked around with the warm enjoyment he so often felt in this ancient city. Ancient, yet new; for the mud walls of its houses were continually crumbling and continually having to be rebuilt by the busy hands of its citizens. Even now men were at work packing mud into the rough shape of cannon balls and binding these with a sort of crude cement made from the residue of the dyeing-pits. Like a plant or a man, the city was always growing and being renewed, bits flaking off the cells being added; and like a plant or a man, if the flow of life were throttled it would fall away quickly into dust and leave no trace behind.

The hooves of the pony kicked up tiny spurts of dust with each footfall. He pranced a little in the sunshine, pretending to shy now at a donkey with a load of green fodder, now at a legless beggar whining in the dust, then at a toothless old woman squatting under a tree beside a tray of fly-speckled cakes. Gresham reined in his pony, threw down a coin and leant over to receive three cakes in his hand, with a ribald quip from the old woman; and threw the cakes to a hungry-looking urchin whose tight pot-belly protruded through his rags.

Sunlight poured down on to his bare head and struck through his thin clothes to his back. He rode on, humming a tune, the music of creaking saddle and jingling bit in his ears. He loved the town; however often he saw it, however long he stayed, to him it always had a sort of magic that made everything appear a little larger than life size, that added a hidden and half-comprehended meaning to the most ordinary events and scenes. He loved the town; to him the crenellated walls of the low houses were as battlements, the tin waterspouts that stuck out over the streets like ancient cannon; the blue-robed, turbaned men on donkeys were as dark-skinned warriors riding their chargers back from battle; the veiled Tuaregs who led their camels down to trade salt for kola nuts brought the very breath and mystery of the desert; and the high red walls of the private quarters behind every house concealed a host of beauties with the limpid eyes, the delicate movements and the soft colouring of gazelles.

New houses had been built by a considerate Government for its servants: rectangular, comfortable and graceless, with corrugated iron roofs and verandas running round three sides. Gresham preferred an older house built in the native style, on no precise plan, with mud walls and high mud ceilings packed over palm poles like flesh over a skeleton. The inside was white-

washed, the roof flat, and several steep, uneven stairways emerged
in unexpected places into the upper rooms. Wide arched doorways were hung with coarse hand-woven cloth and hand-made
rugs lay over uneven floors of beaten earth. It was not a convenient house. Water had to be carried upstairs in buckets,
hordes of earwigs invaded cupboards and drawers, and white
ants continually erupted from walls and floors, leaving a network
of little covered ways to mark their passage; but it was cool,
quiet and amiable, and the servants felt at ease.

He quickened his pony's pace into a canter as he approached.
Priscilla would be back, and waiting; she would enjoy the joke
about the Emir's school.

Priscilla stood by a table over a board on which a pinioned
butterfly lay: a tall young woman with corn-coloured hair
gathered into a loose bun at the back of her head. Her skin was
fair and tender, like a dog-rose, her eyes china-blue; but just now
her complexion was pallid and her eyes shadowed from heat,
exertion and malaria. Her fingers were unsteady as they stretched
a blue and black wing and pinned it to a sheet of cork.

She gazed at the butterfly for some moments, entranced by its
beauty. The colour glowed back at her like a jewel, infinitely
pure and innocent. How exquisite, she thought, and frowned.
What an absurd word, how humiliating to be thus chained to
clichés! One thought in clichés, spoke in them, and in the end
was imprisoned by them; they were like treacle in the hair. The
charming wife of a rising young colonial official: so happily
married: perfectly suited: dining to-night with the Resident:
saw your husband at polo: just off on leave. Her spirit, momentarily freed by the butterfly's wings, sank back into its prison
with scarcely a throb of revolt.

Resolutely, she fixed her mind on the pursuit of the butterfly:
the chase on foot, the capture by the bed of a dried-up river. Hot
sunshine on the rocks, a hot wind blowing sand into her eyes, a
stinking waterhole covered with scum and ringed with cattle
dung. Small boys had gathered, their eyes running; one had a
sore on his leg exuding pus on which flies had settled in a black
clot; his mother had run down, her rubbery breasts shaking like
blanc-manges; the sun was relentless and the grass withered to
an endless drab grey-brown; there had been no colour save in
the butterfly's wings.

A step aroused her, and a moment later her husband was in
the room. He smiled and kissed her, amazed, as he sometimes

was when he saw her suddenly, by the grace and brightness that his humdrum house enclosed.

"Tired, Priscilla? You must rest, after the last go of fever. You've not been out to-day?"

"Only a little way—and I found this."

He admired the butterfly—genuinely, for he had followed and at every stage encouraged her interest in the beasts and insects of this region into which she had found herself dumped: an interest that had saved her from boredom and preserved her from bridge.

"It's lovely," he added, "but you oughtn't to have gone out."

"I can't sit about doing nothing all day long!"

Her tone was brittle. He added, with intent to pacify:

"One day Robin will enjoy this collection."

She withdrew her hand from his. So like him to spoil the moment, to say the one infallibly hurting thing! She walked stiffly to the window, all on edge. Robin's photograph stood on a table; the face of a small schoolboy looked out like an eager mouse, alert, inquisitive, ready to twinkle.

"How could it possibly interest Robin! He's never even seen an African butterfly."

"Oh, yes, he has. I took him once to the Natural History Museum. When we got back——"

Gresham was silent; he knew he had offended. But what a ridiculous offence—the mere mention of their own child! The boy was becoming like a corpse under the floor-boards, something not to be talked about but never quite out of their minds. How wildly unreasonable women were! He sighed; how stale that chiché, and only half true. Of course they weren't unreasonable by their own laws, but their reason followed different channels. Like a river and a bicycle: you could make use of either to get from Oxford to London but your method of progress and your experiences by the way would not be the same.

"I spent the morning with the Emir," he remarked. "He's in his most affable frame of mind, and a new Rodean is to arise in his palace compound."

Priscilla turned back from the window, trying to smother her foolish ill-temper. But it was hard to make her interest sound genuine.

"Are you pleased?"

"Yes, I suppose so. It's what Government wants, so they'll be pleased. And a school can't do much harm."

"Or much good?"

"What good can it do? The girls will get some of the Koran by heart in Arabic, which they don't understand. They might learn to add two and two and to recite the names of a list of kings. Is that doing good?"

"Our own education starts like that, but it goes on, bit by bit. Do you think it's a useless thing? If not, why give it to men and keep it from women?"

Gresham started to walk up and down the room, his feet silent on the thick rugs and the brown sheepskins.

"That's not the point. Do you know what we're trying to do here? Mix fire and water. These people have their own ways of doing things. It doesn't look much, I know. It's a thin sort of homespun civilization, without machines and hospitals and stock exchanges. But it's theirs, and it works. They know how they want to worship God and how to keep alive on the margins of the desert. Why do we knock away the foundations? Wouldn't it be better to find out how to control our own society before telling them how to re-make theirs?"

Priscilla smiled at him, forgetting her vexation. "There you go again, Robert, campaigning for lost causes. These people live in the past, and what you are saying would put an end to all progress. Surely the age of a custom neither proves it right nor protects it from mutation. All things outlive their inspiration and become eventually vestigial. I suppose every one of our customs and beliefs is a sort of potential appendix. . . . Are you ready for luncheon?"

"Ah!" Gresham said, "but then we must let the appendix breed itself out of existence, we mustn't wrench it out by the roots, without anæsthetics. What do you really think? Should we foist all our ideas on these people? They don't want them, they haven't got tired of their own. Are ours really better? Do we care if they're better or not? Any more than the Birmingham merchant cares if his cheap earthenware is better than native pots. He wants to sell his jugs and mugs, therefore he thinks they're better. So they are, of course, for him—his wife couldn't pour her afternoon tea from a native pitcher. So I dare say he believes what he says. And I dare say we really do believe that an African woman is better off stripped of her graceful cloth and stuffed into an ugly Mother Hubbard, that she's nearer to spiritual grace when she wears gloves and carries a sunshade and sits on a hideous sofa reading *Little Women* to her sewing circle."

"But I should prefer reading *Little Women* aloud on a sofa, to grovelling on the floor when my husband came into the room—and a doctor, let's say, to attend me in childbirth than a filthy old hag with a lot of revolting spells. Robert, you're talking like a silly old pasha."

"And you like a politician, which is worse. At least my opinions have the virtue of being old-fashioned instead of mass-produced."

"If you really believe what you say, you ought to resign."

He did not answer, and Priscilla turned to stare out of the window. How foolish: they were almost angry again! The grass outside was brown and there was no view, but a creeper with large cup-shaped blue flowers tumbled over a tub, tangled and confused from lack of a pillar to climb. Resign! She saw a ship, the ocean, the low shore of Africa fading out of sight: as if a great door had blown apart.

"For heaven's sake let's have lunch," she said irritably. "I forgot to tell you, we're dining at the Residency."

"Oh, God. And Freddy Begg has descended from the Secretariat——"

"Yes, they'll both be there."

They stared at each other, united again by the pinch of their common yoke.

Chapter Three

THE hills lay like the crouched body of a starving dog, a brown skin of soil drawn tightly over rocky ribs, each deep declivity streaked with bush. A strong wind broke on the spine, and the air had a sharpness unfelt on the plain below. The view was immense but featureless: away stretched the plain into rippling seas of heat, colourless and supine. But above the skies were open, and buzzards circling high over the rocks and waving grasses were as motes of freedom.

Pagan villages were built here, high among the rocks and the smooth round boulders. Although their women had to slide a long distance down a steep path to fetch water and clamber back with heavy dripping loads, the pagans had not yet become used to the idea of security and preferred to remain aloft. Later, when they grew acclimatized and lazy, they would move down to the foot of the hills and their primitive mud huts and the rest-camp built for the use of visiting officials would moulder together into dust.

The rest-camp stood about a mile from the nearest village, if village it could be called, for it was no more than a group of low thatched huts surrounded by a thorn stockade. Goats, fowls and a few undersized cattle shared it with their owners, and at night the goats huddled under their masters' beds. The men, naked save for a loin-cloth, looked, on the whole, unintelligent and crafty, the women prematurely aged by heavy labour, the children unkempt. In the past these people had been cannibals and Robert Gresham, beneath whose supervision their lives now fell, had little doubt that the living still, on occasion, consumed the dead.

The road to this country of the pagans petered out in broken foothills and his small party, leaving its motor transport in a little cluster of huts, climbed up on foot.

"Just like old times!" Freddy Begg was puffed but chatty as he struggled up the hill. "Not many places left nowadays that can't be reached by car."

"Not enough," Robert agreed. "They're always the nicest places."

They paused for breath on top of a smooth warm boulder. Freddy Begg ran a handkerchief over his face and neck, for he was unaccustomed to strenuous exercise. He was a tidily built, almost dapper man, who looked smaller than he really was by reason of a large head. His sandy hair was brushed carefully over the dome to conceal advancing baldness, his nose was large and rather bulbous and his light eyes, shielded as a rule by spectacles, were weak. Certainly he had missed the gift of beauty, but he looked kind, in an indecisive way, and something of the shrewdness and industry that had won him promotion above his colleagues at a comparatively early age showed in his expression.

The sun blinded their eyes as they turned to look back. It was going down in a golden haze above a flat horizon, dazzling and enormous. The plain lay like some shining Eldorado, an ocean of gold. On the hill, each shoulder cast a sharp shadow on to the flank of the next shoulder, every tree and bush stood out as if it had been cut from cardboard and pasted on. Such evenings had a strange dramatic quality, quite different from the gentle mornings, as if some momentous meaning lay wrapped in all this glory that so suddenly leapt up and was as quickly spent.

"There's something for you to paint." Freddy Begg addressed his wife, who had pulled herself up on to the boulder and stood beside her husband, inspecting the view.

She shook her head. "One can't paint immensity. Haven't you noticed that Africa's inspired no good painters, in spite of its profound effect on sculptors? It lacks form, the colours are blatant. Besides, it's so *direct*, and art is mainly a statement of implications."

Robert leapt off the rock impatiently and led the way up the hill. What pretentious nonsense the woman talked! As for Freddy—he'd been looking at Priscilla in what could only be described as a lecherous way. Well, Priscilla would look after herself; he could not see Freddy in the role of an enchanter. There he was, helping her solicitously up the hill. Robert felt a stab of pity and, at the same time, of guilt. He knew that he should be at her side, but he lost patience so easily with slowness, and the Beggs' chatter made him like a porcupine with raised quills. He quickened his pace, leaving the others well behind. A flicker among the rocks caught his eye and the pale form of a little antelope shone for an instant in the sun, to vanish instantly as it bounded forward into shadow with an ease and grace that lifted the heart. A pebble, dislodged by a flashing hoof, tumbled down the hillside, bounced off a rock and came to rest. Robert felt comforted, and clambered upwards with an ease and speed that even a hillman warrior would not wholly have despised.

The rough rest-house, doorless and with a wide veranda, was ready: that is to say, furnished with a folding table and chairs and with camp beds set up two by two, and all about was the bustle of servants preparing baths and food, and of carriers collecting firewood and water. Washed, changed and tidied, armoured by coats and mosquito boots, the party sipped whisky on the veranda, feeling the pleasures of a mild tiredness and the resting of muscles newly stretched.

"Delightful spot," Freddy observed. "One day we ought to build a hill-station up here."

"With a club, golf course and bridge?" Robert inquired.

"You sound very disapproving. Some of us, after all, enjoy golf and bridge."

"So does Robert, when he's playing well," remarked Armorel Begg. "It's only the idea he disapproves of. Who built this rest-camp?"

"A man called Pailthorpe," Robert answered. "Freddy would remember him."

Freddy, leaning back at ease in his deck chair, frowned in an effort of recollection, and then nodded.

"Yes, he came to grief, poor fellow."

"Why, did he rifle the till?"

"No," said Robert. "He was killed by the local pagans. In those days they were inhospitable to strangers. He's buried just above the camp."

"The poor fellow was rather hasty, I'm afraid," Freddy added. "He came up here without making proper preparations and without an adequate escort, and walked into a hornet's nest. A most regrettable incident."

"Poor man," Armorel said. "I should like to see his grave."

"There's little in it for the tourist," Robert remarked. "But then, there was very little left to bury, as I remember."

"Really, Robert," Freddy protested. "This is hardly a pleasant conversation in front of ladies."

"I'm sorry; we'll change it. Have you decided where you're going to spend your leave?"

Robert did not listen to the reply. He was thinking of the day he had come here with a section of native troops under an inexperienced young subaltern to deal with Pailthorpe's murder. He and the subaltern had been almost the same age: both green, nervous, self-important and afraid, not of the danger to their own lives, which they did not visualize, but of blundering on their first important mission. They must capture the culprits; to fail in that would be to fail in everything. But how? They had discussed the matter and dismissed a dozen schemes, only to settle, out of desperation, on the simplest and crudest of them all. He remembered the long climb up the hill in the cold hour before dawn, and how he and the subaltern had taken off their boots and gone up with cold and painful feet to avoid the sound of nails on stone. He recalled the whispered orders, the tense half-hour while a score of native soldiers crept forward to surround the village; the order to advance, the cries and brief confused battle, the flight of naked figures in a grey dawn and the leaping flames that jumped from thatch to thatch.

And he remembered, too, the grisly business of assembling what little was left of Pailthorpe's body; the horror of detaching a bloody head from the stake on which it had been impaled, the empty eye-sockets and ghastly torn mouth, and, above all, his stricken realization that the eyes had been put out and the tongue severed while Pailthorpe had still lived. Even now he could almost feel a tremor of the sickness that had overwhelmed him then. The remnants of a man he had drunk and trekked with had been collected and shovelled underground, and he had walked down the hill with half a dozen of the hillmen roped together by the neck and a collective fine of sheep and goats driven on before.

He remembered it all clearly enough and Freddy, no doubt, had read about it on a file.

Since then these hillmen had been docile enough, at any rate towards their masters; little of what went on among themselves was known to outsiders. All the same, he wished that the native clerk he was to meet at this rest-camp had kept his appointment. For this clerk was the lynch-pin of Freddy Begg's new scheme of tax assessment, whose workings they had come to study in the hills. And the scheme itself was the fruit of a year's hard work and cogitation, at once Freddy's greatest achievement and his bid for future fame.

His problem had been both delicate and stubborn. In essence, it was this: how to impose upon an ancient and corrupt principality standards of honesty to which none of its people subscribed, without depriving its rulers of their authority.

For the British administration, although in Africa, was dealing here with an eastern satellite. And following eastern tradition, the ruler's authority was complete; in his person lay authority's single source. The idea of integrity in the western sense, as applied to affairs of taxes and money, did not enter the picture. Taxes were tribute, paid to the Emir by right of conquest, collected by his agents and pertaining wholly to him; they certainly were not contributions by the citizens to a common fund. That the Emir's agents should dip their fingers into the honey-pot as it passed from hand to hand was considered not reprehensible but plain common sense. The object of authority was to enrich yourself and to enjoy privilege, not to part with a large share of your riches for the dubious benefit of sweepers and slaves.

The coming of white supremacy had modified these methods, but not abolished them. For, by treaty, the British bound themselves to respect native laws and custom and, by policy, to devolve on to native institutions a large measure of authority. The Emir and his agents, therefore, still collected from each village and

district its annual tax, handing over a proportion to the Protectorate Government. The main difference between the old
method and the new was that the Resident and his officers kept
as close a watch as they could on the collection, and investigated
all complaints. The greatest abuses could, in this way, be corrected, but no one supposed that a really honest system, in the
western sense, had been achieved.

Such injustice was as abhorrent to Freddy Begg as he knew it
to be to his masters in London; but the obvious remedy, to take
taxation out of the hands of the Emir and his lieutenants and
place it in the hands of British officials, was ruled out. For those
distant masters demanded two improvements which were in fact
quite incompatible (unfortunately they did not seem to realize
this): meticulous honesty in the matter of taxes, based on
British notions of morality, and the exercise of greater powers by
those who manned the native institutions—namely, the Emir
and his officials.

A hard search for compromise had culminated in his scheme,
known in the voluminous files in which its evolution was traced
as the Begg proposals. The essence of these was that tax asssess-
ment and collection were to be separated and placed in different
sets of hands, thus enabling each to establish a check on the other.
A much closer grip on matters by the Protectorate Government
was skilfully masked by forms and titles which made it appear as
if these innovations had their source in the authority of the Emir.

The Emir himself had, of course, seen through the subterfuge
immediately. His policy on such occasions was to agree with a
good grace, knowing that between principle and practice lies a
great gulf, and that in Africa many things may occur, or be made
to occur, to reduce the impetus of the best-rolled hoop to a point
where it wavers, loses direction and topples over into the dust.

The hill-dwelling pagans, to whose country Gresham had
brought his colleague, were among those expected to benefit most
from the reforms. In the course of generations they had grown
well accustomed to rendering tribute to their warlike Moslem
conquerors. For centuries that tribute had been paid in slaves,
seized in sudden forays which left a trail of smoking villages,
bleeding bodies and pillaged crops. Against this enemy, an
natural to them as tornado or drought, they had grown their
own defences of mobility and capacity for supporting themselves
in barren, inaccessible spots. Lately, for reasons which they
little understood, the forays had ceased and the form of tribute

had grown infinitely milder. Officials of the Emir came now in peace and were content to drive away a few sheep and goats in lieu of human booty.

Under the Begg proposals, these Moslem officials were to be replaced by a clerk from the Provincial Office, an educated man from the south, who, in consultation with tribal elders, would compile a register of each family and its resources and then assess the family head according to a simple formula involving the numbers of his livestock and the extent of his cultivation. This done, a copy of the register would be handed over to the Emir's officials who would then collect the tax as before, but the payment would be checked against the assessment and defalcations thus brought to light.

The scheme was excellent on paper, but Robert Gresham nevertheless doubted its practical use. The Emir and his agents were spread like a spider's web over the province. Opposition, silent and deadly, would charge every strand of the web. By conspiracy or intimidation the Emir's men would combine with village elders to mislead and cheat the assessors—aliens and infidels whom all agreed to despise. The intricacies of the complex life of Moslem towns would be too deep for any outsider to fathom, against whom the Emir had set his face; among pagans, in whom fear and suspicion were inbred, the safety of the clerks might even be in doubt.

He had put these points before the Resident; but his superior had pooh-poohed his ideas.

"We've had no trouble with these pagans since they were taken over," he had said. "They've always forked out for the Emir, haven't they, without any bother?"

"Yes; but they're still afraid of him. They won't be afraid of a southerner, an English-speaking clerk."

"Nonsense, my dear fellow, you're imagining things. The pagans will toe the line. I'm not expecting any trouble from them; after all they stand to gain, and what's it to them if they deal with a villainous old Moslem or a clerk? It's here, under the Emir's nose, we'll feel the kicks."

So the clerk had gone ahead by lorry and bicycle to make his first assessments, with instructions to report at the rest-camp on the chosen afternoon. Next day the author of the proposals was himself to attend a meeting of elders at which Gresham was to expound the new system and the clerk to make entries in his register, and the little set piece would be played through to the end.

And now night had fallen, but the clerk had failed to arrive. There was nothing remarkable about this. To-morrow, the next day, the day after, no doubt seemed to him very much the same. Nevertheless, perhaps because of the camp's evil memories, Robert Gresham was not quite at ease, and, leaving the others settled with their drinks, he went out to seek for news among the carriers and the camp-followers cooking their evening meal over the crackling wood fires.

Chapter Four

PRISCILLA, leaning back in her chair, looked tired, as was only to be expected; but better that, than to have remained a prisoner in the spent air of the town. Her head ached and her mouth was dry and bitter. In her blood fever had once again been worsted by quinine, but no such victory was final, and the battle-ground became at least as exhausted as the combatants.

To her dismay, she was alone with Armorel Begg. Not that she exactly disliked Armorel. In a sense she admired her: the dark commanding looks, the vitality, the strength of purpose, the social skill. Ruefully, Priscilla acknowledged that if she herself devoted half as much energy and forethought to the advance-ment of her husband's cause, she would be a better wife to Robert. Impossible to imagine that a woman of Armorel's character and astringency should be in love with Freddy, and yet she was as loyal to him as a dog—one of the larger and more forceful breeds, Priscilla reflected, an Alsatian or a Dobermann, perhaps.

There was much to esteem in Armorel Begg, yet with her Priscilla never felt quite at ease. Just now she sat across the table stretching her slender figure in a camp chair. In navy-blue slacks and a wine-coloured silk shirt cut high at the neck she looked her best: trim, tailored, self-assured, her dark glossy hair neatly waved and her pale skin thrown into relief by the sombre tones of her clothing and the background of night. Smoking a cigarette through a long ivory holder, she was combining in her conversation the two subjects on which, in Priscilla's view, she was at her most tiresome: art, for which she had a considerable local reputation, and Robert, whom she always professed to admire.

"One of my deepest unsatisfied ambitions," she observed, "is to model Robert's head."

"Why not? I'm sure he'd be delighted."

"So am I; but nothing would make him admit it. Mock modesty, my dear—bogus, but obstructive. Really, though, he ought to be painted—in the dress of the Renaissance, don't you think? Imagine how he'd look in those puffed sleeves of slashed velvet, the velvet doublets, the gold chains! I always think he should have been born several hundred years ago."

Priscilla shifted uneasily in her chair, and replied coldly: "Like the rest of us, he'll have to make do with the twentieth century. Couldn't we talk about someone else for a change—for instance, Freddy?"

"Freddy's strongest point is that people don't talk about him. There's so little to say."

"The perfect civil servant, in fact."

"Exactly. You haven't congratulated us, my dear."

"Of course I do—sincerely. Freddy's worked hard for his promotion."

Armorel Begg laughed. "Nicely put. So have I, for that matter."

Priscilla could not help smiling in spite of the faint sense of revulsion which the conversation aroused in her. "I suppose it takes two to make a Governor," she remarked.

"Oh, Freddy's not nearly so exalted."

"He will be. Do you like being down at headquarters?"

Armorel shrugged her shoulders. "It's very social, of course. Far too many parties, but one gets variety. I suppose you haven't met the Hamptons yet? Such a charming woman!"

"Is she sitting for her portrait?"

Armorel closed and unveiled her eyes, making them brilliant, and flashed her white, even teeth in a smile.

"You shouldn't be catty, Priscilla. No, she isn't. There's not much in her face to paint, as a matter of fact—uninteresting bones, flat, commonplace. Besides, I'm very busy. I'm taking classes in design and modelling at the African College three times a week. And you've heard of my proposal for a museum of native art? I've managed to get Freddy keen on the idea—a real piece of petticoat influence, I know—and I think we shall get a small grant through in the next budget. You must keep your eyes open for us up here, Priscilla, for good things. We're calling it the Hampton Museum, and Sir Harold's promised to sit for a head to adorn the entrance hall."

Priscilla, immensely impressed, reflected that Armorel was very reassuring; like a mathematical equation, there was always a correct value for the enigmatic x.

"I really do admire you," she said. "You think of everything."

Armorel smiled a little wolfishly. "Including, you mean, myself. Dear Priscilla! You see through me, of course, but not quite far enough. After all, neither of us started at the top of the tree, did we? Frankly, I enjoy climbing it, and the view gets more interesting as you go up. You think so too, but the difference between us is that I have to do all the hard work, and you condemn that as vulgar. You've only got to lift a little finger and the men come running, ready and anxious to do it all for you. You aren't really a bit helpless, Priscilla, but you manage to give that impression, and what's more, to make the helping process seem attractive."

"We needn't psycho-analyse ourselves over it," Priscilla remarked, feeling acutely uncomfortable. "Surely you don't think I condemn people for fighting their own battles? Far from it, and I hate helplessness; I certainly don't want to seem helpless myself."

"I'm glad you agree. All this talk against self-interest infuriates me; it's such hypocrisy. Would any of us be here if the early traders hadn't struggled and died for profit, the first explorers faced all those grisly hardships for fame? It's the same with all of us; we deserve the plums if we survive the struggle. Why not? And why not be honest about it?"

"It's a relative question, I suppose, like most things—how much struggle the plum is worth, and how much one can trample on other people's faces to reach it."

Armorel shook her head. "No, I don't think it's a relative question at all. It's a matter of instinct. If you've got the guts you like the struggle for its own sake; the plum is really a sort of incident, desirable of course, and no more than one's due, but secondary. You don't run a race in order to get to the winning post, you run it to beat the others. To sit down and philosophize over the relative desirability of the plum is a sign of decadence. We're all decadent these days."

"Not you, Armorel."

"Someone's got to do the dirty work. Where should we be if everyone sat down and wondered whether the game was worth the candle? Look at this country—it stagnates, we all know it. But who does anything? We're far too gentlemanly. Take this little museum of mine. Everyone knows that specimens of native art are being lost and destroyed and sold out of the country every day—and of course, no one cares. Well, I fight for this museum—and it's been a fight, I can assure you—and when I win my little victory, people turn round and say: 'She's only doing it to get a place to show off her rotten heads.' Oh, I know what people say! They'd rather see nothing done at all than something done from which I, or anyone else, might get my rake-off. That sort of hypocrisy makes me tired!"

But of the two sitting on the lamplit veranda it was clearly not Armorel who was tired; leaning forward in her chair, her eyes bright with intensity of feeling, she was a picture of vigour. To her companion's relief the arrival of the two men cut short the conversation. They settled in their chairs for another drink, but she sensed a certain coldness between them. The truth was that Robert had annoyed the visitor by some offhand remark to the effect that the new tax scheme looked well enough on paper but would not be liked by the tribesmen. To them, he said, a tax assessor would appear as one more prying and dangerous devil rather than as a new kind of guardian angel.

"That may be so at first," Freddy conceded, "but they'll soon realize that the whole intention behind this innovation is to ensure that the taxes they pay are used in a proper manner, and do not merely go to line the pocket of the Emir and his hangers-on."

"They won't realize anything of the sort," Robert said bluntly. "They're used to being conquered, it's happened to them for centuries, and they'll merely think (as they think already) that one lot of masters has replaced another, and that both are equally greedy. The greatest mistake we make is to imagine that because we know we're different from all the other conquerors who've come to Africa, the conquered know it too; or that because we want to change the inhabitants into good little democrats like ourselves, patient and kind to animals and fond of cricket, the inhabitants really want to make this transformation, or would be capable of it if they did. People don't reverse their natures overnight just by being conquered. This master comes, that one goes, like caravans across the desert; the people are like grains of sand, they give under the tread, but the sweat of the travellers' feet doesn't turn them into gold."

"Well, I don't see things so poetically," Freddy said, with more than a trace of impatience, "but perhaps I look at them with greater balance. Certainly these people have a long history of subjection to their more war-like neighbours. Before the establishment of the *pax Britannica* they were hunted down for slaves. After slavery was abolished the Emir and his immediate supporters turned to extortion. Tribute is forced from these wretched people, poverty-stricken and without resources—and it is still the position to-day—in part (though of course not wholly) to pay for the luxuries of the effete aristocracy of the emirate."

Freddy paused to clear his throat and wipe his spectacles; his listeners had the feeling of people who drop into a theatre with a rehearsal in progress and hear an actor running through his lines.

"That such a state of affairs should exist in a country under our protection is nothing less than a reflection on our enforcement of justice. The weak must be protected against the strong. Now, under these new proposals, the head of each family will pay according to his means. And he will have the satisfaction of knowing that every penny will be spent ultimately for his own good."

Priscilla unexpectedly gave a snort of laughter and then looked ashamed, like a child caught giggling during the sermon.

Robert said: "You don't really think they'll believe that, do you? They think the money goes straight into the pockets of the district officers and Residents. And they're at least partly right. That's where our pay comes from, isn't it?"

Freddy looked really annoyed. "I consider that such flippant and cynical remarks are out of place."

"What would you do, Robert?" Amorel asked. "Let the top dogs go on squeezing what they can out of the bottom dogs just because the bottom dogs won't lick our hands in gratitude if we help them?"

"It's not as simple as that. In the first place, if you drive the Emir too hard he'll simply topple over. The landowners and nobles, the real powers in the land, will turn against him and out he'll go."

"That might be a very good idea."

"No, because however much they wrapped it up, his successor would be their nominee, a far trickier customer to deal with than the present Emir."

"Then why not purge the lot?"

"Because then you'd break up the whole system and there'd be nothing to put in its place; either we should have to create something new and artificial, or run the whole show ourselves.

That might be a good thing or a bad one—but I shouldn't think Freddy would care to take it on."

"Of course we are pledged to uphold existing native institutions," Freddy said crossly.

"Well, what would you *do*?" Armorel persisted.

"I should worry less about injustices to little men and more about a vision of the future," Robert said slowly. "We English set too much store by justice. Because we ourselves regard it as the greatest virtue, we think others must value it as highly. But they don't. They put lots of things above justice—good manners, for instance, and the interests of their family or friends. And they're entitled to their ideas. These kingdoms of theirs were part of a great empire once—not someone else's, but their own. It was primitive, of course, by our standards, and corrupt, but alive. It was a Moslem empire, and all their links—trade, religion and culture, such as it was—were with the north, with the Arab peoples."

"You want to revive their ancient and moth-eaten glories? That hardly seems to be an answer to the reform of a corrupt administration."

"The answer to that, if there is one, is trade. Give these countries more wealth and the burden of tribute, whoever collects it, will lie more lightly on the people. In the past their trade was with the north, across the desert, and they developed their own crafts and industries—small and crude, but vital. Now we ignore them, because we want to tie these countries to the south and handle their trade, such as it is, through our own ports and railways, and sell them things we make ourselves, instead of encouraging their own handiwork."

"That's all so much poppycock, if you'll forgive me for saying so," Freddy replied sharply. "People can't trade with a desert, any more than the costs of camel transport can stand up against the costs of modern shipping and railways, or hand-made articles compete with mass-production. You seem to think that we at the Secretariat live in utter ignorance of economics and geography, and disregard the welfare of the people. I can assure you, you are entirely mistaken."

Robert smiled at his wife across the lamplight and did not reply.

"Very much mistaken," Freddy added. "And I think, if you'll forgive a piece of advice, that you would do better to concentrate on the carrying out of your instructions than to concern yourself with wholly impracticable ideas on questions of major policy which lie outside your province. These matters are in the hands, you know, of quite capable men."

Both women moved and spoke at once and, as if they had been awaiting their cue, a couple of bare-footed silent servants appeared out of the shadows with plates and glasses on a tray to set the table for the evening meal.

Chapter Five

AFTER coffee Robert left the party to see, he said, that everything was properly secured for the night, but in fact to seek the consolation of a talk with Ibrahim, the court interpreter, who came with him often on such expeditions ready to offer, as it was needed, caution, advice, information and sympathy. Ibrahim's wrinkled, leathery face beneath its heavy turban gave nothing away. The eyes were watchful, the voice low and musical, and few men had known him to lose control over his tongue.

Robert felt the need of Ibrahim's reassurance, for he was getting worried about the missing tax-assessor. There was nothing in itself alarming about the clerk's failure to keep his appointment. Time meant so little in this continent that even the European-trained could not be relied on to remember the vast difference that distinguished, in a European's mind, one identical sunrise from the next. But still he felt uneasy. Perhaps it was a stirring of old memories, some essence of the anguish once suffered here that the moon drew out of the rocks, on nights like these, to chill the hearts of the living.

Ibrahim rose when Robert approached, curtsied deeply and sank again to the ground, arranging his robes round legs doubled to the right. Robert sat down beside him in the open by a wood fire and a small boy brought each of them a mug of hot coffee.

They sat for a while in silence, listening to the noises of the night: voices of carriers, crackling flames, the shrill skirl of crickets, the distant barking of a dog. The still air held expectancy but Ibrahim's coiled, sculptured figure gave him confidence.

"I do not think that these pagans seek trouble with the Government," the interpreter said. "They are too much afraid. Why else do they live like baboons among the rocks? They have the hearts of slaves."

"But they will not welcome a clerk, a southerner, whom they do not know."

"By whom, lord, is the tax-gatherer welcomed?"

"You have heard no talk of his arrival?"

"None."

"I think that is strange."

Ibrahim agreed. "If he had come into these hills, the drums would have told of it. Either the clerk has got drunk in the town and failed to leave, or these people tell lies."

"I think it is the second. The clerk is new and has not yet had an advance of pay."

Ibrahim drank his coffee noisily, considering. "To-morrow," he said at length, "you will meet the elders; do so outside the village. I myself will enter the village while the eyes of the men are turned away."

"You will see nothing."

"Perhaps; but I have ears also."

"And what do your ears hear of the Government's plan? Are the people glad to be spared the extortions of the Emir?"

Ibrahim's proud, wrinkled face broke into a smile. With the firelight illuminating his features, the face had a carven look, and his robes lay about him in shadowed folds. He stretched out one thin hand to the fire and turned it this way and that in a gesture of perfect assurance.

"Is a wounded man glad when the leopard drives away the hyena? The jaws of both are cruel."

"But this leopard's intentions are different."

"How is the man to know that, lord? A bite is always a bite."

"The tax money comes back to the people: they wish for schools, dispensaries, wells, the guarding of the peace."

"Beggars may eat at the Emir's palace, but not at the house of the Resident. People think first of their bellies, of the future afterwards, and they believe many foolish tales."

"They are full of suspicion."

"That is because they do not understand the European's behaviour. Your people, lord, are like the wind; they blow first from this quarter, then from that; here they bring sudden storms, there disperse the clouds. No man can foresee whence it will blow to-morrow and none, by intercession, can direct it."

"Yet it is our aim to help the common people."

"For that they look to God."

"They should look also to themselves, Ibrahim. For it is by a man's own efforts that he fails or prospers."

"How can a man prosper, except by the will of God?"

Robert fell silent, hugging his knees and puffing at his pipe. Conversations with Ibrahim, or with any devout Moslem, were always coming up against dead-ends like this. Yet he looked on the interpreter as one of the few wise men of his acquaintance. In his quiet, simple way he saw far into the hearts of men and into their motives. They were friends, but there was a barrier between them; a difference not merely of colour and hierarchy but of belief. For long ago Robert had realized that men are divided with greater potency by faith than by race or pigment, and he felt between himself and Ibrahim the wall, however screened by mutual respect, that must arise between Moslem and Christian. Was that the way to describe it? Between Moslem, certainly, on one side: a wall, perhaps it would be more accurate to say, between the faithful and the faithless, the sure and the unsure. How often he had envied that assurance, like unsplintered rock, that was the core of personality! It was this faith that gave Ibrahim his serenity, his wisdom and his strength, as well as his contempt for those who did not possess it and his conviction that his order of the world was divine. Could there be living faith without intolerance? An old question, still unresolved; the saints gave one answer, but to Ibrahim it would not be a question at all. It was the part of the faithful to convert or destroy. Ibrahim's faith drew Robert to him and yet held him back, like a balance of electrical forces that simultaneously attracts and repels.

Out of his sight his wife was trapped by Freddy Begg on the rest-house veranda. Their hands rested side by side on the low mud wall. Below them, shadowy hills fell away to meet the plain, silvered by moonlight. Soft, magnificent and bewitched, Africa lay now like a land of secret promise, yet for Priscilla it lacked the ultimate spell. Its very immensity repulsed her, its rival still claimed her loyalty. Here moonlight lay on plain and bush and boulder; there, and in the mind, on thatch and rose and hayrick, the silent wagon in the cobwebbed barn. Here no silver mouse went scampering by, and all the elephants in Africa were not worth to her a flicker of that silver claw, that silver eye.

Freddy Begg laid aside his spectacles with some deliberation, and moved closer to his companion. On the edge of the lamplight her skin had the calm and clouded quality of alabaster. Her own looks, when she thought about them at all, seemed to her common and over-English, pink like a rose and, like the rose, inclined to straggle; to herself her thinness appeared as something imposed, not inbred, and her bones too heavy; but to-night, although she did not know it, her beauty was refined into something alien and therefore intriguing. Pallor had enlarged and deepened her eyes, illness pared away the fullness of her face. She had the clear golden hair of a child, and in this distant place, so far from home, she brought to men's minds remembrance of English summers and country gardens, and, without knowing why, their hearts were softened towards her.

Her companion, standing so close that the scent of her hair and face-powder tickled his nostrils, moved his arm to touch hers. As gently as possible, she withdrew; she must be careful not to offend him for Robert's sake, but an amorous Freddy was more than she could be expected to endure.

"A lovely night," he said.

"Beautiful."

"I often wonder, Priscilla, whether you're really happy out here."

She turned to look at him in genuine surprise.

"You've never seemed to fit into the life here as other women do."

Priscilla sighed. "I don't play bridge, you mean?"

"Well, that, and other things. Somehow I feel this isn't the life you'd have chosen."

"How many people do choose their lives? Men, perhaps, occasionally; women, hardly ever."

His fingers, fiddling nervously with the edge of her sleeve, made her shiver. "I never really wanted to come out here myself, you know. You won't believe it, but I wanted to be a journalist. I had my heart set on it as a boy. But my father wouldn't hear of it. He put me into a firm of produce brokers in the City."

"One thinks of sugar and spice, but in real life I suppose it's all inkstains and adding up and ninepenny lunches." Anything to keep him talking about himself!

"I was making out some bills of lading one day and I remember getting suddenly excited by the names of the African timbers

—Iroko, Benin mahogany, Obeche. I wanted to go and see the trees growing, see what they looked like, where they came from—for some reason their names took on a queer meaning for me. I couldn't understand my feelings at all, but I managed a transfer. The impulsiveness of youth, I suppose!"

Priscilla hardly knew what to say. Whoever would have thought to find such a streak in Freddy! "No one's consistent," she said, half to herself. "It's one of God's mercies, I suppose."

"Of course, it was a disappointment. Instead of keeping books in the City I found myself doing so on the coast, where it was much more uncomfortable and unhealthy. I never saw the big trees—at least not until several years later, when I transferred into the Administration."

"And now you're near the top of one of the big African trees."

Freddy, not dissenting, cleared his throat. "If that's so, you must never let it come between us," he said earnestly. "Remember, Priscilla, that even if our paths should separate, I shall always be your devoted friend."

She had a sudden impulse to giggle, dispelled immediately, for he began to stroke her arm with moist, clammy fingers.

"Yes, always! Your happiness means so much to me. Dare I hope that you care a little for mine? Just a word from you, a sign that you return some small part of my regard—my feelings for you are very tender—I hardly know——"

He was beginning to stammer; his face, white and glistening in the moonlight, wore signs of distress; a hot dragon within was propelling him forward into dangerous regions while reason, sense of propriety and shyness combined to drag him back. She could imagine his torture and pity him for it, but to release him was more than she could undertake.

"I value your friendship, Freddy, but your impulses are a little disconcerting. I'm afraid I'm too monogamous, and Robert——"

"Robert! Can't we forget Robert for half an hour?" Freddy felt reckless, carried away far out of his depth. "You know how little he thinks of your happiness, you, whose little finger is worth more——"

"Freddy, please!"

"Of course you defend him, and I admire you for it. I admire everything about you, Priscilla, your loyalty, your generosity —but that can be carried too far. Everyone can see how he neglects you and leaves you to chase wild hares of his own, how he fails to appreciate——"

"For heaven's sake, Freddy, stop!"

But he would not be checked. "There comes a time when one must be outspoken. You're throwing your life away, Priscilla —you must think of yourself sometimes, and others who care for you. If you would only trust me . . . Robert! He can look after himself. Let him dig his own grave!"

The words came into his mouth unbidden; whatever had made him say such appalling things? Emotions entirely strange to him were rushing about in his mind and blood like so many biting ants. He felt giddy.

"I'm sorry, Priscilla, I didn't mean that! Don't spoil everything now—we can help each other——"

He was talking to the air; she had vanished like a startled bird into the night.

He sat down heavily, the pulses throbbing in his temples, his throat dry. What madness had possessed him to say such things! Why had the mere mention of Robert's name caused a sort of nausea, the man's very shape risen before his eyes? Even now he could not shake himself loose from persecution; he could see Robert's figure, insulting in its careless poise, standing between him and Priscilla, between him and her soft lips, her warm skin and peach-like arms. . . . His breathing grew quieter; he poured out a glass of water, drank it, wiped his brow with a handkershief and slowly settled his spectacles into place.

Madness, that was what it was! He was tired, over-worked, he needed his leave, new faces and scenes. The last few days had been a nightmare. He had been in the grip of an obsession; Priscilla's face had come between him and the papers he was reading, he had even dreamed of her at night. Well, it was over now, the storm broken and over. If she had been mean enough to turn against him, she was the one who would have to suffer for it, she and Robert. Life had a habit of setting snares for pride; and if he could be a generous friend, she would discover that he could also be a dangerous enemy.

Freddy Begg frowned and put his spectacle case in his pocket. Already the moment lay behind him, shameful, secret, bittersweet. His will, shaken but not disrupted, drove forward an obedient mind: a report to read, some annotations to be made. Thank God, he could still find solace in his work! And Armorel

would soon be back. Armorel, and the daily burden; she saw
everything; perhaps it was just as well.

He fetched a brief-case from the bedroom and, sitting down,
drew out a wad of papers, took an eversharp pencil from his
breast-pocket and began to read. Soon his surroundings were
almost forgotten, his mind locked with a problem of policy.
Every now and again he paused to mark a paragraph, frowning
slightly in a concentration sharpened and made conscious by
an anger that was sinking deep down into the layers of his soul.
In the yellow lamplight, his heavy nose threw a thick shadow
over a pale, harassed, unhappy countenance.

Chapter Six

ARMOREL sat on a boulder, clasping her knees. She felt
dizzy with the impact of size: the plain bending away
beneath her to the rim of the world, the dark vaults rising to
infinity above. How peaceful here, away from small-talk and
the discord of temperaments, away from Freddy's banalities,
from Robert's self-sufficiency and Priscilla's contempt.

She smiled to herself a little wolfishly; Freddy's face, when
she left him with Priscilla, had been flushed with more whisky
than he was used to, his eye had that moist, sly look. Well, it
would serve Priscilla right. She took little enough trouble to
conceal her feelings towards them both; it would do her good
to come down with a bump from the heights. She could look
after herself. In any case, Freddy never advanced much beyond
a nip at the lady's behind, unless, in his boldest moments, he
achieved a quick fondling of the bosom.

Poor Freddy, how far intention outstripped performance!
But why feel sorry for him? She was the one to suffer. She
knew the symptoms at once, the aftermath of one of his adventures: half furtive, half jocular, the damp kiss, the careful
laying aside of spectacles, the hoarse anticipatory whisper, the
tug at the bedclothes . . . but surely not to-night, in a rest-house
with open doorways and camp-beds that creaked! At least,
she thought, I have no illusions; and the phrase sent her memory
spinning back to a shabby sitting-room in a college hostel where
someone had once half-ironically protested:

"Youth is supposed to be the season of illusions, but you seem to have seen all yours off the premises."

Armorel had answered indifferently: "When you're as young as we are I expect the greatest illusion of the lot is to think you've got rid of them all."

She had been pleased with that remark, thinking it sounded clever; but it was true that she had done her best. Illusions had gone overboard one after the other, like weights thrown out of a balloon: king and country, God and religion, love, marriage and representational art—out they had toppled, and away her unencumbered ego had soared. By now she would have reached the stars had she not known that they, too, were a trick of mathematics and physics. She had seen through so many things in those days that there seemed little left for credit, and her post-war world was like a slate from which the self-deceiving axioms of weaker generations had all been erased.

Yet, looking back, how much they had believed in, how curious and wayward had been those beliefs! The triumph of rationalism, for instance—just as implausible as the kingdom of heaven, and on the whole much less attractive; free love, companionate marriage, sex equality, the emancipation of art; or the classless society, a mere short cut to observance of the tenth commandment by the simple expedient of removing from the rich man his ox and his ass. She sighed; less than ten years had so blurred the edge of memory that she could no longer recall in any detail her convictions and opinions. But emotions—they were a different story. Time had not dissipated but fixed them on her mind with the indelibility of fossils in rock. Even now she could not look back on the awakening of her heart without tasting a pang of the bitterness in which the episode had ended. She could remember each detail of their first meeting: she an eighteen-year-old newcomer agonized by self-consciousness; he a resplendent third-year student—one of the titans: captain of the Rugger fifteen, owner of an ancient car, holder of athletic records, star of the dramatic club. He was gay, he had been to one of the minor public schools, he belonged to a small and unofficial club of nebulous constitution, exclusive membership and no known object save the consumption of beer. Oppressed by the knowledge of her own gaucherie, she had been almost tongue-tied.

"Do you like the floor?"

"Awfully good, considering."

"Quite a decent band."

"Oh, top-hole."

Such dances took place in a draughty hall whose floor was patchily dressed with french chalk, so that performers alternately slithered as on ice or stuck as on glue; but Amorel knew her partner to be on the committee. Upright cane-seated chairs were set in ranks along the bare walls and in them young women clothed, for the most part, in knee-short and ill-cut dresses, tried to avoid expressions of anxiety or vexation. The young men, fewer in numbers, hung awkwardly round the door, their clean white shirt-fronts gleaming, their hair regimented by oil. The bleak light of bulbs dangling nakedly from a raftered ceiling illuminated all.

As if half divining her criticisms, her partner said:

"The hall's pretty grim, but there it is. In America I believe they call those bashful chaps by the door the stag-line, but sheep-pen would be better, I think."

Armorel laughed. "Are there any black ones among them?"

"Oh, *they're* all sitting out in the labs."

"What a place to choose! All among those ghastly things in bottles."

Her partner looked shocked. "You don't think everything in bottles is ghastly, I hope? . . . I say, you dance awfully well, you know."

She could see Maurice Cornforth now as he had looked then: broad-shouldered, self-confident, his sleek black hair smoothed over a well-shaped head, his eyes agate-brown, his skin almost olive-tinted, clear and healthy, and putting her unexpectedly in mind of the translucent bloom of a grain of ripe wheat.

She did not come across him very often after that. Now and again he was to be seen lounging down the cloisters, pipe in mouth and hands in pockets, with two or three of his cronies, and once or twice on a Saturday afternoon she had cycled to the playing-fields to watch him, tousled and mud-bespattered, pounding up and down the football field. But in bed at night she went over every word she had exchanged with him, every gesture and expression, the set of his head, the way he smiled with one half-raised eyebrow; and because he was another's property, and she must keep her feelings hidden, she was at once elated and miserable, hopeful and despairing, and above all distraught.

For Maurice Cornforth belonged, beyond dispute, to a fellow-student of Armorel's and a contemporary of his own: a young woman, Brigid Akroyd by name, who had befriended Armorel on her first arrival. No one, not even Armorel, could for long regard Brigid Akroyd with rancour: she was too good-natured and guileless for that. In appearance she was over-large and rather clumsy, but there was an impetuous attraction about her red, wiry hair, so often untidy, her greenish eyes and creamy skin, and her cheerful grin. She was a young woman of remarkable energy, always working away at her modelling or sculpture, organizing debates, taking part in amateur theatricals or, in due season, going off in boats on the river. For, to make matters worse for Armorel, spring appeared, and then early summer; may trees were dusted with their heady-smelling blossom, the sound of motor-mowers drifted into the open windows of lecture rooms and laboratories, the ugly red-brick cloisters were gay as flower-beds with girls in summer dresses. In the long untidy studio where Armorel worked—a sort of beaver-boarded barn— students grew alternately languid, responding to the sunshine and the whispering of leaves, and frenzied, when skies clouded over and the threat of examinations darkened their minds.

On an afternoon when Armorel found her friend Brigid Akroyd at work on the modelling of a nearly completed head, she examined it curiously, and demanded:

"Why a Negro?"

"Oh, I don't know. Do you like it?"

"It's tremendously alive. But why?"

Brigid resumed her work on the thickening of a nostril. "I can't really remember. Oh yes—I was looking at a book Cornforth lent me."

"Is he interested in Negroes?"

"No, I don't think so. He just had a book." She frowned and worked away in silence for a little. "He's going there, you know," she added.

"Where?"

"Africa."

"What for?"

"To earn a living, I suppose."

"I didn't know." Armorel sat on a block of stone and lit a cigarette. The subject fascinated her; she could not let the chance slip by.

"Then will you go to Africa too?"

"Me?" Brigid looked up in surprise, and then grinned. "Oh, I see. I shouldn't think so. We're not engaged, you know."

"Not officially, but——"

"Anyway, he's not allowed to get married for two years?"

"That isn't so very long."

"Oh, well, lots of things can happen in two years."

Brigid's voice sounded final; she was paring away now at the chin. Her companion sat and smoked, watching her. This indifference! Armorel felt resentment rising in her as she observed the intent expression, the strangely deft and gentle motion of those large blunt-fingered hands. What could Cornforth possibly see in anyone so ingenuous and dull? What right had she to take so much for granted? At that moment Brigid stepped back to examine the head. "I'll join you in a fag," she said. "I can't get it right to-day whatever I do."

Armorel handed her a crushed packet.

"Brigid."

"Yes?"

"Do you believe in letting—well, in going the whole hog with men before you're married?"

"Good Lord," Brigid said, thoroughly startled. "What a thing to bring up! I'm really no authority——"

"No—but do you?"

"I·don't think it's the sort of question——" Brigid glanced at her companion and changed her mind. Armorel had looked fagged out lately, those deep-set eyes more luminous than ever. She had liked the child, and tried to help her, in spite of an awkward and at times almost hostile response; one must admire that curious directness; if she wanted something, even an answer to a question, she stuck to her guns until she got it.

"Well, if you ask me, I think it's all rot. Some people let the thing get completely on their minds, and then they become dreadful bores. But then, I dare say I'm old-fashioned. In America, judging by the films . . ."

Brigid trod on her cigarette and resumed work on her head, the abrupt embarrassment of her manner soon replaced by an unself-conscious absorption. She did not notice the fleeting look on Armorel's face, and if she had she would have been at a loss to analyse it: half amused, part gratified, a little apprehensive.

Chapter Seven

1922

THE summer was rushing by, the may had shed its blossom, a scent of mown grass loaded the air, the pace of life was quickened. While others lounged with gramophones under the trees or cycled into the country, Armorel plodded on at her work, trying to crowd her troubles out of her mind. She was making progress. Crayon and brush were becoming more obedient, that chasm between vision and shapes on paper or in clay was narrowing. Slowly, control of expression was being won; but she was forced to ask herself what was there to express. The excitement which she felt at the start of every enterprise had never yet ripened into satisfaction at its end.

For her major project of the year she had chosen to model a horse: a proud Percheron, standing with flared nostril and arched tail as if about to rise like Pegasus into air. She strove to mingle vigour with buoyancy, arrogance with symmetry. But the achievement eluded her. The Percheron looked too heavy or, transformed, too effeminate; the figure lacked life and cleanliness of line; never did he seem about to soar. She struggled on.

Sometimes the young instructor came and gazed at it, puffing a dirty meerschaum pipe. Generally he was rather dirty all over. Sometimes, to illustrate a point, he would seize a piece of wet clay and work it in his hands with miraculous speed and deftness. There would be the thing he was trying to demonstrate, explained quite clearly in the shape of the clay. So simple! Few of the students liked Emmanuel Roote, he was too rude and off-hand, but they respected him, and their confidence grew with experience. He said little, and that little was nearly always harsh, but Amorel believed that he numbered her among the few who showed promise of competence, and perhaps talent.

One afternoon she found him with a friend, a lanky stranger, inspecting in a desultory manner heads and figures scattered about the big room. They did not hear her enter and she went quietly over to a stack of sketches in a corner of the studio to sort out a few of her own. She had no wish to intervene, but pricked up her ears when she observed them standing over

Brigid Akroyd's Negro, immersed in tobacco smoke and con-
versing, apparently, in grunts.

"Derivative, of course," the lanky man said.

"Of course.   Question of sources.   Get away from all this
blanc-mange and treacle. That girl's got a real flair for handling
masses. Imagination, too. Unexpected."

"Might do something one day."

Roote gave a snort. "Get married, probably. Ruins 'em."

"Pity," said the visitor, and they walked on, approaching,
by way of various half-finished and inept essays, Armorel's
Percheron, standing proudly, and as she thought to advantage,
in a window's full light. But as they advanced towards it her
confidence bled away and she stood with her back towards them,
her heart thumping, stiffening her shoulders for the blow.

Roote's companion pointed with his pipe-stem at the horse.
"Certain feeling for balance," he suggested.

Roote grunted. "Slick. Works hard, nothing there. Run-of-
the-mill art mistress stuff."

"Good likenesses of pet dogs."

"Magazine illustrators," Roote said with cutting contempt.
"That's what they are, the best of them. One possible exception."
Chewing morosely at their pipes, they strolled on.

One of the students came into the room whistling, and started
to bang about with frames and easels. Scarcely conscious of her
actions, Armorel walked slowly over to her Percheron and,
with deliberation, destroyed it utterly, until only a lump of
shapeless clay remained. Taking off her smock, she hung it
on a peg and then walked slowly out of the studio, along the
cloisters and through the college gates. Of what went on around
her she saw and heard nothing, until, walking on through rows
of poky shops and mean streets, she drew clear of the sad and
grimy town.

Turning off the road into a lane away from the rumble of
buses and screech of wheels on tarmac, she walked on through
the no-man's-land where farm and suburb meet, and gradually
the numbness receded, exposing her mind to red-hot rods of
pain and fury; jealousy, disillusionment, self-pity and despair
stabbed at the tender marrow of her self-esteem. She suffered
as only the young can suffer when the secret hope dies prematurely in the heart; and when she returned, late in the
evening, she had revised the terms of the bargain she was resolved
to drive with destiny. She must accept the length of her tether,

but a shorter reach would give a stronger grasp. Looking back, she told herself that she had already travelled a fair way from the cramped, mean home in the Midlands, where her father, a small manufacturing chemist, groused at his health and his family, and her mother, a blowsy disappointed woman, consoled herself for the drab *ennui* of the present with daydreams of a lost youth in a third-rate touring opera company. To climb away from her surroundings had been the first ambition Armorel could remember, and she would not turn back now, nor show to those who might impede her progress a consideration she had never received from others. Counting her assets, she numbered youth, health and a mediocre but assiduous talent; passable looks, a fair intelligence, self-control and a liking for hard work. Many had fared worse and yet had travelled far.

From that moment, queerly enough, her luck seemed to change. Some drawings she had entered for a competition won a prize and Maurice Cornforth, who had for several weeks seemed to elude her, invited her as his partner to a dance. Although knowing herself to be only a stopgap (Brigid Akroyd had been called away to the bedside of a brother belatedly dying of wounds), she accepted with a sense of triumph and danced the evening through with brisk enjoyment; and towards the end, having complained of weariness, found herself in Cornforth's old car, being taken for a breath of air before restoration to her own institutional warren.

Near the town's outskirts the country started to rise towards a crest of rolling downland, and on a spur of these hills was a tree-clad mound—an old Saxon barrow, perhaps—to which people often drove to admire the view. Here they sat, under a beech tree, and smoked in silence for a while, looking at the silvery turf and the lights winking far below. These shone up from an ugly, formless industrial town, but seen as a cluster of lights on the shadowy cloth of night it might have been a crown of jewels or a city of perfect men.

"It'll be a long time before I see those lights again," Cornforth said, "once the term's over. It's a mouldy sort of town, and not much of a university, I suppose, but it's odd how one grows attached to the place."

"Or the people in it. I shall miss you, next year."

He turned to look at her; in the moonlight her face had heavy shadows and a sort of waxy pallor, her deep-set eyes were fixed on his.

"You're a queer kid. We've hardly seen each other."

"You haven't noticed me much, but I've seen more of you than you realize."

"Good Lord." He wriggled uncomfortably. "Sounds like bird watching."

"The courting habits of the male are always interesting."

He said shortly: "Cheap sarcasm isn't attractive. You've got a lot to learn," and put his arm round her shoulders and kissed her. Then he was taken aback by the almost desperate response to his love-making; but it was more than he had bargained for, and his mood was perverse; after a little he pulled her to her feet, threw the rug over his arm and guided her to the car. And on the way home they scarcely spoke.

For the three weeks that remained of the year she hardly saw him, and indeed he might have slipped entirely out of her reach had not Brigid Akroyd, taking pity on a misery that could be sensed but not explained, invited her to join a party of students who had hired a launch for conveyance to a regatta which took place a few miles up-river from the town. By and large, this regatta was a dingy sort of affair, held on a straight stretch of river just above the gas-works where long regiments of terraced houses broke in a screen of ill-proportioned villas over the green countryside. The stream at this point was not a noble one. It slid between muddy banks apologetically, lacking in dignity; the bather's feet slithered into slime and sent up bubbles, the effluent of industries had discouraged all but the dullest and boniest of fish. Nevertheless it was gay, on this occasion, with punts and barges, with thin shells nosing their way over the water, with skiffs darting back and forth like water-rats. On flat green meadows by the waterside crowds came to fill the marquees, flags fluttered brightly, and the painted wagons and creaking apparatus of a travelling fair out-spanned among the flowering grasses.

Dutifully, Armorel watched the races, but they did not interest her greatly and she was glad when at last they were over, and slowly the river emptied of its boats and spectators, and the fair-ground filled. People streamed out from the town, buses rolled into parking places, soon the grass was trampled by the feet of revellers. The merry-go-round creaked and blared, chairoplanes whirled, laughter rose to hysterical shrieks, the voices of barkers by freaks and side-shows grew hoarse but never flagged; people shouted, nudged, squealed, giggled and drifted to and fro. A little past midnight she found herself standing with Brigid Akroyd and half a dozen others at a refreshment booth, tired but exhilarated, their feet aching, sucking at lemonade through straws. It was time now, as all agreed, to make their way home, but two or three of the young men were missing, and the rest good-humouredly awaited them by the booth, leaning against poles and stalls to ease the feet.

At last the missing companions appeared, flushed but triumphant, and waved at their friends. Cornforth wore a dented bowler on the back of his head and clasped a rolled umbrella, trophies snatched from a notable connected with the presentation of the cups—either the Lord Lieutenant of the County or a private detective hired to watch the silver, it was impossible to say which—and intended to decorate the statue of an eminent button-manufacturer, a past benefactor of the University, offering itself in the town's main square as a perennial butt of students' rags. Cornforth's eye was bright and his cheeks flushed, as much with animal spirits and exertion as with liberal draughts of beer; he was exuberant and elated; for this single evening the world lay at his feet, a golden carpet. At such moments even the timid may be predatory, and he was not a timid young man; his roving eye sought new game, and was held by a look no less bold and hungry. Raising the dented bowler, he said:

"Hello, Armorel! I've been looking everywhere for you."

His words were casual but his tone laid bare their meaning, and she stood transfixed, indifferent to the stares and perhaps the speculations of her companions, seeing only the smiling figure poised before her as a picture of enticement and fearing to dispel the tension that had sprung up between them. Then Brigid's voice, louder than necessary, broke the current and set in motion the members of the group.

"We can't stand here all night. Let's get going, those of us who want to go home."

A line of boats waited on the dark oily stream, their noses tucked deep into the reeds. In silence the party, only a little depleted, climbed aboard and cast off from the mooring, their heads full of the music of roundabouts, their feet heavy. For all but Brigid Akroyd, the party had been a good one and their last regatta a success.

Chapter Eight

1924

THE rattle and clink of early milk-carts, the boom of river tugs and squawk of motor cars, the day-long beat of footsteps became the music in Armorel's ears, and she watched the seasons leave their signature on the black slippery pavements or the dappled trunks of leafy plane-trees, and pass lightly over the surface of the changing river. London had been her beacon and to London she came, resolved to make her way by the exercise of a talent she knew to be limited but trusted in to keep her head above water. It was a struggle, only maintained by a small allowance from her father, but she began slowly to scoop out for herself a humble foothold on the lower slopes of the steep ascent. And she enjoyed herself in the meantime. The London of the early twenties, with its confidence and gaiety, its tolerance and energy, was a haven for the young and self-absorbed; like a mighty tree, deep-rooted in history and wealth, it offered the shelter of its strong branches and myriad twigs to birds of every plumage and persuasion, who might twitter and chirp, squabble and court, flaunt their feathers or wilt into oblivion to their heart's content, without in the least affecting the slow invisible growth or decay of the tree.

So in a cramped and dirty one-roomed studio, sustained more by conversation and coffee than by chops and puddings, Armorel experienced the common flux and ebb of pleasure and frustration. At times she would fall into moods of despondency, oppressed by the squalor and threat of futility and fearing a last retreat into the deadening oblivion of the manufacturing chemist's villa in the Midland industrial town. But then she would strike out again among the young would-be artists and journalists and actors of her acquaintance, spending her last shillings on innumerable cups of mud-flavoured coffee, listening to stories of half-eager and half-cynical adventures into new worlds of love and self-expression, and to fiery opinions on current theories of art and the execrable practice of them by various contemporaries.

Armorel's friends were not as promiscuous in fact as their

beliefs instructed them to be, but they were full of experimental ardour, and as time went on she found herself able to treat her memories of Maurice Cornforth with more detachment and to meet without a sense of deliberate effacement the advances of his successors. But she never forgot him. With none other could the glory and the music be recaptured, nor was she able to approach her love affairs with any livelier feeling than a self-analytical interest and something of a technician's resolve to profit by experience. After she had settled down in London she wrote to him once or twice and had a single brief reply, quite non-commital; then she abandoned letters and thought of him less often, but with an intensity that, against her expectations, grew no less poignant as the seasons passed. Not for an age, she knew, could she look for his reappearance; but she was no counter of days, and was taken utterly by surprise when she answered the doorbell one summer evening to see him standing outside, smiling in the way that she had never forgotten, with one eyebrow slightly raised.

He was a little heavier than she remembered, and neater, in a new dark suit and a new homburg in his hand, and his skin was sunburnt, but he looked down at her with the same brown sleepy eyes: a hint of mockery, perhaps, in his expression. For the moment she was literally struck dumb; he grinned, and asked:

"Do I look like a ghost, or have I forgotten to brush the leeches out of my hair?"

She took him to her studio, and could find only a conventional greeting.

"It seems years. I've missed you, Maurice. Are you staying long?"

"Three months, roughly. I owe you an apology, by the way.'

Armorel smiled, and seeing her look he added:

"About writing, I mean. I'm not much of a hand at letters, I'm afraid. And there's never much to say. The natives are black, the sun's hot, plains flat, hills steep, whisky cheap—that sort of thing."

"Then I'm glad you spared me."

"But I enjoyed yours. I was sorry you gave me up."

"Letters are futile, as you said. A choice of sloppy indiscretions or comments on the scenery. I gave up writing, but not thinking about you."

Maurice nodded. "The same at my end, sometimes. But I've always imagined you had your thoughts pretty well under control. The fact is——" He broke off as if undecided, stretching his legs and leaning back in a rickety chair that seemed about to give up and topple over. His eyes, exploring the littered studio, came to rest on a pipe, a pair of male slippers and a tweed jacket with a torn sleeve hanging on the back of the door.

"I see you've got company. I hope I don't intrude."

Armorel flushed a little, and handed him a cigarette. Emannuel Roote and his slovenly habits! She was expecting him at any moment to pack his things and go. He had been there a week—one of fate's malignant tricks that it should be the week of Maurice Cornforth's return!

"I've been waiting two years for this," she said, "but not in unrelieved celibacy. You wouldn't expect that, would you?"

He grinned, and flipped away a match. "I certainly wouldn't, from you."

"Any more than I should expect it in you."

"Then neither of us need be disappointed."

Maurice got up and examined for a moment a half-finished greyhound leaping after an invisible prey. When he looked round his expression was quizzical but also, in a curious way, defensive.

"Would it shock you to know that my companions were black but comely?"

Armorel went quickly over to a cupboard to fetch a bottle of cooking sherry and two tumblers.

"What a very odd conversation." But the oddest thing about it, she thought, was that she did feel shocked.

"You should tell your boy-friends not to leave their bedroom slippers about; they start up odd trains of thought."

Armorel poured out the sherry and said: "Here's luck. Black or what, I suppose they pass the time. Maurice, why did you come?"

He hesitated. "With honourable intentions. Are you free for dinner?"

Something in his tone alarmed her, making her throat dry; his manner was half jocular, half aloof. Nothing was as she had so often imagined it. She was silent, and he added:

"I'm giving a small party."

"How nice! It's a pity I'm engaged."

"We can make it to-morrow."

"I shouldn't dream of inconveniencing your friends."

"One of them's also a friend of yours—or was, once."

Armorel jumped to her feet, almost spilling her sherry. "Have you come back simply to make a fool of me? For God's sake go, if this is your idea of—if this is all——"

He rose too, looking distressed. "Armorel, we must get this straight. I'm fond of Brigid and I still want to marry her, if she'll have me. I know she's got a lot to forgive, but—well, she's a pretty forgiving sort of person, and we're all older now. I had an idea—she did, as a matter of fact—that we'd bury the hatchet and wash out the past, and that if you——"

"Please leave me out of it, Maurice. It's the sort of mutton-headed idea Brigid would have, if you'll forgive me for saying so, but I'm afraid I must deny her the pleasure of brandishing her trophies in my face."

Maurice smiled, but without amusement, for he was angry, and his voice was hard.

"You haven't changed! It's as you please. I've asked a man who came over with me on the ship—a simple sort of fellow, looking for someone to show him round. So think it over, and if you change your mind——" He told her the time and place, and a moment later the door had closed and she was once more alone.

A bitter ending! She told herself that she had long since grown indifferent, that this chance crossing of their divergent paths concerned her no more than a collision with a dustman in the street. In ten minutes they had quarrelled; their temperaments were hostile, their interests discordant, beneath that fine shell of his lay emptiness, quality and ambition alike rudimentary or wanting. She had no wish ever to see him again. Yet why had he come? The question tormented her. She only half believed his explanation. Brigid might have suggested or endorsed the visit, but he would not have made it unless it fell in with some impulse of his own; some pull had brought him back, after two years' absence, in spite of his thoughts of marriage and his half-felt contempt. Something existed; but then she recalled his look when evidence of her freedom—so much less abused than his own—had confronted him, and the subtle change of tone. Something had existed; she could not say whether it lived.

So a leaden and foredoomed curiosity triumphed over pride. He gave no sign of surprise or mockery, but was affable in turn to his three guests. Brigid was but little changed: impulsive, untidy, carelessly dressed, but equipped with an eager sincerity that disarmed the critical. To the fourth of the party, introduced as Freddy Begg, Maurice was a shade deferential, in recognition of the other's seniority and superior status, and the guest responded with a touch of graciousness towards his junior. He was shy and a little solemn, almost over-anxious to make friends and to enjoy what Armorel felt he might well describe as a jolly evening. That both she and Brigid were, in their small way, aspiring artists he found immensely gratifying; evidently he was one of those for whom practice of the arts exercised a sort of glamour, and late in the evening he confided in Armorel, with modest diffidence, the reason for his partiality.

"I had an inclination that way once myself," he explained, "though more in the direction of writing. But it was not to be, and perhaps it was all for the best."

And so with Freddy Begg she did the easy rounds of London in a prosperous summer, for her an altogether new kind of life. The contempt she had felt at a distance for its *bourgeois* and capitalist qualities faded, on closer inspection, to whole-hearted enjoyment. Invigorated by regular meals and spruced by greater cleanliness, she came to look her best: slim, well-built, with handsome eyes, dark hair and strong, lively features. Freddy Begg told himself that he was fortunate indeed to escort such a talented and attractive young lady to places of amusement.

As for her, she began to grow quite attached to Freddy. He had no power to charm, but she was for the moment satiated, even disgusted, with the compulsions of physical attraction, and found it a luxury to enjoy Freddy's companionship in peace and equilibrium. And he flattered her by his obvious delight in her company, and in the small efforts she made to entertain him. Her studio flat, which she knew to be inconvenient and squalid, he seemed to regard, in some obscure way, as romantic and dashing, and at one or two little parties she gave he displayed enjoyment so obvious as to be rather endearing. His face shone, his spectacles gleamed, he was arch with the women and effusive with the young men: altogether something of a figure of fun, and her friends looked on him, only too clearly, as a sort of freak, and took pleasure in filling him up with outrageous stories about each other and about their precarious lives; and as no one went so far as to tell tales about Armorel—understanding, with the freemasonry of the struggling, that she was on to a good thing and not wanting to queer her pitch—he came to regard her as a sort of pearl, or an unsullied snowdrop blooming among the orchids of vice.

All this amused Armorel and, unexpectedly, touched her

also; Freddy was so naïve and simple, so anxious to please, that she could not help the growth of a protective feeling towards him, as towards a child. Where at first she had been amused to hear her friends make fun of him, she now grew irritated at their flippancy, and found herself, at one of the uninhibited studio parties then much in fashion, trying to spare his sense of propriety the shocks it could hardly fail to meet. He had been so anxious to attend the party, to seize his chance to see the gay life at first hand; in fact he had given Armorel no peace until she arranged it, and his persistence had overcome her misgivings. Once in the thick of it, everything was as she had expected: crowded, unventilated, noisy, amorous, alcoholic and hot. Armorel did not enjoy such parties, for her inhibitions were tougher than her stomach, and it was clearly more than Freddy had bargained for; but he stood it all with manly fortitude, looking physically half-suffocated and morally outraged.

Armorel respected his doggedness and for the first time felt really drawn towards him; he was so plainly in a foreign element, yet so determined not to admit defeat. And now, in this monkey-house atmosphere, deafened by competitive voices, jostled by half-drunken strangers, bespattered, as it were, by the entrails of privacy sacrificed on a communal altar, it appeared to her, with all the force of a discovery, that convention is the price that must be paid to dignity for some measure of protection from the vulgarity of the human mind, and that Freddy, in his respect for decorum, had perhaps been wiser than she. Impulsively, she took his hand.

"Freddy, I'm tired; will you take me home?"

A remarkable change came over him; he brightened, he came to life.

"Of course, Armorel; I'm tired too. The atmosphere——"

Honour was saved, they were withdrawing after surfeit, not running away. One of those small explosions of honesty in the mind to which Armorel was addicted drove her to say:

"You know, Freddy, all this—it's bogus, really."

Freddy looked puzzled.

"All these people, I mean. They're not the ones who count. I don't suppose there's anyone here whose work matters. We're just the hangers-on."

Freddy, knotting his white silk muffler at the top of the stairs, frowned and said: "But they're artists, aren't they?"

A young man pushed his way past them and started down

the stairs, and on the first landing he was violently sick. The stench followed them down and the night air outside washed over their faces like sweet water. Neither spoke until they reached the end of the street. Then Freddy said:

"Do you realize that we never thanked our hostess? It seems terribly rude."

"I expect she passed out ages ago."

Lights leapt and swam like glittering fishes in the black, slippery waters of the river. They leant over the embankment to watch them, and the riding lights of a big black barge that glided silently by. The tide knocked softly against the wall below like a child smacking its lips. The river was full of mystery and ancient wisdom, the summer night cool and kind.

Freddy took off his spectacles, laid them carefully in their plush bed, snapped the two sides together and slid the case into his breast pocket.

"My glasses kept clouding over," he said. "It was the lack of ventilation." He paused, and added: "But an interesting experience."

At their feet a gull settled quietly on to the river, faintly luminous against the dark water. The smell of the sea came to them on a gentle breeze—tangy, rough, with a hint of rottenness, infinitely disturbing.

"I shall hate going back when my leave's up. I've had the best time of my life—thanks to you."

"Must you go back?"

"Oh, yes. I'm lucky to have such a good job—established, you know, and pensionable."

She laid a hand on his sleeve. "I believe you'll go a long way, Freddy. You know what you want. I don't think you'll fritter your life away as most people do."

"Armorel." Freddy's throat sounded dry, she could feel the tenseness of his arm under her hand as he gripped the balustrade.

"I've never met anyone like you before. You make me feel I want to do all sorts of things, just to please you. If you'd only give me a chance—I know I've not much to offer—but with your help . . . It would all be so different with you."

Armorel felt flustered, her heart thumped. She had made up her mind, yet she paused on the brink, hesitating to say the word, to make the gesture, that would topple her over into the abyss. The abyss—what a way to think of marriage to a good man! For Freddy was good, no doubt about it: kind, industrious, steady. If, in all his clay, there was no trace of alchemy, that was the price of security. One had to pay for one's needs. Unbidden, Maurice Cornforth's face came before her, and the old longing stabbed her heart. If it had been Maurice beside her now! Then the stars would have sung, the reflections danced under her feet, the very stones of the balustrade would surely have burst into flower. But Maurice had vanished, withdrawn himself deliberately from her life, and she knew that nothing she could say or do would recall him.

"Armorel, could you care for me a little? I care so very much for you! I only want to serve you—be your devoted slave —if you could give me the chance to show you——"

Freddy had lost his calm, he was hopelessly mixed up between emotions he could scarcely classify and the stilted phrases he had read and knew to be appropriate. No time, now, to hesitate, the poor man was floundering, drowning. She took his hand and squeezed it lightly; their flesh touched torpidly, there was no spark, it was like brushing against a stranger in a bus.

"If you want me, Freddy, I'll try to make you as happy as I can."

He lifted her hand and pressed a moist kiss into its palm, dizzy with his good fortune; but in his moment of triumph he shivered suddenly—a goose walking over his grave. He had caught sight of her smile—fixed, withdrawn, like a skull's grin. Absurd! A trick of the starlight, of course; nothing could spoil this moment, the fulfilment of his dreams.

"I shall try to prove myself worthy of you, my dearest," he said. "You've made me the happiest man in the world to-night."

She returned his fumbling kisses, but all the time she could hear the swish of tyres on tarmac, the distant clanging of a tram and the gentle licking of water against the river wall.

Chapter Nine

1929

AS soon as they reached the pagan village Robert Gresham knew that something was wrong. The village itself was like a scab, or a series of scabs, clinging on to the hillside: a circle of round mud huts roofed with thatch, each hut so low that a man had to bend double to enter, the earth between trampled and bared by many cloven and leathery feet. Naked babies with streaming eyes and running noses played in the dust, and scrawny chickens, almost as naked, scratched beside them. It was early; the sun, though hot, was mild, and the air still held a little of that miraculous freshness which made each dawn seem like the first morning of the world. A woman crouched beside a hut, grinding corn between two flat stones, her shoulder blades rising and falling under the glossy flesh as she swung to and fro. An old wrinkled grandmother, her flat breasts hanging down like burnt pancakes, peered out of a hut, squawked at the strangers and dived in again. Everything was oddly silent. A faint film of smoke oozed up through the thatch of the chimney-less huts and rose lazily into the air, like mist coming off a pond on a summer morning.

Robert halted in the centre of the village to confer with Ibrahim, who stalked, priest-like in his long robes, a pace or two behind.

"I have not come to talk to women. Where are the elders?"

Ibrahim looked round him in disdain. "They are cowards, lord, and they have fled to the bush."

Indeed, not a man was to be seen. Young and old, they had vanished, leaving their wives and children in possession.

"You told them to meet me here?"

"I told them, lord. They understood."

A woman came round from the back of a hut balancing a full gourd of water on her head. She stood for a moment staring at Robert, then put down her gourd and bolted into a hut. He did not like the look of things; and to make it worse there was Freddy Begg at his elbow, gazing about him in an impatient way, waiting for the show to begin.

"They must have failed to understand your message," he remarked heartily. "It seems unfortunate, especially as I must return without fail this afternoon. . . . The behaviour of these people would seem to suggest a marked—ah—lack of confidence in the administration."

Robert smiled. "I'm afraid the lack of confidence is on both sides. Flight may not be evidence, but it's strong presumption of guilt."

"Of what do you presume them to be guilty?"

"That is what I have to find out."

The escort of four native policemen moved methodically from hut to hut. The entrance of each one was followed, a few minutes later, by a spewing forth of infuriated women who screeched abuse, accompanied by children of all sizes. The women gathered in groups and stood together sullenly, their ornaments and armlets winking in the sun.

The village clung to a sort of ledge of the hillside, with a ragged pinnacle of boulders at its rear. Robert clambered up them, pushing his way through the bush which grew stiffly on every bit of soil caught between the rocks. Although it was not yet ten o'clock he was soon bathed in sweat, but on the summit of the pinnacle a fresh breeze cooled his face, and he looked out over a bush-clad valley stretching away below. Behind him lay higher and wilder crests and even rockier peaks; mountains, serrated and craggy, rolled away for many days' journey, trackless save for faint paths that wound from one hidden settlement to the next. That they scratched a living from the soil was as true of these people as of chickens. Their cultivation was sporadic and impermanent, they moved from place to place as they listed, in all these hills were to be found no standing villages or habitations, save only a mission station, one of the most lonely in the country, where a handful of Italian monks, deeply isolated from their kind, carried on their ceaseless daily battle against apathy, ignorance and busy pagan spirits.

In the village, the policemen piled together the trophies of their search: an old human skull, some whitened bones and a nameless collection of medicines and talismans used for magical rites. They proffered also the remains of a half-burnt notebook with stiff boards and the buckle of a belt to which a little charred leather adhered. Examining the notebook, Robert made out in careful, rounded strokes the characters Tax Ass, followed by a few truncated words and then a number of blank and charred pages. Ibrahim glanced at it and said:

"God is merciful. This man will suffer no more." And to Robert's question the policeman who had found the notebook replied: "It was among the ashes of a fire, lord, between two houses."

All through the hot morning Robert questioned the women; his rewards were silences, evasions, lies. The men were hunting; they were searching for fresh cattle pastures; they had gone no one knew where. No stranger had entered the village; a man had come but had passed on into the hills; he was no man,

5

but a spirit. The men would return to-night; they would be away three days; no one knew how long their absence would be. Back in camp, Ibrahim produced a carrier who had married a girl of this hill-tribe and had lived for a while with his wife's family, and the offer of a reward prompted him to aver that he knew how to make the drums talk in a way that would be understood. So he was sent off with instructions to tap out in the language of the drums a summons to the men to return to the village at sundown for a parley.

Priscilla had been out all the morning, searching for insects or birds. She looked exhausted but pleased, for she had found a new kind of wild flower and a francolin she had not seen before.

"It went into a hole under a stone. I tried to poke it out with a stick, but it seemed to have gone to ground like a rabbit . . . Robert, what has gone wrong?"

"I'm afraid these idiots have done in the unfortunate clerk."

"Oh, Robert! And you warned the Resident."

"I half expected trouble. Not that one anticipates anything serious, but these people have been making fresh arrow poison; I came across signs of it in the bush. So you'll please conduct our distinguished visitors home this-afternoon?"

Priscilla, combing her hair for lunch, looked apprehensive. "Darling, please be sensible, if you can. I know everything is civilized now, not like the old days, but you're so foolhardy . . . ."

"You needn't worry. As a matter of fact I believe we're in more danger from Freddy than from any number of pagans."

"Freddy! He's not sharpening his assegai?"

Robert laughed. "I wasn't thinking so much of life as of peace of mind, which, after all, may be more important."

Priscilla powdered her face and throat reflectively. She was not concentrating; the powder went on patchily, too white in places. She wiped some of it off.

"Robert, did you know the clerk? Was he nice?"

"Nice? It's hard to say. He was new. He seemed like all the rest, a southerner, anxious to please, passed school certificate and so on. They're much of a muchness, you know."

"Yes, that's the difficult part . . . like the sparrows."

"It can't be helped—think of floods in China, famines in Russia, earthquakes in Japan. Besides, I suspect you're being blasphemous. It's the Almighty's job to grieve over fallen sparrows, not ours."

"Those sparrows! What a stumbling block they are. If God knows each sparrow then he must also be concerned with every fish, every fly—I suppose all the bacteria and even viruses. There's no reason why he should favour only vertebrates. And when you think that there may be a hundred thousand living creatures in every drop of milk!"

"It places a strain on one's credulity, I admit," Robert replied.

"Have you ever broken open the sort of bulb from which the spikes grow on a whistling thorn?"

"Yes, they're hollow, and I don't know what they're for."

"For ants, perhaps, to rest in—like bus shelters, or rather youth hostels, one might say. Have you ever noticed the ants on a whistling thorn? Up and down, up and down, all day long and I suppose all night, from the roots to the tip of each spine and back again, never ending. Those hollow bulbs are often full of them, crawling round and round, in and out. So far as one can see there's absolutely no purpose. They aren't carrying anything, or making a nest, or migrating. They're just crawling on and on, always in a frantic hurry. I suppose there must be replacements, but one can see no differences, it's just a continuous stream: terrifying, like catching a glimpse of the very principle of life itself—continuity, motion, timelessness, anonymity."

"Yet the Prophet also singled out that species. Even the weight of an ant, he said, is not absent from God."

"And Solomon commended them. There must be some reason—perhaps to prevent us from drawing hideous parallels with the human world. Suppose there was someone watching us crawling about our thorn bushes; they would ask: 'How can God possibly know each one of those aimless creatures? And what are they for?' Just as we can't believe in the significance of each of those thousands of millions of hurrying, scurrying, purposeless ants—or of the countless living germs one trumpets out, I believe, every time one sneezes. . . .'"

"Solomon's advice has always seemed to me ridiculous; all one can learn from ants, so far as I can see, is that industry is futile and order a dead end. Give me the lilies of the field, every time. . . . Whatever you do, don't tell Freddy about that clerk, for the present; as it is, his party's ruined."

But it was too late. The news had already spread, and at lunch Freddy said accusingly:

"Armorel has been out sketching, and in the circumstances it was clearly most unwise for the ladies to have left camp."

"I don't think there's any danger," Robert answered. "It was the clerk they wanted, and they got him. They've run away from us."

"Quite so; but in sending the clerk by himself without an escort among these primitive people I'm afraid you showed a certain ignorance of their attitude, or perhaps undue optimism as to their co-operation. We cannot afford to run any further risks."

This was too much for Priscilla. "Robert didn't want to send the clerk," she said warmly. "He was over-ruled, and after all the orders came from higher up."

"Really?" Freddy said icily; and Priscilla, seeing Robert glance at her and give a faint shake of the head, once more regretted her impulsiveness. "Orders, as you put it, from higher up must be translated into practice with due regard for existing circumstances by those on the spot."

"If those on the spot were listened to——"

"We'd better leave them to fight their own battles, my dear," Armorel said. "The man on the spot versus the man with a broad view is as old an argument as the chicken and the egg, and just as boring."

Her tone was unbearably patronizing, and to make it worse Priscilla knew that she was right. Why could she not control her tongue! Armorel, indeed, was wondering idly why Priscilla, in some ways so practical, should be so imprudent. She had offended Freddy the night before and that was foolish to start with; any married woman who aped a sensitive virgin when faced with a little distasteful but expedient bottom-pinching was merely affected. Now she was making matters far worse by doing the loyal little woman act—sheer stupidity. After all, Robert was Freddy's junior in the service now and they must swallow that, however much it hurt their pride; a sharp lesson wouldn't do either of them any harm.

While the camp equipment was packed after lunch, Freddy insisted on having the four armed policemen posted round the rest-house on guard. Priscilla, with interest, observed one of them settle down on a rock in the shade of a small thorn and then gradually drop off to sleep. Afternoons, even in these hills, were blisteringly hot; the very bush seemed to brood and crouch beneath the dead weight of a thermal load. A lovely place, this camp, but strangely unlucky; Priscilla thought of the butchered Pailthorpe lying under the dry turf above. How curious a resting-place for a young Englishman's bones! If you could add them up, these unmarked graves scattered over the plains and swamps of Africa, under the beds of her rivers and bordering seas and in all the continents beyond them, England would seem but a factory for sepulchres, her young men forced outward from their kindly centre by some strange centrifugal force as unaccountable as the impulse that sent the ants hurrying over the surface of their own world, and perhaps as purposeless. . . .

She sighed, and glanced again at the nodding policeman; it was a wonder the rock did not scorch his behind. Surely something moved in the bush above him? She stared for several minutes, seeing nothing but parched grass, spiky bushes and brown rock. Then, again, the branch of a bush quivered slightly.

Absurd! A buck, of course, or possibly a leopard. Ought she to tell Robert? The policeman was still asleep. Behind him a rocky ledge commanded his position, and the camp as well. Was it further than an arrow's flight? She did not know; it would be best to tell Robert.

He had gone back to the village, the carriers said. She scrambled along the pathless contour of the hill between boulders and bush, under the threatening ledge, quickening her steps, for it would be foolish to come to a sticky end, so far from home: a grave embarrassment to Robert, and of course to the poor pagans, struggling to protect themselves in the only way they could—Canute-like, trying to stem the tides of history with their charms, their prayers and their poisoned barbs.

Voices sounded ahead. Robert was coming back, but not alone; Freddy was with him. Now she dared not mention the quivering bush. How right Robert had been! The risk of a puncture by a poisoned arrow seemed to matter little beside the prospect of Freddy's offended temper.

"You shouldn't be walking about by yourself," Freddy told her crossly. "It's not safe." He was touchy as a bear to-day; Priscilla felt, if not exactly guilty, at least responsible. He avoided her eyes, but when her head was turned she could sense that he was looking at her. Indeed, he could not keep his eyes away; the rebuff had only sharpened his desire, and his recognition of its absurdity lacerated his self-esteem. The expedition he had so buoyantly planned had been a dreadful failure, and now Robert, by his lack of forethought, had landed them in this stupid mess; their very lives were in danger, the reputation of the Government at stake. All very well claiming to understand the natives, but this was carrying things too far!

A few hundred yards from the rest-house they heard someone approaching at the double, and the policeman who had been asleep pulled up in front of them. He looked as if he had seen an apparition.

"Lord," he said. "Someone is hiding in the bush." He pointed towards the ridge above them.

"Did you challenge him?"

"No, lord, I ran to tell you."

"Fall in at the rear and have your rifle ready, but do not shoot unless I do."

"I warned you to be more careful," Freddy almost shouted. "And Armorel's alone in the camp."

"No need to worry." Robert was carrying his rifle; now he slipped a cartridge into the breech. "As likely as not it's a wandering goat, but at most it's one of their spies keeping an eye on us."

His manner reassured even Freddy for the moment, he seemed quite unconcerned. They breasted the rise and Priscilla's eyes turned to the ledge above them. She halted suddenly; something was there, crouching beside a small cliff. They all stopped, frozen like rabbits, and from the rear she heard Freddy whisper loudly: "Take cover!" Robert, in the lead, slowly raised his rifle, and Priscilla put her fingers to her ears. The rifle cracked, and rocks flung back the echoes. There was a dreadful scream, the sound of a body falling and a stone, dislodged, came rolling down.

What had Robert done! She looked round; Freddy had disappeared, just vanished. She looked back at Robert.

"You haven't shot him!"

"Come and see."

He led the way to the ledge, scrambling up a steep rise. His victim had toppled over and lay dead, caught against the trunk of a half-grown thorn. It was a large baboon.

They burst out laughing together. The tension over, it seemed a great joke. The policeman came panting up and gaped at the baboon, his eyes round and astonished; then he too joined in. The more he laughed the funnier it seemed, until he doubled up with laughter on the ground, clasping his knees and rocking to and fro.

"All the same, it was quite a harmless baboon." Priscilla was serious again. "And you shouldn't have made a fool of Freddy."

"It was God, not I, who made a fool of Freddy," Robert said.

They reached the rest-camp to see a file of carriers starting down the hill with bulky loads borne lightly on their heads. Freddy appeared half an hour later, in time for the last brew of tea. Stirring in the sugar, he said:

"I think we may count ourselves very fortunate that no worse consequences followed this regrettable affair. It was most imprudent to leave Armorel alone in the camp at such a time. Naturally, when the alarm was raised, I returned with all possible speed to see to her safety."

"Naturally," Robert said.

"Of course you did, Freddy," Priscilla added, with a shade too much warmth. "It was just as well. We were very lucky it was only a——" Her lips quivered, it was terrible, a laugh was forcing its way up like a bubble. She faked a sneeze but of course Amorel, looking aloof and amused, was not deceived. "A baboon." She had got it out, but her voice was much too loud.

"It was indeed," Freddy said stiffly, keeping his eyes fixed on his tea. "We should never have been put into the position of owing our safety to good luck. That casual attitude has resulted already in one brutal crime. I must express the wish—in fact I must give definite instructions—that far more adequate precautions must be taken in future, when dealing with these apparently still unsettled tribes. The prestige of the Government —but I will say no more."

A little restored by his own magnanimity, Freddy drained his tea, thankful that at last a thoroughly unsatisfactory episode was coming to an end. A few minutes later Robert waved to them from the veranda and watched them disappear down a path that twisted and turned among the boulders. Soon the plains below were bathed in the evening's lavender haze, plum-coloured shadows crept gently across the hillsides and the huge sun floated in a golden sea above a crimson-banded horizon.

Chapter Ten

ON her rare visits to the women's compound behind the Emir's palace, Priscilla wondered how she would fill her life inside these high mud walls, daily domestic tasks her only occupation, the trivial happenings of the palace and her children's progress the only food for her mind. In such imprisonment one would see in the wall's innumerable cracks and fissures great rivers roaming through an unknown land; in the rough surface between, woods and mountains; and in the ants and lizards scuttling up and down, elephants and dragons.

But the Emir's women seemed as placid and contented as cows in a spring pasture. Graceful in their gaily printed cloths, barefooted, supple, they moved about the compound on their tasks, exchanging words with each other in high, musical voices. The faces of the younger women were smooth and rounded, soft as purple grapes. They counted themselves among the fortunate: safe, well-fed, valued, comfortable. Here was security, the lodestar of the west, by the east long captured and domesticated; but when we saw it brought to earth, we no longer liked the look of it. Immediately we talked of freedom, and wished to destroy it. Free your women, we said: and those that had done so we rebuked for their prostitutes and beggars. The inconsistency of rationalists! As if freedom and security could be driven in tandem; as well try to mix quicksilver with treacle, imprison the lightning within the stone. Always, one must choose. Here the choice had fallen on security, and among the women, so far as Priscilla had been able to discover, the mole of revolt had not yet started to burrow under the walls.

Her hostess, the Emir's senior wife, was old and rich. She wore her age in her face, crinkled like a ripe passion-fruit, but full of dignity; and her wealth on the walls of her apartments, in the shape of plates. Plates of all kinds; gaudy, garish and hideous in design. They hung in rows on the walls, depicting scenes of English coaching inns, the Houses of Parliament, knaves of hearts, bulldogs draped in Union Jacks. Few women could display so varied a collection—a sign, clear to all, of her husband's wealth and generosity and the high respect in which she was held. The Emir himself led Priscilla to his women's quarters and her hostess prostrated herself, forehead to the ground, on her husband's entrance. As soon as he withdrew she rose and invited the guest to be seated on a chair brought specially for the European—an ugly uncomfortable tubular steel chair, no doubt regarded as the last word in western fashions. The Emir's wife herself reclined on rugs strewn over the floor, her cloth lying round her in graceful folds, and Priscilla felt her own perched-up position to be absurd and vulgar: as if the Albert Memorial had been transferred to Timbuktu.

They exchanged formal inquiries about each other's health and well-being, and touched on the weather and the state of the crops. Conversation flagged; it was, indeed, hard to find fruitful topics with a companion to whom even the streets and markets of her own town were foreign, let alone the world beyond. As to events within her own citadel, propriety forbade their discussion with a stranger. The silence stretched out painfully for Priscilla, but the Emir's wife was serene and unconcerned; for her there was nothing awkward in silence, she wrapped it round her like a cloak.

Priscilla made another effort. "We hear that the Governor may soon pay us a visit. His wife has not been to this province before."

The Emir's wife nodded. "And the King," she ventured, "is in good health?"

"Yes, thank you, the King is very well."

"May God bless his Majesty with long life and prosperity."

"If it is God's will."

"And the Queen: she, also, is in good health?"

"The Queen's health, I believe, is excellent."

"May God be praised, and bless her Majesty with long life and many lusty sons."

"If God is merciful." Priscilla, though she spoke the language fluently, was always a little uncertain of the correct blending of God in the conversation; on the whole, one could not do it too often. She hoped they would pass on to some less formal subject: but once launched on the Royal Family, her hostess seemed content.

"I have heard," she remarked, "that her Majesty the Queen takes her meals with the King, at the same table with their guests. Can this indeed be true?"

"Yes, quite true. It is the English custom for husband and wife to feed together with the guests of their house."

"Even in the palaces of kings?"

"Yes, everywhere."

The wife clicked her tongue in shocked amazement. Mixed feeding, what would these immodest foreigners think of next! But, of course, white people were always eating, it was one of their most extraordinary characteristics. To prepare for tea, her girls had been baking cakes all the afternoon. She clapped her brown claw-like hands and two girls appeared, one carrying a small table and the other a tray with tea. The plates were piled with peculiar-looking cakes smothered in icing sugar. One of the girls poured them each a cup of weak tea, made a deep curtsy, and retired.

Priscilla looked round the room. Hand-woven mats covered the floor and cloths decorated the plain mud walls; there was no furniture. A curtain made by sewing together strips of cotton material woven on the narrow looms of the country formed one side of the room, and behind it doubtless lay the sleeping chamber. Like the women's lives, everything was simple, harmonious and terribly bare. There was no ugliness in the room (save for the plates) and no interest. The inheritance of a nomad people was there.

The Emir's own apartments, to which she had been with Robert, were quite different. They were equipped in European style with hideous furniture ordered, only too clearly, *en bloc* from a catalogue of one of the more prolific British firms. Sofas and chairs, bleekly angular and upholstered in a brown material covered with lozenges, triangles and other geometrical designs, were never sat on, and the fireplace, flanked by yellow tiles and guarded by a firescreen of imitation tapestry, was never used. The Emir was proud of his house, built in concrete blocks tinted to imitate the prevailing red mud, but it was not intended to be lived in, any more than wax fruit on Victorian dinner-tables was intended to be eaten.

Priscilla sipped her tea, wondering what it would be like to be one of a harem. Obviously the system would have certain advantages. She thought of the worn, over-worked older women of her own village, endlessly cooking, washing, mending for their husbands and brood, tied to their cottages by the inevitable baby, struggling to make ends meet; eating with their man at every meal and sharing his bed every night. By comparison. how soothing and easy the life of the harem! The work, shared out between several, would immediately become much less onerous, whether it was cooking or procreation, and there would always be somebody to mind the baby if you had other ploys.

And the gossip and talk! One would never run short of topics. (My *dear*, have you seen how that new chit carries on, as if she were Queen of Sheba? The way she hennas her hands all day! And the antimony on her eyes! I'm told her father is just a small farmer, and our husband got her very cheap—a mere handful of kola nuts and a couple of scraggy cows, I believe. Of course, if it's actually her father; I have *heard* he's a eunuch really, pensioned off by the old Emir. Well, she'll soon find that life isn't all a mouthful of kola, and meanwhile our husband's in an excellent humour. And have you heard Fatima's news? Yes, there's going to be an addition. . . .) Never a dull moment, Priscilla thought.

But for husbands, that was another matter. One wife at a time was enough for most Englishmen, it seemed. Fancy having to keep up two or three! (Mary, did you cook this stew? I *told* you I couldn't stand pepper in it and now *again* . . . I didn't tell you? Of course I did. It was Margaret I told? Oh, hell!) And think of the jealousies, the recriminations. (You know I've wanted a new hat for *months*, and now I see that little half-wit Monica going about in something that makes her look like an unsuccessful table decoration; I wonder you aren't ashamed to carry on like an infatuated schoolboy—at your time of life, too! When I think of all the things I've done for you. . . .) No, English women were too self-assertive and the men, apparently, lacking in ambition.

Priscilla's hostess at last broke the silence in which they had sipped their tea.

"It has been said that the King has been considering our children, and especially the way in which they are to be taught."

So that was it! Priscilla knew that she had not been invited merely as a gesture of goodwill.

"No doubt the King," she replied, "wishes to see the children of all his subjects taught in a way that will enable them to become men and women of industry, good manners and repute."

"It is true, then, that the Governor wishes our daughters to learn to make letters?"

"In England we believe that girls have need of schooling no less than boys."

"Our girls are taught to cook, to clean, to spin and to obey

their husbands," the Emir's wife said with a certain asperity.
"Is that not enough?"

It was curious, Priscilla thought, how every attempt of ours
to improve the lot of the people under our charge was resisted
most stubbornly by those who stood most to gain. Poor St.
George! He galloped about after dragons, but these dusky
princesses, instead of greeting him as their saviour, endeavoured
slyly to trip his horse and blunt his spear, so as to preserve the
very dragons he was intent on slaying. The trouble was that they
had domesticated the dragons. . . .

"A *malam* is to come to teach our daughters," her hostess
went on. "But that is not sufficient to please the Governor.
No doubt he wishes them also to learn stories of your country
and the customs of people there. Of such things even our most
learned *malams* are not fully informed, and naturally it would
be impossible for the English teacher in the town, a young man,
to enter our quarters."

Priscilla felt flattered; absurdly, perhaps, but at least it was
a mark of confidence, more probably in Robert than in her,
that the Emir should have decided to ask her to teach his
daughters.

"No doubt," she suggested, "you need an English woman
for your girls. If the Emir thinks that I can be of assistance, I
shall be glad to help."

The Emir's wife nodded. "That is the Emir's wish," she said.
"Our daughters will be honoured to see so noble an example."

On her way back to the house Priscilla wondered whether
she had been too hasty. What would the Government say?
She was not on the teaching staff, not even a certified teacher;
perhaps she should have asked permission first. Yes, undoubtedly,
that was what she should have done—consulted the Resident,
or Robert at least. She sighed: why could she never think
of what she ought to have done until it was too late? But she
could not have asked Robert, he had disappeared. It was five
days now since she had left him in the hills. Five days, and
no word had come. It was absurd, of course, to fuss; tribesmen
did not make trouble, nowadays, with their masters. (There
was Pailthorpe, but that had been fifteen years ago; the clerk,
but he had not been a European.) Robert knew the people,
the country, inside out, he would not take foolish risks. Yet he
had only four armed policemen against a whole tribe of angry
and frightened men with poisoned arrows, in country where

an ambush would be as easy as falling off a log. Absurd, of course, to fuss, but . . . She had been ill again, fever, she supposed, half repressed by quinine. Her head ached and anxiety gnawed away at her mind. Every morning she said to the cook:

"Doubtless he will come to-day, and we will have ground-nut stew. Be sure to get a fat chicken in the market, and soak some apple rings, for he is fond of apple pie." But the cook was only half attending, he was in the midst of getting married and his thoughts were all of cattle deals and the baskets of kola nuts that must go to the bride's father. And the day dragged by and no one came, there was not even a message.

That evening the Resident looked in on his way back from polo.

"Robert has done it again," he said. "I don't know how he manages to bluff the hillmen these days, most of them are getting wise. But he's sent down four of 'em, nicely handcuffed, and they've confessed to killing that wretched devil of a clerk."

"So he's safe!" Priscilla exclaimed with immense thankfulness, and then felt rather ashamed; to fuss over the safety of his officers would be considered another piece of woman's foolishness by the Resident, who stood as if planted like a short stocky tree in her sitting-room, looking dark and sweaty, the stubble already showing on his chin.

"Though whether we shall get a conviction," he added gloomily, "is altogether another kettle of fish. So far as I can see there's no evidence, unless they tell on each other, and by the time the lawyers have been at 'em they'll know better than that."

"And Robert? He's back?"

The Resident shook his head, twirled the remains of his whisky and soda round in its glass and looked gloomier than ever. He had a fleshy face, and a habit of pouting when he was thinking what to say.

"I don't know what's got hold of Robert, he simply sent a message. Said he wouldn't be back for a few days. On the track of some evidence, I suppose, but there's a pile of stuff on his desk as high as this house. I hope he'll put his best foot forward, I must say."

"Wasn't there any message for me?"

"Not that I know of—at least, not through the office," the Resident added hastily, seeing her crestfallen look. He glanced at her quickly over his glass, and added: "Look here, I don't

altogether like your being here on your own. Won't you come
up to the Residency? Maud would be delighted, I know."

"Oh, no thank you, Commander Catchpole—thank you
very much all the same," Priscilla said hastily—much too
hastily, she knew. "It's awfully kind. But Robert might get
back any moment, and I've got such a lot of animals here——"

It was true. There was a baby antelope which had been
brought to the door a few days before, its legs roped together,
its body flat as a board; she was feeding it out of a bottle, she
hoped it would live. And two chameleons, Pyramus and
Thisbe, on the veranda, needing a regular supply of flies; and
several cocoons in cardboard boxes that might hatch any time,
and of course Robert's ponies.

"It's awfully kind," she repeated, "but Robert is sure to be
back soon."

"Oh, that's all right," the Resident said. "If you want
anything, just ring up Maud any time." He was not at all
offended, but a little disturbed. Priscilla had a habit of wandering in the town by herself, down at the market, in all sorts of
places—and then she roamed about the country on those
collecting expeditions of hers. It was safe enough, of course,
quite harmless, nothing to worry about, but still—not quite
the thing.

"Well, I must be off—see you at polo to-morrow?"

"Oh yes, I hope so—that is, if I—I'll see how I feel." This
would be a good opportunity to ask him about the school.
Priscilla took the plunge.

"Teach the Emir's daughters? Well, I don't see why not."
Commander Catchpole frowned and scratched the back of his
neck, pouting as he concentrated. The way women sprang
things at you, at sundowner time, too! "Of course, it's really
the Education people's pigeon, we don't want to get their hackles
up. And I'm not quite sure whether the wife of one of my
officers—whether it's quite the thing——"

On second thoughts, no. The Education people might object
to poaching, and to have a district officer's wife dinning the
A B C into all these little native kids. . . . Of course, women
did it nowadays, but they were Education, the Administration
was a different thing. Their wives must be above reproach.
Maud did things with the women, reclaimed the girls and so
on, but that wasn't a school-teacher's job. But then, he remembered, he had talked about this school to Freddy Begg.

It was something the Secretariat was pushing, Begg had attached importance to its success. Perhaps, on the whole, if she wanted to mess about with the thing . . .

"I should think that would be all right," he said. "If you're sure you feel up to it. I shouldn't think you'd get much sense out of them; the women, you know, are really cows. . . . Don't worry about Robert; he can look after himself."

That was true enough, she thought, when the Resident had gone, leaving her to another solitary evening by the hissing lamp, turning a book's pages and listening half consciously for the sound of a car. Robert had a sort of genius with the native people. He understood what they were thinking. They rewarded him with their trust—so far, that is, as a man of one race will trust a man of another. With them he was contented, interested, at ease, free from the moods of doubt and questioning that sometimes fastened to his shoulders in his home. Indeed, she thought a little wryly, if she were jealous it would be of these dark easy companions, not of some colleague's wife; but she was not jealous, only lonely, and she wished that he would return. To-night the silence was broken by the sound of song and laughter and some kind of guitar: the cook was having a party, something to do with his wedding, no doubt. She sighed; he would be grumpy and absent-minded to-morrow; but the sound was companionable, it kept away for a little the immeasurable bleakness of a vast and hostile night.

Chapter Eleven

PRISCILLA was giving the gazelle its evening bottle when she heard the sound of Robert's car. By the time she reached the living-room he was there, looking delighted and jaunty, the light of a lamp, just lit, shining on his short red beard. He had been away little more than a week, but kissed her as if they had been parted a year.

"Home! It's a miracle every time one sees it. I'm so glad to be back!"

"It's not much of a home." She stood back to twist up an escaping coil of hair and looked round—how bare and impersonal it seemed! Their few things were battered with packing;

you could not make a great deal of a house if you never stayed in it much longer than a year.

"One doesn't think of the walls and the furniture when one's away. I've missed you so! Are you all right? No more headaches, fever? Any letters from home? Have you managed to avoid the Catchpoles and to exercise the ponies? Is the cook still in the throes of his wedding?"

"Darling, you're so impatient. I think everything is much the same. The cook had a small herd of cattle here last night, something to do with his wedding, of course, they trampled one of the flower-beds and ate the thatch off the garden house, so annoying. I've been all right, but terribly anxious."

"Anxious?" It was genuine, he really did look surprised.

"But naturally, what do you expect? After all, I left you all alone with a lot of murderers with poisoned arrows, and I've had no message even, nothing. You might have been stewed and eaten by now, for all I knew."

"I'm sorry, it didn't occur to me that you'd be worrying. I knew Catchpole would tell you I was on the way."

"But that's days ago, and you didn't come. Darling, where have you been ever since?"

"I ended up near the mission, so I stayed on there for a couple of days."

"Oh, I see . . . . Why, Robert?"

"I like the chap who runs it—a little Italian called Father Anselm. He's interesting, he knows a lot about those hill tribes, and he's got some quality that fascinates me, something we've lost, if we ever had it: a sort of innocence and simplicity. Anyway, it's restful, and curiously refreshing."

This was too much! Priscilla said, rather tartly: "I expect it is, but while you were being rested, Robert, and refreshed, we were all fussing about you and wondering what had happened. You could so easily have sent a message. . . ."

She checked herself, but it was really intolerable! There was the Resident worrying about piles of work and she herself plagued with anxiety—and Robert calmly taking a holiday at a mission, because he liked the Italian Father, without a word to anyone.

"You talk as if I'd been on the telephone," he said. "A message would have taken two days, and there was nothing whatever to fuss about."

"I can't understand you, Robert! You say such fine-sounding

things about getting home, about your love for me, and when it comes to the point you stay away for as long as you please without even bothering to send a note down with the policemen, knowing quite well I should be worrying myself to death."

She started to move about the room, hating Robert for his selfishness and herself for her unreasonable and sudden anger; her nerves were on edge these days and trivialities drove her to despair.

"Do you expect me to give notice in advance of every movement I make? It's not my fault my job takes me away. You talk of home—your idea seems to be to make it a prison!"

"Don't you understand? Don't you know how people feel, waiting, uncertain, alone? Of course you do understand, that's what makes it so maddening. You're not a clod without imagination, yet you don't bother to see—oh, it's too much, I can't stand it!" And overtaken by hysterical tears, she rushed from the room.

Robert paced up and down in black anger, muttering to himself. Scenes! He could not stand such scenes. He had been away for more than a week, not amusing himself, as Priscilla seemed to think—in danger certainly, though he made light of it, on the knife's edge of safety. He had needed that brief rest, if only she'd had the wit to see it, to let the tension ease. She accused him of insensitiveness; had she no understanding? To fly at him thus, within ten minutes of his return—tired from a long drive, hoping for sympathy, affection. . . . His anger ebbed suddenly and he felt deflated, baffled. So much had gone wrong lately: so many quarrels between them, or less than quarrels; a loss of the wordless understanding that had been the very cement of their love.

Priscilla lay on the bed, her face buried in the pillow. What had happened to her, to her life with Robert? For a week she had longed for his return. She had planned their first evening together, his meal, the dress she would wear, the way she would extract from him little by little the tale of his adventures; and now, by her own stupidity and crassness, she had dispelled the dream. It was madness: as if she had, in actuality, been entered by a devil. For it had happened before, nowadays it was always happening, in defiance of her resolution. She was on her guard, yet each time the devil danced through her defences to put venom on her tongue.

She got up, distressed but calmer, and sat down at the dressing-

table. The brush in her hand was shaking, her arm had no more
strength than a wet newspaper. How haggard her face was
getting, how old! Her eyes rested on the portrait of her son, and
the even motion of the brush grew slower, like an engine running
down, until it ceased altogether and her hands lay limply in
her lap. That fresh young face, untouched by mortality, so like
Robert's and yet so different (the same creature in two elements,
as the reptile in water becomes a bird in the air)—how inaccessible
he had become, how unfamiliar! She could not even be sure
that he existed. He may have been dead a week, she thought,
I should not know; and suppose he had, how little difference
to my life it would make, how little to his should I die to-night!
Already our lives have fallen apart, each following its independent pattern, all the links broken. Now she was shut out from
his mind, vanished, like a shape he had seen once in the firelight
of the nursery long ago. She could remember him in a hundred
scenes, he would scarcely recall her in one.

Her own loss she must bear, but why should Robin be cheated
of that right enjoyed by the humblest little woolly-pated African,
even by the beasts of the field: the right to his home? Without
it, he would grow like a tree badly rooted, tall but unstable,
unconscious of his deprivation and yet spiritually maimed.
To Priscilla, her home had been her centre, from it her very
personality had been distilled; even now, so many years later,
her childhood was more real than a nomadic and attenuated
prime, her memories vivid of a warm crowded kitchen with its
open grate, the kettle singing and a smell of cakes baking and
tea spread on the table, the homely hot aroma of paraffin
lamps; of quarrels and laughter, quick anger and secret jokes,
the dark steep stairs and the mustiness of damp walls, frocks
torn on rough-barked apple trees, the rich flavour of bread and
dripping and spring onions for tea.

It came back so strongly to her now, the warmth and friendliness and vitality of it, that Priscilla looked through her pale
reflection in the glass into a vanished world and forgot her poor
existence. Richness, that was the memory—the bounty of love;
and coming slowly back to her surroundings she asked again
with bitterness why Robin should be cheated of all such memories,
and she of the other children she had wanted so much. She
thought again of her own empty life, the crumbling bedroom
hospitable only to earwigs and mosquitoes, the bare silent room
below, the illustrated papers, Robert's preoccupation, the

Catchpoles' dinner parties, her dead moths and beetles. . . .
Self-pity, that was the enemy; hundreds of others, confronted
with the same dilemma, had made the same choice. Africa
enforced it; you could not have home and husband at the same
time, your family was part of the sacrifice. She was one of many,
and now she was being silly, selfish and weak. Dabbing on a
little make-up, she resolved to ask Robert's forgiveness and
retrieve what she could of the evening.

But the sitting-room was empty, Robert gone. Her spirits
sank again. Perhaps he had been too deeply wounded and
retreated to some distant camp or station. There was something
evanescent, unrooted about him that she feared, for one day it
might drive him to an unpredictable and final act. But that
night the car was in its garage, his hat on the table, his place
laid for dinner in the bare dining-room with its high vaulted
roof.

She wandered restlessly round the room, listening again for
his footstep. It was hot and sultry, storms must be in the air,
but at present all was heavy and suspended. Her head ached
and her knees were shaky and her throat dry; was it her distress,
or the return of fever? Pouring herself some whisky, she drank
it almost neat, and its very fumes, pungent and smoky, pulled
her together. Lying back in an easy chair she felt the strength
creep back into her hands and feet and into the pulses of her
blood. Despair, misery, defeat had possessed her a moment
before, now they were routed, she felt almost the equal of life.
Let Robert leave her for the evening if he would, in a childish
tantrum; the gesture was hollow, she was not impressed. She
was thinking of more important things; they raced through her
head, glowing and sparking like fireflies or floating away like
iridescent bubbles to burst just out of reach. And Robert—did
she love him truly, was he the end and object of her life? The
question, kept locked away, thrust suddenly at her. Once on a
ship, there had been a frightful storm; three days it had lasted,
everything was shattered and adrift. The piano in the passengers'
lounge had broken loose, it had galloped up and down, to and
fro, crashing with a sound like thunder against the sides. That
was what the question was like, it had broken loose from its
moorings, it was dashing about among the furniture of her mind.

She poured out another whisky. People condemned solitary
drinking; she condemned it herself, and herself with it; but,
let them say what they liked, solitude was the condition that

placed you most in need of its support. To be gay with friends
was one thing, by yourself, impossible. These long evenings,
with lamps hissing softly like pinioned souls, the high whine
of mosquitoes, the deep intimate silence, the watchful solitude
—without its companionship they would drive her mad. Did
she love Robert? Yes, of course; when he was away she thought
of him constantly, worried about his safety, missed his laughter
and his kindness and stored up things to tell him on his return.
But nowadays, when he was with her, so many things went wrong;
his words grated, his affectations irritated, his egotism seemed
immature and she was seized with a new and horrifying desire to
wound his feelings. He was hers still, and she might be ready
to die for him if need be; but to live for him, that was another
matter. Was it the idea of Robert that she loved, and not the
man?

It was all too difficult and now, she realized, with a glance
at the clock, too late; she could find no solution to-night, but
to-morrow she would face it, and all would be clear.

Chapter Twelve

ROBERT followed a winding path through a field of guinea-
corn whose stalks rustled and creaked high above his head.
Then the path, ceasing abruptly to be rural, plunged into a
tunnel between two high walls. All was black save where, as
he passed a gateway, the glow of firelight melted a little patch
of darkness. Against a deep star-dusted sky the battlemented
walls of the houses showed sharp and angular, as if the whole
town were transformed into a medieval castle; from behind
these walls sounded the fitful music of a primitive guitar and
soft bursts of song.

Moonlight, peace and the timeless feeling of history stilled
the turmoil of his heart. How many loves and hatreds, passions,
jealousies and submissions were going on at this moment, out
of the moon's eye, behind these walls! Yet all was private and
sedate. A hundred generations and more had lived here, bred
and died away, and the walls remained. Men had been tortured,
beaten, mutilated, whole populations massacred, and the walls
remained. Slaves roped by the neck had been driven through

the gates and sold in the market place, men had been chained to the ground till they rotted, plague and leprosy had struck down the noble and the beggar, and the walls remained. For a thousand years prayers had gone up to the gods of men's dark imagination and to the God of Islam, and merciful, the compassionate, and none could say what ears had heard them or what skies had turned them back unheard, yet the prayers continued, and the walls remained.

And now, he asked himself, would the prayers cease and the walls crumble? For surely this enterprise on which he was engaged was the most disintegrative ever known. A thousand years of history, of a balance struck between man and his nature and man and the desert, were caught by the twin forces of this western invasion: the secular force that undermined and uprooted from without, the Christian force that bored away from within. Of the two, the second was the most deadly. So he had suggested to Father Anselm, a busy man who dashed about his mountain mission like some brown, hairy, restless bee.

"You, amongst us all," he had said, "have at once the greatest and the least justification for your presence here. The greatest because you, alone, bring these people a message for the spirit, not the flesh; the least because you, alone, destroy beyond repair. For you touch the fabric of their inner lives. Our daft notions about law and taxes and sanitation are so many hothouse plants that would die inside a generation were we to disappear from the scene. But although the outward signs of all your work would go too—your masses and churches and crucifixes—it is impossible, now, ever to eradicate your influence. For you sow the seeds of doubt which, like the nettle, grow where men have dwelt and thrive where most neglected."

"I have nothing to do with doubt," the priest replied. "I sow the seeds of faith, and so what you say is true, nothing can ever be the same again for those in whose hearts they have rooted. But the word of God drives away doubt, and that is why it is all-powerful."

"Yes, but to build your new belief," Robert insisted, "you demolish every law by which these people live. You destroy their trust in their own gods, and the whole elaborate web they have spun to link their short precarious lives with the infinite, which raises them a little above the beasts and gives meaning to their past and some confidence in their future. You tear away this close-spun web and crush it under the heel of your dogmatism; and they are left like a homeless spider, bewildered, deprived of their support. No, you can't claim that you banish doubts; on the contrary, you destroy belief."

"You do not understand," said the little priest in his friendly, eager manner, his brown eyes puzzled in a brown, bearded face. "We must pull down the false beliefs before we can build in their place the new. So much is obvious. These people have worshipped false gods and idols, sticks and stones. My message is a simple one. It is of the true God, and his Son, who by his death opened to us the way of redemption. To replace the false by the true—is that destructive? Was that not the word which came to Saul of Tarsus, and which he carried to Rome? You are afraid of revolution, but the Church's message has always been one of revolution where false gods must first be overthrown."

"Your case is unanswerable," said Robert, "if your premises are true. But it is your very premises that I question—your certainty that you or any other mortal—or the corporate Church, if you will—can draw a line and say: on this side lies the false, on that the true; this God is real, that one imitation. You treat morality as if it were an egg to be held before the flame of truth for judgment. That one is spotted, out it goes; this is clear, it is saved. But you can't treat systems of belief and morals like that. There is no such simple judgment, no flame by which they may be tested."

"But how you are blind! Such a flame indeed exists, the word of God made flesh, of which the Church is the true interpreter. Sometimes it may seem to burn fitfully, to be cloudy or obscure, but that is the fault of our frail human eyes, not of the flame, which burns through all eternity, and never flickers. And that is the Church's immortal task, to tend the flame and make it visible to the meanest of God's creatures."

Robert shook his head. "Those of us who are outside the Church—and now we are in a great majority—can no longer believe in that single, faultless flame. We may wish that we did, because it would give our lives direction, but that is beside the point; wishes cannot create certainty. Truth does not seem to us as simple as that. Probably it is so complex that it can be expressed only obliquely, in allegoric form. For two thousand years the western world has lived by its devotion to one great allegory. Now that is dying, and the western world must die too, spiritually, unless a new master-myth arises, to express anew the changeless moral laws of the universe. In time, of course, it will happen somewhere, for Christianity was by no means the first attempt and it cannot be the last; in every age and among every people the same tales appear to satisfy the same needs. Man fears death, so he invents life after death; he needs authority, so he bows to God; he is bound by the seasons, so he postulates resurrection; his impotence in the face of nature drives him to create a calendar of saints or spirits he can propitiate with prayer or sacrifice. Where is the difference between killing a black ram to appease the rain-god and lighting a candle to St. Antony?"

"To ask God, if it be his will, to show mercy——" the priest began; but Robert was wound up now like a clockwork train rushing round and round a track on the floor, and would not pause.

"Even our own myth, of the Christ slain and risen, was not invented by the Jews. The tale of the death and resurrection of the god is as old as the seasons it symbolizes. The god Osiris, cut in pieces by the lord of death and joined and resurrected by Isis; the abduction of Persephone to the winter underworld and her release in spring to restore the earth's fertility—these are prototypes for the sacrifice and resurrection of the God you serve, earlier versions of the same eternal myth, varied according to the nature and circumstances of the people who tell it. Persephone waywardly captured in a field of hyacinths, Osiris trapped in a coffin, Christ of the Jews (a hardy and less earthy people), mocked and tortured and avenging his tormentors not with the sword but with the reed-like quality of humility—they are all the same. Or turn to the pagan tribe on your own doorstep—their god-like hero, the rain-giver, was devoured by spirits living underneath a river-bed and restored to life, after proper ceremony, by his uncle the god of death. All follow the same pattern, they are fragments of one great idea. At the start of each planting season celebrations of the pagan god's return can be heard outside your little church, which in its turn rings with thanksgiving for *your* God's resurrection; the forms are different, the ancient myth behind them both, the same. That is why I say that the Church, in hallowing one and outlawing the other, shows arrogance, and shuts its eyes to the facts of history."

"You talk obscurely," Father Anselm said, "and I am a simple man; I cannot easily follow you. And the task I have been allotted is to convert the heathen, not to reclaim the apostate. But it appears to me that it is you who are arrogant and not the Church; for, because you can comprehend only a fragment of truth, in your impatience and foolishness you reject the whole. For truth is like a great light, pure and blinding; even the holy saints saw it but through a glass, darkly, and we sinners catch only reflections now and then. The mysteries of the seasons, of the death and rebirth of vegetation, which men have personified in the death and rebirth of their gods, may be such a reflection; and God, who created these mysteries, chose a way that simple men could understand to present to them the greatest of all mysteries, the redemption of man through the blood of his Son. For myself, I do not probe deeper than my intellect will take me; I have faith in others wiser than I. . . . Have no doubt that we shall one day see the full glory, face to face."

"Have no doubt!" Robert echoed irritably, pacing the room. "There you go again. That is the whole point; that is why I say you are destroying these pagan people, because you inject into their hearts the doubting poison. Have no doubt! Our doubts are within us; we cannot drive them out. But these people were free. Their god was kept sweet by sacrifices, their lesser deities could be consulted and would come to their aid if need arose. The spirits of their ancestors peopled the bush and made it a very lively place—sociable, too, for spirits could not do without their beer and food, and if one of them wandered and got lost it would jump into a calabash of water and let itself be carried back to the family circle. Sometimes, it is true, ghosts, werewolves and evil spirits troubled them, but for every occasion there was a ceremony, for every evil a charm.

"But you are killing all this. The whole pattern of their lives soon will fall away from them like the shell of a rotten pod, as ours has already done. Once we believed as they did; our belief gave us our place in the universe, inspired our art and held together our social life and moral law; it fastened restraints on the arrogance of kings and conferred the dignity of immortality on beggars. That chain is broken now, and we have freedom—freedom to drift and doubt, to stupefy our hungry souls, if we can, by stuffing them with the triumphs of materialism. Where is the man amongst us now who could cry with Faustus: 'See where Christ's blood streams in the firmament! One drop would save my soul——' No, the potency of Christ's blood has faded, we are not to be saved. It is no longer as

Christians that we come to disrupt these Moslem and pagan peoples, and in abandoning that perhaps we abandon our sole justification. But you, who teach them the old creed, have you considered what you are doing? You destroy something irreplaceable and precious; you substitute something discredited and unattainable. For if we, in our two thousand years of Christianity, have failed so tragically to reach the standards set by our religion and have learnt only to abandon its dogmas, you cannot hope to see your savage converts, to whom your teachings are almost wholly incomprehensible, succeed."

Father Anselm looked sad, but unperturbed.

"To deny God," he said, "is but a proof of his all-pervading power, since where there is no authority, there can be no revolt. It is perhaps a stage of development, and it will pass. Tyrants have always hated God."

"I am not a tyrant."

"No, but you are something worse," Father Anselm said, smiling. "You lack the courage, sinful as it is, that a tyrant needs, and that gives Satan his power over men. You are one of the stepping stones on which tyrants rise—a man with principles but no belief, who feels his soul within him but lacks the humility to offer it to God, a man with passion but with no faith."

"Faith!" Robert exclaimed angrily. "You talk as if faith were something one could get merely by wanting it. Of course I lack faith, and so does all my generation; it is the spiritual sickness of our age. Does diagnosis of his disease cure the leper? Paul should have lived to-day; he would have listed his three virtues in a different order. Faith is the most important and the most elusive, for without it there can be no hope, and no cause for charity. Faith lies at the root of all."

"Charity is the soil in which faith grows," the priest said. "Practice charity, and you will find that one day faith has entered your soul. For God is love; and if you love truly, you will know God."

"How can a man practice charity until he has faith? For how can he love God unless he believes in God's existence?"

"He can love his brother, and the love of God will follow, for that which he loves in his brother is divine. Did not Christ himself make that quite clear?"

"To love the individual bound to one's own life is natural, and therefore without merit," Robert said. "The wife, the child, perhaps the friend. But to love one's fellow men for their own sakes, the lousy beggar or, more difficult, the unctuous millionaire—no, that would be possible only if one could see in them a fragment of God, and recognize in oneself a spark of divinity to make one capable of such disinterested love. Faith, I tell you, is at the root of it all."

"You make it too complicated for a simple priest whose mission is to the heathen," Father Anselm said. "The Church has faced many heresies in its time, and pride is at the bottom of them all—the pride that makes every man think he can challenge the might of the Creator with the toothpick of his own mind. A few hundred years ago you would have been burnt for your opinions, and you would then perhaps have questioned whether they were so well founded."

"I might have lacked the courage of the rationalist martyrs; but Galileo's recantation did not halt the planets in their motions round the sun."

Father Anselm bore Robert no ill-will for his heresies; he was far too busy. At the mission station there was all to be done: half-naked children to be taught their letters in the rough-built school, with little apparatus beyond a blackboard and slates; their elder brothers instructed in the rudiments of carpentry and blacksmithing, as new to them as goat-herding to an English boy; the mission farm, with its neat rows of vegetables, its fields of millet, its well-kept cows, supervised and tended; accounts kept, savage visitors interviewed, and masses to be said.

The chapel appeared incongruous in these trackless mountains. Narrow, upright and jaunty, it rose from the peak of a hill to a short blunted spire, a triumph of Father Anselm's carpentry, for he had built it with his own hands, and with the help of his clumsy apprentices. It was painted a staring shade of yellow ochre and stood out against the buff background of the dry hills like a piece of toy village which had strayed from its box. Carvings of remarkable crudity and ugliness decorated the porch, and gaudy images, wearing that peculiar look of smug stupidity which seems to stand for piety in the world of plaster saints, adorned niches in the whitewashed walls.

A hideous chapel, yet there was something endearing about it, for if it was without taste, yet its building was an act of worship, and it stood out bravely on the crest of its hill. In some mysterious way it carried an Italian flavour and round it one looked expectantly for the olive trees, the neat vineyards and the close-cultivated strips of its native land. Father Anselm's congregation was small. Sitting at the back of the chapel while dusk fell quickly over the rugged country, isolating all the more this plot of Christian ground, Robert wondered what shreds and pieces of doctrine penetrated those bowed woolly heads, what sort of hotch-poch of undigested fragments had coagulated inside. The Latin words droned on, incomprehensible alike to him and to the dark congregation, whose thick lips moved stiffly at the parrot-like responses. Strange that the language of that ancient Mediterranean city-state, so many thousand miles away, should be droned out in these hills, so many thousand years later, by these anxious Negro children in whose homes old animist beliefs still ruled; strange, too, that they should praise a God passed on like second-hand clothing from the Jews to the Greeks and Romans, from the Romans to the British and now, under British tutelage, to the pagan subjects of a Moslem state.

But their own gods, he thought, might not so easily give way. They were here, in these bush-clad valleys and hills, watchful and intimate. Like lizards, they would hide under stones and trees and, like lizards, when the danger passed they would creep out again to hold the field, haphazard and indestructible. Father Anselm, seen in his setting, was a brave and a pathetic figure, leading his little sheep-like army forward against the twin and mighty forces of heathen superstition and western repudiation.

But Father Anselm—unaware, no doubt, of his predicament —was not dismayed. Should a single soul be brought to grace through his ministry he would count his purpose fulfilled. From time to time his hopes arose that he was to be accorded such a favour. Robert had been an unwilling agent in the most likely case. Years before, he had confided to Father Anselm's care a small lost boy, rescued in peculiar circumstances from death by sacrifice. He had called the boy Benjamin, and under that name this piece of cast-up human wreckage had been baptized. The boy's home and parents had never been traced; he was indeed an odd scrap of flotsam on the African tide and would have perished unmourned by any, simply vanished, had the curious geometry of circumstance not caused the intersection of his life with Robert's at the moment in time just preceding his obliteration.

Father Anselm had taken him in, fed and clothed him and given him a better schooling than most, for the mission was his only home and no suspicious parents cramped and nullified the western teaching, nor did goat-herding steal time from his studies. He had proved himself a bright boy, exceptionally so: quick in the uptake, retentive of memory, anxious to please. Examinations he tackled easily. He became, in fact, the mission's star pupil. Hitherto Father Anselm had not found among this backward people any worthy of advancement towards the priesthood, and almost his only real ambition was to discover such a pious candidate who would be accepted by the parent mission on the coast for further training and eventual ordination.

In Benjamin he believed that he had at last found such a boy. Certainly the intelligence was there and, Father Anselm thought, the powers of leadership and character; the learning could be instilled; all depended on whether Benjamin had indeed been chosen for a life of dedication. For signs of that the priest could only watch and wait. Several years ago the boy had left the mission in the hills, having reached the limit of education offered there, for the college at the coast. Now, Robert learnt, he had graduated with honours, and the time had come to decide what his future calling should be.

Father Anselm's brown furry face beamed with pleasure when Robert inquired about his protégé's career.

"It is remarkable," he said. "You remember the day you sent him here? So small, so frightened, a mere fragment of suffering humanity! Now the boy shows ability beyond what one would credit from one who made so inauspicious a start. I told you he had passed out of college at the top of his class? And now—what do you imagine? He is going to England! Yes, to an English university; the Government has given him a scholarship. He will come back a giant among his people; and then, if it is God's will, he will dedicate himself to Christ's ministry. Surely a sign of God's grace! What do you say to that, my dear friend?"

"Extraordinary," Robert agreed. "He was, as you say, a frightened little shred of humanity—quite doomed, had it not been for a mere accident, a chance in a million."

"Yes—one is greatly tempted to believe that he was chosen of God, to further his purposes. Now he goes from my little school in the hills to an English university, Oxford perhaps! He is a good boy, he will study well. And when he returns . . ."

Father Anselm smiled happily; he was indulging himself (a rare event) in a dream. He saw Benjamin as a lamp shining through the heathen darkness to show the path of grace to a long procession of souls; perhaps a blessed destiny awaited as one of the founders of a great new African church that would arise to the glory of God from the humble beginnings in which he, Father Anselm, had a small part. . . . He pulled himself up; it was wrong to entertain such extravagant thoughts, but not wrong to be thankful that he had been chosen to guide the first steps of this most promising recruit.

Robert was a little less confident. The plunge into so confusing a world as that of an English university dislocated people; few could keep their balance on the tight-rope stretched between the old world and the new.

"Don't expect too much of Benjamin," he suggested. "Sometimes England scrambles all their ideas."

"He has been well grounded—that is to say, as well as lay within our power. It was a preparation, Benjamin has a destiny before him—Benjamin Morris, he has become. I don't know why he took the name of Morris—something was needed for the papers, I suppose."

It had been a pleasant interlude at the mission, with Father Anselm buzzing to and fro in his bee-like manner, smiling, happy and absorbed. There was a sense of peace on his hill-top, a sort of serenity one did not often encounter: certainly it was not to be found in the stuffy lanes of the town where Robert walked, with dusty feet, recalling his conversations. The cool hills seemed a universe away. Even the air here was debauched by odours from slime-covered ponds, from cattle and camel dung, from spittle-spotted dust and the market-place latrines. Moonlight bathed the old town, rimming each wall with black shadow. To the moon it must lie open like a honeycomb, exposing each cell crowded with human maggots, eating, talking, making love, restless always, even in repose. It didn't matter, Robert thought, where you went, east or west, Europe or Africa, at the time of the Crusades or the time of the bomber, it was all the same. 'Let him be rich and weary,' God had said, and man obeyed—rich sometimes and weary always, the price of divine blackmail; 'if goodness lead him not, yet weariness, may toss him to my breast.'

No rest at home either, for Priscilla's mind had lost the tranquillity he had loved and shared. He knew the reason well enough. He had rooted her up like a primrose to plant in this harsh inclement soil; and like a primrose she had withered, so far from her native woods. She belonged too much to England, this was not her home. And half her heart, at least, had stayed behind with Robin. A heart built generously, like our forebears' houses, with room for a brood: and only one to fill it, and that one out of reach. Too late, he acknowledged that in bringing her here he had destroyed the thing he loved, and now between them, however hard they tried, the unfulfilment, the resentment and the remorse lay between them like a sword between lovers.

A line of camels passed, roped nose to tail, plodding silently under the high walls. The man who led them called out a greeting in a deep, melodious voice. They had come down from the north, from the desert, with loads of salt to change for kola nuts from the plain. Such examples of an old and vital trade as a rule stirred his imagination, but to-night his thoughts were turned from the sand and scrub and old cities to memories of a green English spring ten years ago, when a curious quest, undertaken half jokingly, had ended, and in finding what he sought, he had lost what he had most treasured.

Chapter Thirteen

1919

ROBERT smiled to himself and leant back in a corner of the railway carriage. It was six years since he had been in England—years of war; and now there had been staged for his welcome one of those days the exile dreams of but very seldom encounters, a day that comes but once or twice in a year, when spring is everywhere, in the sap and the blood and the insects' wings. Just to look at it through the window of the carriage was intoxicating. Spring fever—he had forgotten that such a thing existed, but the foolish quest on which he had embarked was proof of its potency. He had decided on the spur of the moment, when the sunshine in the streets and the soft spring breeze had made him realize that he could not stay in London an instant longer. It was then that there had come into his mind the resolve to keep a promise he had made to himself half jokingly, and half a world away. Out of his pocket he pulled the faded yellow photograph that had travelled with him to many distant places, through thunderstorms and sandstorms, rivers and floods. It was still undamaged, the face with which he had grown so familiar looked back at him with gaiety and candour. How absurd that dress appeared to-day, those high collars and the long hair piled on top of the head! Now skirts were up above the knee and waists down below the hips, the hair cropped and stuffed into extraordinary bell-like hats swooping down over the ears. Hideous! They did not look like women at all, but dolls, marionettes. The girl of the picture would not be dressed like that.

But of course he had no chance of finding the girl of the picture, no chance at all. He knew two things about her: six years ago a man called Roger Fawkes had carried her photograph, and the signature in the corner was Priscilla. Then the war had come down like a fog. Now it had cleared away and she might be anywhere—Valparaiso, Teheran, Pekin; married, of course; certainly a married woman, widowed as likely as not, with children, living goodness knows where. Even if she hadn't married, she would be utterly different; everyone was, after the war.

But it was no day to think of failure. The buoyancy of the air keyed him up to a pitch of expectancy and delight and carried him over a three-mile walk from the country station to the village where the Fawkes lived—or had lived, for he did not know whether they were dead or alive—along lanes enclosed by tall brilliant hedges whose every leaf seemed like a banner newly hung to celebrate the victory of spring.

In a village of thatched roofs and bright gardens he was directed to the manor where the Fawkes, it seemed, still lived. An old brick wall, ravaged by ivy, curved back to admit an opening in which was set a big wrought-iron gate with a coat of arms above. Once through it, the road became full of pot-holes. The park stretched on either hand, golden now with buttercups and guarded by oaks, chestnuts and beeches. Like the men who had planted them, they had been given light, space and air in which to grow to their fullest size—born, as it were, with silver hairs on their roots. While, in the neglected cut-over woodland, saplings fought each other for light and nourishment and sometimes grew up stunted and out of shape, privileged acorns, favoured by mere accident of birth, unfurled to the oak's full stature. The house came into view—a disappointment, Victorian brick where you expected something Palladian. In front a very old man with a drooping tow-coloured moustache was pushing a hand-mower slowly round a weedy lawn. A grey-haired butler, just as old but not quite so bent, responded to Robert's tug at the bell-handle; and the caller, now rather nervous, found himself standing by the french window of a room smelling of lilacs—a pleasant, sunny place, its faded grey wall-paper almost hidden by portraits, its chairs and sofas covered in glazed chintz.

He turned to greet an elderly woman whose grey hair escaped in wisps from a large straw hat. She had a kind, dreamy face that had once been handsome but had now, in late middle age, gone soft; the lines of character had as it were petered out into un-certainties. Her eyes behind horn-rimmed spectacles looked vague and faded. While he gave his name and apologized for the disturbance she scarcely seemed aware of his presence at all, her eyes roamed round the room examining the different arrange-ments of lilac, but then she waved him into a chair and sat down herself on the sofa.

"The fact is, I knew your son." He had plunged. "It's a long time ago now, and perhaps I'm stirring up painful memories. But I haven't been in England since, and I thought perhaps —I was with him when he died——"

Lady Fawkes started to fiddle with some green string that hung out of a large pocket in her gardening-apron.

"Yes," she said abstractedly. "Is it a long time ago? I suppose so. Time runs on so fast. We heard very little, but then, there is seldom much to say. You were in his regiment, I suppose?"

Robert was puzzled. "Not his regiment; I was in the same service, I arrived to take over the station from him just before he died."

Lady Fawkes frowned. "Service . . . station. . . . Oh, I see. I'm afraid we are talking about two different people. You mean Roger, of course?"

Robert nodded.

"Yes, you are right; it is a long time ago. His brother was killed, you see, and I thought that you were speaking of him."

A clumsy start, a bad omen! Robert's morning mood seemed callous now, but he could not retreat.

"You'll think this an odd thing to ask, and perhaps it needs an explanation. After your son died it was my job to seal up his papers. But one thing was overlooked. I found it later—too late, I thought, to send it on. I've kept it ever since. Here it is."

He laid the cardboard-mounted photograph in front of Lady Fawkes. She looked at him for the first time with attention.

"You mean that you kept one of his private possessions?"

"That sounds unpardonable, I know. Perhaps it is; but I've come here to return the picture, if you want it, and to ask you a favour. Will you tell me who it is?"

There, it was out. He felt absurdly nervous, as if he were making a proposal. Lady Fawkes looked down at the picture and frowned. "Oh, yes, that's Priscilla. A girl he—a friend. As you say, Mr.——it was a long time ago. Are you sure you won't stay to luncheon?"

She rose, but he refused to accept his dismissal.

"Lady Fawkes: I've carried that photograph about with me for six years. Of course that was foolish, but it became a companion, a sort of mascot, and I made myself a promise that one day I'd find out who she was. Perhaps that sounds impertinent, or soft in the head? I can only ask you to humour me."

Lady Fawkes had walked over to the french window and stood looking out, her back towards him. Was she so offended she would not even say good-bye? Slowly he picked up his hat.

"Wait," she said, without turning. "You are right, what you ask is impertinent, but you sound sincere. You were with my son when he died?"

"Yes."

"I will tell you the story, though it is something I have not spoken of since."

"If it distresses you——"

She came back and sat down on the sofa, knotting her hands in her lap.

"The girl in that photograph was brought up in this village; she was a few years younger than my son. Her father was a carpenter on the estate. Her mother, I think, had been better educated—she is a woman of strong character, and had high ambitions for her children. She used to take in washing to help see them through their schooling. She had a family of six or seven. Priscilla was the youngest and cleverest; I believe she passed examinations which would have qualified her for a university. They were good people, in their way, God-fearing and respectable; but, of course——" she waved her hand vaguely in her lap.

"My son fell in love with Priscilla. He was barely of age. Of course, we could not allow it, his father and I. The difference in their positions—his youth—a passing infatuation—Priscilla's mother was as much against it as we. She wanted her daughter's happiness, as we our son's. Neither could have been happy if they had been allowed . . ."

"So your son was sent abroad?"

"Yes. His father and I believed that he would get over his infatuation, as young men do. Perhaps that would have happened, but he never came back."

For Lady Fawkes, that was the end of the story.

"And Priscilla?"

"She was vèry young. With her I think it was an adventure, a fairy story to which she expected no end. She got over it soon enough; she was to be married, I believe, to a young farmer, one of our tenants—a promising young man. But he was killed at Ypres, I think it was. I hope that satisfies your curiosity, Mr.—I'm afraid I didn't catch your name."

Again Lady Fawkes rose, but Robert delayed her with one more question. "She's gone away, of course?"

"Yes, she went away—war-work of some kind. But she is back now, I have heard, with her mother. I believe that she is teaching in the village school."

Remarkable, that the beginning and end of his quest should lie here together, like two ends of a loop, in this little west country village! It seemed almost too easy, he thought, striding back through the park, and so different from all he had expected. It had been a shock, he admitted to himself, to rearrange her in his mind as a village school-teacher, a washerwoman's daughter; but people thought less of all that nowadays, and in a sense the circumstance added to her charm, as a flower out of place in a field appeals more to the imagination than its sister nurtured and fussed over in a garden.

Smoke rising from every village chimney made him realize that it was dinner-time and, furthermore, that he was hungry, The village inn provided bread and cheese. Afterwards he wandered into a wood and lay for a while on a carpet of moss among the bluebells. To breathe in their scent was like a slow, luxurious drowning in a sea of infinite blueness and magic, with the blue heads bowed all around him in silent multitudes and gleams of sunlight striking down the crusty silver-grey trunks of the trees. He lay there, dreaming and idly watching birds and butterflies, squirrels and ladybirds, until he judged that schooling would be over for the day.

A rosemary bush sprawled beside the porch of the cottage, shedding the tiny petals of its misty flowers, the colour of dusk. While awaiting an answer to his knock he rubbed a few leaves in his fingers and sniffed the aromatic flavour that brought a tang of the sea into this inland garden; it was sharp and firm, a corrective to the sensuous perfume of bluebells and the headiness of lilacs. The door opened and a woman in a flowered cotton dress stood there, with the sun in her face. Robert stared dumbfounded, for here was his picture made flesh and blood. Yet how different from the yellow pasteboard in his pocket! As if, from an old faded drawing, one could reconstruct a rose. She was taller than he had imagined, and more strongly built. Her hair was corn-coloured, her eyes like the bluebells he had left in the wood, her cheeks flushed, and in her expression that same open, candid look.

He had no idea what to say or do; the careful little speech he had prepared simply vanished. He fell back on mere bluntness. Pulling out the photograph he thrust it towards her and said:

"Please don't think I'm very impertinent, or even off my head. Do you recognize this? I've come to see you because it's been sitting in my pocket for years, and I've a natural wish to look at the original. Will you forgive me? I really can explain."

She turned the photograph over several times in her hands, bewilderment in every look and gesture.

"Who are you? Surely I've never seen you before?"

"Will you let me come in and explain?"

They sat in the parlour. It had the stiff, cold look, the smell of damp and polish, of a room that is seldom used. A piano stood against one wall and on it was a photograph of a young man in uniform, sitting very upright with his cap and cane by his side. Sounds of clattering pots and footsteps came from the kitchen and a warm smell of ironing filled the air.

Robert sat on the hard sofa and told his story quite briefly. "If this visit seems extremely silly," he finished, "please try to excuse it on the grounds that I've carried this bit of cardboard about with me in all sorts of odd and lonely places, and it's reminded me of many things I hoped still existed, but which I often thought I should never see again."

"Roger Fawkes!" She stared out of the window into the sun-

flooded garden. "I never thought I should hear him spoken of
again. His mother was right, and we were children, but if he'd
never met me and stayed, as he had a right to do, in his own
country——"

"To be alive at the beginning and at the end of a war are two
different things," Robert protested.

"In any case, you'd better have a cup of tea. Do you mind
the kitchen? It's full of washing, for it's ironing day, but if you'll
forgive the muddle . . ."

She led the way across the passage into a room which looked
at first as if nothing more could be squeezed into it. Piles of
folded linen lay on the table and those parts of the wall not
hidden behind cluttered cupboards were hung with prints and
with enormous enlargements of old photographs, portraits of
various kinds. Robert had to stoop to enter the door and wondered what he would do with his legs; but, once inside, the
room seemed, in some peculiar way, to be no more crowded
than before. As they entered, Priscilla's mother straightened
her back to greet them: a stout, shapeless woman, but in her
weathered expression all the character of a Dutch portrait.
It must have been a fine face once, with strong features and a
broad forehead set over eyes that had kept all their shrewdness
and clarity. She took Robert in at one glance: a lanky young
man with a thin, bony face burnt dark by sun, clean-shaven,
with very blue eyes, looking friendly but awkward; no doubt
a good enough young man, but of the kind that had brought
no good fortune to her children.

"The kettle's on the boil, Priscilla," she said. "Best make the
tea. How do you do, sir? You must excuse a muddle in the
kitchen, it's my ironing day. I don't know why Priscilla should
bring you in amongst it when she can have who she likes in the
parlour, but girls will follow their own notions and that's all
there is to it. Will you sit down? There's no fancy cakes or thin-
cut bread and butter for tea, as I expect you're used to, but you're
welcome to all we've got."

Robert, who had lived for years on tinned food when he could
get it and (more often) concoctions that put him in mind of
paste-and-sawdust or fried wasps when he could not, had
forgotten that butter could have such richness, bread such flavour,
jam such excellence. The cottage was cramped and inconvenient
and smelt of damp, but its cosiness, after years of exile, seemed
too happy to be true; homeless himself, this was like a dream of

home. How had he ever managed to enjoy his own bleak existence, as he had in stretches, and in part? When he tried to tell them a little about it everything he said made it sound horrible, more like a penance than a life; but of course they were against it from the start and perhaps their hostility coloured his accounts; they knew it only as a heathen place which had got in before the Germans could to take one of the village's young men.

After tea Priscilla's mother dismissed them, saying she had her ironing to do, and they walked along a lane whose hedges held the dry, enticing scent of the may, and then followed a footpath through fields deep with buttercups that dusted their feet with gold. Finding a bank beside a small brook, they sat leaning against the bole of a big ash; bluebells confronted them from the bank opposite, and clumps of late kingcups glowed by the margins of the stream. This was the English countryside as one sometimes dreamt or imagined it, an idealized version, not the real thing, playing one of its tricks on the exile to taunt him for his betrayal. He murmured, speaking his thoughts aloud:

"All done with wires and mirrors! To-morrow, we shall be back to boarding-house porridge and railway waiting-rooms."

"What are you talking about?"

"The weather, like a good Englishman."

"Splendid! I feel more at home with everyday conversation."

"Is my conversation so very odd?"

"Perhaps not your conversation, but your whole arrival out of the blue——"

Robert rolled over on to one elbow to look up at her. Chin cupped in hand, she was gazing intently into the stream, as if absorbed in piscatorial studies. He observed her skin to be soft and fair, her mouth generous, her brow clear, her movements calm; but then she pushed back a wisp of hair with a quick motion of the hand, and knowing his gaze to embarrass her, he shifted it to the kingcups bending over the stream.

"The only odd thing about it," he said, "is that I feel as if I'd known you all my life."

"You know nothing about me, or I of you."

"On the contrary, I know most of the important things. Even a square of pasteboard——"

"That ridiculous photograph! Doesn't it occur to you that you had no right to it? I didn't give it to you, and surely a dead man's property——"

Immediately he was contrite and even alarmed. Pulling the worn and faded picture out of his pocket, he held it out to her.

"You're perfectly right. In a way I suppose I stole it. Will you accept my apologies, and take it back?"

She glanced down at it, and then again at the stream.

"I don't want it now. It had best be destroyed."

Slowly, without replying, he tore it across several times. She looked at the pieces, and smiling a little, said:

"You have a short way with old friends!"

"I was obeying orders."

"I should imagine that you're more used to giving them."

"Am I so very dictatorial?"

"No, but self-assured, as people of your kind are."

"People of my kind! Please don't push me into the oblivion of a sort of category. I'm anything but self-assured at the moment, but in my profession one gets a certain surface glaze. That's why it's good for us to come home and find ourselves back with the small fry, where we belong. Like tiddlers in the stream." Getting up, he walked to the edge of the brook and peered in. "Are there tiddlers here?"

"Yes, but they stay mostly under the reeds."

He stretched his arms and breathed in deeply. The air had a sparkle, the sun danced on rippling water, the brook's murmur and the bird's chirruping filled the world with sound. It was almost too much, an embarrassment of riches; he felt as if he might burst into flower, or float up into the tender blue sky. Such days should last for ever, such moments expand to cover weeks instead of seconds. He looked down again at the water.

"Lucky tiddlers! They can stay here all their lives, lying on a sort of air-cushion, now and then digesting a tasty midge. A perfect existence!"

"Until little boys come with nets and bottles, or a great cow, like a sea-monster."

"That would provide the spice of adventure. Otherwise they'd get bored—the same banks, the same reeds, and I suppose the same water."

"You think tiddlers believe the next brook's sweeter than their own? They may have more sense. I think we make too much of moving on. You've been to all sorts of peculiar and outlandish places; my mother has scarcely been more than a dozen miles from this village in her life. Which do you suppose has found out the most?"

"If you pushed that argument to its limit, you'd say that a goldfish in a bowl might know more than a whale in the ocean."

"Perhaps it might, if it was a thoughtful goldfish."

"Wouldn't you allow it a single companion?"

"Two would get into an argument."

"Why not a love affair?"

"I see you don't know much about the habits of fish. . . . I must be getting back." She stood up, brushing fragments of grass from her skirt. How young and supple she looked! Every movement seemed to him full of magic. Their words had been light and quite unreal, a little flurry of dust to screen a wordless and far more cardinal exchange. Nervously, he took her hand, and she neither withdrew it nor responded, but looked at him with an expression he could not understand—almost of compassion, or perhaps reluctance.

"I must go back to London to-night. May I come and see you again?"

Gently, she disengaged her hand. "I'd rather you didn't."

"Do you dislike me so much, and so quickly?"

"It isn't that. We live in different worlds. You must go back to your savages, I belong here."

"Till your fins grow stiff and your scales muddy? There's a world outside the bowl."

"I know that. Is it any better?"

He was disconcerted, unable to reply. Suddenly impatient, and dreading the escape of time, he bent down and kissed her lips, and she fell back a step, putting a hand to her heart as if to check its movement, silenced by a sudden resentment. Of this he was quite unconscious, for a cloud of pure elation had carried him aloft high above the golden-dusted meadows and the tangled thickets of other people's minds; it was as he had thought, life was too strong an advantage and the dead must always give way.

A cow came down to the brook and thrust her nose deep into the clear water, sucking noisily. They looked round to see her staring at them without curiosity, water dripping from her muzzle, her tail swishing at the flies, and both smiled at her as if she had been an angel alighted among the kingcups, come to tell them of ambrosial pastures and milk of paradise.

"You've made a mistake," Priscilla said. "I'm neither bound to the past nor a slave of the present—I mean to remain as I am, in love, but with freedom."

Walking homeward beside her, Robert felt strong enough to ignore her disavowal. He merely said: "What a fantastic day! When I started, armed only with the photograph——"

"Please don't mention it again!"

Her vehemence startled him. "Why not? It's brought me good fortune——"

"No, no, it's unlucky. Dead men's property—a thing come by in that way can't ever bring good fortune."

Robert smiled with a touch of superiority. He had come from the land of superstition and fetish only to find in this quiet village, among his own people, the self-same irrational beliefs—or, rather, the parent fears from which sprang the whole dark jungle of taboos and charms.

"What a lot I still have to learn about you, Priscilla! But then, I have a lifetime to do it in."

She shook her head, and at the cottage gate said good-bye without warmth, and without asking him in. But he strode back to the station triumphantly, her image before him, thinking that as he walked his heart unravelled and knowing that the slender thread would guide him back.

Chapter Fourteen

1929

THE Treasurer sat a little awkwardly on the edge of a wicker armchair, his robe gathered about his feet, a teacup on the table by his side. He found European houses inconvenient and complicated, cluttered up with furniture which was not only in the way but offended the eye by breaking the clean sweep of the walls, but he knew such coruscations to be necessary for a European's prestige, and he had himself furnished a wing of his house in this fussy style. He never actually used it, but visiting chiefs were duly impressed with such ocular evidence of the esteem in which their Emir and his ministers were held by their white overlords.

"The Emir regrets your departure," he remarked politely, after a number of fish-paste sandwiches and iced cakes had been consumed. "He was gracious enough to entrust me with a message. He wishes you a safe journey, and as a token of his esteem, I have brought a present."

From a reticule in his robes he fished out a small leather bag. Out of it, after a good deal of fumbling, came a heavy silver ring whose boss was fashioned, by a crude but inventive craftsman, into the head of an eagle with tiny obsidian eyes. With genuine pleasure Robert slipped it on his finger and thanked the Treasurer, wondering what he would be able to think of in return.

"Perhaps," the Treasurer suggested, "if God wills, you will come back to our kingdom." He was a wizened, monkey-like man with a pock-marked face and a shrewd, bright eye. His reputation was that of the most astute of the Emir's ministers and no one doubted that his wealth was prodigious, for he was not the man to bungle the opportunities he had worked so hard to seize.

"You know it is the custom of the Government to move its servants about, and I have already been here for longer than usual."

"Is this custom not a peculiar one? We, the Emir's ministers, are known to you, and our loyalty to the Government understood; the Emir himself listens to your opinions; you leave us, and this knowledge will be locked in your breast. The judge who comes in your place will grope like a blind man, for everything will be hidden from him."

Robert smiled; this was indeed an accurate description of the fate of a newcomer.

"He will soon learn to see. Perhaps that is the plan, that each of us must train our eyes to see the truth even when it is hidden."

"To train judges in that way is expensive," the Treasurer said dryly. Certainly, Robert reflected, the old man was not ill-pleased, for each change of master meant an opportunity to try old tricks. Clearly the Treasurer had something on his mind. A mere courtesy call would not have lasted so long. But no one here could state his case simply, there had to be a long preliminary sounding and testing before the real business emerged. Deciding to take a random plunge, Robert observed:

"I have heard that the Emir's school for girls has started. Let us hope that it will be well spoken of by the fathers whose daughters attend."

The Treasurer nodded a small head swathed in heavy wrappings. "The school has started, yes. The Emir's care for the welfare of his subjects, even the females, is appreciated by his

people, who thank God for his mercy in sending them so beneficent a ruler."

"I am delighted to hear that they are pleased."

The Treasurer raised one skinny hand, weighted with rings,
as if to deprecate so hasty a leap to conclusions.

"That is the feeling of all devout and loyal men. Unfortunately, God has seen fit to allow certain less respectable persons
to reside in the Emir's kingdom. How shall we question his
wisdom, seeing that he permits the scorpion to lurk in the ground
and the adder to bring forth its young?"

"Unfortunately God allows such people to exist everywhere.
What is the sting in the tails of these scorpions?"

The Treasurer shrugged his shoulders and gently waved a
hand. "There are certain persons who condemn the Emir for
sanctioning such an undertaking within his own palace walls.
They say that such treatment of females is against the teaching
of the Prophet, and that the Emir himself has been corrupted by
Christian practices. This talk is wicked; but evil words, like
weeds, sometimes prove more prolific than plants of good
repute."

"Every innovation has its decriers. Like mourners at a funeral,
they wail over the virtues of departed customs. But are they not
old men who dread new ways, and need not be too much regarded by intelligent rulers?"

"It is not only old men who scan the Prophet's writings to
find support for their inclinations. And it is on the interpretation
of the Koran that the Emir's actions are questioned!"

"But a very respected *malam* has agreed to teach the young
women."

"In your country, do all learned men agree?"

"Certainly not," Robert admitted.

"And so with us. Some say that the *malam* has been corrupted
with gold, as well as with more refined inducements. These
evil persons include young men of high position—known to you,
judge—whose influence matches their rank."

Robert felt unreasonably annoyed. On the verge of his departure, he was being warned of an incipient palace revolution.
Well, someone else would have to deal with that.

"Since we are out of reach of the longest ears," he suggested,
"it would not be indiscreet to mention names."

"You have taken note of a young man called Aboubakar?"

"Surely he is a nephew of the Emir?"

"The same."

Robert was taken aback. Aboubakar he regarded as one of the most enlightened of the younger generation of Moslems of the ruling class. A man of considerable wealth, he had elected to take an appointment in the Native Administration from a desire, Robert had hoped, to serve his people and to train for a position of responsibility. He had carried out his duties with intelligence and, so far as Robert knew, integrity. But he was too closely in touch with the more liberal trends in Islam to oppose his uncle's experiment on genuine grounds. Clearly he was—if the Treasurer did not lie—exploiting the situation for some end of his own. An old story: the succession rested on a shaky record of bloodshed and treachery and probably almost any one of the Emir's innumerable nephews could, without much difficulty, establish a claim to the throne.

"He can scarcely win wide support on such an issue," Robert suggested. "The Emir's rule is just and enlightened, and among the younger of his subjects the suitable education of females is surely considered to be consistent with the word of God."

"True; but a small fire lighted among brushwood may, if skilfully fanned, consume even very large trees. The education of females is not the only matter on which the Emir finds himself obliged to change our present customs."

Now, Robert thought, we are getting down to the root of the matter.

"You mean the changes in tax assessment," he said.

"You have read my mind, judge."

"Since the people will benefit by these changes, they should bless rather than blame the Emir for bringing them about."

The Treasurer contorted his face into a positive cobweb of wrinkles and displayed several yellow fangs.

"It is not for me to remind you, judge, that in this world the bestowal of gifts, while it may enrich the recipient, impoverishes the giver, who must wait for the next world for his rewards. Unfortunately few men have reached a state of holiness sufficient to fix their minds upon the next world rather than upon this."

Robert accepted the rebuke in silence; the Treasurer was in fact telling him to use his intelligence. And of course the Treasurer was right. A system which robbed the Emir's nobles and district heads of what they considered their just perquisites was bound to be heartily disliked. At best, from their point of view, it would involve them in a heavy outlay for the bribery of a whole new class of person, the educated clerks, who would form an unwanted wheel in the machinery and were infidels and sons of slaves. It must, indeed, be galling to disgorge large sums, for the satisfaction of an alien government's whims, to individuals who would formerly have had their throats slit at the first sign of sauciness.

If, to the anger of cheated nobles, you added the resentment of religious conservatives, and ignited the two with a spark generated by an ambitious young man, clearly you would have an explosive situation. And the poor Emir had no choice but to sit on the powder magazine. On the one hand his British over-lords urged him into these reforms, on the other powerful men of his own entourage blamed him for actions he was reluctant to take. His nephew, Aboubakar, seemed to have the ball at his feet.

Of course, there was always another possibility: the wrinkled old Treasurer might be trying to pay off some personal grudge. You never could feel down to the bottom of the well; this wary, half-hostile, half-respectful, friendly yet basically antagonistic relationship, like that of chess players, between rulers and ruled lay always between you and a true understanding.

The trouble (if trouble there was) would be his successor's pigeon, not his, Robert thought thankfully; and probably his successor would have some other interest, new roads or the improvement of water supplies, that would leave him little time or inclination to play at politics. How easy it was, at the end of a tour, to let everything slide! Already the affairs of the emirate, so portentous in his daily life, were beginning to seem insubstantial. All the same, he mentioned the matter to the Resident that evening.

"Aboubakar?" Catchpole said. "He's one of our bright boys, isn't he? Sort of chap we show off to visiting Governors? Well, I shouldn't be surprised, they're all the same—murder their mothers for a bag of beans."

"We'd better keep an eye on him," Robert suggested. "After all, it was we who dished up both the tax assessment scheme and the girls' school on the Emir's plate."

A frown came over the dark, florid face of the Resident. "By the way, that tax business. You didn't put up at all a good show for Begg, I'm afraid. Had rather a snorter from the Secretariat this morning." He pushed over a file with an official dispatch on top of the papers.

'Moreover it would appear,' ran a paragraph which the Resident prodded with a stubby finger, 'that in areas only recently brought under administration, where in the past an antagonistic attitude to Government has prevailed, the decision to introduce a native tax assessment assistant into the area without due preparation of the people for his reception, on the one hand, and the protection afforded by the presence of a European officer on the other, was premature. I cannot feel satisfied that in this instance the interests of the Government have been served with due regard to the balance of factors operating in the particular circumstances of the case, and in the event a most regrettable incident, involving loss of life, has occurred. I must instruct you to convey to the officer in question an intimation that his conduct of this most important experiment in fiscal reform, which may be regarded as a significant step forward along the road to ultimate self-government, cannot be considered as having been in true accord with the best traditions of the service.'

Robert read it through and shrugged his shoulders, but his eyes were angry. "The best traditions of the service! That's a good one—the last bleat of the bureaucratic nanny-goat! Oh, well, what's the odds? Begg's scheme will go through. It won't work in practice, but the cries of the toad beneath the harrow will never reach the Secretariat, and Begg will get his C.M.G."

The Resident frowned. He disliked cynicism at all times, and especially in his subordinates; but in this instance he knew that the raspberry had landed on the wrong plate.

"The scheme's all right," he said, "but we slipped up over the application. Begg went off the deep end about it when he came back, and I told him that you hadn't wanted the clerk to go up to that hill village on his own at all—in fact that you'd definitely advised against it. It was my decision, not yours; at the time it seemed perfectly safe—anyway, he seems to have forgotten what I said. I'm sorry, old boy, and I'll put the thing right on paper in my reply."

"Don't bother, sir," Robert said stiffly. "It won't make any difference. . . . What's happened about the four poor devils who killed the clerk?"

"They've been committed for trial."

"What a hope of a conviction!"

"The police may dig up some more evidence before then."

"There's none to dig up. Just another nice surprise when the guilty parties come walking back up the hill, free as air. Everyone will think the murderers found some particularly potent magic, stronger even than the Government's. How we manage to run this country in the face of the contrary efforts of the High Court is beyond me."

"It's no good crabbing British justice," the Resident said shortly. He, too, deplored the vagrant nature of the legal system as applied to primitive races, for quite often it let down the administration, made fools of his officers and demolished a lingering native belief in the punishment of the guilty. But he felt bound to support the existing order of things. "After all, it's the finest system in the world."

"There's nothing wrong with it except that it won't take yes for an answer and generally lets criminals off scott free."

"It's not our job to alter things," the Resident said, frowning. "We're administrators, not reformers. Remember that, old boy, and we'll all get along better. It's no good supposing that the officer of the watch knows better than the man who sets the course."

"There'll be no holding our ship with that old sea-dog Captain Begg in charge," Robert said.

Chapter Fifteen

THE lamps were lit when Robert reached home, and Priscilla was on her knees before a packing-case, sorting books. Their lives, he reflected wearily, seemed a constantly repeated tale of packing, storing possessions, sorting them, counting them and unpacking them all over again. All the complications of living! Squatting down beside her, he joined in, making two piles: a smaller one to keep, a larger one for the hospital. The lamplight made a golden halo of her fine, unruly hair. Her cheeks, usually so pale, were flushed to-night, she looked eager and excited. Yet there was something about her colour that made him uneasy: it was too vivid, too diffuse. The widening gap between all that he had meant to do for her and the little he had achieved—and that little perhaps corrosive in its last effect—depressed him anew, and he cast round for some gesture, even the lightest motion, that would illustrate his warm intent. He remembered, suddenly, the eagle ring, and pulled it from his pocket.

"The Emir gave me this to-day. It's an old design, rather Egyptian, I think. Will you take it?"

Priscilla turned it over in her hand. "It's very sweet of you, Robert, but I couldn't wear it, it's far too clumsy and big."

"You could keep it as a sort of souvenir."

Priscilla laughed. "I don't hanker after Benares trays, or, in our case, crossed spears, native drums and horrible masks on the wall. 'That was a ju-ju I ran into in Bongo-Bongo, old boy.' No, thanks, Robert—you keep it. The Emir's your friend, not mine."

Discouraged, he put it back in his pocket. Of course, she was quite right, a heavy ornament like that was useless to a woman, but she had looked at it as if a scorpion had lain in her hand.

"You hate living out here, don't you," he said, more as a statement than a question.

Priscilla frowned at a book. "Of course not, Robert, why should I?"

"Because it's not your cup of tea."

"Oh, I don't know. It's rather like living with your mother-in-law, you never feel the place is really your own."

"The nesting instinct," Robert said thoughtfully. "As dangerous to thwart as any other, I suppose. They should breed a race of cuckoos for the job."

Priscilla slapped two books impatiently into the packing case, wishing that Robert would talk less sententiously of the obvious.

"I've got nothing to complain about," she said. "Most women only have one home at the best, I get a new one every couple of years. . . . Talking of homes, I've found one for Pyramus and Thisbe—with the Catchpoles, poor dears. Poor Pyramus, poor Thisbe, I mean."

She went on sorting books, oblivious of Robert beside her on the floor hugging his knees and staring at the lamp. Then she caught sight of his face. He looked tired and unhappy; and she realized, with a stab of self-blame, that she had barely noticed lately what had been happening to him. His beard was red in the soft light, he had trimmed it smaller; she was tired of it now but he had grown it, she remembered, on some half-facetious

suggestion of hers. Poor Robert! She had given him little
tenderness lately. She put her hand over his: but discerned,
as she did so, a hint of the specious in her gesture, a note of
falseness in her own voice.

"You look sad, darling. Are you sorry to be going?"

He shook his head. "I haven't made much of a show of it here.
It's time for a change."

"What nonsense, Robert! Of course you have, you always
do. Have you had some kind of trouble?" It was dreadful,
here was Robert, full of sadness and conflict, and she hadn't
even noticed what was going on. Of course, there had been that
murder, and the episode with the baboon. . . .

"Has that little toad been trying to get his own back?"

"If you mean Freddy Begg, I suppose he has, but it means
nothing."

"Little beast! Oh, Robert, and it's all my fault! I didn't
tell you, but he tried to make love to me, and I had to snub
him, he was so deplorable. And then, of course, you made a
fool of him over that baboon." The recollection made her smile.
"It was so funny the way he vanished, whiff, like a djinn. I
told you he'd never forgive you. What has he been and gone and
done?"

Robert laughed at her agitation. "Nothing; or at least, only
written one of his ineffable dispatches, but his complaint was
against my laxness, not your virtue."

"One thing leads to another. Oh, dear, I'm such a muffin
of a wife; I try hard, but I always seem to offend the wrong
people, and when I do score a success it's with the wrong side
too. Look at Armorel, she seems to pick out the right people
by their scent, like a bloodhound. I wish I was more like her."

"Thank God you're not!"

"And now she's modelling the Governor's head. Think of
all the ideas she'll put into it while she kneads the clay—like
witchcraft, almost."

"It may have the opposite effect. To hear Freddy's praises
sung for hours on end, twice a week——"

"Ah, but Armorel's not such a fool. She won't talk about
Freddy's virtues, other people's shortcomings will be her theme.
If you go on scooping away the soil all round a molehill you can
make a mountain of it in time."

"Well, let her. You don't think I married to get a sort of
trumpeter to blow my praises in Governors' ears?"

"No, but I don't think the brass is effective in our sort of orchestra; you need someone who's really clever with the strings."

Robert brought her a drink and raised his own glass.

"Here's to us, and a good leave. D'you know that it will be our first Christmas at home since we married?"

"Not Christmas; we shall be back by then."

"No," Robert said. "We shan't be coming back."

Startled, she looked up at him from the book-strewn floor. "What do you mean?"

"I've decided to chuck in my hand."

"But, Robert, you can't! Your career—your whole future—and we've no money. What would you do?"

"Good heavens, this isn't the only occupation in the world for an able-bodied man of, I suppose, a reasonable education! If England's no good we can try Canada or America."

Priscilla was dumbfounded, but behind her dazed expression some emotion was struggling to emerge. Hope, perhaps? Her cheeks were more flushed than ever, her eyes brighter.

"The place doesn't matter," he added, "so long as we can all be together. It's a poor sort of life we lead—changes, partings, separations. Robin's a total stranger to both of us. In any case I don't think you ought to come out here again."

Priscilla shook her head. "We've been into all that. I won't be turned into a millstone round your neck. Besides, I don't believe you really want a settled home. Fundamentally, I think you're happiest when you're foot-loose and free."

"As I've told you before, I'm happiest when I can entertain some hope that I'm making you happy."

She resumed the packing impatiently, slamming books into the case without looking at their titles.

"Do let's stick to the point! The point is whether you want to start something new half-way through your life—and whether you could. My happiness is only incidental."

He took her arm, half-angrily, and shook it. "Sometimes you're so thick-headed, Priscilla. Your happiness is as much the point as the sun is the point of the solar system. . . . But of course it's not the only thing. Life here is changing, it isn't the same world as the one we came out to before the war. You were your own master then, more or less—not a puppet on the end of a string jerked hither and yon by the bosses. It was a hard life at times, but at least you could see where you were going—or thought you could. Now, you can't be sure. The goal doesn't merely recede, it turns into something quite different from all you'd imagined, and something, to put it mildly, very dubious. . . ."

He looked round the bare dark-walled room, at the pools of lamplight in the soft gloom. Something stirred in him— regret? Thankfulness? Foreboding? He did not know.

"Robert." She was looking at him in an abstracted way, a little crease in the middle of her forehead. He realized that she had scarcely been listening at all. "Your beard!"

He put a hand to his chin.

"Would you mind taking it off?"

"Not if you want me to. Why?"

"It makes you look like a goat."

"Oh, damn my beard," he exploded, and buried his head in his hands, leaning his elbows on the window-sill, at once furious and wounded. While he struggled to amend their lives, and hers especially, at the cost of his peace of mind, she talked of beards, and made him feel ridiculous. Such harsh frivolity! He felt an arm slide round his shoulders, her hair brush his cheek.

"Darling, please forgive me." Her voice was contrite. "Of course I love your beard. Only I thought you wouldn't be needing it at home."

Was his imagination over-sensitive, or did he detect a note of lightness in her voice, almost of liberation? Had she, he thought bitterly, accepted his sacrifice so quickly, so casually— just swallowed it like a mouthful of cake? She took for granted too much! But she slid her hand into his and kissed his cheek.

"No, you're quite right," he said. "I shan't be needing it at home."

PART TWO

Chapter One

IT was raining when they got out at the station: a slow, soft,
steady drizzle that seemed a very part of the grey air and
cloud enveloping everything—the dirty grey platform, the choco-
late-brown station buildings, the glistening rails, the few ghost-
like people haunting the platform in dripping raincoats and
turned-down hats.

It had been raining a week ago, too, when Priscilla had
met her son, nervously and with apprehension, at another
railway station. Tall for his age, lanky, his navy raincoat flapping
round his bare knees, his face fresh and smooth as a pink sugar-
coated almond, he looked to her stranger's eyes more generic
than individual: a boy, with a boy's mysterious interests and
delights which were to her more secret than those of savages.
Ever since their meeting she had been constrained with anxiety
lest she commit some unforgettable *gaffe* thàt would shame her
in his eyes. When she had seen him last he had been a child,
interested in catapults and wigwams and devoted to a canary;
now he was reserved and a little supercilious, moving in a
busy world of his own. The canary had been given away,
wigwams certainly were buried under mountains of contempt,
catapults—she was not sure about them. Now the right topics
were probably locomotives, dormice, cricket. Priscilla sighed;
they were all things of which she knew nothing; already he had
outgrown her.

They drove along flat narrow roads, the hedges each side
dripping with moisture, trees sighing and swishing overhead.
The thick, rich greenness of it all! Everything looked as though
it would burst and the juices come gushing out: fat pastures,
sappy trees, swelling flowers in cottage gardens, even the faces
of the village women they passed, full and round. Beside them
she herself felt desiccated by dry winds and parching sun.

Robert was thinking the same thing. "Every time one comes
back, one forgets that anything can be so green."

"Or so restful; one never has to screw up one's eyes." She

smiled. "Only one's courage." She was deeply alarmed by her husband's relations, whose lives seemed to take place on a different plane from her own.

"The car smells of manure," Robin said.

"I expect it's just the horse-hair coming out of the cushions."

"Is great uncle Hubert very poor?"

There was a pause. Robert reflected that he really couldn't answer. He knew little about his uncle Hubert's affairs. His own father, Hubert Gresham's younger brother, had believed him to be rich and mean, practically a miser; but then Gabriel Gresham's bitterness against his family had been deep and perhaps justified.

"Your great-uncle has a lot of expenses. Anyway this is the second-best car."

"What's he done with the best one?"

"I don't know. He's promised you a pony to ride."

Robin nodded, and wiped steam off the window with his cap. "I hope it won't be a very fat one. Do you think it will be a roan?"

"I don't know."

"I hope it will. I'd like it to be a roan."

His lips moved. Priscilla looked at him nervously. Was he praying for a roan? Or reciting something to himself? Did he pray still, or had he grown out of it? If he spoke Chinese he could scarcely have been more of a stranger.

They were driving up to the front door along a lime avenue. The house was not really large, but it rambled. The nucleus was sixteenth century, in mellow brick and timber, with two wings and a projecting porch. Bits had been added on through the centuries, down to a bay-window in the 'eighties, but from a roof which strayed over a dozen different levels rose thin twisted Tudor chimneys, patterned in brick. Sometimes when Robert was wandering in the terraced gardens and caught sight of them over a tall hedge they would start off in his mind images of the place as it must have been when it was new, a sort of villa admired for its modern conveniences by the upstart tradesmen and perhaps despised by the baronial classes for its cosy vulgarity: indeed even the gardens (hung as they doubtless were with gilded bird-cages and ornaments of coloured glass dangling from boughs and topiary) with their fussy little knot-gardens and beds, must have looked distressingly chi-chi.

Wigg, the butler, greeted them gravely, as if they had just

returned from a week-end visit. His pink, full face never looked any older, indeed it would have been hard to gain from his appearance any clue to his age. He was totally bald. His first employer, Robert's grandfather, being hairless himself, had regarded it as disrespectful in an inferior to flaunt a possession denied to the master, and so the whole of his staff, from coachman to cook, had been shiny-pated. The virtual impossibility of finding bald women had resulted in a household almost entirely staffed by men, until at last his wife, driven half distracted by the dirt, drunkenness and brawls of her domestics, had resorted to deception and kept several young women tucked away over the stables. Even this was a constant anxiety, for it was necessary to complete the housework by eight in the morning and then to keep the girls out of sight, and also to protect them from the interest of the male staff, whose lack of hair was certainly no indication of weakened virility. In fact to her dying day Robert's grandmother had believed that bald men made up for their loss by an extra dose of masculinity in other directions.

Hubert Gresham came out to welcome them. He was tall, bony and stiff in his movements, with a strong-featured face and a surprising mat of yellow hair. Having inherited the family baldness, and long ago grown sick of egg-like skulls, he had taken to a toupee, and was now too lazy or too indifferent to change it for one more suited to his age. So there he was, an erect figure with a lined and weathered face surmounted by this most unlikely shock of bright hair, dressed in a tight pair of riding-breeches, an alpaca jacket and a yellow waistcoat that his father before him had worn.

He greeted them in a manner which appeared indifferent, but which Robert recognized as cordiality.

"You'll find few amusements," he warned them. "We're not gadabouts here. But so long as you don't expect me to entertain you, you can stay as long as you like. . . . Good gracious me, who's that?"

He had caught sight of Robin, who blushed, and looked mutely at his father.

"Surely you expected Robin, Uncle Hubert?"

"Robin who?"

Robert laughed. "None of our family is good at relations, but you do know we've got a son."

"So you have, so you have, but a baby. . . . You don't mean that this is yours? Well, I'll be blowed! One can't keep up with things nowadays. You remember that sequoia Father planted in the old shrubbery? It's fifteen feet high now if it's an inch!"

"It was planted before I was born; it must have had a good forty years."

"Yes, yes, I dare say, but you should see it now. Astonishing!"

Still muttering about the pace of events, he led them in his curious stiff-jointed motion through the panelled hall to the staircase, and they followed their bags along warren-like passages. While they were unpacking Robin's pink face looked round the door.

"I say, the floor's wavy, it goes up at one end. Is there a secret room?"

Robert smiled, remembering, in his own boyhood, clambering down a ladder into a dark cubby-hole smelling of cobwebs and mice.

"Yes, there is; I'll show it to you after tea."

Robin's face shone with excitement. "Is there a ghost too?"

"One thing at a time," Priscella said. "Would you like to explore the garden? Put on your goloshes, and don't forget to take them off when you come into the house. . . ."

The quick clatter of his feet died down in the passage; his parents smiled at each other. Priscilla's smile was a little forlorn. Once more she found herself almost counting the hours; one more day was slipping from her little stock of days. Robert, guessing her thoughts, said:

"This time, no more of those harrowing farewells. We'll be able to keep an eye on him."

Priscilla shook her head. "When it comes to the point, everyone's chained to his particular treadmill."

"No, I really mean it this time. I shall speak to Uncle Hubert to-night."

But that night Uncle Hubert sent word that he was tired and would not appear for dinner, and he left early next morning for one of his long, mysterious days in the City.

It was cold and showery, the heavy August foliage was drenched, the corn shocks leant on each other's shoulders like weeping maidens, only birds and slugs rejoiced. Occasional gleams of thin silver sunshine illuminated the sodden flower-beds and leafy trees. Robert strolled round the garden with quiet enjoyment. The yew-screened terraces, the lime walk, the sunken garden held few golden memories for him and many leaden ones, nevertheless he was glad to be back. Familiarity shed a sort of lustre on the scene. Here was the oak tree whose acorns he had gathered for a little pig, the runt of the litter, that he had adopted; there the dilapidated outhouse where a robin had nested in a derelict cupboard. How closely, he thought, children invest a piece of landscape with their dreams and memories, until it becomes a very part of their lives! The child and the landscape grow together, and afterwards he cannot look on it unmoved; though so much of the meaning has faded, he is looking back into the making of his own soul.

The house and its occupants had been dominated, then, by the personality of his grandfather. A sort of cold paralysis had assailed him when the old man, with his smooth marble face and blue darting eye, had thrown a remark in his direction as you might throw a scrap to a dog. The servants, too, had lived in a state of trepidation. There had been one, Roger the valet, a stocky fat-faced youth, prematurely bald; once, when his master had fallen into one of his rages, Roger had stretched out a hand as if to check the onslaught and the old man, with all his venom, had spat full into the palm; and later he had summoned the valet to give him no apology, but to press a golden sovereign into the same hand.

In those days people did not shrink from rule by fear and they did not mind being hated. His grandfather had been a bully and many had smarted from his rages; consideration for other people's feelings he would have regarded as degenerate weakness; yet the fear with which his juniors and inferiors regarded him had been mixed with admiration. His wife and even his servants had stayed with him and his friends, although he gave them scant encouragement, had never deserted him. It was something that was hard to understand. Perhaps it was because he was so indifferent to the opinion of others that so few people really hated him, since hate, like love, requires some response to sustain it. One of the few exceptions had been Robert's mother, who had entertained towards him a contrary passion no less great than love. She had crossed him twice. The first time was when she had run away with his son Gabriel; that round had seemed to be hers. The second and final round was his.

He had been a man of many quirks and oddities, not the least queer being an aversion, real or pretended, for the sight of feminine flesh. Women he had always disliked, regarding them as regrettable biological necessities; since they had to exist, the only remedy was, in eastern fashion, to keep them covered up. Being, he believed, a reasonable man, he did not require them to be veiled, although he would no doubt have preferred it, but he did banish any unnecessary display of flesh. All his feminine guests were warned to wear dresses with long sleeves, and to keep their hands gloved. Every visiting female found on her dressing-table, on her arrival, a pair of gloves, and with it a note enjoining her to wear them at all times in her host's presence. Every evening a new pair was laid out.

Susan Gresham had been a young woman of force of character to match his own. Seeing the note on her dressing-table, all her anger and resentment had flared up. She was not to be treated so by any tyrant! She had appeared at dinner in a short-sleeved gown and without gloves. A storm had followed: he had ordered her from the room, she had refused to obey. (Robert had been told of it, years later, by Wigg; the scene had lived in the memories of its witnesses as vividly as a day-old event.) He had ordered the footmen to offer her no food. All through the meal she had sat, her plate empty, silently storming. Next day she had left early, never to return. She had crossed him twice; he never gave her another opportunity.

By comparison his elder son Hubert seemed less than half a man. He had lived on in his father's house, never marrying, and retrieving, Robert believed, by his careful and mysterious dealings in the City, a fortune wrecked by the extravagancies of his father, who had died heavily in debt. Yet Hubert was not without his peculiarities. On the day following his visit to London Robin, intent on climbing trees, found him on his hands and knees beside a pile of dead leaves, gathering miniature toadstools.

"Are those to eat, great-uncle?"

Uncle Hubert looked pleased. "Certainly, my dear boy. They are excellent, especially when stewed in red wine with a little paprika." He got to his feet and dusted his knees. "You are interested in fungi?"

Robin looked at the ground and muttered something; he was trying to pluck up courage to ask about the pony, which had not yet appeared.

"I'll show you my collection. A world in miniature, full, like our own, of creatures struggling and striving, and all para-sites—just as we are, you know. Have you ever paused to con-sider how many meals you will eat before you die?"

Robin looked up with bewildered but awakened interest. This was a fascinating and, in a sense, encouraging thought.

"If you live to be eighty, as I expect you will, and consume three meals a day, you are faced with the prospect of eighty-seven thousand six hundred meals, not counting tea, before your digestion gives up the struggle. And each one of these an expression of the parasitic nature of man. For the simple chemical operation on which all existence depends cannot be performed by that wondrous creature man, so he must go to the humble plants to rob them of the fruits of their industry. Mere parasites, you see, like the fungi—but endowed, in my opinion, with very much less beauty."

He led his great-nephew to an attic over the old part of the house where he had made among the rafters a sort of museum of moulds. Robin gazed in creepy fascination at fungi of every possible shape, some crinkled, some smooth, some like revolting fleshy growths of diseased tissue, some like thick leathery pancakes, some again like delicate waving seaweeds on the ocean's floor. He spelled out their curious suggestive names: Jew's ear, Druid's saddle, fairies' butter, witches' broom. The allurement of the sinister hung over these really quite innocent toadstools and growths. His great-uncle Hubert related with gusto scraps of curious information about his treasures: here was a grey fungus caterpillar shroud eaten as medicine by the Chinese; there a pile of near-mushrooms esteemed by the Romans as one of the four greatest luxuries (the others, he explained, being oysters, thrushes and a small bird fattened on figs)—the very vehicle, and this made it seem highly dramatic, of the emperor Claudius' death.

"All, my dear boy, have this in common," Uncle Hubert exclaimed, waving a hand to comprehend the whole attic. "They draw their nourishment from the juices of decay. The rotting tree-trunk, the crumbling root, the damaged branch, alike in dissolution—these are their habitat."

The old man's face was alight with enthusiasm, his large fingers, fidgeting with slides, were quick and delicate in their movements. His air was almost that of an evangelist.

"To burst out with a raw kind of life in the spring is easy enough, a common sort of performance. The rush of sap, the rash of primroses (such plain little plants, with flowers like acid drops) and then hordes of buttercups which make the fields look like scrambled eggs—I hate the spring No form, no moderation.

How much more intelligent and subtle to flourish when the year declines, in the damp steaming woods of autumn, to shape their delicate forms and gentle colours from the sap of putrefaction! Contrast the variations of the fungi's form, the richness of invention, with the few crude shapes of spring—the bell, the plain rosette. Or compare the subtlety, the range, the variations of a single theme to be found in October woodlands, with the raw colours of spring—suburban sofa-covers or a draper's window. Remember this, my dear boy—there is more beauty to be had in decay than in creation!"

Robin's interest was absorbed by a crinkled fungus like a cauliflower ear, growing out of a dead branch. He was trying to ignore his great-uncle without appearing rude, for there was something repugnant not in the fungi, which fascinated him, but in the flow of talk.

"As you grow older you will observe that our human world. being divided into sexes, is hopelessly obsessed with the combination of these two sexes, in their individual units, in order to secure the continuance of the race. You will find that from your late childhood until your death you will be surrounded, and very likely yourself obsessed, with this unfortunate need. You will find it to be the constant theme not only of your own life but also of literature, of drama, of art, even embedded in religion; and I can assure you, my dear boy, that like anything else indefinitely repeated, it becomes exceedingly boring. And what makes it even more tedious is that it is quite unnecessary. Our fungi, you see, produce their spores without any of the fuss and bother of sex. Think of that, my dear boy! The more you consider it, the more you will come to realize that there is only one solution for the future of the human species, if indeed it deserves a future at all—it must find a way to get rid of its obsession with sex by changing over to the system of vegetative reproduction."

Through a dirty window, heavily edged with cobwebs as if with grey lace, Robin could see blue sky and a gleam of sunshine. Quite suddenly he plucked up courage to ask about the pony. He was frightened of his great-uncle, but the pony was desperately important, and somehow, in spite of the old man's queerness, he was less frightened than he had been before he came into the attic.

And, to his surprise, Uncle Hubert only smiled at him.

"Of course, my dear boy, you shall have your pony. We'll see about it at the farm this afternoon."

Chapter Two

AT last the fine autumn weather came. Each morning was steamy, with a pearliness in the air that made everything look faintly misty, as if seen under water; the edges of objects were bevelled rather than sharp. Partridges fed among the dusty stubble, wagons creaked under their harvest loads, the moist smell of fecundity hung about orchards and fields. People smiled and their voices were gentle under soft blue skies. The rich fruition of harvest, the seeded grass, loaded trees, replete animals, these spoke only of plenty and masked the poverty beneath: untilled field and undrained pasture, crumbling barn, emptying villages, the first breath of winter touching the cheek.

In the house they dined in a small panelled room off the old hall. All the rooms now were untidy and austere, and none too clean. Uncle Hubert did not pay attention to dirt and Wigg had long ceased to bother himself with detail, so the rough girls from the village had little supervision. The walls were encrusted with family portraits, stags' antlers and spears captured in imperial forays; on the floors worn Persian carpets jostled the pelts of tigers and bears.

Uncle Hubert never sat long over his port. He was a sparing drinker, though sometimes he would remind his guests of the debt mankind owed to the fungus world for its part in the making of wines. On fine evenings he would disappear into the woods, walking by moonlight; his comings and goings were always a little mysterious. But on this evening Robert nailed him down. Speaking distinctly—for he never quite knew whether Uncle Hubert was listening—he explained his circumstances and his need for a change of career.

"And you are how old?" Uncle Hubert asked.

"Thirty-seven."

"Your present salary?"

"About a thousand a year."

Uncle Hubert sipped his port, looking suddenly business-like. Although he masked it well, considerable ability must be needed to sustain his connection with so many unspecified concerns; in his home, he never mentioned these matters at all.

"I could get you a position, if you want it," he said at last, "with one of the companies of which I am director. But you can't expect a good one, you know. Men of middle age who have spent their lives ordering blacks about are not a very marketable commodity."

Robert shifted in his chair. "One does rather more than order blacks about. One learns a bit about administration, finance, how to deal with people, to take responsibility. . . ."

"But not about commerce, the vulgar business of making and selling?"

"Perhaps not. But isn't it mostly common sense?"

Uncle Hubert laughed. It was a high-pitched laugh more like a giggle, oddly thin for so large a man.

"You have much to learn if you think that. It is partly following tradition and partly thinking of innovations before your neighbour, a curious mixture. What school were you at?"

"A school in Switzerland."

"Yes, of course; Gabriel's wife could afford nothing better. Well, Robert, you may have your way if you want it, but you would do best to think carefully first."

"You can get me a job?"

"If you want one, yes."

Robert was delighted; it was all much easier than he had expected.

"And the pay?"

"Four hundred a year—at the most, five."

"But we couldn't live on that! We should need a house— Robin's school fees——"

Uncle Hubert shrugged his shoulders. "I don't suppose your mother had as much. But it's as you wish."

"I shall have to think it over."

He felt his uncle's eyes on him—light, curiously blank eyes that left no impression and yet were shrewd. Was it his imagination, or was there something mocking in the look? But Uncle Hubert only drained his port, wiped his mouth on a napkin and added:

"Perhaps you think I should do something for you, but you know that my father's arrangements prevent your getting a penny."

"I know that quite well. I was not asking for charity."

Uncle Hubert gave his thin, high laugh. "You have something of Gabriel's looks, but more of your mother's character. A stubborn, pig-headed woman! But she made her bed and lay on it to the end, that I will say, without whining."

Robert half-pushed back his chair. "If you think your father's inhumanity can be excused——"

But Uncle Hubert, with a malicious smile, was gone, leaving Robert alone with the port. He settled back into his chair, touched by a sense of futility. The years of hardship and labour that had been needed to turn him from an infant to a man only that he might, in his turn, be trodden under by circumstances! Uncle Hubert's words were nicking at his mind, paring away his confidence. Thirty-seven . . . untrained . . . ordering blacks about . . . a foreign school. . . . How much ability and luck would be needed to balance those dead weights? If his grandfather had not borne so deep a grudge—if his father had been less precipitate—his mother more pliant—fate less harsh. . . . He smiled into his glass. Absurd repinings! If human beings were not as they were, fiery, obstinate and perverse, then fate would not be so harsh; like flies under a tumbler, people buzzed in the invisible prison of their own characters—as his parents had done, long ago.

His notions of his father as a young man sprang from a photograph, cherished by his mother, of Gabriel Gresham in the uniform of a lieutenant of Hussars: as handsome a young officer as you could hope to find, with a gay, twinkling look about him, clear eyes, a chin and jaw that suggested some of his father's stubbornness. And to his father he had been all. He was the one who rode and shot with the dash and ease of a master, born with the quick wit and the taste for joking, in contrast to his sombre, clumsy brother. One of those blessed with looks, intelligence, charm and position, none denied him a fair future: an eligible *parti*, heir to a property, a promising young officer in a regiment of repute.

Looking back, it was easy to guess how the cracks had started, a little here and there, unnoticed at the time but weakening the whole structure. Expensive tastes, debts, gambling, ill-luck, a hot intemperate nature insufficiently curbed. All that was an old story, and something he could have scrambled through. But he made a mistake from which there was no retreat. He fell head over ears in love with his Colonel's eighteen-year-old daughter, and the two eloped.

That in itself need not have been fatal. But it happened that the daughter was engaged to a young man prominent in society, and within a week of her wedding, when she was persuaded to elude her chaperone at a ball, step into a four-wheeler with the dashing but now penniless young lieutenant, and disappear. The scandal was great and public, accompanied by the sordid intervention of the police; for it was found that an expensive emerald necklace, the gift of the bridegroom, had vanished from its place among the wedding-presents.

It would have been hard to say which of the two fathers was the more incensed. The bride's had the better cause, but Gabriel's the greater capacity. His anger burnt within him like a live coal. Months later, the pair regained their cruel notoriety. They were arrested by the French police over some squalid affair of unpaid bills. The proceeds of the necklace had gone in the casinos and Gabriel Gresham had laid himself open to a criminal action should he return to his own country.

His father paid his debts, redeemed the necklace and severed himself for ever from his favourite son. Gabriel and Gabriel's future children were expunged from the will and his very name outlawed. One attempt was made by friends to bring about a reconciliation. The young wife came to England to return the necklace, which had been taken almost by accident, out of youthful folly and with no intention to defraud. But Susan Gresham was touchy, proud and frightened; and, being excessively young, chose to conceal her fears under a display of aggression. She had no notion, then, of her need for amnesty, and could be as rash and obstinate as her father-in-law. In such circumstances it was madness to defy him, but she saw herself less as a supplicant for mercy than as a wronged party come to treat on equal terms. The absurd but terrible scene over the gloves followed and their enmity was sealed.

Thereafter the doom of this young couple was assured. Extravagant, innocent, spoilt and gay, they were equipped only for a life which they were now denied. But they did not surrender. Beneath Susan's childish temerity the lineaments of a woman of dogged character began to appear. Penniless, they drifted from place to place, earning a precarious livelihood now at this and now at that; still in love, and a fortune always just in front of their noses. Robert was born in Brussels in a mean half-furnished flat and a brother two years later in Paris, but the second baby died.

Gabriel had from his boyhood shown an aptitude for engineering. Studying as best he could in the intervals of scratching a livelihood, he was able to win a French qualification and, after various ups and downs, he at last secured a well-paid position in

Chile. Once more confident and gay, believing their troubles to be ended, the couple set out for their new world. The child did not go; they were to send for him later; and it was at this point that Gabriel's mother, with an effort into which she put all her wit and stratagems, managed to introduce her outcast grandson into her husband's house and so at least to secure his well-being.

Of his parents' life in Chile, Robert knew little. It was something of which they did not afterwards speak: rough, he imagined, crude and hard, but not without exhilaration and the sparkle of adventure. Would they, he wondered, have succeeded in mastering their fate, or were they like spiders in a bath, clambering a little way up the slippery side and always losing their hold? He could only speculate. A mining accident so gravely injured Gabriel's spine that it was a year before he walked again, even then painfully, and his way to salvation was closed.

When Robert next saw his father he was already a cripple, dragging his legs after him and leaning on sticks. As for his mother, lines of bitterness and fatigue had marked her face, her gay lark-like manner was all gone.

They had come, with the last of their money, to Lausanne for treatment, and here they stayed. Gabriel grew worse. His body stiffened, walking became a torment, and at last his injuries drove him into a wheeled chair. The range of his world narrowed to a few hundred yards of pavement and his spirit fretted without respite in its chains.

The maturity of Robert's parents was one long sacrifice to pride. However desperate their state, Susan Gresham would not beg. By ceaseless toil and by a dozen petty means she scraped together, year after year, sufficient money to support her husband and son. Two rooms, thread-bare clothes, worn cheap shoes, food bargained for in the market to the last cent, all these were the background of his childhood—these and, over-shadowing all such details, the tormented, bitter spirit of his father caged in a body afflicted by a creeping paralysis which spread with icy languor to every member but the heart.

That Susan Gresham grew hard, embittered and even cruel was no less inevitable than the body's making of scar tissue over a wound. Robert's boyhood was without tenderness or gaiety. As he grew older he longed only to get away from his cramped home, haunted by the suffering body and pinioned spirit in the wheeled chair, now querulous and morose, and ruled by the hard-faced, hard-willed woman who silently nursed her husband,

cleaned and cooked, and spent her evenings at book-keeping or
linen-mending to earn the money for the week's rent and the
day's bread.

He had felt only thankfulness when at last his father died
peacefully in his wheeled chair, an empty bottle of sleeping-
draught on the table by his side. He remembered the doctor,
bearded and plump, seated by a table and turning the bottle
over in his hands and saying presently, but in stern tones : 'Your
husband's affliction would scarcely have permitted him to lift
the glass to his mouth without assistance.' And his mother looking
at the stranger stonily, full in the eyes. 'Both my son and I were
out, doctor, when it occurred.' And the doctor glancing back at
her, at the empty wheeled chair, at the lanky ill-clad boy;
shrugging his shoulders, hesitating and, with a little flourish,
signing his name to a paper on the table.

Pride on the one hand, a vindictive spirit on the other, had
first exposed them to the thrusts of fate and then kept open the
wounds. And so Robert had resolved to keep clear of all intemperate emotions. He had seen in his own experience how lives
were crucified on such unyielding timbers. Now it was his duty
to see that Robin did not suffer, as he had done, from the failure
of his parents. The boy had suffered already, perhaps, from the
insecurity of the homeless. But worse than that was the parasitic
kind of poverty that sucked all life and spontaneity from the host.

He rose to find Priscilla, sitting over an early fire in the drawing-
room, and told her that the first round of his contest had gone
against him.

"And now," he added, "the serious search begins."

Chapter Three

IN spite of the gentle days and the calm autumn weather and
the company of her son, Priscilla's health was not mended.
She suffered still from headaches, fits of breathlessness, apparent
fluxes and torpors of the blood. She had the dread of doctors
common among country people, who regard physicians less as
healers than as purveyors of bad news. But Robert insisted, and
she sat one morning in an austerely opulent consulting-room,
nervously fingering her unaccustomed gloves.

The verdict was not encouraging. Too much malaria, a diet of quinine, an unfavourable climate had combined, it seemed, to do some injury to her heart. Africa was to be ruled out, at least for the present; excitement avoided, stringency observed towards alcohol, cigarettes and all strenuous activities.

"And of course, no more babies, you understand."

"I was told that after my only child was born."

"Quite so. If you are careful, Mrs. Gresham, and exercise common sense—for it's largely a matter of that—there's no reason why you should not live a normal healthy life for many years to come."

"Thank you, doctor."

"But I must emphasize that any violent exertion, any sudden shock, and especially any prolonged strain such as you have been subjected to through malaria might prove too much. . . . There is little we can do in such cases, you know, save to appeal to the patient's good sense and to alleviate pain. The patient's fate is largely in his own hands."

He stood up, an erect, decisive, almost aggressively clean-shaven man. Priscilla's fingers rested for a moment in his hard, dry hand, she murmured thanks and was passed from hand to hand like a package into the street.

Walking towards the scene of her appointment with Robert, she felt irritated with the doctor and furious with herself. Ridiculous, to manifest such weakness! Like all healthy people she looked on illness, and her own especially, with exasperated contempt. As for doctors, their first thought was for their own professional pride. Why urge you to treat yourself like a piece of Chinese porcelain? The body was for use in the daily wear and tear of the household, not for confinement in a corner cupboard; it must take its chance of getting cracked or broken. Doctors were the worst of all confusers of means with ends. The preservation of life was their end, the patching of the cracked vessel, no matter what its content; they could not see that life was but the means to an end, its preservation secondary to its use. . . . But what should she say to Robert? Foolish to alarm him without reason, and he did take on so.

Absorbed in thought, she all but collided with a man. Both stepped aside, but in the same direction; they barred each other's path. Looking up, she smiled in apology and found, by one of those chances that occur so much more often than would seem justifiable by the laws of mathematics, that she had bumped into Maurice Cornforth, who had once shared with herself and Robert, a doctor and a vet, the distinction of being the only Europeans in a lonely and desiccated African post.

He raised his hat, smiling broadly.

"Well, Doctor Livingstone of all people, alone in the jungle; and what a jungle it is, too! Are you enjoying your leave?"

"Very much, thank you. When did you get back?"

"Two days ago; I've hardly had time to shake the mould out of my trousers and buy a bowler hat—still in the tailor and ticket agency stage, and trying to remember how a telephone works."

They stood there, people swirling round them like waves about a rock, wondering what to say next. Both knew the conventional gambits inside out: I came over with old Jones, I hear young Smith is getting married this leave, I'm going to a show to-morrow with Robinson. But, for different reasons, neither of them felt that it was worth while.

Smiling, his hat in his hand, Maurice Cornforth looked down at her, the sun adding a sheen to his dark smooth-brushed hair. The good looks of his youth had thickened into a sort of burliness. His clear complexion had darkened with exposure to sun and wind, there was something of a hard-bitten look about him and his brown eyes, large and quick of expression, were a little wary. Priscilla, looking into his face, saw a hint of dissipation in the heavy lids, the full sensual mouth and the crowsfeet beginning to appear under the eyes; but his smile was broad and simple and his eyes danced; it was impossible not to feel that he was a good fellow, friendly, dependable, lively and by no means lacking in charm.

As for Maurice Cornforth, he saw in this encounter, as people do in events which please them but which they have not dared to arrange, the workings of fate. For years he had seen Priscilla as it were behind a red flag of warning. Knowledge of her integrity, of her husband's position and of his own weakness had compelled him rather to avoid her, or at least not to seek the meetings he would have otherwise contrived. This chance encounter was like an unexpected present, or a fall of rain in a season of drought. Standing by his side in the sunshine she looked slender, neat and self-possessed in a plainly cut russet dress with touches of white, and a hat that seemed to nest in her golden hair; but a nervous picking of fingers at the button of her glove, a slightly quickened breathing, betrayed, or perhaps underlined, that self-possession.

"Are you in a hurry? Will you come and have a drink?"

"Thanks, but I'm on my way to meet Robert."

She paused, curiously reluctant to let him go. Just at that moment, in the late September sunshine, in the gay street crowded with hurrying figures and bright colours, life seemed infinitely desirable, its sweetest element the affection of friends. And it would be difficult to face Robert. A way out, or at least a post-ponement, suddenly presented itself.

"Why not join us for lunch?"

"Oh, I don't want to butt in; thanks most awfully all the same."

Priscilla smiled. "We're not on our honeymoon, you know. Will you walk as far as the restaurant, at least?"

They picked their way together through the crowd. Maurice was rather garrulous; he chatted on.

"I'm pausing on the brink before plunging into a tankful of relations. But I don't want to stay long in London. In fact I've taken rooms in a fishing village for part of my leave; it's on a marvellous little bay, and the pub has a good line in beer. One can catch mackerel and hire horses from a farmer and drink with the locals, and let the world go by."

They found Robert waiting at the restaurant and Maurice, over-persuaded, joined them. Priscilla saw at once that she had made a mistake. Robert was touchy and morose. He said little, occasionally glancing at her with a curious blend of vexation and concern. She herself, to her own intense annoyance, felt shaky and slack. Maurice saved the situation by prattling on about his voyage over, his last station, mutual acquaintances and plans for leave, making her laugh at nothing in particular, as he had when they had shared the same outpost.

The lunch ended at last and, saying good-bye, he took her hand; the firm touch did not leave her quite unmoved.

"Enjoy yourself at your fishing village, Maurice—what was its name?"

He told her.

"But that's quite close to my mother's home! I shall be going down there next week."

"Then perhaps we shall run across one another. If you've nothing better to do, come and catch mackerel one day."

"Or come over to tea. I'll give you the address." She scribbled it on a piece of paper.

"Thank you, Priscilla, I will."

He was gone, and she turned to face Robert, slipping a hand under his arm.

"Why did you insist on asking him?" Robert's voice was edgy with impatience. "You know I was waiting to hear the doctor's report."

Priscilla sighed, the warmth she had felt towards him ebbing away. Robert was all fire or ice! No comfortable fireside glow. His anxiety made him chilly and severe, in this public lounge, amid the potted palms. She craved for a cigarette and, after a brief struggle, yielded.

"Five guineas' worth of froth and very little beer," she said. "There's nothing the matter except a bit too much fever and quinine."

Chapter Four

TO return to the village was like plunging into a slow-moving stream that never chafed or faltered. Here, like the bent fruit trees in the orchards, people had flowered, fruited, withered and returned to the soil that made them, and the hardness and symmetry of their lives had laid on their surroundings a patina which neither time nor the slow wasting of rural England could rub away.

In this mellow October, a gentle but resplendent sun poured down on roofs of golden thatch and lichened tile. Dahlias blazed in the gardens, children still in summer dresses passed by with fingers stained purple by the late blackberries. Although to youths talking of motor-cycles, or even old ladies going by chara-banc to the seaside, the gathering of the harvest no longer held a personal meaning, an ancient sense of satisfaction persisted in come subtle fashion at this crown of the year.

Priscilla busied herself about the small tasks of cottage and garden with a zest to whose prick she had for some time been a stranger.

"You've no idea how wonderful it feels to be able to get one's own cup of tea and sit down to a meal witthout someone always behind one's shoulder!"

Her mother smiled a little grimly. "I've an idea what it's like, but none of it's being wonderful."

"No, of course, it's been your whole life. Now you're getting on and you've earned a little leisure, it's time you listened to reason. There's no need for you to live here by yourself, doing all your own work——"

Her mother replied with finality: "I've hoed my own row since I was fourteen years of age and I'm too old now to change my ways. You have your black sambos and I'll keep my own pair of hands."

"But your rheumatics——"

Her mother changed the subject abruptly. "Will you be bringing Robin here? I've not seen him since he was learning to walk."

"Yes, of course. If I'm to stay here this winter there'll be the Christmas holidays, and then Easter."

The older woman shook her head. "It's not right, Priscilla."

"To let Robert go back alone? If it happens it will be against my will, and only to obey the doctor."

"A doctor should come between man and wife no more than anyone else."

Priscilla almost shared the same feeling. She told herself that these ideas were foolish. Such separations were frequent among their friends, who seemed to suffer little from them, and to start smoothly again from where they had parted. But instinct told her that she and Robert would not find it so easy. If so, the fault must lie on her side. Disturbed and puzzled, she thought often that she must have this out with herself, but whenever she reached this point her mind recoiled and shot off at tangent. The days were too formless, busy and pleasant, and on each occasion she added: to-day there's no time, but to-morrow will bring an opportunity. So the days slid by. Seagulls flew inland to inspect the fresh moist furrows, apples were shaken from laden trees, the last wasps buzzed angrily on window panes, the slow fires of autumn smouldered in the woods. The crowded kitchen was full of the smell of jam boiling in saucepans, and small bright bubbles clung to the skins of plums in glass jars.

One afternoon a time-worn two-seater drew up by the cottage and its driver walked up the brick path and knocked at the door. Priscilla's mind leapt back ten years, as she went along the narrow passage to answer the summons, to the afternoon when, pulling open the door, she had seen the tall figure of Robert on the threshold, the spring sunshine gilding his fair hair and his face alight with an anxious smile. But this time it was not Robert. Maurice Cornforth greeted her, smiling, looking like a friendly brown spaniel asking for a bone.

"I've taken you at your word, you see. My fishing village is less than twenty miles away. I've come in a frightful rattle-trap, but it's got me here."

"Do come in."

"I'd love to. May I come to tea? But it's early yet; why not sample the rattle-trap?"

Priscilla hesitated. She was sorry now that she had given him her address. Not that Maurice was unwelcome, but he brought with him complications.

"Half an hour, then, and back for tea."

The car started with a leap like a nervous horse and spun forward with a high singing note. It was the sort of car that could not be left to itself for a moment; the driver's hands were busy all the time. Priscilla watched them: broad, brown hands with little silky golden hairs on the backs of the fingers. Maurice sucked at a pipe. His sunburnt face was almost florid, his eyes the clear colour of water running over peat. In grey flannels and tweed jacket he had the look of a grown-up under-graduate. He gossiped about their acquaintances, chatted about his village and the small pub where he was staying.

"Aren't you lonely there?"

Maurice laughed. "Never, at the seaside."

"Meaning that the walrus can always pick up little oysters on the sands?"

"He isn't always hungry, you know. But we've got a mock turtle—you ought to see her. Platinum blonde, crimson toenails. lives in an arty-crafty cottage. . . . Will you come over? If it's fine we can catch mackerel in the bay."

"Thank you, but it's really too far——"

"I'll fetch you in the car. I'd like you to try our speciality at the pub—shrimps and sloe gin."

"It sounds horribly indigestible."

"Not if you have enough gin."

Priscilla shook her head. "It's very nice of you, but it all sounds too adventurous."

Maurice looked round at her and grinned. "I'm not inviting you into the Bight of Benin. I'll protect you from the onslaughts of mackerel and deliver you back safely for supper."

Tea in the cottage turned out to be a gay and cosy event, but when he had gone Priscilla's mother looked at her quizzically and said:

"So that's one of your young men?"

"Don't be absurd, Mother! I haven't any young men, as you know very well."

Priscilla's mother, washing the teacups at the sink, only smiled.

"Robert knows him better than I do; we had a tour together in the same station."

"He's a pleasant-spoken young man, but he has his eye on you, Priscilla, as you know well enough. It's no business of mine, but Robert—there are men who see no more than they want to, and others who see what isn't there. I reckon Robert will see no more than what's thrust under his nose, but then, like as not, he'll be off."

Priscilla was really angry. She flushed and exclaimed:

"You're simply talking nonsense! There's nothing for him to see. Maurice Cornforth means no more to me than this teapot." She slammed it down so hard on the draining-board as to endanger its bottom. Utterly ridiculous, that an old acquaintance could not come to tea without these implications! Some trace of this rebellious mood still lingered when Maurice reappeared one morning a few days later, tempting her to mackerel fishing by praising the weather and the sea.

It was a golden morning, reflecting the last of summer. The sea lay benign and inviting, the bay cradled in two generous arms of green and chequered land. A whitewashed village sat at the cliff's foot with the settled look of centuries, and black fishing boats rested on the narrow beach. There was nothing in the world like the sea! Priscilla responded to it as others to music; she felt herself unfolding, her blood warming to its exhilaration.

But after lunch the breeze freshened and fishing boats tossed out in the bay. They decided against the mackerel, and instead followed a path that wound up the cliff and over sweet-smelling turf above the sea. Inland lay a prospect of patterned fields and wooded coombes, green and smiling. Gulls wheeled and cried, now and again a rabbit frisked its white tail as it bolted for cover, and below them, compelling the eye, lay the flashing and eternal sea.

They walked briskly, saying little, and taking as their objective a fairly distant point, the highest on all this stretch of coast, where the sea lay on three sides, and here they rested on the turf by a patch of heather. Priscilla felt pleasantly tired, warmed through by the exertion and freshened by the wind that had whipped her fine hair about her face and plucked at her skirt as if anxious to sweep all human excrescences off the smooth cliff-top, but now that they were down to rabbits' level, had abated. She lay at peace, savouring the rich bouquet of the air: smells of turf, thyme and heather, a hint of the earthy scent of woodlands, and above and all through all the salty, spicy tang of the sea. Idly she wondered at the poverty of language when it came to the country where the nose is king; you could enlist a dozen words to convey the shape and colour of a rose but could say of its scent only that it was sweet. All she remarked was:

"Everything smells so fresh!"

He breathed in deeply; and became aware, through and beyond the rough sea-smell, of a scent more delicate and subtle, like a single thread of gold shot through a brocade: the scent, perhaps, of the hair that blew about her face, of the powder on her skin, of her flesh itself. One arm, the colour of pale honey, lay idly by his side. He slid his hand lightly from wrist to elbow, and when she turned towards him his look seemed to pass into her very bones.

"Maurice, please!"

Spoken as an entreaty, her whisper fell on his ears as an invitation. He leant over and kissed her. She did not resist, indeed she could not, and he pulled her into his arms; and she, caught up on the same gust of hard and biting passion, yielded to the moment and let her senses ride her body uncurbed by the will.

But it was only for the moment; breaking away, she jumped up and ran a few steps to the edge of the cliff. Her flesh was burning, her heart, beating like a bird caught in a net, full at once of exultation and turmoil. Behaving, at her age, like a callow girl, betraying Robert, at least in her heart! She pushed her hair away and the wind, sane and impersonal, cooled her skin. Maurice was standing by her side. The wind had caught the ends of his tie and was tossing them about, and driving his trousers-legs in folds against his shins.

"Of course the right thing is to apologize, but I shan't do that. I'm not sorry, I'm glad, because now you know the truth."

"I don't believe in post-mortems. . . . Let's go back."

But he only stood there with a stricken look, and said:

"Priscilla, you must understand: I love you with all my heart."

She was dismayed. Maurice was in deadly earnest, standing there oblivious of the wind and the murmur of the sea and everything save her nearness and inaccessibility.

"We must forget that this ever happened."

"Forget!" Into two syllables went a world of protest and affirmation.

"What else? You know me well enough to know that Robert —that I——"

She paused, aghast. Her lips had simply refused to complete the sentence, her voice had petered out. 'I love him'—of course it was true! She had always loved Robert; it was impossible that the rock on which her life was built should have crumbled unnoticed into sand.

She barely heard his voice above the wind that tore the softly-spoken words from his mouth.

"And yet you were not indifferent."

His last card! But he stood there half-swallowing the words, and she felt a prick of pity to see him so entangled in unexpected impulses and half-forgotten codes that he simply threw his ace of trumps away.

"One can't build one's life round a moment of sensuality."

"At least we needn't talk like adolescents! You know well enough what this could mean."

"We must go home, it's getting late." She turned and hurried back, without looking to see whether he followed, and despising her own folly. Useless to run from an inner enemy! Yet the motion gave her an illusion of safety. Plunging down the slope and up the slippery turf on the other side she was sharply reminded of another and more brutal weakness, and her legs, turned leaden, would no longer obey. She was forced to the ground, gripped by a fearful pain and struggling for air, an icy panic chilling her blood.

"Priscilla, what's wrong?" Maurice was at her side. "You're terribly pale! Here, I've got a flask."

She drank gratefully, and the spirit flowed down like a fire to melt the ice in her veins.

"You're stony cold! My coat——"

"No, no, I'm all right. I get these turns. . . ."

It was passing; and soon she was breathing normally. But the attack had left her weak and shaken.

"Let me get help to carry you in."

"Good heavens, no." Priscilla got to her feet, trying to control her knees. "I shall be quite all right, now. This is very stupid. Maurice, I'm sorry——"

"Don't be foolish, and hang on to me."

Concentrating on the mere business of motion, everything else was laid aside; but she was half aware of the strength and warmth of his arm, the hardness of his muscles under the rough coat. As soon as she could manage it she walked alone, perhaps with too much ambition, for the last pull up the village street again over-taxed her and she arrived panting and deathly pale drawing on the dregs of her strength.

The landlady of the inn took matters in hand, fussing with hot-water bottles, sal volatile and eiderdowns. Soon Priscilla lay in a sort of stupor under a pile of coverings, breathing now more quietly.

"We ought to get a doctor."

The heavy red-faced landlady, looking down from the other side of the bed, shook her head.

"Poor soul, she's white as a sheet! There's no doctor in the village, sir, but if you run down to the post office and telephone there's Doctor Sadler will come over . . ."

Priscilla's eyes flickered and opened; there was a strange withdrawn look about them that almost made Maurice shudder. He realized how strong had been the resolve that had carried her home.

"I'll go for the doctor, and shall I bring your mother over? You ought to stay quiet for a bit."

Priscilla shook her head with a sudden gust of vigour.

"I don't want a doctor, please. I shall be all right if I can rest here a little."

Maurice and the landlady looked at each other.

"Best see how she is, sir; maybe the lady's often taken with these attacks. I remember how my sister Maggie. . . . Well, she's easier now. Sleep will do more for her than a doctor, I dare say."

"I'll sit up with her, then, and call you if there's any need."

She darted a curious glance at him as she went out. Not his type at all! She had seen him in the bar getting off with the little peroxide piece from the cottage up the hill—an old hand at the game. She knew his kind. But he was in deadly earnest now, no mistaking it. Someone else's wife! Well, it was no business of hers.

Maurice stretched his legs in an old creaking chair by the open window. The light was already fading, over the sea the sky was lavender and primrose, the first evening star had risen above the hills. A paraffin lamp, turned low, threw a soft circle of light.

Priscilla lay outside it. He could see a faint blur in the shadows, like a white rose at night, and a glint of hair. She was utterly still, and if he listened carefully he could feel rather than hear the soft beat of her breathing.

Now she was asleep in his bed; he smiled wryly, and told himself that she would never lie there as his companion. His mind went back to the times when they had ridden together in those bright mornings through cobweb-spangled grasses, or laughed at trivialities when the day's heat was spent, drawn together by a sense of exile. He had loved her then, but circumstance had silenced him. Other women seized their opportunities! Most women, if it came to that, as he knew perhaps too well. He neither disguised from himself his inclination nor dissembled its source: a deep sensuality, a physical curiosity, a search without finality that sometimes dismayed but always led him on.

And now, it seemed, he had reached the end of the road, only to find that it had carried him back to his starting-point. All his experience, his long apprenticeship of the body, seemed to have brought him to this moment of certainty and frustration. His life amounted to little, yet he could offer her something! But this she rejected, choosing the sterile path. . . . Angrily, he rose from the chair and stood beside the window, resting his forehead on a cool pane. Robert Gresham! What had the man done or been to deserve such sacrifice? Living in his own world of ideas, happy in a life that was slowly destroying Priscilla, he had allowed her to waste her youth and poison her health, leaving it to a junior, to whom he did not even pay the compliment of suspicion, to ride with her over the plains and take her into the life of the country. No doubt he had loved her in his way—surely a cold, selfish, inhuman fashion.

Sighing deeply, he walked over to the bed and looked down for a long time at her sleeping face, shadowy in the half-darkness, pale as a mask in wax. Gently, as if to lift a butterfly, he touched her hair, and then turned and stole out of the room. As he opened the door the friendly murmur of voices from the bar came to his ears, and he hurried down towards their warmth and companionship.

Chapter Five

FOR a little while after Priscilla awoke in a strange lumpy bed she imagined herself back in her mother's cottage and in her own childhood. Sunshine slanted through the window as it had so often streamed into the little box-like room she had shared with her sisters. Almost she could smell the mixture of damp walls and frying bacon, almost hear the sharp click of a pony's hoof-beats and a rattle of pans, and her mother's voice calling. She would dress quickly and go out into the garden barefooted, to feel the bite of cold dew on her feet, the rough touch of grass, and hear the bird's chorus.

Wide awake by now, she sat up, realizing that she was in her clothes and that whatever she must recall within the next few moments would be repugnant. Her legs were shaky, she had to hold on to the foot of the bed, but her breathing was normal and her head clear. Relieved, she found her bag and made a half-hearted assault on her crumpled appearance. She must get back at once.

Humiliating, to be so trapped in this unknown inn, dependent on the man she had been compelled to hurt!

Over a cluster of roofs a glimpse of the sea brought back yesterday's scene in all its vividness: she could smell the heather and feel the breeze. Abruptly, she rose and walked to the window, and there, leaning on the sill, she faced at last the truth of her feeling for Robert. It was as if a tower had dissolved into rubble, and from among the ruins she wondered whether indeed she had ever truly loved him, but had not, overborne by his determination, married him in the belief that love would grow from seeds of interest and respect. And Maurice—what could she say to him? She was a bad liar. Yesterday on the headland he had carried her with him into a world of enchantment and now she could not think of him without a quickening of the blood. She knew him for what he was, a loyal friend, a generous and easy-going creature, with more virtue and less inconstancy in his nature than he himself believed; but hard-drinking, promiscuous, with a touch of the bar-propping bagman about him. And for that, to betray the steadfast trust of Robert. . . .

A knock on the door, and Maurice entered, freshly washed and shaved. With his strength and vitality he filled the room, but his eyes, shadowed by fatigue, seemed large as a moth's, and as defenceless. He raised his eyebrows a little.

"Up already! Surely you didn't ought?"

"I'm perfectly all right this morning. And I'm sorry to have been such a fool. Putting you in this position——"

"Please, Priscilla! You go on as if you'd done it on purpose."

"I should have known better, I suppose, than to bring it on. Will you please take me home?"

He hesitated, searching her face. "I'd much rather you saw a doctor. I don't think a motor drive——"

"No, please, Maurice. I'm all right now; I know the form."

Dubiously, he agreed. But in the car she seemed well enough, and the crisp air of an early autumn morning brought colour to her cheeks. They drove for a while in silence, at least so far as the human voice went; the car chugged and clanked, panting up the short steep hills. Sun shone on the rich gleaming grass and the golden stubble, on the tossing trees, and cattle fat from summer's pasturage, and sleek birds, and ash trees dripping gold in hedgerows and men at work in the fields.

"You know, you must see a doctor about these turns."

"Oh, I have."

Maurice looked round quickly at her profile, alarmed.

"What's the verdict?"

Priscilla hesitated. Impossible to tell him what she had kept from Robert! Yet an impulse to confide in someone was strong. At last she said:

"Nothing out of the way. My heart, of course; too much malaria; I'm supposed to go slow."

"And if you don't?"

"Well, then. One loses a few years of this world, or gets a few years' start in the next, whichever way you look at it."

"I see. I'm sorry, Priscilla."

She smiled at him, and for a moment their eyes met. Quickly she added:

"Please don't say anything to Robert."

"But surely he knows?"

"Yes, in a way. But I don't want to alarm him with harrowing details. He worries so."

"I won't say anything. I shan't see him, I hope."

"Don't let's make too much of this." She laid a hand on his arm. "I'm a respectable married woman believing in the old-fashioned virtues, if that's what they are; and you—well, you're a philanderer, Maurice, we might as well face it; an occupation which I suppose never reaches a dead-end."

"I see."

"Please don't be angry."

" 'And I shall find another girl, and a better girl than you——' "

"I'm sorry, Maurice. But there's no half-way house."

"And the whole way?"

She shook her head. "I'm afraid not."

It was only what he had expected, but the answer chilled his heart. Poetic justice! He had taken his fun where he had found it; futile to sigh because the moon was out of reach. Let the punishment fit the crime! He had no cause for complaint.

They had come to the outskirts of a small seaside town popular with holiday-makers and tourists. Houses of extraordinarily varied ugliness peered at the road through gardens of lush but stereotyped beauty.

Maurice slowed down to negotiate some children on bicycles and remarked:

"This is a sort of elephant cemetery, where retired senior officials come to die."

"Let's hope we don't run into a rogue Governor, then."

"Oh, Governors never die, they simply turn into county councillors. Let's have breakfast at the Angel."

"Well, it would be nice: I'm rather hungry."

Priscilla found herself ravenous. Already the colour was back in her cheeks and life, so closely threatened, had regained control. Amazing resilience! Maurice felt his eyes drawn back and back to her over the metal pots and coarse earthenware crockery. Every moment counted now, yet he could hardly bear to sit opposite her so calmly, in this stuffy dining-room with its drooping waiters, and customers munching like cows with heads bent over their plates.

"I must fill up with petrol. Will you join me at the car?" He escaped.

Pausing at the reception desk, he was startled by a voice behind him.

"Good morning, Cornforth; fancy running into you!"

Horrified, he turned: and there, sure enough, sleek and affable, tidily dressed in a dark London suit, stood Freddy Begg, holding out his hand.

"What a coincidence! Are you staying here?"

Maurice glanced quickly round. Armorel was invisible—invisible but not, he was sure, far away. Of all the strokes of bad luck!

"My wife and I have had a few days here." Freddy was being very gracious. "Quite delightful, and so fortunate with the weather. We came largely to see an old friend who's retired down here—Sir Bertrand Hockling, our last Governor. Perhaps you knew him? But no, I suppose you would hardly—a delightful man. Keeps up his interest in things amazingly. I found that he knew more than I did about what was going on!"

Freddy Begg laughed gaily. Maurice had his eyes fixed on the dining-room door.

"Are you staying long?"

"No, sir, I'm not staying here at all—only passing through."

"Ah, I see. Well, I mustn't keep you, and I must have breakfast myself. We return to London to-day."

He turned to speak to the cashier. There seemed only one chance of escape. Maurice strode into the dining-room and found Priscilla preparing to leave. Together they entered the lobby. Freddy's back was turned and his head bent over the desk, and for a moment it seemed that they would pass unseen; but Priscilla paused to close her bag, the moment flew by, and Freddy turned from the desk.

The beginnings of a smile of greeting formed on his face, now peeling slightly from sunburn: and then froze. A comical look of astonishment spread over his features. He took a half-step towards them and opened his mouth as if to speak; and then abruptly, as the situation presented itself beyond doubt to his mind, turned on his heel.

Climbing into the car, Priscilla caught sight of her companion's expression.

"Is anything wrong? You look as if you'd seen a ghost."

He shook his head, thanking providence that, by failing to see Freddy, she had been spared a new shock. He could say nothing to distress her, yet matters could scarcely be left like this. Excusing himself, he ran back into the hotel, to see the backs of Freddy Begg and his wife disappearing through the dining-room door. He was just in time to touch Freddy on the shoulder.

"Forgive me, sir—may I speak to you?"

Freddy started, and turned. He stared at his accoster, and

under his pasty skin reserves of blood gathered slowly, bringing an unaccustomed pinkness to his cheek.

"I have no wish to discuss your private affairs!"

With a subdued but malevolent click, the glass-plated door closed behind him. Out of the question to follow and make a public scene! Maurice turned away, angry and full of foreboding. In the car he said:

"You'll tell Robert about this?"

Priscilla shook her head. "No. It would upset him dreadfully."

"Suppose someone saw us together? It would be a pity to be hung for a sheep when we haven't even stolen a lamb."

"But surely there's not much risk of that? The point is, I should have to tell him about my absurd performance yesterday, and I'd almost rather he thought I'd been on a lamb-stealing expedition, as you put it, than that."

With this he had to rest content.

In the hotel dining-room Armorel spread her napkin on a smartly-tweeded knee and looked at her husband coolly, with a slight lift of the eyebrows.

"Have you found a friend?"

Rather irritably he answered: "No. It was that fellow Cornforth, as a matter of fact."

Armorel's eyebrows went up a little more.

"Who was he with?"

Freddy gazed at her through his spectacles with a twinge of distaste.

"What makes you think he was with anyone?"

"His reputation."

"One should not attach too much weight to that."

Freddy studied the menu carefully. He looked, she observed quite ruffled. After the waiter had taken the order she added: "I believe it was someone you know."

"Really, Armorel, I prefer not to discuss the matter."

So she was right! Freddy's mouth had hardened into the obstinate line she knew well, and he broke his toast with a snap that was almost vicious. Indeed, he was thoroughly upset. To see Priscilla, of all people, in a seaside hotel with a man of Cornforth's reputation! It was doubly shocking: the wife of one of his officers (and, with all his faults, a promising one, quite on the cards for a Residency) with a comparatively junior policeman, subordinate alike in seniority and status; and Priscilla, the fas-

tidious, beyond reproach, caught out in a cheap seaside intrigue!
Suppose there was scandal, publicity, a divorce? Ghastly thought!
Seeing Armorel looking at him with an appraising expression
(like a spider, he thought, speculating on the succulence of an
entangled fly) he added, to reassure himself:

"In any case, to be seen coming out of the dining-room of a
hotel is not proof of anything compromising."

Armorel gave her wolfish smile, and poured some coffee.

"I imagine that a good many women have breakfasted with
Maurice Cornforth, but very few of them after a night of innocence." Her smile lingered on, sardonic, reminiscent.

Something in his wife's tone aroused in Freddy an unexpected
desire to protect Priscilla. She had looked so fine-drawn, so
unhappy. That conceited fellow Cornforth had no doubt tricked
her into some foolish indiscretion. A rotter if ever there was
one! At any rate, Armorel should not know, let her ask as much
as she pleased.

But Armorel changed the conversation.

"I hope you found your talk with Sir Bertrand profitable."

"A wonderful man, that, wonderful! He keeps in the closest
touch. . . . Yes, he was very helpful."

"And still on good terms with our masters?"

"Naturally, there is often occasion to call on his ripe experience.
He's lunching, I believe, with the Permanent Under-Secretary
next week."

"I hope he'll remember his cue."

"Really, Armorel, you sometimes say the most uncalled-for
things!"

Armorel only smiled. Freddy had proved so apt a pupil that,
like a proficient linguist who forgets his laborious ascent through
verbs and declensions, he no longer recalled the devices by which
his success had been contrived. That she had been the main
contriver she believed he had expunged from his mind. She
hoped so; should the reins chafe, Freddy was quite capable of
resolving to gallop off on a line of his own, but not capable
enough, in her opinion, to choose the right line, or at any rate to
follow it with sufficient perception to its end. He needed a belief
in his own destiny. She thought that she had succeeded in giving
him this; and that, when he bowed before destiny's shrine, he
did not recognize in its goddess the features of his own wife.

"Shall we be going?" he said. "We don't want to risk being late
for our luncheon appointment, and my meeting's sharp at three."

Looking back from the car, Armorel memorized the name of the hotel, smiling a little at its ironic flavour; should it be the fallen angel, she wondered? A successful trip: with a little *bonne-bouche* of mystery to top it off. Well, the days stretched ahead, and in her own good time she would find the solution.

Chapter Six

IT was a part of Armorel Begg's genius to recognize in their early stages those trends in public opinion which would one day become fashionable. Like a truffle-hunting dog, she could sniff the buried treasure which, dug out and acclaimed, would be eagerly devoured. Thus while the older generation still, for the most part, dismissed such subjects as 'a lot of gup' or 'so much eyewash', she recognized in native welfare and all its ramifications one of those trends destined to progress from the status of a bee in someone's bonnet to that of the rock on which British policy was grounded.

One of the means which she employed to detect and study, in their early stages, these policy-making trends, was to keep in touch with the small but passionate group of men and women in England who formed themselves into little societies, which in turn passed ardent resolutions condemning insults or injustices offered to (as they held) or imposed upon aborigines. Freddy had at first been reluctant, during his periods of leave, to follow Armorel's lead in mingling with what he called 'those Bloomsbury people' at meetings or discussions in draughty temperance halls or over-crowded flats. He disapproved, he said, of spoiling his leave with shop; but she knew that was not the reason. He loved shop above all things and was merely compelled to pay lip service to the convention that barred it from dinner-tables and other out-of-hours occasions. The real reason was that such societies and their members were considered by the authorities to be cranky, pernicious and shabby, and that he feared contamination. His masters might even suspect him of saying things which should not be said before outsiders, and this, he knew, was (and rightly so) the most unforgivable of sins.

Armorel admitted the risk, but did not think it was serious, and after a short struggle she had won her point. Freddy had attended a meeting and been at once astonished, bored and intrigued. It had been shocking to find that individuals with so little knowledge of realities and of no account in the world should set themselves up as critics of the experienced and distinguished men who were his masters, and of the service to which he belonged, which he never for a moment thought of as anything but the most efficient and disinterested in the world. Sheer curiosity brought him back. When he returned to his post he found that certain aspects of these meetings could be worked up into a nice little semi-comical story, and that, more important, his knowledge of what 'those Bloomsbury people' were up to enabled him to carry conviction as an authority on that mysterious and wayward force known as 'public opinion at home'. Once or twice, shaking his head, he had observed: 'Public opinion at home would never stand for it,' or, on other occasions, he had minuted: 'In view of the probable demands of British public opinion . . .' and had found his views respected in the highest quarters, and several times confirmed by events. After this he began to take seriously the process called by Armorel 'keeping in touch', and when on leave made a point of attending one or two meetings of her favourite society. That his judgment had been sound was agreeably confirmed by Sir Bertrand Hockling, who was himself to take part in the next discussion, together with a Member of Parliament notoriously hot in his views on the iniquities of empire. Sure enough, there he was on the platform when Freddy arrived—a fine figure of a man, tall, well-built, grey-haired, urbane, with a bright eye and a lean aquiline face that might have belonged to a successful doctor. There was in his speech and bearing, too, more than a hint of the bedside manner. What a contrast, indeed, to the politician by his side: a cadaverous, untidy, sour-looking man with unkempt clothes, a lock of greasy hair falling over his forehead, burning eyes and a sallow, dyspeptic look.

Armorel, inspecting the audience, raised a neat gloved hand to greet several acquaintances. Among them was Robert Gresham, sitting with a dark-skinned companion at the back of the room. She looked at him appraisingly. Why was he here? Had he tumbled to the practical value of these circuses? She dismissed this explanation; Robert was too much in the clouds to pay such calculated attention to his own interests, and Priscilla quite useless to him in that direction. Useless all round! He was talking to his companion, his head thrown back, his bony face illuminated by a flash of laughter, his eyes extraordinarily keen and blue. To be sitting with an African, at such a meeting—how infallibly he did the right thing, but (and this was so irritating) always without premeditation. What others strived for, he strolled by and picked up without ever knowing that the rest of the world was after it; and then, as a rule, simply threw it away.

At last the Member of Parliament rose to launch his thunder-bolts, his eyes glowing, his dark hair drooping over his face. The evils of empire, the exploitation of the weak, the depravities of capitalists were lashed by his viperous tongue. Soon sweat was pouring down his face, he was shouting at his audience as if they had been a horde instead of a handful in a bare damp-stained room. In his mind a holocaust was proceeding. Smug, red-faced men in white flannels and solar topees, with moustaches brushed up from the lip and hard pig-eyes, were toppling over on all sides like grain before the reaper. They lay in the dust, squirming, squealing, and spurting not blood but streams of golden sovereigns. Standing on top of a pyramid of soft pink bodies a man of great physique, masculine and imperious, bare-armed, bestrode his prostrate enemies, and all around to the far horizon immeasurable legions of bowed black figures arose, casting aside their chains; but all were faceless. From their throats came a murmur that rose and swelled like the roar of the sea and the noble figure of their saviour was lifted upwards by a great wind into the sky.

The speaker reached his climax, the vision faded, there came into view a small drab audience listening phlegmatically to his oration. He sat down amid tepid applause. His listeners had heard it all before, but they were faintly stirred, sniffing a little of the spilt blood of the pukka sahibs. The speaker wiped his face and smiled a trifle grimly. He had breathed once more the heady air of the mountain tops. It was worth it, even for this poor bunch of middle-class fools! Why did he bother with them? His constituents in their grim north-country factories and slums did not care a rap for the fate of all the blacks in Africa; it was nothing to them that their representative championed good causes. He got little enough out of it himself—a few guineas here and there. But it was a path. He was becoming known as an authority. They were going to put him on a committee. People would listen to him with respect, he would become a public figure. And one day the great tide of millions of blacks would lift him off his feet and carry him on the crest of a great wave to glory, high above the petty bitter struggle—the great liberator, the man who freed the black masses, the modern Wilberforce. . . .

The applause faded and Sir Bertrand Hockling got to his feet. He stood before them with a half-smile on his clean-cut lips, rocking a little from heel to toe. One by one, with the politest possible stabs and in the most self-deprecating manner, he pricked the politician's balloons. It was, perhaps, an easy task, but he did it in such a manner as to leave no cause for bitterness. Phrases rolled from him as smoothly and evenly as sheets from a printing press : trusteeship for the native, a sacred trust of civilization, the blessings of law and order, raising the standard of living, advance towards ultimate self-government, the principle of indirect rule. Freddy, leaning back with the tips of his fingers pressed together, was lost in admiration for the skill with which Sir Bertrand demolished his opponent—left him without a leg to stand on. How enviable to speak with such poise and polish!

Robert listened with a growing sense of irritation. The man was blowing bubbles : below the iridescent surface of his words, all was hollow. This spinning of fine phrases and principles— what did it mean to the district officer sweating on his bicycle, the black man hoeing his guinea-corn in the bush? Sir Bertrand was like the beautifully polished mouthpiece of a bellows, emitting great gusts of hot air. At last he finished. The meeting was opened for discussion and Robert, to his own surprise, found himself on his feet.

"Listening to these able speeches," he said, "as a man with a narrow sort of experience, carrying on in a corner of Africa the work which one speaker has condemned and the other commended, it appears to me that both miss the mark. Suppose you described to two people who had never seen one the appearance of a horse. Suppose those two people then seized pencil and paper and drew a horse. You would get two pictures, each different from the other and also, I imagine, from the actual appearance of a horse. That is how the pictures drawn by the two speakers appear to me."

He heard a slight stir in the audience, a snicker or two of laughter. He hurried on.

"The first speaker would have us believe in the existence of a quite imaginary person, the innocent native, downtrodden and abused, always a passive agent and dwelling in a once arcadian society free from the vices and corruptions of our own.

"Of course I needn't stress the absurdity of this idea. True innocence is as much a figment of the imagination as absolute guilt, the sentimentalist and the Calvinist are but the same person in twin moods—and both moods are false. There has been no age of innocence in Africa, nor are the people children, as we are so often and so wrongly told. Like ourselves, they have lived through countless generations struggling to hold in check the vices and evils of the human heart, to cage the lust for power, the cruelty, the love of violence, to reconcile the selfish disruptive impulses of the individual with the needs of society.

"They have achieved some measure of success, like all living societies, since those that fail entirely do not survive. In some ways perhaps they have done better than we. But on the whole they are not less cruel than we are, but more so; oppression of the weak by the strong is not less but greater; slavery is not our invention but a centuries-old custom of their own. In our faith, our technical mastery of nature, our morality and our political experience we have found provisional answers considerably superior to theirs. That is why we have a lot to offer them, transcending any disadvantages that contact with us may bring, such as shortfalls in perfect justice, unrest of the mind and the payments they must make to support us in the style to which we have become accustomed.

"But the second speaker, it seems to me, has fallen into the same trap from an opposite position. He, too, does not look on the African as an ordinary human being who shares alike our troubles and our faults, but as a sort of cypher in a complicated game. It is the game of government and administration, the game or power; and people are the pawns, to be moved hither and thither about the board. The player is of course convinced that he knows just what is best for the pawns. It is a difficult game, for the pawns are not automata; they have curious powers of obstruction and unreasonable whims; this means only that they must be handled with greater care and skill. And the stakes are high. Successful manipulation of the pieces brings great rewards: promotion, public regard, titles. At the end of the game, when he puts down the last piece, he may sigh and think: 'Well, I have not done too badly. I have avoided any false moves. I have been in a few tight spots and out of them again with credit. The board is pretty tidy, and now it is someone else's turn.' I don't think he often worries deeply about the feelings and destinies of the pawns, or the final purpose of the game."

Robert heard a faint creaking and stirring around him; with a flash of pleasure he thought of Freddy sitting in front, stiff with disapproval. Encouraged, he went on:

"I should not presume to suggest where the truth lies. But I do say this: neither approach will enable us to perform our task. Were we to clear out to-morrow, or the day after, as the first speaker would doubtless have us do, the exploitations, oppression and sharp practice which would follow would put the worst efforts of the white man far into the shade. But if we stay, and are not to be failures, we must come to grips with many ugly and difficult facts of which the second speaker gave us no suggestion.

"To-day there are a thousand things that cry out to be done every hour; an honest man is overwhelmed by a sense of his own impotence and of the shortness of time. His tragedy is that the fine phrases used by the second speaker to describe our policy seem to him to cover up an empty void. He finds himself compelled to carry out measures which he does not believe in or, more often, unable to discover what he is expected to do at all. He must refer back to headquarters matters on which he should know his own mind, only to meet with vacillation and indecision. He is swamped by a tide of instructions telling him in great detail how to carry out his duties and all the things he may not do.

"To my mind he would do well to scrap the lot and turn to an older and simpler form of instruction, which lays down more completely, and certainly much more concisely, than any memoranda I have read the principles on which his conduct should be framed. I refer to the biblical injunction: 'What dost the Lord require of you but that you do justly, love mercy, and walk humbly with thy God.' "

Robert sat down, surprised at his own outburst. Armorel turned round to give one of her flashing smiles, but Freddy's back was rigid. His whole attitude showed his displeasure. That was perhaps too mild a word; he was really outraged. To get up in public and abuse the very service to which the man belonged! And in the face of one of the most distinguished public servants the Empire had known—a gratuitous insult, a disgraceful display of bad form! Really, Freddy thought more calmly, Gresham was impossible. You tried to help him, you were prepared even to ask him to lunch with Sir Bertrand Hockling, and he behaved in this shocking manner. Fortunately, Sir Bertrand was doing what he could to restore the situation with a few good-humoured, neatly turned phrases which showed up the absurdities of his critic's strictures. A masterly reply!

And then the meeting livened up. As if they had been waiting impatiently for the fall of the flag, people leapt on to their hobby-horses and rode them with single-minded enthusiasm round the room. The conditions of a leper settlement in the Cocos Islands, the neglect of dogs in Malaya, the lack of school privies in Tobago, the licencing of brothels in Hong Kong, these and many other abuses were thrust under the chairman's nose.

Robert turned to his black companion, wondering what he made of it all. The young man was enraptured. Leaning forward in his chair, his eyes fixed in turn on each speaker, he was alight with interest and glowed with passion at the mention of every injustice. Like a gourmet presented with a score of rare delicacies, he gave himself up to the enjoyment of a feast of words.

To see this student whom he had first encountered as a pagan child had been one of Robert's fixed intentions when he came on leave. He was curious to discover the effect of English teaching and customs on this homeless youth brought up at Father Anselm's isolated mission. In an interval of job-hunting he had sought him out—a pleasing interlude, for the job-hunting was not going well—and had found a changed young man. Benjamin Morris seemed to have shed not only the freshness of boyhood but also much of his friendliness and enthusiasm. You could not quite say that he was surly, for his natural good manners had not been altogether destroyed, but he was certainly far more reserved, even suspicious. Outwardly self-confident, very ready with his tongue, yet he carried an elusive suggestion of one who had lost his way. The eyes were sad, or so Robert thought: dark, round and sometimes full of fire, yet there was a flat and baffled look about them, as if drawn from an inward core of defeat.

But this was fanciful, no doubt. Benjamin had no cause for sadness. He had done well, amazingly well if one remembered his origins. He was one of the chosen few, a man in a million, and one with an excellent conceit of himself.

At last the meeting ended and they walked out together and along the street. On the kerb they passed Freddy Begg and Sir Bertrand Hockling waiting for a cab.

"Yes, I remember him vaguely," Sir Bertrand was saying. "I recall his lean and hungry look, but I must confess I understood little of what he was talking about. But I've no doubt it was very profound."

"A clever fellow, of course. But awkward to handle."

Sir Bertrand watched the two figures, the fair and the dark, out of sight.

"His black companion looks like a brand ready for the burning. I wonder who he is? A sign of the times!"

"As our educational policy progresses there will be an increasing number——"

"Quite so, quite so. The trouble is, they get too big for their boots. So far our educational system seems to turn out mainly political agitators. And political agitation is a devilish thin diet on which to feed the half-starved multitudes."

"That is only a passing phase, Sir Bertrand."

"I hope so, I'm sure. The question is, when the smoke clears, who will have passed? Ah, well, no doubt these things will adjust themselves. . . . At last, a cab."

They climbed in and sat side by side, their soft black hats resting lightly on their knees.

Chapter Seven

'FAIR and false, like a Campbell'; with how much more truth, Robert thought, could those epithets be applied to restaurant cakes! That creamy, seductive exterior and then the flat tasteless middle, sawdust-like. . . . He sat contemplating a plateful while Benjamin Morris sipped his tea genteely, one little finger extended.

"It was from Father Anselm that I learnt you had gone to the university," Robert said. "He spoke of you with affection. He hopes for great things one day."

Benjamin smiled, perhaps superciliously.

"I think Father Anselm's ideas and mine no longer agree. I believe he hoped I would become a priest."

"And you don't intend to?"

Benjamin's expression was now supercilious beyond doubt.

"I interest myself in more important matters."

Robert abandoned his cake and proffered his cigarette case. He noticed that Benjamin's fingers were long and slender, his hand was not broad like a Negro's. Glancing again at the shape of the head, the set of the thin shoulders, he thought, not for the first time: this young man has fiercer blood in him, Arab perhaps

—a queer unstable mixture. His skin, though dark enough, had the copper tinge that spoke of the north, his bones lacked the heaviness of the southerner.

"Might I ask what those interests are?"

Benjamin fingered his teaspoon, ill at ease.

"I do not think you would be pleased."

Robert laughed. "There's no need to make a mystery out of it. Your interests are political. You join with other students to hold meetings at which everyone abuses the Government, the British, imperialism and the colour bar. You have a few white friends who help you and give you a little money. You see vague, glorious visions of freedom, which you confuse with power; you think of riding in large cars, ordering about obsequious bush-folk and sitting at ease in Government House, and so you plot to throw out the British neck and crop and run the country yourselves."

Benjamin was startled out of his pose of disdain. His eyes widened with alarm, the whites showed as he stared at his companion.

"Then you have listeners and spies——"

"My dear fellow, this isn't Russia! It's part of our peculiar philosophy that we offer the protection of our law to the very people who plot to destroy it. You can hold your inflammatory meetings to your heart's content, so long as you stop short of high explosives."

"But your information——"

"If you throw pepper in a man's face he'll sneeze, and if you try to govern him, sooner or later he'll want the power for himself. It's a law of nature to which you, like the rest of us, conform. Everything really hinges on the interpretation of 'sooner or later'. You say sooner and we say later—somehow we've got to agree on a half-way house."

Benjamin looked relieved; a flow of words always suggested a sense of security. He hid his nervousness under a cloak of self-assertion.

"I do not think we shall agree, Mr. Gresham, so long as you stick to that word 'later'. Frankly, we are tired of being told that we are children who cannot manage our own affairs."

"Nothing could possibly be more irritating. But in your own case, I doubt if you can manage them very well from London. It's a long way from Africa, where the dirty work is being done."

"Just at present I am busy here." He drew from his pocket a note-case and from the note-case a little pile of cards, and one of these he handed over. Robert read: 'African Freedom League' and an address in Holborn, and underneath: 'Secretary, Mr. Benjamin Morris'. No doubt the subscriptions of the few sympathizers paid a little salary and the rent of a bare room up four or five flights of stairs.

"Father Anselm will be disappointed that you have decided against the Church."

"I think I have absorbed enough British culture to have outgrown that, Mr. Gresham. We are no longer taken in by the clever British idea of using God as a mouthpiece to support imperialism. Sometimes, you know, we feel that you have appointed the Deity as a district officer."

Benjamin trotted out the gibe with the air of someone exhibiting a treasure. No doubt his undergraduate audience had often applauded. Robert realized in a flash of sympathy how doubly sweet that praise must be to this emotional, confused, sensitive young man perpetually at odds with himself and with the world.

For it was no easy task to realize in a single career the aspirations of a people. Benjamin must walk alone, a pathfinder. Behind him the life of his own people proceeded in its immemorial pattern. His sisters and cousins planted and hoed among the crops under an exacting sun, and in the cool of the evening returned to their crude shelters, to the rounding up of goats, the fistfuls of porridge, the long droning talk that, like a cow in pasture, was hedged in by the petty events of the day. But all this, with its certainties and limitations, was not for him. His were the wide plains and infinite mountains of the world; sometimes his head swam with all the knowledge that had been crammed into it. On these mountain heights it was very lonely. The west, with a gesture of liberality, had welcomed his mind, but could not shelter his spirit. So there he was, suspended, a rootless and divided man.

Benjamin's memories of his life at the mission school dwelt mainly on the bad patches; on the rare punishments, the menial tasks that should have been done by women, the painful knocks at football (which he hated), the mission's niggardliness in failing to supply shoes. Had he been quite honest he would have admitted that he enjoyed his schooling. Quick at lessons, he found it easy to shine, and agreeable to bask in the gratification of his teachers. It was at this stage of his life that praise first became a necessity to him, like a drug. This need sprang from his isolation. To a man sure of himself and his place in society, knowing himself neither worshipped nor despised, praise is a sweet-meat, pleasant but dispensable; to a man cut off from his roots, nourishing himself on his own person, it becomes a staple food.

Towards Father Anselm he had held no conscious feeling of affection, but an unconscious belief that he was a manifestation of God. Like God, the priest was omnipresent, all-pervading. From him food, shelter, instruction, guidance, all derived. That brown, bearded, twinkling face was always among them, his eye saw everything, and his tongue was never harsh. The face could be stern instead of merry, but it was never turned away. If Father Anselm had moments of weakness his pupils did not see them; that he was fallible they did not suspect.

One of the deep and sudden changes that intersected his life occurred when he left the mission in the hills for a college in the crowded sea-port capital. The sultry heat, the heavy vegetation, the flimsy houses crowded together like termites' cells, the narrow streets deep in dust or mud, the jostling laughing people of every race and tribe—all these were new and full of fascination, but very strange. Boys from the coast moved in groups who spoke the same language; to them the climate and the hurrying scene were an old story. But Benjamin found no one who spoke his own tongue. And he discovered that in some respects he lagged behind his fellows. A wide gap in his knowledge was uncovered by a master, who spoke sharply, impatient not so much with the boy as with the quirks of mission education; and Benjamin felt humiliated before his fellows. Dismayed, he set to work to redeem his failure, but the first crack had come to the structure of his confidence, and his belief in Father Anselm was shaken.

It was soon borne in on him that not only was Father Anselm no terrestrial god, but that God himself was not so much a fact as an argument. At the mission he had learnt to believe in the literal truth of the Bible. The stories in it had seemed interesting and real, the explanations satisfactory. Now, quite suddenly, he learnt that the very people who had brought this teaching and proclaimed it, in the same breath said it was false—not, it was true, the same individuals, but men of the same kind. At college the two doctrines existed side by side. Benjamin went regularly to church and the familiar ritual, the assurance which the very presence of the priest provided, endorsed his belief; then, in the classroom, he would learn of natural phenomena and human reasoning which denied it all.

It was not, however, in the classroom but through his relations with one of the teachers that his doubts were confirmed. This young man, newly arrived from England, had come to Africa from those motives of idealism mixed with frustration which so often propel individuals into new paths. Himself one of those who never quite fit in to society, too prickly and aloof for the rough-and-tumble, he had known much unhappiness, and this had so sensitized his spirit that the very shadow of injustice, bullying, arrogance—or, indeed, anything but meekness—injured it like clumsy fingers laid on burnt flesh. The fact that he was by inclination a missionary but by conviction an atheist deepened his frustration. As a teacher of young Africans, he believed that he had found a cause worthy of his devotion. And in this young Englishman Benjamin at last found a friend. Flattered by the attentions of a European, he listened with the avidity of one attending a revelation to the teacher's talk. Not that the young chemist had any conscious wish to tamper with another's soul, but his very talk and outlook were iconoclastic. And he believed that only by awakening the young African to the realities, as he saw them, that lay below the surface of colonial benevolence could the exploited win their freedom, and that to stimulate that easy-going race to a sense of its own abuse was to serve humanity. Had he been an old-fashioned liberal he would have talked about divine discontent. But he was not; he was a modern, and spoke instead of social consciousness and the solidarity of the working-classes.

Benjamin borrowed from his collection books which exposed the iniquities of all the usual forms of government and lashed the existing order of things. He learnt, to his growing amazement, that not only was Christianity a tissue of superstition shot through with ethically sound propositions, but that practically everything else which he had taken for granted was in fact a mere stage on the way to something else, and based on the proclivity of a small ruling class to abuse its power. The over-lordship of the European, the authority of emirs and chiefs, the constancy of society and the might of an empire to which, he had vaguely realized, he himself belonged—all these, he now discovered, were corrupt, illusory or doomed. The fixed stars of his heaven were now revealed as lamps waved deceitfully before him by those who wished to hypnotize or oppress.

To him, as an African, the whole idea of change was a new one, and especially the idea of changes consciously directed and controlled. He embraced it with all the fervour of a convert to new ideas arrived at not by gradual synthesis but by revelation. The Christian faith, white supremacy, tribal tradition, all these, being opposed to change (which now became his religion) must go. He joined gleefully in the attack. And now that the mask had been broken, he began to notice things he had not seen before. The children of the villages were poor, barefoot and unlettered: they were being cheated of shoes and schools. White men rode in cars, Africans walked on foot; white men lived in mansions, Africans in shacks. The Church tolerated this. Was that an example of its teaching that all men are equal in the sight of God? Therefore the Church was a corrupt instrument of the ruling power. And, while at the college white and black teachers shared meals and quarters and lived together amicably enough, Benjamin began to resent other differences which he had hitherto taken for granted. Africans were seldom invited into the houses of white officials, they did not belong to the club. Europeans, and especially the ladies, had a habit of looking through an African as if he wasn't there.

He had not seen it before, but now it occurred to him that a sense of superiority in one race implies the inferiority of another. Not that he disliked Europeans when he met them. His headmaster was quiet and polite, for his friend the teacher of chemistry he felt a real affection, and in others he had known, like Father Anselm and Robert Gresham, he had met only kindness and disinterested help. The discrepancy between his personal experience of Europeans and the idea of them he was beginning to build up in his mind did not worry him. His life was too full of discrepancies for him to take account of one more.

It was not until he reached England, successful in his scholarship and with the eager help of his teachers, that this idea of racial difference swelled up, as it were, almost to bursting point in his mind. At Oxford, he was not unhappy. He worked hard, and work was to him an active pleasure. The prodigality of everything, the enormous quantities of books, people, cars, clothes, food, indeed of all material things, impressed him beyond measure. And yet the very settled and indifferent calm of his surroundings deepened his sense of inferiority. Against the ancient beauty and wisdom of the colleges his own people appeared as empty savages, crude, dirty, ignorant, lacking in the rudiments of civilization. But they were not to blame. They had stayed in the dust because no one had come to raise them, because Europe had locked away these treasures in its own heart.

On the other hand his personal friendships with English undergraduates and the indifference with which people treated the colour of his skin acted as a prolonged and subtle form of flattery. The world could see that he, a black boy from Africa, could hold his own with the best of the race that had appointed itself as ruler. Young Englishmen, steeped in learning and masters of debate, were not ashamed to accept his hospitality. He dined and drank wine at their tables. This deepened discrepancy between his personal experience of white-skinned folk and his political idea of them as a race caused him to divide them into two branches, as it were: English Englishmen who were on his side, and colonial Englishmen who were against him. A few of the latter might escape contagion (and among these happened to be nearly all the Europeans he had met) but that did not alter the truth of his discovery. He became an even more divided and explosive person: a conceited young man with a racial inferiority complex.

One summer, coming to London during the vacation, he sought a room at a small but (though he did not know it) fashionable hotel. The clerk, after a slight hesitation which aroused his quick suspicion, told him that all the rooms were full. He scented at once an evasion and, hanging about just out of sight, heard the clerk allot a room to a man who had entered after him. Incensed, he repeated his demand; the clerk icily refused; a scene followed. The manager, emerging from his concealment like a spider in response to an agitated web, and seeing that tact was unavailing, brought matters to a head by a brutal statement: coloured men were not admitted.

This was Benjamin's first direct collision with the colour bar, although he had sensed its existence under the surface of other relationships. He was deeply wounded, angered and, in a curious way, at the same time relieved, as at the bursting of an abscess. At last, freed from the silken cords of kindness, he could hate without reserve.

Attempts to take legal action, eventually abandoned, brought him into contact with a group of people, both black and white, who were closely concerned with the wrongs suffered by coloured peoples and with their redress. Benjamin found the atmosphere of their meetings, and of their gatherings at a café in Soho, heady and exciting. The rolling words they used set up delicious vibrations in his mind. Here at last were people of his own kind, who offered dreams of racial glory into which his own ambitions could merge. Here was a chance to revenge the many kindnesses he had received as well as the few insults: a chance to advance up the road to power which had for so long beckoned to his spirit.

Here, then, lay the origins of that African Freedom League whose card Benjamin handed to Robert Gresham over the tea-table. Installed now as secretary in a dingy but nevertheless genuine office, Benjamin was filled with pride in his achievements, especially those yet to come. One day the world would ring with the name of the league, and people would say: "Yes, it is a power in the land, thanks to its brilliant secretary, the man behind the scenes; he has supporters all over the world who would follow him to the gates of hell—a modern Napoleon!"

Robert pocketed the card, remarking:

"I congratulate you. You have become a sort of prophet, you know, of a new religion. Your league has a fine name, but may I ask—freedom from what?"

"From oppression, of course. If you will forgive me for saying so—from you."

Robert smiled. "That cuts both ways. Many of us, you know, feel ourselves to be slaves to the interests of your people. I wish you luck, but please remember that oppression isn't something we British invented. You will oppress each other much more efficiently, as indeed your history shows, as soon as you get rid of us."

Benjamin moved impatiently in his chair. "That is an old argument, if you will forgive me again. I admit that we have been oppressed by chiefs and emirs, and who is it now that keeps them in their positions? It is not us Africans! It is you, the British, who keep them in power, and then turn round and say to us—look how you oppress each other!"

"Then you think you have found a remedy for that ancient human failing, the lust for power and the trampling of the weak by the strong?"

"We shall use power for the good of the people! Once let us throw off the foreign yoke, and we shall show our true democratic spirit. We do not wish to exploit each other, we wish only to live at peace and control our own country in our own way."

"All reformers start by thinking that, but reformers, least of all people, can resist trying to make others do as they think best. And what else is that but tyranny? For all tyrants, you know, believe that what they wish to see done is best for the people, or the country, or the kingdom of God. But never mind, you must find out for yourselves; and as for us, we must answer for our own Frankensteins."

Benjamin looked at his companion warily. Robert never talked down to his audience and that was one reason why nearly all Africans liked him. Often they did not understand a word he was saying, but they never minded that. In fact they rather enjoyed it, for they were thus relieved of the mental effort of trying to follow, and for the most part they took an almost Elizabethan pleasure in words for their own sakes, in the flash and flow of syllables. Their enjoyment was spoiled by ignorance of the meaning no more than one's pleasure in the onward dash of a river is spoiled by not knowing whither it is bound.

"What we need is education," Benjamin said with sudden vehemence. "We need schools, schools, schools. And do you deny that these are kept from us? You know my province, Mr. Gresham, where you have presided. In that province we are told by the Government that there are perhaps one million people, and among all that one million there is one single school for girls. It is in the Emir's palace, where only the Emir's daughters can go, and the daughters of a few nobles. The poor man cannot send his daughters there. Is that democratic? Is it just? Is it not tyranny?"

"It is a strange thing to label as tyranny our attempt to break down the ancient prejudices of a Moslem state. Girls had no schools of any kind before we came. If it is a choice between no education at all and a small beginning, which would you have?"

Benjamin shrugged his shoulders and smiled. "You are too clever for me, Mr. Gresham; you will justify it all, I am sure. But that is not the only thing. People are growing tired of the Emir and his reactionary ways; I do not think they will submit much longer to his extortions."

"You keep closely in touch with events. I hope that you will soon return to deal with these matters at first hand. It's more satisfactory."

A shade of embarrassment showed in Benjamin's manner.

"One day, perhaps. I have certain plans. . . . But I do not expect to be popular with the authorities. You know my views, Mr. Gresham; I do not agree with the existence of Emirs at all. All your talk of indirect rule—it is so much wool pulled over our eyes. Shall I be hanged for that, do you suppose?"

He laughed, as they rose to go, turning aside from an awkward subject. A little warning light, the result of long years of watchfulness, sprang up in Robert's mind. Benjamin knew more of the affairs of the emirate than he would admit; it was evident that he was in touch with one of the dissident factions. Clearly, the intrigues went deep. Then, for the hundredth time, Robert remembered that all this was his business no longer. The Emir's manœuvres, the plots of these distant orientals, even the threads that linked them to this dark Caliban by his side, were nothing to him any longer.

Outside the café they parted; and Robert, as he watched the other walk away, reflected on the strange quirks of life that had crossed the thread of his own destiny with Benjamin's so many years ago. In a fast-changing world, Africa had turned head over heels and he was not sorry to be leaving it. The future belonged to the Benjamins, no doubt, and it looked like being a future of more selfishness, more oppression, more muddle, rather than less. As he brooded on events to come, memories of the past returned to him with surprising freshness. He recalled, even, the day when he had first set foot in Africa: a different continent, a different world, before the war had come down like a guillotine to slice off the head of an age in history—and above all a different Gresham: young, ardent, full of dreams. And as these memories assailed him on this London pavement, moist and shining from a steady drizzle on a late October afertnoon, the flat musty smell of the coast crept back into his nostrils: a subtle compound of mud and mangroves, palm oil and sweating bodies, heat and the sappy growth of bush and forest; and the sight of that earlier and simpler land came sharply to the nostalgic eye of his mind.

Chapter Eight

1913

MUD caught at the keel of the surf-boat as it drove into the beach. The shore beyond was nondescript and flat, with dark-leaved trees growing down to the edge of the mud. The steamer had nosed her way over a sand-bar and some distance up a slow-moving river so wide, and with banks so low, that it might have been taken for a lagoon. Robert Gresham glanced back at her: small and already remote, her derricks were waving slowly like a snail's horns and the chug of her donkey-engines came to him faintly over the sunlit muddy water. Now she seemed friendly, like a fragment of home. Ahead, and for the first time under his feet, lay a new continent: indifferent, implacable, alarming.

Yet a sense of elation filled him as he jumped ashore. England, with its self-sufficiency and smugness, its settled and unchanging ways, was all behind. He was glad to be free of a country that rewarded only the conformer. For the misfits, the unfortunate, it had little pity, as he well knew; to the young aspirant without wealth or position it offered a hedgehog's welcome, or, at best, conceded an office desk and a life of arithmetic and boredom. Here was a new world, open to men of spirit to grasp its prizes with no rarer qualities than courage and fortitude. Here, all rested with the man, and as Robert stepped on to the beach, wetting his feet in the warm sea water, he felt that he carried his future with him in his bare hands.

Coal-black and stalwart, naked save for loin-cloths, the beach-boys tossed his boxes from the boat as if they had been so many packets of feathers. Robert envied them their nakedness. His own new tropical suit, freshly pressed that morning, already stuck to him in damp patches, his collar had wilted and sweat streamed down his face from under the cork-lined helmet. The heat seemed to strike at him off the beach with a demonic gusto.

There were his boxes, lying in a pile on the cracked mud. Such a mountain of luggage seemed ridiculous for a young man starting life on less than four hundred a year. 'He had forty-nine boxes, all carefully packed, his name printed clearly on each.' No exaggeration, had the Bellman been landing here on Government service.

The only other passenger to disembark, a trader, came up and shook hands.

"Well, I'll be saying ta-ta, and good luck. Look me up if you ever come my way."

Robert felt an unexpected desire to delay the trader's departure.

"What do I do with all my kit?"

"Hire some of these kru-boys to take it over. There's the

Commissioner's office." He waved towards a cluster of palm-thatched roofs just visible above the struggling trees.

"It seems ridiculous, all this for one man."

"Oh, well, you're expected to be the little gentleman, you know. Impress the natives, and all that. Not but what a bottle of gin impresses them a great deal more—they're ready enough to pay for it without a lot of palaver, anyway, which is more than can be said for the Government's taxes. Well, bye-bye."

By the time he reached the Commissioner's office, distinguished from similar palm-thatched, mud-walled buildings by the flag that drooped in front, Robert was soaked in sweat and not a little discouraged. No one had come to meet him, he felt unwanted, an intruder.

In the Commissioner he saw a thin, angular man with a sallow face. The whites of his eyes were yellowed over and his skin, too, was ochreous—dried up, like a squeezed lemon. Quinine and fever, Robert supposed; and suddenly it crossed his mind that one day he, too, might wear that desiccated look.

"My name's Gresham," he said awkwardly, hat in hand. "I've just arrived."

The Commissioner looked up from the papers in front of him. "You've chosen a damned awkward time to do it," he said.

His desk was piled with work, accumulated while he had grappled with a bout of fever. He was short-handed, half his officers seemed to be on leave or sick, and he had just received a stiffly-worded dispatch from headquarters about trouble in a remote corner of his province that had demanded a military patrol. Peaceful penetration, he was thinking bitterly—that was what people wrote in offices, surrounded by cracked ice and electric fans. He glared sourly at the newcomer, seeing a tall young man with a narrow face and high cheekbones and a soft, fresh skin, clean-shaven. The hair gleamed like a new sovereign —cut too long, affected. The Commissioner frowned. The eyes confronting him were blue, the clear northern blue of seas and ice—too light, too tender, for these latitudes; the face, like all young men's faces, appeared to the Commissioner to be half-finished, like unfired clay, still indeterminate. Irritated, he lit a cigarette, his hand shaking. What possessed authority to send out these half-weaned youths with their puppy fur still clinging to them! This was a job for men, not sucklings; he had no patience to act the nursemaid at his time of life.

He got up and stood with his back to the newcomer, gazing at a map on the wall.

"You're to be stationed here." He stabbed a position somewhere in the middle with a nicotine-stained finger. "There's a launch going up to-morrow morning. You go as far as the launch goes, then on with porters."

"Yes, sir. And my kit—it's on the beach at the moment?"

"You'll sleep to-night at the district house, and transfer to the launch first thing in the morning." He opened a drawer of his desk, took out a small black book and handed it over. "Repeat the words after me."

In a flat, bored voice the Commissioner recited the oath of loyalty and Robert muttered the words after him. They were empty of meaning. He had pictured it all differently: a friendly welcome, the companionship of equals, from superiors encouragement and some vision of the high civilizing mission on which all were engaged. And now, in this hot, bare little room, with this yellow monkey, he was swearing away his freedom with no more ceremony than if he had been guaranteeing a horse free from glanders.

The Bible went back into its drawer, the Commissioner rustled his papers and Robert felt dismissed.

"What sort of station is it, sir? And to whom do I report?"

"You'll take over from a man called Fawkes. He's going on leave. Your superior officer will be the Senior Commissioner on the river, fifty miles away—Mr. Pawley. And now, Mr. Gresham, I must wish you good afternoon."

The district house was built of sun-baked mud with a deep roof of palm thatch, and round three sides ran a wide veranda full of deck chairs. The big room inside was cool, by comparison, and airy. The mud walls were hung with the horned skulls of animals and on the tables copies of illustrated English papers lay about. The place seemed empty save for a few gechos spread-eagled on the walls; but a young man emerged from a large arm-chair and crossed the room.

"You're just off the *Skylark*, I suppose? Welcome to the white man's grave. My name's Pailthorpe."

Robert shook hands gratefully. He saw a brown-haired, stocky young man with a silky moustache and the healthy complexion that betrayed him as a comparative newcomer, and brown eyes that were bright, inquisitive and merry.

"This calls for a drink. Thirsty work, getting ashore. Boy!"

A steward in a white coat appeared immediately, carrying a tray with two full glasses. At this touch of friendliness Robert's spirits rose and some of the morning's elation returned. His chance would come when he was out in the bush, away from lemon-livered Commissioners, with fellows like Pailthorpe for his colleagues and a man's job to be done in carrying law and order and justice into the wildest places, and taming savages who had known only bloodshed and superstition in the course of lives that were nasty, brutish and short. He found himself questioned closely about London's affairs—the latest musical comedies, the doings of actresses, the newest music hall jokes. Pailthorpe knew more than the newcomer about stage gossip and new plays; already he was starting to plan his first week's theatre-going on his next leave. Robert liked him immediately for his easy friendliness and lack of pretension, and though he was full of blood-curdling stories about the horrors of the bush he seemed himself to be in the best of health and spirits.

That night ten people sat down to dinner, their white jackets newly pressed, their collars starched, their chins freshly shaven. Lamps hanging from the rafters of the barn-like roof were miniature suns, each the focus of a universe of insects which circled round with the persistency of planets, but with none of their restraint. Two young Army officers were in high spirits, fresh from a patrol and full of their almost bloodless triumph over an obstinate village.

Buller-Cartland, the yellow-faced Commissioner, took the head of the table. He spoke little, and his immediate neighbours were subdued. But over the port he became more forthcoming and told a story or two; and turning to Robert he said:

"You're last from school. Tell us what's going on at home. Did you see the Australians?"

"I'm afraid not, sir."

"I heard that a poor grouse season was expected."

Robert fiddled with his glass. Buller-Cartland annoyed him intensely, the unfamiliar school-like atmosphere even more.

"Very likely, sir."

Buller-Cartland grunted and poured himself another glass of port.

"Well, then, perhaps you can enlighten us on the hunting prospects. Some of us hope to be back by then."

Robert's irritation got the better of him. He had not come to Africa to be made a fool of by a yellow buffoon.

"I'm afraid I'm useless as a sporting guide," he said. "I suggest a subscription to the *Field*."

There was a shocked silence, while Buller-Cartland glared. He put his glass down slowly and said:

"And I suggest a return to school until you learn not to be insolent, young fellow-me-lad. Decent manners appear to have been omitted from your education. May I ask which school is privileged to have enjoyed your patronage?"

"One you've never heard of, I'm afraid. I was educated in Switzerland."

"I see."

The two words held an ocean of contempt. At the same time Robert felt that he had been almost exonerated. If anyone had the shocking taste to go to school among foreigners, the tone implied, ordinary standards of conduct could not reasonably be looked for.

The young officers, only mildly drunk and ready for horseplay, started a diversion. The table was pushed aside and furniture arranged in barricades across the room to make ready for a steeplechase, and the young men peeled off their jackets and lined up at one end. Buller-Cartland jumped on to the table to startle the gechos on the wall and the insects in the thatch with a blast on a hunting-horn, followed by a series of hunting noises.

Then he caught sight of Robert, standing quietly against a wall, and waved an arm.

"Come on, all in!"

Robert did not move.

"All in, I say! No shirkers!" Buller-Cartland was rocking to and fro on his feet, his face yellower than ever in the lamplight. In the shadows of the veranda a few white-coated figures looked on impassively.

Robert stood rigid. Compliance with orders to join in after-dinner horseplay was no part of his contract.

Buller-Cartland threw back his head and hurled a frightful screech into the rafters, waving at the cluster of young men. They looked at Robert uncertainly, suddenly turned from horses into hounds and shown their quarry. Well, they could do what they liked, if this was their amusement; a few of them, at least, would have bleeding noses. Unexpectedly, he felt himself gripped by the arm and pulled towards the others, and Pailthorpe hissed into his ear: "Come on, you fool, don't bait the man, for God's sake!" The subalterns, with a shout, hurled themselves at the first barricade of chairs. There was nothing for it but to join in. Robert dashed round with the rest, leaping over sofas and clambering under tables, and then with the others gathered, flushed and sweating, round an out-of-tune piano to sing old songs while the doctor thumped the keys. Stewards brought tall glasses of beer and as the evening advanced the young men grew subdued and rather sentimental, chanting ballads and love-songs in deep untuneful voices and thinking of their distant homes.

Strolling on to the veranda, Robert turned away from the creek and the river with its half-sweet, half-rotting smell of man-groves and stared into the darkness that concealed the vast interior. A hundred, a thousand miles and more it stretched, bush and jungle and desert, away beyond imagination to the swamps of Chad, the forests of the Congo, beyond that again to the headwaters of the Nile, the mountains of the moon and the land of lakes, to reach that ocean which lapped the Indian shore. Confronted with such immensity, his irritation seemed petty, even the elation of the morning absurd. How could one man's foot shake the earth of such a continent? At his back, the party in the district house gradually subsided. Robert found his pyjamas laid out and the mosquito net slung, and his new friend Pailthorpe, waiting to see him settled in, apologetic about his intervention.

"It doesn't pay to get a black mark at the start of a promising career."

"Nor does one come out here for a schoolboy romp."

"It all helps to keep the white man's end up, you know."

"I suppose it does."

"You get pretty lonely and fed up in the bush, sometimes, and when you get down to a spot of civilization you feel like kicking up your heels. . . . Well, you'll find it all out for yourself."

Pailthorpe's eye fell on a pair of mosquito boots beside the bed. "By the way, always look inside your boots before you put them on."

"Snakes?"

"Scorpions, mainly. Well, pleasant dreams."

But for a long time Robert was kept awake by the croaking of frogs and the shrill purr of crickets and all the other nameless sounds which, strident yet muted, blended with the night so fully that the darkness itself seemed to generate them, as a kind of breathing. Now was the time when beasts and even vegetation awoke, freed from the prison heat; the time also when black men danced and werewolves, it was said, prowled under the moon. An old traveller's tale came unwanted into his mind: of a haunted rest-house, a stench of death, and an ancient ghostly sorcerer crawling through the dust with a rope trailing from his neck. The vicious whine of thwarted mosquitoes filled his ears. He stifled his own trepidation. Werewolves, insects and men, let them come at him as they might, he was more than their equal; the Buller-Cartlands would eat the dust while he strode forwards into fame and glory. He fell asleep, to dream of the surly Commissioner crawling towards him on all fours with a rope in his hand; and, turning at a warning cry from Pailthorpe, he found himself face to face with an army of scorpions.

Chapter Nine

1913

THEY had marched all day along a narrow path that caught at the feet, unable to see more than a yard or two on either hand. Tall grass and rampant bush immersed them. Sometimes they had plunged into the deep shade of a forest belt, cool after the sun's bite. The trees were immense, their dark foliage a world apart, inhabited by a host of creatures preying on each other in an endless battle of wits. Here everything was hidden and self-absorbed. Orchids and ferns sprang from bark and crevices, long rope-like tendrils dangled as if from the sky, hornbills with crowned heads walled up their mates in hollow tree-trunks, butterflies as big as humming-birds drifted by. Then suddenly, as though a curtain had been lifted, they would pass back into the glare and monotony of the bush and the brown grass that waved above their heads against a hard sun-flooded sky.

They reached their destination when the sun's heat was abating and the dusty earth seemed to lie exhausted before collecting itself for the activities of the night. A clearing opened up out of the bush and just ahead lay a gentle rise, with a creek at the foot. On it stood the usual thatched bungalow, and a pole in front with its usual drooping flag. A house, larger and squarer but otherwise the same, lay a little farther back and a number of

thatched rondavels clustered round. Robert surveyed it all
without enthusiasm, but with considerable relief. Footsore,
parched and exhausted, he would at last be able to report to
Fawkes and discover, beneath the shapeless mists in which he felt
himself to be moving, the solid outline of his duties.

He put on a spurt to reach the veranda, thinking with pleasure
of an approaching sundowner, his servant at his heels. As he
reached it, a raggedly-dressed house-boy appeared.

"Tell him I have come to see his master."

The two servants started a brisk conversation in a strange
tongue. There seemed to be a hitch of some sort. At last Robert's
man reported:

"Master no see."

"What do you mean, no see? Isn't Mr. Fawkes in the
station?"

"He say, master live for die topside."

Irritated by this ridiculous baby-talk, Robert crossed the mud-
floored veranda and walked into the living-room. It was empty
and untidy; doors opened out of it on either side. He hesitated,
chose one, and opened it. An ugly smell halted him in the doorway. Under the window stood a camp-bed and on it lay a
man.

Robert crossed the room and looked down on to a bloodless,
wasted face, the hair matted and rumpled, a week's growth of
beard on the chin. Nose and cheekbones seemed almost to be
poking through a parchment of skin—an arm lying on the blanket
was withered, too, brittle as a stick. The bedclothes were dirty
and the whole room stank. Revulsion, fear and pity struggled
in his mind. The man was dead or dying and he had no notion
what to do. A quick inspection showed him that life still inhabited the wasted body; the man was in fact breathing in a
stertorous but subdued way, whether asleep or in a coma Robert
could not say.

"He live for die," the servant repeated with finality; and
Robert knew that, but for a miracle, he was right.

He did what he could to clean up the room and the sick man.
The body was frail and its scraggy lightness sickened him; there
could be little fight left in this assembly of bones. After a meal
served out of tins, he took up his post on a camp chair near the
bed and tried to read, but his mind was in disorder. Mosquitoes
pinged in his ears and through the open window insect hordes
began to gather, banging against the glass of the lamp with little

plops, retreating with angry whirrings and renewing the attack.

For a long time he watched them, fascinated by their sacrificial persistence, wondering why nature had endowed them with this desperate passion and the light with so compelling an attraction. How lightly the fear of death weighed against desire! What flame was it that had pulled into its orbit this young man, dying so far from home and in such indifferent company? A vision of his country's greatness or his own glory, love of adventure, or need for escape? Now Robert would never know, and perhaps the sufferer himself could not have supplied an anwer. What was his own flame, that had brought him to this distant savage country with his life before him, perhaps to lose it, as this young man was doing, still unspent? Even that question he could not fully answer. The very flame, perhaps, that drew the explorer, the mountaineer, the inventor, the sailor. Death was an incident, the pursuit was all. Man had no need to wonder at the insect; his own motives were no less obscure, his immolation as mysterious.

Towards midnight the sick man stirred and began to toss about in his camp-bed. The fever had returned. Soon his limbs were shaking and sweat glistened on his hollow face, and sounds tumbled out of his mouth in a wild confusion, quite meaningless. Presently he began to thresh about with his arms and legs and Robert had to hold him down to the bed, surprised at the strength that still shook the limbs.

After a while the fever ebbed and Fawkes sank again into sleep or coma. Robert wrapped himself in a blanket and resumed his vigil in the chair. The whine of mosquitoes took on a loathsome quality of personal spite. Fever! He supposed he would get it too. Was this what it all led to, this pain-racked skeleton on the bed? He was filled with a sudden hatred for this indifferent and graceless land. A single white man would spend his force like a boy set to punch a haystack. There was still time for him to avoid capture; he would get out before he was ruined, like the doomed Fawkes, betrayed into a living death, or death itself! Fortunate to be warned in time. . . .

He awoke to see a beam of sunlight slanting into the veranda and to hear birds calling from tree to tree. Someone was striking a piece of iron with an iron bar to wake the station; the note sounded clear and resonant through the morning air. The lamp still burnt beside him, now dim and sulky. He blew it out and walked stiffly over to the figure on the bed. It lay very still. In the light of sunrise the skin was grey and ghastly; the jaw sagged open and the eyes stared sightlessly ahead.

Robert sat down heavily on his chair, overcome by a sense of failure. Had Fawkes woken from his coma in those last few hours, tried to give a message, sought a final reassurance? He would never know; but he was tormented by the fear that he had failed a fellow creature in his moment of ultimate need. The sun, climbing quickly, sent a beam right through the glassless window and over the bed, shaming everything into a dusty squalor. Quickly he spread a towel over the dead man's face and walked into the sparkle of the morning; and that evening he buried Fawkes under a tree, stumbling through the unfamiliar service in the presence of the paraded policemen, and knowing himself to be now in sole charge of a district as big as an English county, or ten times as big for all he knew, with no idea of his duties, and hemmed in by a hidden circle of watchful and suspicous eyes.

At sunrise and sunset a police corporal hoisted and struck the flag outside the district office and a bugler sounded reveille and the last post. In between times the twelve policemen drilled, paraded and came or went on patrols; litigants, idlers and malcontents squatted in the veranda waiting to state their complex and interminable cases; the sad clerk scribbled and blotted at his desk and the interpreter picked his nose, gossiped with loiterers and conducted long and involved trading deals. Little else happened in the station, at least of its own accord. The white officer was like some tiresome irritant or bug. Let him go on trek, or fall sick, or die, and everyone heaved a sigh of relief and settled back to the enjoyment of his leisure spiced with some part-time and interesting pursuit such as negotiating for the purchase of a new wife, consulting a fortune-teller or attending a marriage feast.

Robert sealed up Fawkes's few possessions in one or two boxes. When these had been roped ready for transport to the river, he found something he had overlooked. It had sidled into a chink in a badly-made drawer and caught in a crack. He drew it out: an unframed portrait, post-card size. Something in the frank open expression, the widely-set eyes and the soft mouth caught his attention. It was the face of a young girl, not out of her teens, and signed, in childish writing, with one word: 'Priscilla.' In this torrid atmosphere, in the loneliness of a termite-ridden bungalow, this crude portrait had in his imagination the freshness

and purity of a wild rose in an English hedgerow when white
mists begin to rise before a midsummer sun. He looked at it for
a long time and then slipped it into his pocket. Inexcusable, he
thought a moment later: but to restore it he must break the seals
on the boxes, and for this he felt a deep distaste. No, he would
keep the photograph, a companion in this hostile land—and
perhaps one day restore it to its first owner.

One evening, returning from a stroll after bush partridges,
he found a crowd of people gathered round the veranda. At last,
he thought, stepping out briskly, the Senior Commissioner had
come. But it was not Pawley, only a black-skinned crowd from
whose midst arose a shrill female voice overborne but not
silenced by the comments of the spectators.

As Robert approached these voices ceased and the crowd
opened up to let him through. An elderly woman stood there,
clad in a dirty cloth. Black and skinny, her limbs were shaking
with agitation. Under one arm she clasped a piece of sacking
wrapped round something of boulder size.

From the interpreter Robert demanded an explanation. This
man made several vague gestures, shook his head and said:

"Sir, I think she mad."

At this the woman burst forth again and, stepping forward,
flung her package, with a flurry of speech, at his feet.

A sickening stench of decay rose into his face. There, at his
feet, lay a human head, blotched and pulpy, half decomposed.
It seemed to be staring up at him with a ghastly intimacy from
protruding greenish eyeballs. He buried his face in a handkerchief, his stomach heaving.

"Take it away," he gasped; and a policeman, shaking off the
woman who clawed at his arm, pushed it with his foot into the
sacking and bundled it up again.

Still fighting his nausea, Robert tried through the interpreter
to get to the bottom of the hysterical woman's story. The
interpreter's English was shaky and it came out in a sort of
jargon.

"This woman's son make bad palaver. He go to bush, no come
again. She go fetch, find head crying in bush. She bringing
head, white judge see."

Robert was completely nonplussed. If only Pawley would
come! He sat on the veranda over his first whisky, the woman
safely lodged in the hut described as a jail, and wondered what
to do. In this no-man's-land where the writ of the Government

scarcely ran beyond the clearing where the station stood, he knew that rash action might still lead to disaster embarrassing to authority as well as unpleasant for him. But to sit still and take no action until his superior arrived would be an open admission of indecision and defeat. Of the two, the first alternative was the least discouraging.

Taking with him the interpreter and four policemen, he marched at dawn next morning to the woman's village in search of clues and thence followed a trail, faint but promising, to a more distant village in a part of the country not yet brought under administration. Meeting here with nothing but sullenness and hostility he withdrew, half expecting to retreat into an ambush of warriors in the wilderness lying beyond the little circle of cultivation that surrounded the unfriendly village. They fell into no ambush, but met with a disaster almost as bad. Their guide deserted them and the interpreter, at first confident of his knowledge, led them astray. After tacking several times in thick bush and hesitating between the choices offered by innumerable forks in the paths, they followed a branch that finally petered out altogether and found themselves hopelessly lost.

Robert, armed with a pocket compass, took over, trying to conceal his tenderfoot's ignorance and the chilling panic in his mind. There could be no more forlorn and desperate feeling, he soon realized, than to be bushed. The wilderness was so vast and timeless, man's strength so short-lived, there could be no contest more unevenly matched. He might lead his party within twenty yards of a clearing and see nothing through the curtain of prickly vegetation. But he had his compass and to that he clung, leading his five followers steadily forward in the direction in which he believed the station to lie.

Darkness fell as they struggled on, by now blistered, bleeding from scratches and ready to drop. By nightfall their water-bottles were empty, their throats parched and their morsels of food exhausted. Having nothing to cook they lit no fire and spent a hard, hungry, comfortless night in the open, within a rough thorn zariba to protect them against wild beasts.

They started off again at dawn, thirsty, footsore and half-exhausted, first chilled by the night air and then roasted by a vicious sun. Now Robert's fear, which soon became a barely controllable sense of panic, was that he had overshot the mark. A few square yards of clearing in a continent of bush seemed so hopeless a target that it was almost frivolous to seek it. But sooner or later, he told himself, they must surely come to signs of human life, and once an hour he paused to rest and to fire his rifle twice into the air and listen for an answer. None came; and, with ammunition running low, he and his followers had several times perished miserably from thirst and exhaustion in the mind before—the afternoon well advanced and their pace reduced to a despairing crawl—one of these volleys brought an answering crack. Electrified with hope, he fired twice again: two more explosions answered. With shouts of relief the weary policemen plunged towards the sound, and half an hour later the lost party was welcomed in the Senior Commissioner's camp.

Pawley was a heavy, hirsute man with muscular arms, a barrel of a chest and a large, fleshy face, mahogany coloured, with slightly protruding pale-blue eyes. Everything about him was rather bigger than life size—his torso, his voice, even his tattered felt hat. In other circumstances he might easily have been imagined in a loud check suit calling the odds below a banner. Robert greeted him with trepidation.

"Well, young fellow," he said, raising Robert's arm like a pump-handle, "where in the name of Moses have you been? You've had us all running round in circles, and a lot of wild rumours went about that you'd been chopped up by the local beef-eaters."

"Well, sir, there was a murder, and I went to investigate."

"A murder! There was damn' nearly a massacre. Young fellows like you aren't popular, I can tell you, when they get themselves cut up and the powers-that-be have to send out a military patrol. You'd better have a clean-up and some grub and tell me all about it."

Robert guessed that relief at the party's safety had tempered Pawley's natural anger at his subordinate's rashness. Over a delectable dish of scrambled eggs he told his story. Pawley listened carefully, sucking at a pipe, and pronounced the trouble due, beyond doubt, to a ju-ju murder. The stories that Robert had heard of sorcery and intimidation had hitherto seemed unreal, mere pages from a boys' annual; but now he learnt that black magic in these parts was not a queer superstition but a hard fact in the daily life of every villager, no more unreal to him than winter's frost or summer's thunder to his English counterpart—or, indeed, the evil eye to Robert's own ancestors. In fact, he began to realize, witchcraft was a sort of business, controlled by a small group of bold men for their own profit and glory. This, at any rate, was Pawley's view. Robert asked:

"What do they get out of it for themselves?"

"What does a crooked company promoter get out of the mugs who swallow his bait? Wealth, in one form or another. You'll find the victims of a ju-ju are often rich men, as things go in these parts, or belong to rich men's families. The ju-ju priests get hold of their property, or else the victims fork out to buy off interference—blackmail, in fact. Or they kidnap and spirit away the children and get a good price for them, up or down river. The slave trade is still the most paying trade in Africa—if you can get away with it. Our job is to see it doesn't pay."

Robert took to Pawley at once, recognizing a fellow-traveller in the world of giants and demons that lay under the surface of things. For in Pawley's eyes the ju-ju priest, in his loathsome painted mask and queer rag-and-bone aprons, appeared almost as terrible as to the eyes of the awestruck savage. Although he treated with contempt such heathen quacks, there were times when he half-believed in their occult powers; but whereas the savages were far too frightened to intervene, Pawley went about sniffing the air for battle. Regarding himself as the bluffest and most prosaic of men, he was a secret crusader, perpetually dashing off to rescue ignorant victims from the thralldom of superstition, his lance always couched to strike at cruelty or oppression; and the floor of Africa was strewn with the debris of his encounters, for he was a most energetic man, with a constitution that had withstood years of onslaught by micro-organisms of every imaginable kind. If he recounted some of his adventures with a certain amount of bombast, seeing every petty chieftain as a crowned king and each dabbler in black magic as Faustus reincarnate, Robert did not find this absurd. He had seen very little of the wilds, but enough to guess that only by nursing a vision that magnified his own part and romanticized an apathetic scene could a lonely Englishman's purpose be sustained.

"When I'd been in Africa five years," Pawley told his junior, "I used to say: 'I know the native inside out.' And after all, if you've trekked with the native, fought him, doctored him, slept with his women and damn' nearly been eaten by him, maybe you do get to know him better than some of these college professors who write books about him or politicians who've never been nearer the bush than Epping Forest. But now I've been here for nearer fifteen years than five, I sometimes wonder whether I know the native at all."

"Is there such a person? There are millions of them; like us, they can't all be alike."

"They're not; the northerner's a very different fellow from one of the coast boys. But when you get down to brass tacks, there's not all that difference in the way they behave. It's the law of the tribe, you see. If you don't toe the line, out you go. Tribal law's a straight-jacket, and there's no one strong enough to break out. If they try—well, our ju-ju friends soon put a stop to that."

Talk of ju-ju brought him back to experiences of his own in the twilight world between reality and imagination, the world of the exploitation of fear. Pawley, coming out at an historical moment when, after centuries of uninhibited trade, the European nations were for the first time extending the arm of law and government into the still unchanged interior, had seen Africa as it had been for centuries in the moment preceding its dissolution. He knew the close tribal society, as no men after him were ever to know it again—he himself, as its reformer, among the chief agents of its destruction. He loved what he had known, and killed what he loved. His tales of battles and trickery, of werewolves and oracles, of queer curses and spells and of his own miraculous escapes lost nothing in the telling, and kept Robert, tired as he was, out of his camp-bed until a late hour of the night.

Chapter Ten

1913

ONLY by guile and patience could a white man hope to track down one of those oracles, controlled by clever men initiated into the secrets of many ancient rites and practices, which terrorized for long periods whole districts of the bush. Pawley was an old hand at this game. That such a powerful oracle was at work in this district he had long known. People had disappeared mysteriously, conversations had ceased suddenly as he approached, now and again he had caught on the faces of bushmen, even of his own carriers and messengers, the grey look of terror worn by men who fear not merely for their lives but for

their souls. And he had good reason to believe that this particular oracle was sending slaves up the river to a kingdom in the
interior whither the arm of British authority had as yet scarcely
reached. Once he had missed by a few minutes, in a surprise
raid, the capture of a party of such boys. He had in fact secured
the canoe in which they were travelling but the boys themselves,
no doubt bound and beaten and perhaps mutilated, had been
spirited away into the bush and, try as he might, he had found no
trace of any one of the victims.

Pawley was compelled to play a watching and waiting game.
From a half-spoken hint here, and overheard word there, he had
gradually to piece together enough information to force some
terrified individual into an admission that would put him on the
right track. An expert colloquial knowledge of the language
helped him, and occasionally he caught scraps of conversation
not intended for his ears from which he was able to surmise at
least the whereabouts of the oracle's headquarters (it was
exceedingly mobile) and an idea of its mode of operation.

That it was in the district under Fawkes's charge he knew; and
just before Fawkes's illness he had been able to confront a man
from that part of the world with sufficient evidence of his complicity to force him, scared out of his wits, to promise co-operation.
With informers Pawley had to walk extremely warily. Once
before one of his messengers, acting as a spy, had come near to
the heart of the mystery and within a day of the planned *coup*
he had disappeared—snatched away under Pawley's very nose
a few hundred yards from district headquarters, and never heard
of again. After that Pawley resolved to use no spies.

But now, by a mixture of threats, bluff and bribery, he had
got this man to agree to lead him to the oracle's lair. The informer was engaged as one of Pawley's carriers, and the caravan's
route planned to pass close to the spot where this man believed
the shrine to be. When they were close at hand, the informer was
to halt the caravan by setting down his load, and Pawley would
turn back to settle the trouble and send the column ahead. After
that it would be a matter of speed, luck and judgment. As for
the informer, his terms were to be placed under close arrest on
reaching the station and sent immediately to the coast, where
he would change his identity and receive a large reward.

Pawley, finding that his new and green assistant had set off
precipitately on the trail of a murder clearly the work of the
oracle he was after, swore extensively and long. There was now a

double danger: that the ju-ju priests, emboldened by their successes and their apparent safety, might destroy this ignorant and interfering white man—a stroke which, could they escape punishment, would raise their prestige to a point where Pawley's fight would become almost hopeless; and the lesser but still annoying risk that his young assistant would scare away the birds by stumbling too close to their nest. At best, the foray would set everyone on the alert.

Robert's disappearance seriously alarmed him, and it was therefore with enormous relief that he saw the ragged and exhausted little party stumble into his camp late in the afternoon. A descent on the oracle's hiding-place was then planned for the next day. Early in the morning camp was struck and the party set off, the informer carrying a load of tent-poles. The column marched for several hours through the bush without incident, halting every now and again for a breather and sometimes passing near villages, when buxom women hoeing among the crops straightened their backs to stare or smile, looking at the travellers with the round soft eyes of gazelles while their babies slept under a tree; or glistening young men, attending to a yam vine or striding out in search of wild honey, would shout a greeting.

Presently the villages thinned out, and they marched for some time without sight of cultivation through coarse brown grass that almost met above their heads. Then came a shout from behind, the signal they had been waiting for with a growing sense of tension. Pawley turned and went back, followed by Robert and the policemen. Several loads were on the ground and the headman was helping with readjustments.

"I shall rest here for a little," Pawley told him. "Take the carriers on."

They sat down in the shade of a tree and watched the porters heave their loads on to each other's heads and start forward again along the path. Pawley puffed his pipe in silence, watching them out of sight. Six policemen had stayed behind; they squatted a little distance away, taking snuff.

"Did you spot the branch path?"

Robert shook his head. "It all looks just bush to me."

"It's well concealed, but a man can't cover his tracks completely any more than an elephant."

At first the path was so faint that Robert could barely make it out, but he followed Pawley, whose bulky figure slid in and out among the vegetation with surprising ease. In perhaps twenty minutes they emerged unexpectedly in a small clearing beside a towering cotton tree. Several huts stood in its shade, too small for dwellings, and close to the trunk was a larger hut, not round like the others, but long and thin. A strange assortment of objects littered the ground: bones, rags, broken pots, feathers, eggshells. But there was no sign of a human being.

"Cleared off." Pawley was deeply disgusted. "Missed them again." He swore briefly. "They're as cute as a cartload of monkeys."

He sniffed loudly; over everything hung a faint reminder of the stench that had so sickened Robert when the severed head had fallen at his feet.

"Reminds me of a place we wiped up in nineteen-o-five," Pawley added. "Found the remains of over fifty people and bits and pieces of God knows how many more in a pit. Nothing like that here." He sounded rather contemptuous, as if he were dealing now with small fry.

A cry interrupted his reminiscences; one of the policemen was holding up a human hand. Pawley, looking like an angry bull, strode up to the rectangular hut. It had a small, low doorway sheltered by a palm-thatch screen. He dived in, and Robert followed.

Inside, all was dark. The contrast with the glare of the open was so great that neither could at first see anything but the almost extinguished embers of a fire glowing like a bloodshot eye. Flecks of light filtered through the palm thatch and danced under the roof, making the surrounding gloom appear more complete. The smell here was much stronger, forcing Robert to pull out his handkerchief and hold it to his nose as a filter.

Pawley wrenched away the door-screen to let in a beam of light, and switched on a torch. The long, low-roofed hut was full of litter, but empty of votaries.

"The birds flew in a hurry—this is their nest all right. I'd give a year's pay to have caught them at their little game."

Wooden drums, black and broken pots, sticks and rope twisted from forest creepers lay about in disorder. Could this curious mace-like object, Robert wondered, stuck about with pieces of dirty rag and membrane and bone, be taken seriously as a symbol charged with demonic power? It looked like an urchin's plaything assembled on some deserted building lot, the product of a vacant mind. Yet there on the floor beside it lay rotting pieces of a human body that had been sacrificed and dismembered. He walked round the hut, touching objects here and there with his foot, afraid of what he might find. At one end stood a rough three-legged stool and near it a heap of rags and cloths; and as he prodded, he encountered something solid. Bending down, he pulled the cloths away to reveal the body of a naked boy.

Pawley, summoned by his exclamation, picked it up and carried it outside. His dark, fleshy face looked angry as he glared down at the body, whose back was marked from top to bottom with weals and cuts on which blood had congealed.

"Bloody murderers! Look at this poor kid—heads they sold him as a slave, tails they enjoyed themselves by beating him into a jelly."

He knelt over the body and gave it a quick examination.

"He's alive. Wouldn't have been if we'd turned up a couple of minutes later. One leg broken, you see? They break both arms and legs and then disembowel them; it's considered unlucky if they die first."

The boy was a skinny creature of perhaps eight or nine, rather light in colour. His body was limp, his woolly head sagged like a dead animal's as they lifted him on to a stretcher made from poles and forest creepers. Before they left the clearing Pawley put a match to piles of dry grass heaped against the long hut and soon the flimsy buildings sent thick plumes of smoke billowing into the sky.

"That's that," he said, "for the time being. These birds will build again. I'm going to get them on the nest one day if it's the last thing I do—they've given me the slip once too often."

To Robert, the scene was fantastic and barely credible. It was the contrast that struck him most. At one moment he had been sprawling under a tree watching the carriers re-arrange their loads, a bottle of beer in his hand, talking about London (even Pawley had wanted news of the latest musical shows); at the next, inside that plain flimsy hut, he had stumbled about among senseless paraphernalia belonging to the dark ages of man's mind. He had thought before of witchcraft and black magic as picturesque survivals of old cults among simple people. Now he saw them as something at once more ageless and more evil: as instruments used by the ruthless and ambitious against the ignorant and weak. And what made it all particularly gruesome was the lack of dignity and form. Here was no devil's mass, no Faustian bargain nor even the trappings and order of an Inquisition; here was only a stick plastered with rags and eggshells, a bloodstained whipping-post, fragments of rotting flesh—the obscene made frivolous, the reduction of human torment to the stature of an idiot's jest.

The rough district headquarters, when they reached it, offered the luxuries of hot baths, a well-cooked meal off a table and a cool roof overhead. During the march the injured boy had come round and he lay now on a palliasse in the shelter of a store, in pain and feverish, but still alive.

"Our only trophy," Pawley spoke a little grimly. He had dressed the boy's back with skill and put his leg in home-made splints.

"What will you do with him?"

"Hand him over to the missionaries. That's the only thing we can do. If I ask for his parents, he'll be claimed by some bogus father who'll keep him as a slave. The mission will patch him up and I suppose turn him into a bum-sucking imitation white man—neither fish, fowl nor good red herring, poor little Benjamin."

The writing of a note to the mission fell to Robert, and on impulse he added: 'Name, Benjamin.' It seemed to suit the boy and no doubt the mission would approve of it.

It was the custom for the police corporal at sundown to recite to the officer in charge a tally of the number of people in the station, according to categories—so many policemen, messengers, Europeans, servants, prisoners and so forth. On the night of their return he reeled off his report as usual, standing to attention on the veranda; but Pawley noticed immediately that something was wrong.

"You have not mentioned the jail."

"The jail is empty, sir."

"I ordered you to arrest the carrier who had trouble with his load to-day."

"The carrier has gone, sir."

"Gone! Gone where? When did he go?"

"I do not know. I went to arrest him as soon as the loads were counted, but he was not to be found."

A search was immediately started. Several men thought they remembered the carrier returning to district headquarters; certainly his load had been brought in. After that the trail came to a dead end. All questions met with blank stares, muttered negatives, shakes of the head. The carrier had vanished into thin air. Pawley swore a great deal, he even stormed at the interpreter and others of the staff; he vowed vengeance on them all. But nowhere did he detect the slightest weakening, the faintest clue.

Over his sundowner, he was savage. "They know what's happened," he said. "Every man jack of them knows. And not one of them will say. They're scared stiff. That's the sort of thing we're up against. I'll get those beggars one day, by God, if I have to become a werewolf to do it."

That night a double guard was set over the sick boy in the store. He was unmolested; but the carrier was never heard of again.

Chapter Eleven

1929

SIR ROSSLYN POWERS had sat through a thoroughly gloomy lunch with a City friend usually prosperous and genial, but now a prophet of disaster. The panic on the New York stock exchange he pronounced serious, and worse would follow: rising unemployment, bank failures, the instability of sterling, international tension—there seemed no gleam of hope. Sir Rosslyn himself could not follow all the arguments; he looked on the whole subject as a little squalid and vulgar. One had to balance budgets, of course, and keep a rein on expenses; and trade, though dangerous, was a thing to be nurtured—rather like an elephant that was useful, in fact indispensable, for carrying the palanquin of government on its back, but needed careful watching for signs of running amok; beyond that, economics was best left to the commercial world and to the long-haired professors. But now, if his friend was right, economics was in some way going to mix itself up with serious affairs. Even the Government might be shaken.

He looked out of the window on to Whitehall. A cold autumnal wind was blowing and coveys of dead leaves went whirling by. Crowds hurried past, holding on to their hats, bending slightly into the wind; the flags on the Cenotaph fluttered and pulled at their poles. It all looked perfectly normal, just as it always did. The sight reassured him. Surely, by the year of grace 1929, the highly-skilled men in the Treasury, the bankers and the politicians between them, understood these matters well enough to put them to rights. Looked at in that light, it seemed obvious. His City friend had lost his head, that was all—allowed himself to be panicked by the Americans. Given time, the trouble would adjust itself. After all, the law of supply and demand . . .

A messenger entered to announce Mr. Begg, and Freddy followed. He looked fit and sunburnt after his holiday, spick and span in a neat dark suit. Sir Rosslyn rose to shake hands, full of cordial greetings. He was more impressive seated than on his feet, for he was a small dapper man with a round and rather flat, leathery face, on which two large ears seemed to have been pinned. He wore a short bristling moustache and the impression he created was one of tidiness, efficiency and a sort of cold inhuman precision of mind.

Banishing unpleasant and, as he felt, adventitious thoughts, he settled down to discuss the affairs of the Protectorate to which Freddy had hitherto devoted his abilities. For these abilities Sir Rosslyn had a considerable respect. No man in the Colonial Service drafted a sounder and more business-like dispatch. Few were so hard-working and dependable, so little liable to lose their heads and allow themselves to be deflected from their steady course by the impulse, which came over most people from time to time, to chase their own hares. Take this slump, for instance— he was sure that Begg would not allow himself to be disturbed by that, but would pursue steadily and sensibly his chosen path. Moreover, like most men marked down for success, he had a special flair of his own: the knack of finding compromises. However divergent two policies might seem to be, however irreconcileable two points of view, Freddy Begg, given a little time, could be relied upon somehow or other to find a middle way. In the complicated affairs of countries of mixed races and traditions, there could be no attribute more valuable than this. Begg, as Sir Rosslyn sometimes declared (and it was almost the highest compliment he could pay) had both feet on the ground. For all this, the Service had its rewards.

"Coming now to questions of personnel——" he said, and broke the news. Freddy was to be transferred to a small dependency with a rank second only to that of the Governor himself.

Freddy flushed with pleasure, the more so as it took him by surprise; he had never dared to hope for such rapid promotion.

Chief Secretary at forty! It could mean only one thing: that he was marked down for advancement and that, unless he made some foolish blunder in the next few years, the highest of all prizes, the crown of gubernatorial glory, would come within his grasp.

He thanked Sir Rosslyn warmly, but he hoped not too warmly, and exchanged a few words about the new world he was to conquer. It was a neglected, obscure territory of which he knew nothing, with a Governor of whom, from what little he did know, he had no high opinion; but it was a start. In a few sentences Sir Rosslyn gave a succinct outline of its principal affairs. His mind was like a filing cabinet, with everything accurately docketed and stored. He could tell you, without hesitation, the figure for the Customs revenue or expenditure on medical services of any of the half-dozen or so territories under his control. He knew the names of every officer of senior rank. This was all the more remarkable in that he had never visited any of the countries concerned, or, indeed, been farther afield than a single holiday trip to Sark. His charges were to him abstractions, each distinguished from the other by the order of importance allocated by its Government to more or less similar problems.

His own problems were to keep the pot from boiling over at any particular place, and to shuffle his pack of senior officials in such a way as to distribute them as fairly as possible over the whole field. Thus, if you had a comparatively strong Governor, it would not be right to give him an outstanding Chief Secretary, your best Financial Secretary and a top-notch legal man as well, leaving some other colony bare of talent. A nice balance was called for. He believed that Freddy, with the zeal of the ambitious and the relatively young, added to his industry and talent for compromise, would be able to patch things up so as to prevent any outbreak of open dissatisfaction. In all this he did not feel that personal acquaintance with the countries concerned would be helpful—in fact the reverse; and when the head of the Office had once suggested a visit he had smilingly declined.

"One must preserve one's detachment; a personal visit might expose one to the risk of bias."

Although concerned with the appointment of only the most senior officers, he seized all opportunities that came his way to compile a fund of information about the younger men, due in a few years for promotion, who would one day fill the higher posts. Moreover a neighbouring country which had suffered decimation of its senior ranks by a series of accidents was being forced to call on the Protectorate for the loan of a few experienced officers to fill one or two vacant Residencies. Several names had been suggested to Sir Rosslyn Powers and he took this opportunity to consult Freddy Begg on the merits of their owners.

His short list of candidates was headed by the name of Robert Gresham, whose personal file was open in front of him. It revealed a good record. In ability, character and experience, all tests were passed, and there were several suggestions of exceptional qualities. Against this must be set one episode that suggested a high-handed nature, an inclination to value his own opinions above those of his superiors. Sir Rosslyn needed a personal opinion.

"He is an able officer, undoubtedly," Freddy said, pressing the tips of his fingers together and leaning back in the deeply-padded leather armchair. "His strong point, I should say, lies in his relationship with the native peoples. He has the knack of winning their confidence."

"As a Resident, it is equally important to get the best out of European subordinates."

Freddy pondered. The fact, which he fully admitted, that he had a personal bias against Robert Gresham made him all the more anxious to do his colleague full justice, even to give him the benefit of the doubt. At the same time, duty must come first.

"So far as I know, he is well liked in the Service," he ventured. "Sometimes I have had the impression that he chafes a little under authority, but greater responsibility might well prove the remedy for that. All the same——"

He checked himself in time. It would not do to put into words feelings which were really quite irrational. The idea of Robert's promotion was distasteful, but he was greatly afraid that personal prejudice was creeping in. On the other hand there was that recent and unfortunate business of his open opposition to the new taxation proposals, and his dereliction of duty—it was scarcely less—resulting in the murder of the native clerk.

"You speak, of course, in absolute confidence," Sir Rosslyn said.

"To be quite frank, I have found him to be—how shall I put it?—a little over-enamoured of his own opinions, which have not always coincided with those of his superiors."

Sir Rosslyn nodded. This was exactly what he had deduced from a sketchily recorded episode in the file. It had occurred during the war, when Robert Gresham, after serving for a while with the military forces, had been placed in charge of a large area of conquered German territory, an area in which many enemy estates were found. A letter on an old file which Sir Rosslyn had caused the registry to disgorge enshrined his request for a grant of five hundred pounds which he had wished to use to re-start a factory for expressing groundnut oil, together with a refusal from the Office, which was doubly bound by a Treasury minute and by a policy decision taken at the highest level.

There the matter should have ended; but it had not. A minute on the file, bearing a date two years later, recorded a personal call made by Mr. Gresham on the individual (since retired) then in charge of ex-enemy territories; and the handing over by Mr. Gresham to this evidently startled person of a draft for some ten thousand pounds. This sum, it appeared, represented the profits made for the Government by a factory which never ought to have been operating at all, and never would have been if its activities had been known about in London. A spate of minutes had followed this unexpected and quite illicit windfall, which had caused considerable consternation all round; but it had been finally decided, in collusion with the Treasury, to keep the matter hushed up and to accept the draft under some non-committal heading such as General Suspense Account. Gresham, referred to more than once as 'this over-zealous officer', had escaped without an open reprimand, but his action quite clearly reflected a high-handed and dangerous disregard of clear instructions from the highest authorities.

Sir Rosslyn wished to say nothing that might influence Freddy Begg, and he did not mention this forgotten incident. Aloud he said:

"Over-confidence is a not uncommon fault among younger men; as a rule the sobering effect of time and experience disposes of it quite effectively."

"Quite so. And one doesn't want to discourage initiative."

"On the contrary, we encourage it—always provided, of course, that it is directed into the right channels."

Sir Rosslyn flipped through the papers, thinking quickly. Initiative was all very well, but you could not have people striking out lines of their own all over the colonial empire. Major policies

were decided here in London and it was the job of the Colonial
Service to enforce them. But Sir Rosslyn made a point of looking
at matters from all angles, and one of these was a candidate's
domestic state. A man's wife could make or mar him in those
senior posts where hospitality and social effort were a part of his
duties. Moreover, a Resident was a picked man, with opportunities open to him to go forward to the highest positions. In
the selection of each one the authorities looked for the qualities
of a potential Governor; and it would be short-sighted not to
pay some heed also to the qualities desirable in a Governor's wife.

"Gresham is married, I believe?"

Freddy felt very ill at ease. He knew what Sir Rosslyn was
driving at, but not where his duty lay. A Resident's wife must
set the tone, be looked up to—beyond reproach. Suppose she
should be wagged at by malicious tongues, slandered—or, worse
than that, not slandered but truthfully accused! Involuntarily,
his mind went back to that chance meeting in a seaside hotel. A
Resident's wife and that notorious policeman! Dreadful! And
the possibility of open scandal could not be ruled out. It was his
duty to utter some word of warning, but he could scarcely bear
to do it—to descend himself to the level of the gossip-mongering
he so much deplored. All he could bring himself to say was:

"Yes, his wife's a very charming woman, though perhaps—
I doubt if the climate——"

Sir Rosslyn came to his rescue.

"Poor health?"

Immensely relieved, Freddy clutched at the lifebelt. "Yes,
that is no doubt the trouble. Her health is poor and I understand that it's unlikely she will be able to accompany him back
to his post."

On such matters Sir Rosslyn made up his mind quickly. Too
independent—one might take a chance on that. Wife doubtful—
nervy? discontented? immoral?—no help, in any case. Plenty
of fish in the sea. . . . He laid aside the file.

"I have good accounts of a T. R. Scammell, now stationed at
—let me see——" He frowned at the file; one could never be
certain of these obscure African names and he did not like
to display even a suggestion of ignorance in front of subordinates.

Freddy brightened. Scammell was a man he could heartily
recommend: conscientious, hard-working, sober, steady, and his
wife a most estimable woman—no beauty, perhaps, but always

ready to shoulder her share, most interested in native welfare, and certainly beyond reproach.

"Scammell," he said. "Yes, the very best type of officer, I should say."

Chapter Twelve

FREDDY walked back in an elated frame of mind to the furnished service flat he had taken for part of his leave. The wind stung his face and whipped his light overcoat, causing him to clasp his well-brushed hat. It was cold—the first taste of winter. The evening papers' posters screamed some gloomy message about the failure of a foreign bank. Thank goodness, we in England needn't fear that sort of thing! His thoughts hurried back to his own pleasurable situation. He was positively glowing inside, as if he had just dashed off a large liqueur brandy. This, perhaps, was the turning point of his life. Other awards might follow, of grander and more glittering prizes; the bugles might yet sound for him at the gate of some Government House; but this was the moment when the bolted door was opened to him and he was permitted a glimpse of the delectable gardens.

How pleased Armorel would be! Quickening his step, he thought that this at least would merit her rare praise (for Armorel had high standards); and he valued her praise above that of all others. With gratitude, he thought of all she had done to further his career. If at times her advice was irksome and her certitude provoking, he had to acknowledge that without it he would not have seen the unbolting of that heavy door. She had saved him from many false steps. A wife in a million—and he, it was fair to say, a faithful and considerate husband. Unbidden, the image of Priscilla came into his mind—almost a tragic figure, beautiful and bad. Unlucky Gresham, to have a wife who not only betrayed him but poisoned his career!

He found Armorel in an excellent humour. Curled up on the sofa, her legs tucked under her, cigarette-smoke drifting about her spare pale face, she greeted his news with almost exultant satisfaction.

"Don't be modest about it," she replied to his self-deprecating remarks. "You may have got promotion, but they've got a

Chief Secretary who knows his job. I dare say it will be a new experience for them as well as for you. . . . Have you met the Governor?

Freddy shook his head. "Some kind of General, I think. It's seldom successful when they look outside the Service."

Armorel was thoughtful. "That probably means India: I'll look them up in the book. Bubblephor makes wives very correct; perhaps I ought to invest in gloves."

"We mustn't expect too much, of course. I believe the hurricanes are bad and there's a tiresome and vociferous local element. Still, perhaps in two or three years . . ."

Armorel rose, smiling. "Isn't it terrible to be such climbers? But nice when you approach the top. Clever Freddy!" She kissed him on the ear. "I'm going to change."

Freddy gave her behind a gentle pat. "I'll just look through my letters."

The word gave her a slight prick of conscience. One letter had come for him by the afternoon post which he would not see, because it was at this moment concealed in her room. Undressing for her bath, she smiled wryly. To stoop to tampering with her husband's letters—it was undignified, petty, not a thing she made a habit of doing: but unpremeditated. The afternoon post had come while she had been drinking a solitary cup of tea. Glancing casually through the letters, she had been arrested by a handwriting that she had not seen since her marriage. Suddenly petrified, holding the letter, she had been filled with the most extraordinary sensations. Once that handwriting had possessed the power to stir the very depths of her heart. Once she had picked up every letter with hope and let it fall with disappointment if it did not bear that script; and, on the few occasions when she had been rewarded, she had sat for a long time with the envelope in her hand, at once summoning up the resolution to open it and prolonging the joys of anticipation.

It was more than five years since she had married Freddy and in all that time she had never seen Maurice Cornforth, nor had they corresponded. She could meet him now, she knew, perfectly calmly, indeed with a half-contemptuous backward glance at her own infatuation. Nowadays he hardly ever entered her head. Yet, for all that, her memories of him were the most poignant and bitter of her life and even to-day this unexpected sight of his handwriting had the power to quicken her heart and unnerve her hand.

Not that she had sighed for the moon. She had made her bed and on the whole she had not found it distasteful; knowing in advance that you could not have your bun and your penny, she had not hankered after the bun. And the penny had been a bright, solid coin. Her avocation of intriguing and planning was one at which she was adept and which she enjoyed both as a test of skill and as relish for a sense of cynicism. To love Freddy had been beyond her power, but a half-amused tolerance and a certain respect had proved a fair substitute. She had borne him two daughters, and if she saw them seldom (they had to be left at home) that on the whole suited her, for with children she was at a loss and often bored; and she had been interested, but not at all surprised, to find that her feelings for her own offspring had been no different. Everything had turned out for the best. She had no doubt whatever that as the wife of an unambitious and underpaid policeman she would have been neither happy nor successful; love in a cottage was not her cup of tea. Nevertheless she knew also that, if Maurice had wished it, she would have followed him to the meanest cottage at the farthest ends of the earth.

And now this letter had come. Why had he written to Freddy? So far as she knew, the two had not seen each other since their voyage together five years ago and the evening when, introduced by Maurice, she and Freddy had met. Policemen had little truck with Chief Secretaries. What could he possibly have to say? A small draught of suspicion blew through her mind. Could Maurice have found some reason for raking up the past? Impossible! It was probably some suggestion of a lunch together to renew an old acquaintance. Yet that, in a man of Maurice's status and seniority, would be a form of self-advertisement out of keeping with his character.

Armorel was a woman who, if faced with two courses, would choose the boldest. Tearing open the letter, she took out a sheet inscribed in a small, rather neat handwriting, and read it through.

'Dear Begg,
I feel I cannot leave you with the false conclusion you must have drawn from our chance encounter at the Angel Hotel. The lady you saw me with had not (as you evidently thought) involved herself with me in any compromising way.

'I drove this lady over to the village where I am staying for a

day's fishing and unfortunately she was taken ill. Being unfit to
travel she had to spend the night there and I took her back in my
car next morning. We merely stopped at the Angel for breakfast
on the way. It was a chapter of accidents, but no more than that.
I am aware that you may doubt my assurance, and can only give
you my word that it is so. Also I think you know that the lady
is ill and had been forbidden to return—perhaps that will act as a
partial confirmation.

Yours sincerely,
Maurice Cornforth.'

So there was the answer to the little riddle that had piqued
her curiosity! Running through the names of her acquaintances
at present on leave, she had immediately hit on the solution.
Only that week Freddy had mentioned casually that he had
heard Priscilla's health was to prevent her from returning.

Priscilla Gresham! Armorel was astonished—the last name in
the world that would have occurred to her. Priscilla, so irre-
proachable and pure, one half of a supposedly perfect matched
couple—it was incredible! Yet, as she thought about it, perhaps
less improbable than amusing. True, Maurice had denied it,
and perhaps there was substance in his claim that she had been
taken ill; but he was not the man to take another man's wife out
for a day's fishing just for the healthy open-air sport. If a heart
attack had caught her out, perhaps that was not surprising;
excitement brought on such things.

And now, reading the letter through again at her dressing-
table as she prepared for Freddy's little celebration, she smiled to
herself. Maurice and Priscilla! She was amused beyond measure.
Cæsar's wife with feet of clay; Cæsar, his head in the clouds,
cheated by a common seducer! It was a delightful morsel. She
had needed just such a tonic, for the flood of memory released by
her first sight of the letter had left an unaccustomed flatness in
its wake, a touch of *malaise*.

In the meantime, here was the letter: how was she to pass it
on to Freddy? She could hardly admit to opening his correspondence. In any case, he would be a fool if he took the letter at
its face value. Frowning a little, she reflected that this was
probably exactly what he would do; he did not like to think ill
of others and, if anything shocked him, he preferred to believe
it untrue. Coming to a decision, she rose and slipped the letter
into a pocket of her writing-case. After all, it could make little

difference now. Priscilla could have affairs if she liked, but she must not expect that her looks and charm, and whatever it was in her that so appealed to the lingering sense of chivalry in men, would enable her to dodge the consequences. Like others, she had made her bed. . . .

Chapter Thirteen

1924

AS she dressed slowly—there was plenty of time—Armorel's mind went back, unbidden, to her first meeting with Priscilla, five years ago. She and Freddy had found themselves sharing the Chief Engineer's table with the Greshams and a couple in forestry—she had forgotten their name; and it was mildly amusing to find that, although her marriage was less than a fortnight old, it was Priscilla (a wife of several years' standing) who was usually mistaken for the bride. Armorel, sensitive as always to atmosphere, observed that her husband and this lean, fair-haired young man treated each other with a certain embarrassment on Freddy's side, and with a hint of constraint on Robert's. Intrigued, she set herself to probe the little mystery. But her husband was evasive.

"I ran into him during the war on one or two occasions."

"Did you like him?"

"Like him? Oh, yes, he's quite a good fellow."

"I didn't think you seemed altogether pleased to see him."

"Pleased to see him?" Freddy had a trick, which she was already beginning to find irritating, of repeating the last part of her previous sentence in his reply. "He's not a particular personal friend. As a matter of fact on the last occasion we met, we had a slight—er—difference of opinion. But of course it was nothing really, purely an official matter." And he would not say more.

Armorel had started married life by thinking her husband transparent and entirely tractable, and already she had met with several surprises. It was true that Freddy's mind was like a clock behind glass, predictable and regular, but he had in him a streak of obstinacy she had not bargained for. It was true also that he was in love, bowled over by his good fortune, but he displayed a tendency to divide his life into private and official compartments and to prohibit traffic between the two. This revealed in him a certain rigidity of character she had not expected, a brittleness which she knew must be dissolved if her plans for the future were to mature. The discovery of these flinty seams in her husband's nature was on the whole a pleasant one, promising to redeem her marriage from the dullness that she had faced from the first as its direst possibility. A battle always pleased her and she felt confident that her weapons of detachment and superior subtlety, used with intelligence, would triumph in course of time. Meanwhile, the present was agreeable enough: the long, empty but entertaining days spent at ease in a deck chair dipping into a book or watching passengers go striding past; the pacing of the narrow deck, a damp salty wind in the face; drinks before meals among the worn leather armchairs and small fixed tables in the smoking-room.

Armorel got out her sketch book and covered the pages with quick impressions of lascars at work on the ship's business and the faces of her fellow-passengers. Among these, one in particular attracted interest, both for his position at the Captain's table, which fixed his social pre-eminence, and for his looks, which were distinguished. His handsome, clean-shaven face glowed with self-assurance, his eye was keen, his movements well controlled and he dressed with that simple elegance that conceals care as well as expenditure. Every morning his silk shirt, monogrammed over the pocket, was fresh, his perfectly pressed white trousers clean and new. She noticed that he was treated with deference by the younger men and by the older ones with a heartiness reserved for those indisputably classed as good fellows. And when they ran into him one morning on deck, Freddy greeted him with every sign of pleasure.

"I was delighted to hear of your appointment—if I may say so, sir, there couldn't have been a more popular and deserved promotion in the Service. I hope you enjoyed your leave?"

"More than I can say," the other answered, his smile revealing the whitest and most even of teeth. "It's quite superfluous to ask you the same question. You're the one to be congratulated, my dear fellow."

Freddy flushed with mingled pleasure and marital pride. "This is Mr. Hockling, my dear, our new Chief Secretary."

"A great pleasure, Mrs. Begg. If Freddy does his duty as a husband as well as he does it in the office, you'll have everyone congratulating you on picking a winner."

"I hope his sense of duty won't be his only motive, Mr. Hockling."

Dutifully, everyone laughed.

"Clearly this is one of those occasions when duty must become a delight. I hope I shall have the pleasure of seeing quite a lot of you and your husband, Mrs. Begg."

Armorel felt that the encounter had been a success. It had taken place just after she had emerged from her cabin for a morning walk, her make-up still fresh; a crimson chiffon scarf loosely tied round her head threw into relief the glossy darkness of her hair, the depths of her full deep eyes and the chalky pallor of her skin. In the new clothes of her trousseau, with leisure now to tend her appearance, she was looking her best: slender, clear-skinned, in the early flush of life (she was as yet only twenty-three), but with a subtle hint of experience which removed all trace of youth's insipidity.

It was to a large extent to Bertrand Hockling's favours, she gathered, that Freddy owed his present position, but on this subject he was reticent. Freddy had come to the West Coast on the staff of one of the big commercial firms; during the war he had transferred into the Administration; Hockling had assisted in or arranged this transfer; that much she knew. Now she learnt a new fact about this episode. On the boat was a large, heavy, jovial man, in complexion and consistency rather reminiscent of a beefsteak, who greeted Freddy with every appearance of delight, slapping him on the back and offering him a drink. Freddy accepted and introduced his wife; he could hardly have done otherwise without being openly rude.

"This is Mr. Babcock of the Coastal Trading Company; my wife."

They sat down together at a table in the smoking-room, but Freddy's manner was chilly.

"I've known your husband since he first came to the Coast," Babcock said, with great cordiality. "But he deserted us, Mrs. Begg—I'm giving you fair warning, you'll know what to look out for, eh?"

He laughed heartily, but Freddy stared glumly at his gin-and-lime.

"So you're staying on the Government side of the fence,

Freddy. Like the company, eh? Well, I'll admit it's more genteel. All the same, you might find the pickings better on our side, you know. Now you're a married man you'll have to think of these things.''

Freddy answered very stiffly: "I've nothing to complain of in the Government service."

The other let out a guffaw. "Then, by God, you're the only one of 'em who hasn't!"

They finished their drinks and Freddy did not offer to buy a second round. This, though Armorel did not then realize it, was as deliberate a snub as could well be given at such a time and place. When no doubt could remain that it was intended, the victim put aside his empty glass and said dryly:

"I won't keep you any longer from your official friends. Good-bye, Mrs. Begg, it's been a pleasure to have met you. Don't worry that I'll betray any secrets of Freddy's disreputable past."

He walked off, smiling but clearly angry, and leaving Armorel puzzled.

"What did he mean?"

"Of course, you mustn't take him literally. He's a good fellow in his way; but if I were you, Armorel, I wouldn't see any more of him than you can help."

"Surely you don't mean that he's a well-known seducer?"

"Of course not, nothing in the least like that!" Freddy tried not to look shocked; sometimes Armorel quite upset him with her outspoken remarks.

"What's the matter with him, then?"

"Nothing's the matter, my dear. It's merely that the commercial element keep themselves rather apart and that our ways and Babcock's aren't likely to cross much, later on. Nothing snobbish about it, of course. It's just a case of different interests and a rather different type of man, perhaps, employed by the commercial firms."

"But, Freddy, you started off in a commercial firm yourself!"

"Yes, my dear, all the more reason——"

He broke off, embarrassed, but he had said enough; Armorel understood perfectly. These other men, the Hocklings and Greshams, had not entered the Service by way of a commerical back-door at a time of staff shortage during the war; they had come in by the front entrance and the mud of trade did not cling to their boots. A service such as the one in which he was now embedded, when it unbent, welcomed the footloose cattle-puncher or the erstwhile ivory poacher more readily than the counting-house clerk.

She had too much sympathy for his fears and ambitions to despise him for entertaining them. While resenting the complicated and almost cabalistic system of social grading, she accepted it, as one accepts unreservedly the rules of a game one is resolved to play. In fact her discovery of Freddy's secret enhanced rather than lowered her opinion of him. In cutting himself adrift from his previous associates, he displayed a correct reading of the rules; and from that moment she looked on him as an ally rather than an instrument. So far, she reflected with pleasure, the surprises offered by married life had all been on the favourable side; even his expected inadequacies as a lover were being remedied more quickly than she could have foreseen.

While fine weather held and the sea was kind, she would perch with her sketch-book on some convenient protuberance of the superstructure, and acquaintances would pause to watch her flying pencil, now directed with considerable technical skill. Absorbed in a struggle to pin her momentary vision to the paper, she seldom noticed them until her pencil flagged; and one morning, looking up, she was delighted to observe the fresh, clean-cut face of Bertrand Hockling hovering above her shoulder.

"That's really a ripping sketch," he said, his head on one side. "I can see you're a real pro."

"You're kind, but that's an overstatement. I meant to give it up when I married, but I can't resist trying to make something of all this."

"It's your first trip abroad?"

"Yes, and it's very exciting."

Hockling looked at her pensively, rubbing his chin. To him, twenty years her senior, she looked a mere girl, fresh and appealing, but more intelligent than most of these young, innocent and doomed brides.

"I can imagine no better equipment for your new life than the artist's eye, that can see the magic in everyday things—even pink grass, sometimes, and square trees. The best part of life is hidden from those of us condemned to bury ourselves in offices. . . . What are you looking forward to most in Africa, Mrs. Begg?"

Armorel played with her pencil, brought up short by the question. She had never considered it before. Security—an end of poverty—a home in which she could be master—scope for her

talents—new faces—position—success? None of this could be
openly mentioned. Hesitantly, she answered:

"I've no very clear ideas. I want to help Freddy in his work.
The trekking part—is that what it's called?—sounds the most
fun. I'd like to see new places, and how the natives live. But if
Freddy goes on working at the head office, I suppose there won't
be much chance of that."

Hockling smiled. It rather amused him to hear the Secretariat
described as the head office. At the same time the ignorance and
innocence of these raw young English girls saddened him. They
had so much to learn! And little of it either edifying or useful.
In ten years all but the toughest would look so very different—
washed out—yellowed by quinine, nerves frayed by idleness and
heat.

"We shall have to see that Freddy gets a few tours in the bush
to satisfy your interest in native life," he said. "You've never
done anything like that, I suppose?"

"No, not really. Of course when I was a child I used to go
camping sometimes. . . ."

Hockling grinned. "Girl Guides? You'll find this a little
different. One advantage, there's no need to light a fire with two
matches—there's always a pair of black hands ready to do that
part of it."

Armorel flushed a little, furious with herself. She was appearing naïve, gauche—all the things she most despised. This man
had the effect of making her seem childish and uncertain.

"Can you ride a bicycle? In my young days ladies, if they
came out to the Coast at all, used to be carried about in hammocks,
like the wilting, helpless creatures we believed them to be.
Nowadays they cycle furiously, wiping the floor with their
men."

"I'm glad I shan't be expected to lie about in a hammock."

"You'll be well treated, don't worry about that—too well,
perhaps. But it's a man's world you're going into, you know;
women are the ornaments—the glitter, not the solid stuff underneath. . . . You must always take your sketch book, and I hope
that one day you'll show me the fruits you gather in our famous
bush."

Restored, Armorel plucked up courage to say: "I should
love to. I like doing heads best of all. Would you let me try my
hand at yours?"

Hockling looked at her in surprise. "My head is hardly worthy of such an honour. But then Van Gogh, as I remember, delighted in an old boot! Of course, I should be charmed, if you think it worth your attention."

Dressing for dinner that night Armorel could not resist telling her husband of her success. To her surprise, he was luke-warm.

"One must be careful not to give a false impression."

"Of what, Freddy?"

"Well, of—perhaps it's of small account. But I would rather you didn't spread abroad among the other passengers any mention of your arrangement with Hockling."

"Good heavens, Freddy, you talk as though I was proposing to sleep with the man!"

Freddy was horrified. He looked at her with a sense of outrage which, against his will, melted into admiration. She could not help making such remarks—almost on their honeymoon, too! It was the fault of the coarse bohemian life from which he had rescued her. And she had made this arrangement with Hockling simply to help him, her husband! All for him! A rush of grati-tude almost brought tears to his eyes.

Manipulating his tie, he dwelt on her reflection in the glass. His marriage still seemed to him a miracle. How had he come to possess anyone so lovely and so clever, capable of such tenderness and such passion? What could she possibly see in him, a very ordinary, plodding sort of fellow—dull and stodgy, as he knew only too well, in comparison with brilliant men like Hockling, or even those like Gresham, with the gift of the gab? She was too good for him, the whole thing was too good to be true. One day he would wake up to find a note on the pillow and Armorel gone, snatched away by some handsome, witty rival.

And now she was spending her energies in promoting his interests, thinking of him. A helpmeet indeed! It filled him with a sense of wonder. Impossible to explain the need for caution in this particular case. Hockling was known to everyone on board as one of the gods, and it did not do to be seen too openly courting favour on Mount Olympus. Freddy knew well enough that every passenger was under observation, as it were, by each of his fellows. He had heard comments before on others who had been con-demned or held up to ridicule for sucking up, for being on the make, and he had always been careful to avoid this breach of the elaborate and unwritten code by which his life was regulated. One could hardly put all this into words. But then, Armorel had too much sense to do anything foolish. He would watch and wait, and perhaps drop a hint if he thought she was overstepping the mark. Meanwhile, he could not resist a glow of pride. Even the great Hockling had found his wife irresistible!

Chapter Fourteen

1924

THE ship ran into a stormy patch and for a week pitched in turbulent seas. Saloons were empty, the deck deserted save for a few hardy and muffled passengers who staggered round keeping fit, and at meal-times pursued their food all over the table until they cornered it against the fiddles. Most passengers remained in their cabins, yielding to the storm.

When the seas at last subsided, the weather was found to have undergone a complete change. They were in the tropics, steaming into the Gulf of Guinea. For the first time the newcomers felt the sticky, languorous tropical heat creeping into saloon and cabin, into their very marrow. Blankets were abandoned, they slept under the light touch of a sheet. Combing their hair, the women wondered at its glutinous quality, and at the end of the day the brush felt like lead in their hands. After dark the passengers leant over the ship's rails searching the creamy waves for phosphorescence under a sky brilliant with stars. They felt a new magic in the air, an insidious softness, and in the the heavy noons and windless nights, a new threat.

A canvas tank was rigged up on the well deck for bathing, stewards carrying long drinks were always on the move, the passengers had become talkative and friendly. Armorel got out her sketch-book again, but although she started many impressions, she seemed able to complete very few. One day, finding her chair next to that of Robert Gresham, who was lying at ease with his head thrown back and his eyes shut, she started to draw. Presently his eyes opened and watched her with amusement.

"I hope you don't mind this. To be honest, I've wanted to draw you for a long time and I thought you were asleep."

"I'm flattered."

"You needn't be, really. It's the shape of your head."

"Thank you. How fortunate you can't draw what's in it! Or do I insult you? As I suppose that's what the moderns attempt."

"I only try to draw what I see, not what goes on in the subconscious."

She sketched for a while in silence, intrigued with her problem. The head lent itself to a bold geometrical treatment, angular and hard. But the expression was elusive: how to get that indrawn, hungry, evanescent look? It fascinated and baffled her. After a little she snapped the book to impatiently.

"Mayn't I see?"

"It's a failure. You're a difficult subject."

"I'm sorry. The sodden effect of a heavy breakfast, perhaps."

"No. You have a lot of expression, but one can't tell what it means. Like a stone tablet covered with hieroglyphics."

Robert laughed. "A noble ruin! But when you find your Rosetta Stone, the hieroglyphics generally turn out to be some-one's household accounts, or a recipe for embalming."

"I'd be willing to risk it."

Robert shook his head. "You'd waste your time. If you want a subject, why not try my wife? That would be a real test—to put on paper sweetness of character that isn't insipid."

"Women are tiresome. Their faces are much less definite than men."

"Not their characters."

"They keep those more hidden—in self-protection."

Robert smiled at her and picked up his book, stretching out his legs. For the first of many times, she was piqued by some elusive quality in his nature. He slid out of things, turned from the personal to the general and, at the moment, hid behind his wife. Of course it would be waste of time trying to make an impression, no less than to dent a stone; he had no eyes or ears for anyone but Priscilla. The thought irritated Armorel; collecting her things, she said, in what she intended to be an off-hand manner:

"I must look for my next victim. Mr. Hockling has asked me for a portrait."

Robert, lowering the book, raised his eyebrows.

"A royal command!"

"You sound sarcastic. Don't you like him?"

"I barely know him. I swim about among the lesser fry, he's one of the big salmon—or perhaps I should say a porpoise."

"That doesn't sound very polite."

"It's intended as a compliment. The porpoise, you know, is

pre-eminent among fishes. Perhaps it sounds better to say a lion among beasts, or a king among men."

"I don't understand why there's such a fuss about him. Mr. Hockling seems a very nice, friendly sort of person, not stuck up at all."

"I quite agree. But when you belong to a hierarchy, it's wise and proper to show a decent respect for those at the top."

"I don't agree with that sort of thing." Armorel felt a revival of the egalitarian spirit that had ruled her earlier years. "Anyway, it's out of date. People want freedom nowadays, not to be ordered about."

"People always want to believe in themselves. That's the advantage of a hierarchy—it sets up a ladder from the fishes down there in the sea to the archangels in heaven. Man can go clambering up, there's no limit to the heights he can reach. Whereas if he brings every thing down to his own level and resigns himself to eternal equality with the pickpocket, he's for ever chained to his rock."

Armorel got up, out of her depth and annoyed with him for pushing her there. She could never tell whether he was serious or half joking and this, too, was disconcerting. Yet she felt herself susceptible to his attraction. All she could think of to say was:

"In this weather, climbing up ladders sounds much too exhausting."

"It might be less so than scrambling for a breathing space in the scrum. . . . Don't go, here comes Priscilla."

He sprang to his feet, ready to adjust a perfectly well-arranged deck chair. But Armorel made her escape. When those two were together she felt insignificant and shut out. She had nothing against Priscilla, but could not feel towards her any warmth or liking. She resented, in a woman but little older than herself and (she guessed) of no social position, a lack of that insecurity, that striving to please, which bedevilled her own serenity of mind. Priscilla did not seem to care whether she made a good impression or not; she even seemed oblivious of the fact that she was making an impression at all. She was absorbed in Robert and fascinated by her surroundings. At times Armorel felt contempt for her almost childish unsophistication, at times envy for her quite effortless poise.

"I wish I could do something useful, like sketching." Priscilla had watched her ship-board acquaintance out of sight.

"Useful? Yes, I should say that's exactly the word."

"What do you mean?"

"She's going off to draw Bertrand Hockling. He'll be a sitter in both senses of the word."

"Robert, you're being catty! That's not like you at all."

"Yes, perhaps I am. But there's something about Armorel that puts my back up, I'm afraid."

"She can't help being a bit prickly. She's young, and after all——"

"After all, you mean, she's got Freddy Begg on her hands? But she's the very wife for Freddy. By the time she's finished with Hockling, he'll be Governor designate of the Laxative Islands."

"The what?"

"There really are some islands called that."

He lapsed into a sleepy silence, his hat pulled over his eyes. Neither of them had heard Freddy emerge from a hatchway on to the deck and, seeing his wife, advance towards them with a tread subdued by rubber-soled shoes. Hearing Armorel's name he had paused, without premeditation, to catch the rest of the sentence; and Robert's comments had fallen on his ears with the impact of a physical blow.

His face pink, his ears flaming, he turned and walked to the far side of the ship where, leaning against the rail, he wiped his misted spectacles and sought composure. Rage against Robert mingled with a horrible conviction that the strictures he had just heard were only an echo of a chorus that was filling the ship. Dreadful phrases were passing from mouth to mouth—place-hunter, back-scratcher, even (ghastly vulgarity!) bum-sucker; Freddy could almost see the sneer on Babcock's face. The worst of it was that Hockling himself would think the same. And it was all so unjust! Armorel meant it for the best, in all innocence; how could she guess at the delight in back-biting that poisoned the air? He saw himself banished to some dreadful fever-ridden outpost while others, Robert Gresham perhaps, carried off the cherished prizes. At all costs, he must stop this rash undertaking.

But Armorel was caught up in deck tennis and then a shandy-gaff party, and it was not until the siesta hour, when passengers were driven from roasting decks to stuffy cabins to sweat quietly on their bunks until tea-time, that he found an opportunity to warn her. To his dismay, she was not at all impressed.

"But, Armorel, you must take my word for it! People are talking already."

"Does that matter?" Armorel lay on the bunk in her slip, looking cool and unmoved.

"Of course it matters! Don't you understand that Hockling himself will think you're trying to curry favour?"

"It's not currying favour to sketch someone's head. Good heavens, Freddy, what a storm in a tea-cup!"

Freddy paced the tiny cabin in exasperation. "Armorel, in this you must be guided by me, and I must positively forbid you to go on with this proposal. I can assure you, I'm not being a fool. This is a new world to you—naturally you can't be expected to understand——"

"Oh, stop treating me like a child!" It was intolerable, being dictated to by Freddy! His obstinacy had gone too far. Infuriated, she slipped on her dress and retired to a secluded corner of the boat deck to meditate on his revolt. This, she realized, was the first and perhaps the decisive test. It was unthinkable that she should allow him to become the arbiter of behaviour. She had not resigned herself to his mediocrity for that! Still fuming, she played with the idea of retaliation. There was Babcock; she had read the signs in his eye; at the lifting of a little finger she could have him on a string. . . . But she checked her thought; that was not the method.

Tea over, passengers gathered on the boat deck for various games and sports. Hockling was among them; and Armorel, marching up to him, said:

"Have you forgotten your promise, Mr. Hockling?"

He looked blank.

"I've got my sketch-book ready."

"Of course! I'm afraid I had. When would you like——"

"Now, if you don't mind. I work quickly."

He looked none too pleased and started to excuse himself; but, seeing her intense expression, shrugged his shoulders and perched himself on a corner of a covered hatch. They were in full view of passengers awaiting their turn at quoits or deck tennis, and ship's officers off duty, emerging from their cabins for a breath of air, strolled by, hands in pockets, glancing with mild interest at this display of artistic endeavour.

Armorel's nerves were keyed up to their highest pitch. There was no time for hesitations and changes of mind; it was all or nothing. And Hockling, when she came to it, was easy. His face was not only handsome and well-proportioned but fundamentally simple; there were no baffling hints in it, no great depth of expression. Everything was on the surface and the surface was well-defined, smooth, like a piece of neatly-designed functional machinery. The face took shape, a little bolder, a little sterner than in life. Adding a few deft touches, signing her name with a flourish, she handed it over with a smile.

"I say! That's really top-hole."

"It isn't very polite to sound quite so astonished."

"I wasn't surprised at its excellence; but the speed! You're really, if I may say so, a very talented young woman."

"Then you aren't annoyed with me for doing it?"

"Annoyed? Good Lord, no; why should I be?"

"My husband said you'd think I was trying to curry favour."

Hockling threw back his head and laughed, but with a trace of embarrassment.

"And why should you pay me that compliment?"

"Because you're so important, I suppose."

"Tell Freddy from me that he's starting married life on the wrong foot, casting aspersions at his bride."

Hockling's tone was light, but he had a speculative look in his eye. Of course, the thought had crossed his mind. It was an old gambit and he had developed a wary watchfulness towards it. Was this young woman very naïve or very deep? By bringing into the open a forbidden subject, she had exorcized it, and prevented him from placing on her conduct the interpretation she had spoken of. If this was indeed premeditated she had at once committed the offence and made sure that she would get away with it. Clever—too clever, surely, for a girl of her age and inexperience!

"May I keep the portrait?"

"Of course. There's no charge."

"Thank you, Mrs. Freddy." He smiled at her; really, she was very attractive. What on earth could she see in Freddy—a good office wheel-horse, a glutton for work, but scarcely an Adonis! The youth that mysteriously informed her supple figure, the rounded limbs, the smooth unblemished complexion, pulled him powerfully; the mark of passion lay on those half-parted lips and dark eyes. Young enough to be his daughter, of course, but if he had been a free agent . . . He sighed, and added:

"I shall send the sketch home to my wife."

Freddy was nowhere to be seen. She found him later, after

sundown, sitting on his bunk in his shirt-sleeves, holding a book. He barely looked up when she entered, his face was sullen as a thunder-cloud.

Three cocktails in the smoking-room with friendly companions had heightened Armorel's elation and her sense of success; she felt light-headed and in command of life. The cabin's air was sticky and, deciding on a shower, she started to undress. Freddy closed his book with a snap.

"So you chose to disobey me, Armorel. Of course, if you're determined to turn yourself into a public spectacle like a pavement artist, there's nothing I can do."

"For God's sake don't be so stuffy! I told Hockling that you thought I was trying to curry favour, and I'm to tell you from him——"

"You said that to Hockling!"

"Yes, I did. Why keep things covered up? I don't believe in it!"

Freddy was speechless. He had gone quite pale and stood motionless, gazing at her through his spectacles with a helpless look, as one might regard some monstrous reversal of nature, like a waterfall going upwards or fish perching in trees.

"So you needn't worry any more! However much people talk, he won't send you to Timbuktu to live down your brazen wife."

Freddy sat down again on the bed. Finding his voice at last, he mumbled:

"I'm sorry, my dear. Perhaps I spoke hastily. I had heard——"

But he could not go on. It was bewildering; she had mentioned something that simply wasn't talked about and completely won the day. He felt himself linked to some unpredictable and wayward force, as if chained to the lightning. Marriage was turning out to be quite different from anything that he had pictured.

As for Armorel, she was trying to resist an impulse to rock with laughter. So it was as easy as that! First Hockling, and now Freddy—both bowled over, helpless, all their fight gone, like a sheep on its back. A most delicious sensation spread over her body, every nerve tingled, her blood was on fire: she felt herself in the grip of a sort of passion that sprang from the very crevices of her soul. Power! In a flash of illumination she knew that this was what she had always sought and would go on seeking, the god she would worship to the end of her days with a devotion sweeter than the satisfaction of bodily passion or the stimulation of wine.

Laughing aloud, she felt a sudden pity for Freddy, lying prostrate, as it were, at her feet. She owed him something for this terrifying pleasure! Bending over, she kissed his lips, and was rewarded by feeling him electrified at her touch. Injury, resentment and revolt fled from his mind. Armorel was headstrong but irresistible, she meant it all for the best—the most wonderful wife in the world! Reaching up with an unsteady hand, he pulled off his spectacles and laid them aside.

Chapter Fifteen

1929

FOR Priscilla the short November days and the long nights dragged by. Her son had returned to school and she to Hubert Gresham's to be with Robert; but Robert was often away, still hoping to arrange for the future in the few weeks that remained before the end of his leave. It was on Priscilla's insistence that he had promised not to resign until he was sure of an alternative. And he had not yet resigned.

To one of his nature, repeated attempts to wrest from men of authority promises which they did not wish to give was a prolonged agony. Every rebuff was like the twisting of a knife in his insides. And rebuffs were monotonously regular. It was not only his qualifications that were at fault, it was the times. The crisis generated in the highly-charged atmosphere of New York was searing the world like a lightning flash, and in the vacuum behind it fear, distrust and impotence rushed in. People shook their heads and shrugged their shoulders and said that the storm would pass and things return to normal; slumps had happened before and were followed by booms as surely as summer followed winter; all one need do was to hang on. But Robert, who knew nothing of these things, had the feeling that he was in the presence of a sort of cataclysm, and that when things settled back, the whole shape of the world would be altered.

He would return to his uncle's house dispirited, his nerves injured by their treatment. Priscilla herself was discouraged by

the gloom of the house, by the scowls of Wigg, who resented her
attempts to tidy up, and by her sense of failure. She found Robert,
by turns touchy and tender, more than usually difficult.

"Surely you'd better give up the struggle! It's bad luck,
hitting on this particular moment; but why go on bashing your
head against the wall? Isn't it better to go back——"

"And leave you?"

She shrugged her shoulders. "Heaps of people do it. I'm much
better, I could follow later."

He glared at her morosely, his eyes bright. "I believe you want
to get rid of me!"

"Please don't start that."

"You take it all so calmly! Every day I'm sweating blood to
find something that will keep us together, and getting turned
down like a packet of damaged goods, and all you can say is that
I'm wasting my time!"

"I'm only trying to face the facts. I know all your tender
spots are being bruised and prodded, but it doesn't help to give
way to self-pity——"

"Self-pity!"

"Isn't that what it is?"

"Damn you, you're impossible! Is that all the sympathy——"
He broke off, pacing the little sitting-room which they had to
themselves; and, visibly pulling himself in, turned with a smile
and held out a hand.

"Of course, you're perfectly right, that's just the trouble! A
disgusting form of self-indulgence. I'm terribly sorry, can you
ever forgive me?"

Perching on the arm of her chair, he took her hand; and,
feeling its coldness, looked down with a sudden contraction of the
heart. Surely there were blue shadows under her eyes, too little
warmth in her fingers; she, too, was distressed and worried, and
he came back with nothing to offer but recrimination!

"We shall work things out somehow; we're not the only ones.
So long as we're together . . ."

How Robert went to extremes! He jumped from one emotion
to another like a monkey from tree to tree. It was unreasonable
to expect her to follow.

"You do love me still, Priscilla? Lately you seem to have
changed——"

"Yes, of course." She pulled her hand away from his and got
up quickly from the chair. "We must dress for dinner."

He looked at her searchingly, but in her distress she scarcely noticed his perplexity. If only he would not ask questions! She was so constituted as to loathe the need for lies; even half-truths made her uneasy. Alone in the bedroom, she was filled with self-reproach. These scenes, these bursts of bitterness and pleas for reassurance, were becoming more and more frequent in their lives. Something had gone out of their marriage, and she knew where to lay the blame; it was her love, not his, that had changed. It was not her fault, these things happened, but they could be mastered and controlled; and it was disconcerting that when she did indeed discipline her emotions she should be rewarded not by a glow of virtue but by feelings of dishonesty and guilt. Suddenly impatient and angry, she jumped to her feet and, taking from a cupboard a bottle of brandy, poured a generous helping and quickly drank it down. Humiliating to be so dependent; she drank it not for pleasure but to buy simplicity and support. There was a price; that would come later.

She entered the drawing-room smiling, the strained look gone from her expression; and Robert thought that he had never seen her appear more lovely or serene.

In a few days his luck changed suddenly. He came back from London enormously excited, hot on the trail of a position which, though out of England, was in a climate not inimical to children nor cursed with malaria. It seemed as if his persistence and painful effort might, after all, bear fruit. He departed for the north for a final interview with the managing director of the firm, full of confidence that at last the long and bruising search would be over.

It was on the next afternoon that Wigg came to her and said:

"There is a gentleman to see you, madam, in the library." His tone indicated his disapproval of the visitor, but Priscilla was not prepared to find Maurice Cornforth inspecting ranks of leather spines, inhaling the musty effluvium of untouched volumes. She stood still near the threshold, not offering to shake hands, and feeling her heart quicken its beat.

"I've come to say good-bye," Maurice said.

"You're going back already?"

"Not quite; but I'm going north and shan't be back in these parts before I sail."

"Maurice, you promised——"

"I know, but isn't it permissible to say good-bye? And there's something I must ask you before I go——"

They stood facing each other across the table, uncertain and confused. Her eyes searched his face, dwelling on the details: little lines of tiredness or dissipation under the heavy-lidded eyes, the way his strong dark hair sprang from the forehead, the half smile on his lips.

The tension was broken by the opening of the door, and Hubert Gresham walked in, erect as a soldier, surmounted by his ludicrous yellow thatch of hair, his clothes looking more than ever as if they had been worn by a character in Dickens. Searching for a book, he barely noticed the occupants, and would perhaps have ignored the visitor altogether if Priscilla had not made the introduction. Once the newcomer was forced on his attention he delivered a look of close inspection.

"Ah! Down here for the hunting?"

"I'm afraid not, sir. My quarry won't play."

"I beg your pardon?"

"Hunting doesn't come my way. I shall be in Africa by Christmas."

Uncle Hubert shook his head. "Unhealthy and demoralizing. In my opinion we should have left it all to the French, and reconquered North America. But my nephew enjoys it. He extracts a sense of grandeur from his position among these sable potentates, who show him a deference which has not been seen in this country since the fraudulent substitution of dirty scraps of paper for the gold coin of the realm. In fact I should not be surprised to hear that he keeps slaves—very well treated, no doubt."

In spite of herself, Priscilla was nettled. "Half his time used to be spent in seeing that people didn't keep slaves."

"A great mistake! One is faced with two alternatives, slaves or machines; slaves can be kept in order, machines enslave their masters. One has only to contrast our present situation with that which prevailed in Athens. . . . You are fond of reading?"

He addressed his question to Maurice, who had unthinkingly picked up a book from the table.

"When I get a chance, sir. But I'm afraid my tastes aren't very intellectual."

Uncle Hubert peered at the book which Maurice was holding, a best-seller of a few years back dealing with the family saga of a haberdasher. He frowned and made a clucking noise.

"Frippery! I never read books about the middle classes." Turning on his heel he vanished swiftly and with his usual silent tread.

It was a windy November day, with gleams of silvery sunshine striking through gaps in the storm-tossed clouds. Underfoot, grass was damp, borders bare and tidy save for wet bronze leaves that drifted about. Trees tossed their branches, to which a few leaves still clung in ragged decoration, like steers in a field throwing up their horns. Priscilla led her guest through a bare rose garden to a yew walk, their feet flattening small spindle-legged toadstools that had sprung out of the mossy path. They found a bench, weathered to a silvery grey, beside a yew hedge beaded with moisture. In their nostrils was the rich full smell of moss and moist earth and dying leaves and on their palates the sharp, bitter taste of winter that was beginning to creep out of the ground. The air was warm, yet with a cold core to it, like the feel of bones under living flesh.

They sat in silence for a little, conscious of the irrelevance of words. Priscilla fixed her thoughts on the vagaries of time. Months, years, flowed by unremembered, and then a few moments gripped hold of one's mind, to be lived over a thousand times. What would one's life consist of, at the end, but a small tally of such moments, like a handful of gems, the crystals of experience—that, and nothing more, the rest crumbled away. And might not such crystalline moments freeze the very air, imprinting on it a sensation to be caught by the minds of later comers and transmuted into apparitions? Centuries after perhaps her ghost would haunt this quiet yew-sheltered corner, living again in this moment of intensity.

Maurice broke the silence, saying quietly, as if he had followed her thoughts:

"Do you remember the evening when we climbed up that steep round hill, high above the plains, without shoes because it was so slippery? And then we flushed the leopard lying on a ledge near the top—almost trod on him, if you remember; and he looked like a yellow flame flashing across the rock, and simply melted away?"

"Yes; and we sat and watched the sunset, and it turned the puddles in the rocks into pools of blood."

"And then it got cold and the air sharp, but the rocks were still warm under our feet——"

"Like those ice-creams you have with a hot sauce, rather exciting. Why did you think of that?"

"Because on the way back you let me lift you down a little precipice and that was the first time—I suppose really the only time—you've been in my arms. And because I knew then that I loved you, for better or for worse."

"So long ago as that! Nothing you said——"

"What could I say? I knew you too well!"

"It would have been better if we'd gone on like that."

"Priscilla, will you listen?" She felt compelled to look at him and saw a new and desperate Maurice, his expression hard with intensity; and, meeting his eyes, she was afraid not of his feelings but of her own.

"This is our last chance! You know as well as I do that it isn't what we do that we regret, it's what we don't do—the timidities and things we funk, they're what come back at us. And for you—suppose there's not much time left, surely you've the right to take what life offers while you can! I'm not much, God knows, and I don't know why it should have happened, but there's something between us——"

"Little enough! Aren't you going too fast?"

Maurice smiled with something of his old expression, and the lift of the eyebrow she knew so well.

"I'm no good at making speeches, but there's no need. What's between us I think is love; together, I know we could find happiness, if that isn't too big a word. We could enjoy life together—more than either of us has ever enjoyed it before. Isn't that something?—everything, perhaps. And you've got a good deal of happiness due to you, and maybe little time left to collect it——"

"Evangelism in reverse! Really, Maurice, your invitation is a little sepulchral."

But her attempt at flippancy was not convincing, for he had exactly expressed her own thoughts; and, sensing his own advantage, he pressed on.

"I've got a bit of money put by; we could go off together somewhere, a place where we could sit in the sun, the south of France, perhaps, and after that——"

"You seem to forget that I'm married!"

"There's such a thing as divorce."

"And such a person as Robert."

Maurice moved impatiently on the seat. "And as yourself. Isn't it time you thought of that?"

"Is happiness to be found by chucking one's responsibilities overboard?"

"We could talk here all day, it gets nowhere. Priscilla, this is our last chance!"

She glanced again at his face, and in it read a look of pleading and hunger that all but dissolved her resolution.   She was afraid of what her own expression would reveal. This was a new kind of love, this ache, this drumming of blood in her ears, this longing to lie in his arms; new and murderous to all her promises. She leapt to her feet.

"You must give me time!"

"Time! Time's your enemy. Try to bargain with it and you're done. If just for once you'd do what you want to and hang the consequences——"

"But it's not my own life I'm playing with! No, Maurice, I must have time to think."

He got up too, wearing a look of defeat, and walked silently beside her towards the house.   But her thoughts were more favourable to him than he imagined. He was right, this was her last chance, and she knew it; and all her impulses urged her to make her bid for happiness before it was too late. Suppose she vanished to-morrow, just walked out—after an interval of turmoil, wouldn't the waters settle back calmly enough? Robert to his work, where his heart really lay; Robin, already beyond her reach, to his school pursuits and friends; wouldn't both be as happy, happier rather, once the shock had spent itself? Indeed it seemed that she was actually harming Robert's interests at present, forcing him to abandon his career and walk into a blind alley because of her physical weakness, and that to leave him before the harm was done might, if the truth were told, be best for them both.

But Robert was in the north, on the verge of committing himself to a new enterprise which he had sought, with great labour, for her sake. What a way to reward him—to vanish in his absence, simply turn her back and walk out of his life!

All at once, as they reached the house, she decided—decided not to decide, but to let fate do it for her. Events had fallen out almost as if ordered by the whims of destiny; let destiny then complete the affair. If Robert returned with success in his pocket, their new life settled, she would have no choice but to follow him. But if he failed it must be because his fate lay where she could not follow; and if she could not follow, then she would be free.

Turning to Maurice, she said: "I know what I'm asking subjects you to a kind of torture, but you must give me three days."

He shrugged his shoulders. "Anything you say. Only remember——" There was too much to be conveyed. "Promise me one thing."

"Of course."

"It's in case you decide against me—and against yourself, I believe. If you ever need a friend, if there's anything I can do, promise you'll send word. Wherever I am, I shan't fail."

Priscilla smiled. "You're very comforting, Maurice. It's always nice to know there's a ship ready to rush towards one's distress signal. But I don't think I shall sink."

Maurice touched her hand lightly and was gone. Slowly, she walked through the old stone porch and into the panelled hall that smelt of damp and floor polish and the mustiness of age, and the smoke of beech logs burning in the open fireplace. The crackle of flames and the steady ticking of a grandfather clock were the only sounds. So quiet, so settled, so old! The very windows, looking out on trees or fragments of garden, seemed built to keep out the light. The heavy door, swinging to behind her, closed with a muffled click, and the footfall of Wigg, passing through at that moment with a tea-tray, fell softly on the worn rugs and dark oak boards. The silver kettle and his bald head shone together in the greyness. He walked with the stealthy tread of a jailer, and the rattle of teaspoons sounded in her ears like the clink of keys.

Chapter Sixteen

IT was dark when the train from the north came in and dark when Robert climbed into the high old-fashioned car, smelling of horsehair upholstery, beside Priscilla. She could not see his face, but his whole manner was jaunty.

"I believe Uncle Hubert keeps this car for toadstool cultivation—it smells positively leprous to me. . . . Well, I've explored new reaches of the commercial jungle. I met a sort of Tarzan, swinging from the tree-tops by his toes, directing the activities of hordes of hairy-chested denizens."

"And there really was a job?"

"There was indeed. Good pay and prospects and a busy useful life in the Canadian overworld, selling very high-class shoes."

"Congratulations! Certainly if anyone deserved success . . ."

She tried to put warmth into her voice but in her own ears it sounded leaden. Robert as a shoe salesman! Absurd! He talked on eagerly as the car, in the hands of an elderly chauffeur, rumbled on with dignity and a good many creakings through the moist darkness.

"He was a captain of industry, I suppose—a fascinating chap: heavy, blunt, deliberate, quick, and very North Country. And no panelled pretentious offices, such as Londoners run to: all cluttered up and dingy, but a feeling of things going on all round you—telephones ringing, cables coming in, decisions going out. Very impressive!"

"It would have the charm of novelty, especially as regards decisions, for anyone in the Government service. But all this for shoes?"

"Oh no, shoes are only a small part of it. Produce buying— tanning—rubber—leather—he's a sort of octopus, I suppose. He's got factories, and now he wants to start selling the things they make; a new 'venture, a sort of gamble, I think. 'The swanky trade, that's what I'm after,' he said. 'Top prices, top quality, top clientèle—start at the top and work down. You learn at school that water doesn't run uphill. Nor does the reputation of a product. But sell the Prince of Wales, and every pimple-faced errand-boy will want to ride on the same donkey, whether it's a matter of cars or hats or boots.' The job is to start things off on those lines in Canada—sell shoes to the Governor-General, I suppose, and work down."

Priscilla could find nothing to say. She could not for a moment imagine Robert happily engaged in such pursuits, yet he seemed remarkably buoyant and pleased. He rattled on.

"We got on famously together. After a bit he said: 'You seem a level-headed sort of chap' (I imagine that was high praise); and he asked me to dinner. We dined at half-past six at the big hotel, all plush and potted palms and brass cuspidors; and what a meal! Oysters of course, joints of meat, hunks of ham, slabs of cheese, and pints of champagne. He told me the story of his life and enough about success in business to make me a millionaire if I could understand or remember half of it. He started by buying bankrupt cotton firms in the last slump and somehow sorting them out and selling shares later on when things recovered. He says that this slump will be worse and last longer, but he's not worried—he'll do the same again, I dare say."

"As a new master he sounds more lively than the Colonial Office, certainly. When do you start?"

"We came to that over liqueurs and half-crown cigars among the potted palms and marble pillars. By this time we'd got very matey. He offered to appoint me his sales manager for Canada, after training, of course—I was to work in one of his factories for a bit and then his office, and so on. So I thanked him and said: 'I like the sound of it, I like your methods and I might even like the job—but I'm not taking it.' He was surprised."

Priscilla turned in astonishment to look at him, but she could see nothing in the darkness except that he was grinning. For a moment she wondered whether he had been drinking, his behaviour was so odd. He must be mad! But, no less cheerfully, he went on:

"I wasn't able to explain to him and I don't think I can to myself, even now. It just came over me suddenly, perhaps as a result of the oysters and champagne; and I've never been more certain that I was right. Sitting there in that stuffy, solid atmosphere, prosperous business men all round, with a sort of hush over everything, I felt stifled, and thought of Midas—for that was what this man had become, a modern Midas, everything about him was solidified. I was afraid, quite terrified; I could almost feel his hand on my heart, beginning to freeze it into gold."

The car was entering the lime avenue and its headlamps conjured suddenly into existence the crinkled trunks that lined the long tunnel opening before them. Priscilla was speechless; the unpredictable nature of her husband had once more caught her off her guard.

"Absurd, of course, but all visions and voices are absurd, and for a moment my head was crammed with visions. I saw the old town where we've both so often walked and ridden together——"
He broke off, unable to find words to fix the shape of the pictures that had flashed through his mind: the dusty red streets crowded with men in long blue robes and folded turbans, the black-clad women gliding like lizards, water-carriers with dripping gourds crying out to the thirsty; the market thronged with its hawkers and veiled milk-sellers and tall Arabs selling embroidered saddle-cloths and the cruel long-cheeked bits, the noise and bustle and animation; and the quiet courtyards where men sat in silence at their narrow looms treadling with skinny legs, the rhythmical clatter of the sizers of cloth beating their clubs in unison against

the ground, the sour smell of the dye-pits, even the quacking of ducks scavenging on green-coated slimy pools—all that queer amalgam of dignity and squalor, tradition and change, vigour and decadence. It had come over him then, in some queer way, that they alone were living and he and his kind were dead—that sitting round in their plush and marble halls among the cigar-smoke, his companions were corpses embalmed in greed, on the brink of disintegration; and that the stream of life had carried the men of the walled city on and out of sight.

Priscilla exclaimed: "Surely you must have thought of all that before!"

"Yes, of course, but thought is a feat of balance, weighing pros against cons. This wasn't thought, it was conviction, something that springs up, ready-made. Everything else went out of my head, save a sort of home-sickness for a place that's never been my home and never can be, and for people who will always be foreign."

At dinner Robert was more cheerful than he had been since his gruelling search had started. His mind made up, his future decided, and—this, perhaps, was the essential point—that choice not commanded by circumstance but settled by his own free will, he was light-hearted and good-humoured. The sudden change, and the whole outcome, merely bewildered Priscilla. Had he tried and succeeded she would have felt bound to him; had he tried and failed she was to have been free; now he had succeeded, and thrown the price away. That should have left her more than ever unenslaved; of his own free will he was leaving her and Robin to follow his own bent; but for some baffling reason this did not seem to be the case. It was too confusing; she needed time to think.

Uncle Hubert withdrew after dinner, as he often did, leaving to them the small sitting-room used when there was no company: an untidy, comfortable room with a low ceiling and ancient mullioned windows, now curtained, looking on to a sheltered court. A wood fire smouldered in the open hearth, spreading a thin mist of smoke that blunted the outline of things and tinged the air with acridity. Priscilla, on the sofa, bent over her knitting in the indifferent light. A quiet, domestic scene: but her mind was rent with indecision, and Robert's no longer satisfied. Leaning against the stone fireplace, he remarked.

" 'I don't know whether to laugh or to cry.' What a lot of life there is in that remark! The trouble is, I don't know whether *you'll* laugh or cry; whether from your point of view this is a sort of amputation, as it is for me, or whether you'll be glad to get rid of me and be left in peace."

"Don't be absurd, Robert; of course I——"

"No, don't say that." She looked up in surprise, his voice was so peremptory. "That sort of response is automatic, like the jerking of a dog's hind legs when you tickle its tummy. We've got past that now, both of us."

Leaning back against the big stone fireplace, he watched her fingers' rhythmical motions with her knitting, and the light shining on her hair. Now that the way ahead was settled, he could scarcely bear the thought of his loneliness and above all of her peril: if death itself should strike, he would be out of reach. Turning back to inspect the fire, he said gently:

"And you, Priscilla, what do you want to do? You'll go back to your mother's?"

Her fingers paused in their motion and she, too, stared at the fire. She had made a bargain with herself, heads or tails, and it had fallen out that she had won her freedom. Robert had, in a sense, renounced her in favour of his black sycophants: she could leave him now with little sense of guilt. Better take what life offered than sit with folded hands and wait for the blow! Robert added, prodding logs with his toe:

"I believe half your heart has always stayed there. You'll be happier in your own village than anywhere in Africa—if you'll only take care of your health. . . ."

In face of her silence, he felt a need to hold her by talk; a foretaste of loneliness, like the first chill of autumn, touched his heart.

"I shall become one of those," he said aloud, "who live from leave to leave—something I've always rather despised. So much for condemning others without first meeting the temptation! And I shall become a terrible plague to the locals, who prefer above all a man who gets on with his polo and doesn't thrust his head into all sorts of beehives. To kill my own boredom I shall make everyone's life a burden."

Talk of this sort jarred on her nerves. She retorted impatiently:

"That's all rather a pose. You're perfectly happy putting your fingers into other people's pies; why not admit it?"

"Is that the only motive you'll allow me—an itch to interfere?"

"Surely you don't deny that the reason your work absorbs you is because you're dabbling in other people's lives—playing at being a little tin god?"

Robert kicked a log sharply with his toe and shook his head. "I deny that completely. One interferes, certainly; but even the occupants of Mount Olympus, who were highly whimsical in their interventions, had some idea of what they were after. We have none. And neither Mount Olympus nor Heaven came under the orders of an immense, impersonal machine that spewed forth a sort of perpetual snowstorm of regulations and memoranda."

"But you're a part of that machine. It isn't a sense of purpose that makes you feel so God-like, it's a sense of power."

"There's little enough of that to be had!"

"Every time a man bows to you, or asks your advice; whenever you deliver judgment, the respect which people show as you walk by—all these are juicy little mouthfuls for the power-sense inside. No wonder you get fat!"

"Those are very trivial things."

"Do you call it a trivial thing to change men's lives? You're a part of the new super-state, which is having a sort of trial run in the provinces before being put on in the capital—here, at home. You can no more give it all up than an addict can renounce his drug—nor should you, I dare say, for you'd soon wilt without it."

"It's all very well to run down the itch for power, but one might equally condemn the fear of responsibility. Someone's got to do the dirty work of running the world and it's far from being all beer and skittles. Look at England—a sort of universal policeman, with all the urchins in the world trying to knock off his helmet, and no one even thinking of a word of thanks. Wouldn't he be better off if he took off his boots, put his feet on the mantel-piece and told the rest of the world to go to blazes? If you really think chaos, civil war, famine, corruption, oppression and a sort of general free-for-all are better than the present state of affairs, then send us back to cultivate our own back garden, which many of us would much prefer. But not otherwise."

Priscilla was silent, frowning at the work in her hands. It was useless to argue with Robert and of course he was right, when it came to practical politics. Her own feelings were the result less of logic than of a deep unreasoning resentment against the whole system of which he was part. She hated it not for what it did to nations or history but for what it did to herself, and to people she had known or still knew: to the families it had parted, the young men it had killed, those it had embittered or broken; and she hated it for the home she had never had, the children she had never borne, the death which awaited her round the next bend in the road.

Robert was staring at the smoking logs with a look of concentration, feeling the need to explain his motives and for once searching for words.

"All that's in a way beside the point. Years ago I made a promise and took on a job. The work is far from finished—it never will be finished, I suppose—and so the promise still holds. You remember the curse that fell on the half-hearted ploughman? —the curse of self-reproach, of course. So if I push on to the end of the furrow it won't be so much from a lust for power as from fear of the trouble I should get into if I turned back."

"So you believe that promises count?"

Robert smiled. "Why ask that? You do, at any rate."

"You can't assume that I shall always keep them."

He looked round, surprised; her eyes were on the fire and her fingers fiddled with a piece of tangled wool in her lap.

"I should never want to hold anyone to a promise that had become a kind of bondage."

"You're holding to yours."

"Ah! But I want to hold to it. That was what I found out among the potted palms and cuspidors."

"And let the rest of the world go hang!"

"And one's own peace of mind. It's an old choice."

Priscilla smiled a little. "You're giving an unfashionable answer. A sense of duty goes with stove-pipe trousers, mutton-chop whiskers and families of sixteen."

He shrugged his shoulders. "I've never managed to keep up with the latest fashions. . . . It's my fault that our marriage is going to become such a miserable disembodied affair, and if ever you decide that a husband you'll see for a few months every couple of years isn't what you bargained for, well then——" He bent down to put more logs on the fire. "You're free, as you've always been, to choose your own way."

She did not answer, and when he had built up the fire he added: "I shall go out for a stroll, I think."

Mechanically, she responded: "It's colder, don't forget your coat."

When he had gone Priscilla jumped to her feet and roamed about the room, picking up books and putting them down again, patting out cushions and re-arranging the logs on the fire. She almost hated Robert now. Of his own free will he had chosen the course that would set her free; he had almost thrust upon her what she had half resolved to steal. Yet how cunningly he had poisoned the cup! Both had made promises, he to Cæsar, she in the sight of God. If he honoured the lesser, could she default on the greater vow? For him to say that she was free did not make her so.

Perhaps, she thought, it is stupid to fuss about one's own self-respect. Humility, that old forgotten virtue, might require of an individual that he set less store on his own opinion. If the choice lay between one form of egotism and another, did it matter much which form one chose? But even that way out was closed. It mattered, because until her last breath was drawn she must live always with one unsleeping comrade, her conceit of herself. Others would come and go; passion wear thin, love shrivel into toleration, ambition shrink to a poor hankering after safety; but this companion would never vanish or fade.

She had left her little riddle to be solved by the falling out of events. In the end not fate but character, Robert's and hers, had decided. There lay the point of intersection between destiny and will: no choice could be free, since the shape of the instrument that must make it was already determined; the fluid metal must take the curves of the mould, the leather bear the stamp of the die.

Going to a desk littered with papers, she took up a pen. She had scarcely dared to think of Maurice. Now, pen in hand, she knew that he, not she, would be the true victim, and as she signed the brief letter she seemed to hold an executioner's weapon in her hand.

PART THREE

Chapter One

1933

IN their owner's eyes the *Chanticleer's* offices formed a beacon of modernity rising from the wastes of a change-resisting, down-at-heel town. The concrete blocks and corrugated iron of which they were built proclaimed their up-to-date superiority to the hovels crowding round them, no better than ant-heaps, and, like them, of mud. It was true that two rooms and a narrow veranda were, as yet, the full extent of the building, and true also that the money had given out before a floor could be installed; in spite of such temporary imperfections, the owner and founder of the *Chanticleer* felt for his achievement a pride that could not have been surpassed by the mightiest press baron of Europe surveying his latest glass-and-chromium cathedral.

In his eyes the two rooms were but ante-chambers to a great edifice from whose tower the whole city lay spread at his feet. In apartment after apartment, as he walked round every morning, his men were toiling and hurrying, pausing only to stand to attention and then bow to the ground as he passed; in the whole town, the whole Protectorate, there was no such noble building and the newspaper it enshrined thrust into every corner of the land. Even the Governor, his breakfast borne to him by a procession of white-robed servants, would say sharply, before he plunged his spoon into his paw-paw: 'Where is my copy of the *Chanticleer*? Do you not know that I cannot eat breakfast until I have seen what the editor has to say?' And a boy would come running with a copy on a silver tray.

As he cycled to his office Benjamin Morris looked forward to a busy day, for the *Chanticleer* went to press that evening; that is to say, the editor tucked the typewritten sheets into his brief-case and left them on his way home with the owner of a small hand-press. The printer was a Moslem of sketchy education, and the demands of his faith, and his own indifference to time, combined to make the text haphazard and the date of publication vague. Now, Benjamin reflected with chagrin, Ramadan was approaching; for a month everyone would be sleepy, edgy and unreliable, and he would find it more difficult than ever to din into the printer's obstinate head the need to produce the weekly batch of *Chanticleers* within a few days of the proclaimed date of publication.

Passing through his outer office, he nodded briskly at the general clerk, Mr. Robbins: a long-faced, solemn young man with a somewhat ecclesiastical manner and a suit from which his long arms and legs stuck out like stalks. He was a southerner from the coast, well educated and exceptionally reliable, save when he managed to evade his creditors for long enough to buy a bottle of gin. Benjamin did not really find him sympathetic—no fire, no fervour, his mind was a heap of wet grass instead of the dry tinder which ideas, like sparks, would ignite—but he knew his work and had been hired at a cheap rate, owing to an incident of which Benjamin had come to hear connected with a debt, a rapacious money-lender and the accounts of the European firm for which he had previously worked.

Benjamin settled himself at a desk deep in papers, in a room whose uneven floor of beaten mud contrasted oddly with the plastered walls on which hung shiny school maps, pictures from the illustrated English papers and groups or snapshots taken at Oxford, depicting the editor gowned for study or clothed for sport. As he applied himself to his papers his staff began to drift in and soon the outer office was full of chatter and commotion. There was Mr. Montgomery the accountant, a round fat little man whose reputation as a raconteur stood so high that even Moslem passers-by, who disapproved of these foreigners in their city, would drop in to hear his latest imitation of a quarrel between the Emir's vizier and his favourite. A cousin of his was employed as Mr. Robbins' assistant; two or three messengers hung about, supplementing their miniscule pay by gifts from those anxious to see their names in the paper, and going off now and then to the post office on news-gathering expeditions. Finally there was the sub-editor, Mr. Fitzpatrick, who occupied the grandest desk in the room and carried on a crafty and un-flagging battle to have it moved into the sanctum of his master.

Activity quickened as the morning wore on and the heat in the *Chanticleer's* office mounted. Benjamin himself was busy re-writing a pungent editorial on the infamous state of the town's water supply, which had remained unchanged for about five hundred years; some brilliant new metaphors had come to him during the night. Mr. Fitzpatrick, with the advice of Mr. Montgomery, was trying to slip a report he had written himself of a cousin's Christian wedding into an obscure position where it might escape the editor's eye, between the market reports and a bush story sent in by a man whose brother had been turned into an owl. The editor, courting Moslem readers, frowned on reports of Christian ceremonies; but this one had an unusual feature, and Mr. Fitzpatrick, printing in capitals the headline: 'Minister swoons from over-eating', hoped that it might creep by.

Outside a small crowd of men, young and old, waited lethargically in the shade of the narrow porch, squatting on their haunches: men with grievances to relate, with help to be sought in litigation, with enemies to blacken or friends to advance. They were in no hurry; if necessary they would wait all day, watching the street's endless panorama: the little donkeys trotting briskly, like grey mushroom-stalks under their voluminous white-robed riders; women walking barefoot to market or returning with baskets balanced on their heads loaded high with provisions; water-carriers with their big dripping gourds; grubby children, tall, dark-faced camel-owners, the pot-maker with his wares, the stump-armed beggar whining for alms. The watchers lacked neither sights to entertain nor topics to discuss, and soon the dust at their feet was bespattered with the chewed pulp of kola nuts whose bitter juice had cleansed their mouths and assuaged their thirst. Sooner or later each would enjoy his moment of drama and celebrity; until then, all could wait.

Now and again Benjamin, in the throes of composition, would stride to the window and observe the group huddled in the shade of his porch, some turbaned and Moslem, a few Christian and trousered, each group keeping a little apart. All these people were waiting to see him, Benjamin Morris, founder and editor of the *Chanticleer*—looking to him to redress their wrongs and offer them advancement—to him, and not to the Resident or the Emir! They sensed already which was the waning and which the rising star. Let them wait; he was a busy and important man, one moment of whose time was worth a year of theirs; but he was beneficent also, he existed to help others. *Noblesse oblige!* He turned back to his desk strengthened and refreshed to wrestle with his duty.

For life had been no bed of roses since his return. He had found many changes. The old Emir had gone—gone at last, toppled over like a rotten tree eaten away at the roots. That

Benjamin had been one of the eaters he would scarcely have
admitted; he saw himself more as a cleansing fire. But that he
had been in touch with those who had intrigued against the
Emir he did not deny. They were men of enterprise and public
spirit, engaged on a noble crusade to rid the kingdom of a
reactionary ruler who thrust aside reforms, licked the feet of the
European, exacted grinding taxes and, worst of all, kept in
office his own clique of relatives and friends.

Opposition to his mis-rule had crystallized round the person
of one of his many nephews, Aboubakar, a forceful and able
young man with a smattering of western education super-
imposed on the usual Koranic foundation. The steps taken to
undermine the Emir by his party, supported on the one hand by
Moslem conservatives and on the other by firebrand reformers,
had been devious and many, and Benjamin was by no means
acquainted with them all. In the old days the matter would
have been simple: a quick knife-thrust in the night or, should
the Emir scent in time what was in the wind, the raising of an
army and a brief and thrilling struggle for the throne. Now,
European rifles were on the side of the Emir and could not help
but prevail; therefore by subtle and well-planned means the
Europeans must be won over.

Fortunately the old Emir had played into his enemies' hands.
There was, for instance, the matter of the girls' school which,
in defiance of orthodox Moslem opinion, he had started in his
own women's quarters. At first all had gone well, and the daily
attendance of an old and respectable *malam* had gone far to
silence the mutterings of those who believed that women's
schooling ran counter to the Holy Writ. Then, one day, a
Government inspector had arrived. New to the province and to
the Moslem world, a young, impatient free-thinker, he had
bubbled over with an ill-concealed contempt for the travesty
of education he had found in these Koranic schools. He had
demanded the right to inspect the Emir's establishment. The
Emir, more nettled by his brusque uncivil manner than shocked
by the proposal, had refused to sanction this violation of the
purdah. The inspector, on his side determined not to be fobbed
off by reactionary religious prejudices, had insisted; and in a
fit of anger the Emir had retorted by closing the school.

This was a single incident, of course; but a fiery report sent in
by the inspector had thrust under the Government's nose one
more piece of evidence of the Emir's reluctance to countenance

the reforms yearly becoming more fashionable in high quarters. Benjamin himself, who was in correspondence with Aboubakar, had been able to make his contribution. His efforts had resulted in several Parliamentary questions directed to reveal the dire state of a corner of the Empire containing upwards of a million people and without a single school for girls. This theme had even formed the basis of a short but trenchant article in one of the anti-Government newspapers.

But such contributory gnawings away at the tree's roots were insufficient, as Aboubakar and his friends well knew, to topple it over. For only two misdemeanours would the Government bring itself to depose a ruler; for murder, and for misappropriation of funds.

No quirk or oddity of the ruling power was harder to understand than the British attitude towards public finance. That the rulers of a country enriched themselves was self-evident; it was, after all, the reason for their assumption of all the burdens and dangers of office; as well accuse the sun of being hot, or the leopard of seeking food for its young. The British themselves favoured this obvious principle—everyone could see for himself the wealth and splendour of the Governor, and where did he draw his money save from taxes?—yet they decried it in others. The only explanation that would fit their conduct appeared to be an intense and morbid greed. The payment of tribute was a recognized need, but never before had there been such a skinflint conqueror. Others had been content, so long as they received a fair payment, to leave the system of collection alone; only the British continually pried and admonished, deciding not only the amount of the tax but the method of gathering it and the share each individual should receive—afraid lest they should be cheated of a few pence.

It was with a good deal of satisfaction that Aboubakar had perceived that this very rapacity could be used against them. That the Treasurer was feathering his own nest no one doubted or condemned; if this could be demonstrated to the Government, and if the Emir himself could be implicated, the plot was as good as concluded; for the Emir, already in the Government's bad graces, would be speedily deposed.

Aboubakar had therefore set himself like a hound on the Treasurer's track; and the means by which he had obtained his evidence, and the extent to which that evidence had been genuine or faked, were matters of which Benjamin knew nothing. Nor did he know the full story of the end. That the Treasurer had suspected the plot was obvious, and the attempt on Aboubakar's life, thwarted in the nick of time, had clearly been his retaliation; but the assassin had escaped, and a suspect caught a few days later had either allowed himself to be beaten to death without betraying his master or (much more likely) had been the victim of a mistake. After that, matters had moved quickly. One of Aboubakar's spies had brought word of a counter-plot to burn down the Treasury and so destroy the evidence that had been slowly pieced together. Aboubakar had decided to risk all on a bold stroke. The Treasurer's own house had been fired and, in the confusion, he himself strangled and his body hurled into a pit, where it lay hidden until the following morning.

Then a hue and cry shook the city for days; everyone was nervous, excited and deliciously stimulated; wild rumours flew about the market and through the streets. British policemen arrived, hundreds were questioned and a trail of hints and half-confessions seemed to lead back to the Emir's palace. Finally a man came forward to confess that he had been entrusted with the secret task of handing over a heavy bag of coins to two masked men, who had let fall enough to suggest their complicity in a plot, emanating from the palace, to assassinate the Treasurer. But there the trail ended, and the masked men were never identified. The Treasurer's papers, meanwhile, had been impounded by the Government and irregularities of the gravest kind had been revealed. There was no doubt that the Treasurer had been consistently defrauding the public purse over a number of years and in a manner so skilful that it had eluded the eye of the British officials. There was no doubt also, in the official mind, that not only a number of subordinates but the Emir himself must have connived at the frauds.

Many consultations followed, to which the Governor himself was a party. It was decided, in the end, not to proceed against the Emir, but that he could no longer hold office was abundantly clear. The Government was always extremely reluctant to interfere with an existing native authority; but in this case not only was the Emir implicated in fraud and even in the suspicion of a murder designed to save himself from exposure, he had quite clearly lost his people's confidence. The time had come for him to make way for a younger, bolder, more popular and more progressive man. The Emir himself relinquished his office with dignity and restraint—although, in a speech to the council called to accept his abdication, he denied all complicity in the crimes.

Unpredictable as the white overlords were, no one supposed that they would make such an elementary mistake as to leave the old Emir alive and unimpaired while transferring their support to the new. But that was exactly what they did. In the old days not only the Emir but all his sons, numbering perhaps thirty or so, would have been dispatched, or at the very least blinded: a custom admittedly harsh, but found by experience to be necessary if the greater evils of endless intrigue and civil wars were to be avoided. The British, however, merely removed the Emir, together with his wives and smaller children, to an isolated part of a mountainous territory some hundreds of miles away. Although he was kept under close observation he was not a prisoner, and his new headquarters were not so remote as to preclude the coming and going of friends. Nor did they molest his sons; in fact it was doubtful if they even knew the identity of all of them and several were actually employed in Government service.

Aboubakar was the obvious choice for a successor. He was duly chosen, and ruled in his uncle's stead; and the authorities congratulated themselves on an awkward corner satisfactorily turned.

It was Aboubakar's rise to power that had caused Benjamin's return to his native land. The two were not friends—between a believer and an infidel of a slave race no equality could be assumed—but they entertained for each other a good deal of respect. Aboubakar had long ago marked down this young man with such an exceptional degree of western education as a useful tool in his future dealings with Europeans; and Benjamin, a man without a family (that rarest of African freaks) was highly susceptible to the flattery implied in the attentions of the Emir's nephew, a rich and eminent prince. The outcome of correspondence between the two, coinciding, as it did, with a further and this time fatal financial crisis in the affairs of the African Freedom League, was that Benjamin, armed with a few hundred pounds of capital unexpectedly subscribed by one or two of the League's European supporters, arrived in Aboubakar's capital to become founder and first editor of the *Chanticleer*.

It was soon clear to him that his vision of great reforms under an enlightened new ruler were not to be realized. Indeed, things seemed to be growing worse rather than better. Europeans put it all down to the slump. No one could get a fair price any longer for the fruits of his labour; the pulse of trade, the city's life-blood, slackened; stringency crept into every compound, want and uncertainty crouched at every door. Even the Government pared its business; and men who had departed on the pilgrimage intending, as from time immemorial, to work their way across a continent to the sacred city and back again, found themselves suspended at some distant and inclement spot, penniless, and unable to move in either direction.

But a purely economic explanation was too prosaic for Benjamin; he had more piquant reasons. His alliance with Aboubakar precluded him from laying these misfortunes at the new Emir's door, although he soon sensed that the failure of taxes to lighten and of wealth to flow had quickly tarnished the glitter of his patron's initial popularity. But the Emir's masters had no such protection. Almost everything that happened, or did not happen, could be attributed either to their tyrannous greed or stiff-necked sloth; and Benjamin made full use of his opportunities. After all, he argued, overseas trade was a foreign invention; Europeans had financed the merchants, established the canteens, built the railways and summoned the ships; it would indeed be ingenuous to believe them when they turned round and complained that they could not control this creature of their own making, that they were equally injured by its disorders. Such explanations were a typical piece of British hypocrisy, and Benjamin had no doubt at all in his own mind that the whole slump had been arranged in order to force down prices paid to the poor African grower by the rich foreign merchant; and he said so, boldly and repeatedly, in the *Chanticleer*.

For himself, he felt for the first time the glow of achievement. At last he was able to take sweet revenge for the nagging sense of inferiority brought about by association with a people and a scale of values not his own, by a fate that had obliged him to be for ever a poor guest in the house of a rich man. Now he, Benjamin, and he alone, had found how to fight his masters with their own weapons, with barbs that could prick under their armour of certainty; and this knowledge was as sweet to him as honey, as exciting to his senses as a draught of warm beer.

Chapter Two

BENJAMIN'S editorial on the town water supply was soon done, and he whipped through the pieces of copy brought to him for final selection, weeding out the majority, especially those selected by Mr. Fitzpatrick from the English papers. News from a western world which scarcely one of his readers had ever seen or envisaged he knew to be quite unimportant. Of much more interest were the usual rumours and bits of gossip flying round the town—that the Emir's youngest wife had been caught with a lover, that a man had betrayed the whereabouts of a swamp into which cattle were driven to escape the tax-count, that a son of the old Emir had vowed not to lay scissors to his beard until the injustice to his exiled father had been redeemed.

At last the patient squatters by his door were to be rewarded. Shouting to Mr. Robbins to bring in the callers, he lit a cigarette and leant back in his chair, cocking his knees against the desk and running a pocket comb through his short woolly hair. He had grown into a thin and bony individual whose well-proportioned caste of feature and relatively thin lips suggested a streak of Arab or Berber blood. His shoulders were a little rounded, he had an air of pent-up energy and excitability that contrasted strongly with the easy-going yet dignified poise of his fellows. To invest himself with a learned appearance he wore horn-rimmed spectacles, although he could see rather better without them.

Mr. Robbins walked to the outer door and surveyed the waiting group with a lugubrious expression. The procedure was well known to everyone. A small fee was due to the clerk for arranging an interview, and the highest bidder won first place. On this occasion, a tall and bearded man who had been standing aloof from the others marched up to the door and placed in Mr. Robbins' hand, with a most disdainful air, a coin worth at least double the usual sum. Taken aback, Mr. Robbins made way for this imperious individual, who wore the robes and turban of a Moslem with an embroidered scarf flung loosely over his bearded chin.

Without pausing to be conducted thither, the visitor walked

haughtily into the editor's office. Hastily slipping his comb into his pocket, Benjamin greeted him and offered a chair, but his visitor, glancing at it as if it had been a piece of ordure returned a grave greeting and a remained standing, his arms folded over his chest.

"My name," he said, speaking in his own language, "is Abdulahai; I have come on business of state. God is great!"

Benjamin inclined his head slightly and examined his visitor under cover of sharpening a pencil-point. The face seemed familiar, yet he could not place it: one of those dark, graven, strong-featured faces so often found among the Moslem nobility, hard as bronze, with the single purpose of the warrior and the spareness of the desert ascetic. He looked the sort of man who would use the husks to make his coffee.

"It is written in your journal," he went on, "not once but many times, that your concern is to see justice done to the people."

"It is well known that the fearless voice of the *Chanticleer* is always lifted——"

But the visitor cut him short with a gesture.

"Then you have surely seen that since the greatest of all injustices was done to the rightful ruler of this kingdom the people have not prospered, but have fallen into poverty and despair. Is it to be wondered at, when they are vassals of a thief and a usurper? To-day the honest craftsman cannot buy milk for his children, the leper begs in vain for a few farthings; even the rain comes fitfully and the locusts gather. God is great, and what is this but a sign of God's displeasure?"

"Even the *Chanticleer* does not number God among its readers——" Benjamin began; but again his visitor interrupted, ignoring his flippancy.

"Let us come to business! Men of honour and influence in this town are grieved that a dog so base as the present Emir, and a cause so false, should have the support of a person such as yourself, of much learning, whose words are quoted in the market-place and whose opinions are respected by the ignorant."

This recognition of his power by one who affected to despise him fell sweetly on Benjamin's ears.

"I give my support to those who deserve it," he said. "The poorest and lowliest man in the emirate——"

"No doubt," the impatient visitor again interrupted. "It is not denied that you exercise an influence that can be to a ruler either a staff or a scourge. You content yourself at present to be the staff of a man who stole from his uncle the robes of authority. But his days are numbered; God has judged him. Men who flatter those whom God has condemned will themselves he destroyed. It would be wiser to become his scourge."

Benjamin was not surprised by this suggestion. He had guessed from the first that his visitor was an emissary of the deposed ruler's party. All at once it came to him why Abdulahai's features seemed familiar: they bore a strong likeness to the old Emir. No doubt this was one of his sons. In spite of the resentment aroused by the air of patronage invariably present in the manner of Moslem nobles, Benjamin was impressed by Abdulahai's frankness. A person who so openly proclaimed his hostility to the ruling Emir must be very sure of his strength.

"The men for whom I speak," Abdulahai went on, "are not without wealth, nor do they expect the services of their supporters to go unrewarded. They will pay you, and my business is to discover your price."

Abdulahai, as he himself instantly realized, had made a false step. His contempt for these upstart slaves who had rolled like dogs in the filth of western heresy was such that he could not bring himself to treat with them as equals, arriving at the point after full discourse and in a gentlemanly way. Instead he had handled this infidel as if he had been a clerk in one of the canteens, and of course the man reared up like a spurred horse.

"The *Chanticleer* is not for sale!" Benjamin exclaimed, pushing back his chair. "How dare you insult me, the man of justice and voice of the people! Do you think that I can be bought like a cow in the market, or like one of your concubines?"

Abdulahai, incensed by such impertinence, stepped forward with flashing eyes and raised arm; but then let the arm drop and curbed his anger. He was here to win an ally, not to bandy words with a conceited and contemptible clerk.

"You mistake me," he said haughtily. "Or perhaps I am ignorant of the customs followed by foreign *malams* such as yourself. I ask you only to support the cause of justice, and I repeat that those who do so will not lack their reward in the next world, nor, if they are impatient, in this."

But Benjamin was deeply injured. He sprang to the door and flung it open.

"And I repeat," he said loudly and in English, so that those in the outer office could hear, "that you waste your time in tempting the editor of the *Chanticleer* with bribery! You will excuse me, I am busy; Mr. Robbins, please usher in the next caller."

Abdulahai's hand leapt to his belt and for a moment Benjamin quailed before the murder in his eye; but then swiftly, as if neither the office nor its *canaille* existed, he strode from the room, his very robes seeming to swish and quiver with outraged dignity. Mr. Montgomery's face dissolved into delighted laughter. This was the most delicious titbit that had come his way for weeks; how the market would cackle to-morrow! Mr. Fitzpatrick looked perturbed and Mr. Robbins grave. Already he had ascertained that this was indeed the old Emir's son, and leader of a growing faction that opposed Aboubakar. Later on, Mr. Robbins would pay him a visit. If Abdulahai had offered the lion too little there might be pickings for the jackal, perhaps.

Benjamin turned back into his private office and paced the floor, still fuming. The impertinence, the cold insulting effrontery, to come to him, editor and owner of a great newspaper, to ask his price as if he were a mere seller of sandals! A man of no education, unversed in world affairs, ignorant of any civilized language; a man who fell down on his knees to babble dogma to an empty sky, who would travel for thousands of miles to kiss a dirty stone—a mere meteorite! And this worshipper of a lump of mineral would patronize him, Benjamin Morris, conversant with the experiments of every scientist from Bacon and Mendel to Morgan and Haldane, familiar with the works of Spinoza and Voltaire and Shaw! What did this barbarian idiot know of the third law of thermo-dynamics, of Ricardo's theory of rents or the Freudian interpretation of dreams? He had never even heard of such things! He, Benjamin, could quote from a hundred books of whose very existence Abdulahai was utterly oblivious, from the aphorisms of French essayists to the weighty conclusions of German philosophers; and, cudgelling his remarkable memory, he quoted aloud: "The teleology of nature is thus made to rest on a transcendental theology, which takes the ideal of supreme ontological perfection as a principle of systematic unity. . . ." But the entry of his next visitor interrupted his declamation.

By the time he had completed his day's work, stuffed the typescript of next week's issue into his brief-case and mounted his bicycle to pedal, by way of the printer's, through the hot torpid afternoon, his anger had quite subsided. In fact he had begun to wonder whether he had not been over-hasty. The look in Abdulahai's eyes, the instinctive motion of his hand towards a concealed dagger, came back to him with unpleasant clarity, and the recollection of several highly uncivilized incidents entered his mind: the late Treasurer's murder, swift stabs in the darkness that sometimes ended a quarrel, the finding of anonymous bloated bodies rising to the surface of slimy pools. Yes, perhaps it had been unwise to insult so openly a man of Abdulahai's standing.

And in one respect at least the fiery young man had spoken truly: the condition of the town had not improved since his uncle's accession. All sorts of hopes and visions and promises had simply fizzled out. The new broom had swept nothing away. No need to put it all down to the displeasure of God! The new Emir had brought it all on himself by ignoring the opportunities that lay right under his nose. Although nothing had been openly said, Benjamin had taken it for granted that a man of his own exceptional talents would find positions of the highest honour and influence thrust upon him when he returned to a city where none was his equal in education and knowledge of the world. He had expected that the Emir would, as a matter of course, consult him on questions of high policy; it had been, in fact, the virtual certainty that he would become a power behind the throne that had decided him to return.

But matters had not so fallen out. Whenever Benjamin had sought an audience he had been treated with courtesy, but never had Aboubakar consulted him of his own accord. It was the Emir, certainly, who had secured for him a site in the town and made a trifling contribution towards his expenses, but now that this sum was exhausted it had not been renewed. And he had been offered no high position in the Emir's employ. The more he thought about it, the more he wondered whether the pig-headed Aboubakar had not forfeited his right to the *Chanticleer's* support.

His way to the printer's lay past the house of a man of whom Benjamin knew nothing save that he had an unmarried daughter of slender figure, graceful carriage and lustrous eyes. On two occasions he had happened to encounter this young girl, once emerging from the outer door and once entering it, accompanied each time, of course, by an older woman whom he took to be her mother, or a female attendant. Like her elderly chaperon she was swathed from head to foot in fine black muslin with a spangled cloth draped over her shoulders. He could see little but her eyes, shaded with kohl, and part of a smooth light bronze complexion. Nevertheless she had made a deep impression. In all his life, Benjamin thought, he had seen no eyes so soft, so deep and so alluring. The hand, too, was fine and delicate—the hand of a girl of quality, dyed with henna to a lovely and exciting shade of red. From the size and position of the house he judged that her father was a man of substance, a merchant probably, who would expect a costly payment for his daughter. But even if he, Benjamin, came to pay suit in a car with a uniformed driver, even if he offered glittering jewels and herds of sleek cows, he would be rejected—he, an Oxford graduate, a newspaper proprietor, a distinguished man—rejected by an ignorant haggler in a savage market-place!

To-day he was unlucky, the gate was shut. As he pedalled slowly by he searched the small unglazed windows that overlooked the street for some sign, perhaps even the glimpse of a cloth or flutter of a hand; and suddenly he was rewarded. A face appeared at a window and the eyes, those deep and shining eyes, gazed out—surely straight into his! Was that not a toss of the head, a gesture of recognition? He could not be sure, for the head withdrew immediately, and at the same instant his bicycle wobbled alarmingly, obliging him to hop off. He stood there transfixed, gazing up at the hollow window. But she did not return; and after a little he reluctantly mounted his bicycle, feeling almost as if his feet were caught up in glue. He wanted to stand there all the afternoon, gazing at the window. How absurd! All this for an ignorant little girl to whom he hadn't even spoken, and would never be able to speak! Gripping the handle of his brief-case, he pedalled resolutely on.

A legless beggar in the shadow of a doorway watched him out of sight. Then he glanced at the house, naming to himself its owner and the owner's daughter now of marriageable age, and adding one more little fact, hard and bright and tiny as a bead, to the queer and enormous assortment of unimportant facts that filled his mind. Years of poverty and degradation had taught him that, just as scraps picked out of garbage may be eaten, so the trivialities of other men's lives may have their value. His mouth, adorned by two yellow fangs which hung like lanterns from rotting gums, opened in a grin, and then twisted into a whine for alms as a long-legged man on a short-legged donkey went jogging by.

Chapter Three

MORE than four years had gone by since the Beggs had seen the low, leafy outline of the Protectorate's shore come into view and reveal its detail of iron-roofed sheds, white houses screened by verdant trees and Negroes in tattered attire lounging by the wharf, and since their nostrils had breathed in its flat and marshy odour. Both were delighted to be back. They had enjoyed their interlude; the setting had been beautiful, the work fresh, the people exotic; but to return to the friendly faces and familiar customs of the country they knew so well was, when all was said and done, a sort of home-coming.

And it was sweet to Freddy Begg to return as chief to the Secretariat where he had toiled for so long in various junior positions. Leaning against the rail in a new and still uncrumpled tropical suit topped off with a neat black tie, and watching the approaching shore, his mind went back to his first arrival, more than twenty years ago. What a poor timid creature he had been then! A third-class commercial clerk, glued to his books, under-paid and thrown into confusion by a mere word from the general manager. Freddy smiled a little, polishing his glasses, recollecting with a flash of surely merited satisfaction the Birthday Honours' list with its mention of his C.M.G. Once he had been ashamed of his connection with the Coastal Trading Company and of his beginnings as a clerk. Trade and economics had scarcely been decent then, but now they had become fashionable, and this early experience of his was counted not a blemish but an asset. Talking to Coverdale, the general manager, he would say: "You'll correct me if I'm wrong, but as I recall it, when I was on your side of the fence, the main difficulty there . . ."; and Coverdale, smiling, would reply: "I can tell you, it's a relief to deal with someone in the Government who knows his onions on the commercial side." *Autres temps, autre mœurs!* Yes, it was pleasant to be back: the bustle, the greetings, the news of old friends.

That night they dined at Government House, delighted with the spaciousness of the well-kept rooms, with the unobtrusive yet ever-present sense of ceremony, the shining silver, the polished table, the banks of flowers perfectly arranged. Freddy's late Governor had spent much of his time in deep-sea fishing or exploring the outer islands in a yacht, returning, from time to time, to work off his social obligations in a few big parties at which everyone was deafened, distracted and bored. These little intimate dinner parties, the well-drilled service, the easy flow of conversation between a few carefully chosen guests, had been beyond his powers, or those of his untutored wife; but the Hamptons—now, alas, on the verge of retirement—were artists at their social task.

After coffee, Sir Harold Hampton took Freddy to his study for a brief review of the Protectorate's affairs. Sir Harold's shrewd, grey, kindly face was growing old. The strain of the last troublesome years had whitened his hair, deepened the furrows round his eyes and mouth and taken the stuffing out of his shoulders. He looked ten years older; Freddy was quite shocked. At the end of his career he had been condemned to see much of his work undone and all his plans for the future vitiated.

Perhaps he was more gloomy than he had need to be; at any rate, Freddy was not given a rosy survey. The country's coffers were empty; trade had fallen off, taxes dwindled, salaries been docked, wholesale dismissals reluctantly enforced, all schemes of expansion cast aside. Worst of all, there were signs of native disaffection. It was not to be wondered at, Sir Harold added. The simple illiterate peasant understood nothing of economic trends and believed the fall in prices to be a deliberate attempt to cheat him of his just reward. Two quite spontaneous strikes had already occurred; small producers had burnt their produce rather than accept the ruling prices; cuts in salaries among the semi-educated clerical classes were deeply resented. The people, in fact, were in a tricky mood, distrustful of all explanations that the Europeans—themselves baffled and insecure—could offer; and Sir Harold greatly feared an outbreak of trouble unless something could be done, and done quickly, to improve prices and restore trade.

In the next week or two Freddy, bringing himself up-to-date by means of conferences and files, found much to confirm his master's pessimism. A stony prospect was indeed in sight. Bags and bales of various kinds of produce were piling up in warehouses because no one in the world's markets would buy them, even at their present shrivelled prices: over-production, people said. Elsewhere they had been forced to burn perishable goods that were rotting, and outraged producers were refusing to sell; that meant the cancelling of orders for imported cotton goods and bicycles and shoes which could no longer be afforded, and a people sullen and resentful because they could not get the things they wanted any more.

In the Protectorate, the people seemed so far to be accepting the inevitable with a fair grace. Freddy was inclined to think that Sir Harold, grown tired and discouraged, was a little panicky.

"Thank goodness, our fellows can be trusted to keep the native steady," he remarked to his wife. "I don't think we shall have anything serious to fear so long as our men can explain things and keep an eye on the disaffected elements."

"How can they explain it," Armorel asked, "when they haven't the faintest idea what's happened themselves?"

"A fair point; and I've already arranged to circulate a brief memorandum explaining just how this economic crisis has arisen, and the reasons why we may look to the future with sober hope. District officers can then pass on the salient points to leaders of native opinion."

Armorel smiled; she had long ago given up trying to disillusion Freddy. His belief in the efficacy of memoranda and the power of reason was not, indeed, detachable, but built in to his nature and a source of its strength. Whatever happened, Freddy would not panic, or be rushed off his feet. People knew this, and their knowledge gave them immense confidence in his judgment.

Armorel was glad to see that he was settling down nicely, digesting an immense volume of papers, seeing everyone, reading, listening, absorbing, cogitating, with his usual energy and application. Soon, she had no doubt, he would be ready with a scheme for pulling the Protectorate through the slump, just as he had hitherto produced a scheme for meeting every other difficulty that had confronted the Governments he had served. That he should succeed now was almost a matter of life and death. He had reached the crisis of his career. Either he must go forward into gubernatorial glory, or decline into the limbo of mediocrity. His promotion to the Protectorate had been a sign that he had acquitted himself well in the trial canter, as it were; now the real test had come.

Four years in new surroundings, Armorel believed, had done much to equip him for the strenuous times ahead. They had brought him out of himself, given him self-confidence and a certain polish, made him more human and approachable and

less afraid of venturing from the centre of the strictly official
road. He had become more tolerant, too, of others' weaknesses,
and fond of after-dinner stories, provided they did not overstep
the borders (as he put it) of good taste.

A certain measure of this improvement Armorel put down to
an affair which she had handled, she considered, with good sense
and not a little skill. The population of the island to which
they had been transferred was colourful and varied, mixed blood
the general rule. Some of the island's girls, with their creamy
skin, their dark glossy hair and brilliant eyes, had a breath-
taking and evanescent beauty; and to one such, who had acted
for a time as a decorative but inefficient typist, Freddy had felt
himself powerfully drawn.

For some time he had struggled against temptation, tormented
by the girl's proximity and by his dread of a rebuff and his feeling
of guilt. He grew edgy and morose, his concentration weakened
and even his work began to suffer; half his time was spent
inventing excuses to be with her and then, when he succeeded,
he could make no headway, and reproached himself at once for
his unworthy aims and for his ineptitude in advancing them.
Fortunately for everyone, Armorel soon noticed his distraction.
Inquiries placed the girl as the daughter of a coloured school-
master in a mean part of the town, and of a mother who had left
her brood of brats to vanish with a Negro seaman. The father
was desperately poor, the family of no account, and Armorel
felt sure that neither the morals of the typist nor the status of
the family would come between Freddy and his objective.

For some time Armorel had considered that a discreet adventure or two, properly handled, would be good for Freddy;
like a tonic, it would freshen him up, improve his self-confidence
and his temper. Up to date, he had shown a distressing timidity
and lack of enterprise, and now he was reaching a dangerous
age and seniority. His infatuation with the typist might give
him his chance before it was too late; but she realized that, so
long as he was battling with temptation, he would be in no
state to make prudent terms with the devil. Freddy, as usual,
needed her help.

In the course of a few weeks, all was arranged. Freddy often
worked at home in the evenings, and at Armorel's insistence a
room was set aside in case he should wish to keep a typist until
an hour when her solitary journey through the meaner streets
of the seaport town would be inadvisable; and she herself

suggested that her daughters needed her in England for the summer holidays. At first Freddy protested, for he always felt lost without his wife; but once he had adjusted his ideas, he was in a fever of anxiety lest something should occur at the last moment to prevent her departure. Armorel kissed him good-bye with the satisfactory feeling that she had done everything to ensure his comfort that could be expected of a conscientious wife.

She lengthened her stay to six months, and returned to find a subtle change in Freddy: he seemed, just as she had hoped, more self-confident and lively, less hesitant and self-deprecating. Mentally, it was as if he had thrown out his chest. There was no doubt that he was pleased to have her back, and he was ready with a dozen bits of news, and a list of the people they ought to ask for dinner. At the same time—and this was more than she had bargained for—he seemed rather less eager to consult her; a shade, perhaps, indifferent to her opinion, more self-contained.

"I've missed you a great deal, my dear," he said. "Without you, the house isn't the same at all. But I've been working very hard. H.E. has been away a good deal—he's really excessively fond of deep-sea fishing—and I've had to deputize, and then with all the reorganization that's so badly needed . . ."

"You look well on it," Armorel said, observing him critically. "I hope the arrangements for your secretarial help in the evenings worked well."

The barbed edge to her voice warned him of her meaning. Their eyes met, and his turned away. He understood that she knew of his aberration, she knew that he realized his exposure. But no further word of the subject passed between them, then or at any future time.

Now that they were back in their old haunts, such adventures were all behind him, tender memories; serious matters loomed ahead. After a few weeks of careful study Freddy was, if not perturbed, at least concerned about the immediate future. Everyone shared his disquiet, but to him fell the onerous duty of setting the course through stormy seas.

His difficulty was that everyone agreed on the diagnosis— the fall in prices; and on the remedy—their restoration; but no one was able to bring this about. Thus the real redress lay quite beyond the power of anyone in the Protectorate, and naturally this produced a feeling of impotence and defeatism; but Freddy, once more, refused to give up. After reading and digesting all that had been written on the subject—and it was an enormous amount—he saw ahead of him one possible way out.

The Protectorate's crops, as he well knew, were at present being unskilfully grown by peasant farmers with no knowledge of modern methods—in some cases they were simply plucked or shaken from wild trees. They could not stand comparison with the produce of skilfully controlled plantations found in territories belonging to other and less enlightened nations, where the native was doubtless exploited, but nevertheless secured higher rewards for his work. The produce of the Protectorate, on the other hand, always fetched the lowest prices on a world market which was becoming increasingly pernickety about such things.

For some years technical experts had campaigned for an improved system of marketing based on the grading of the produce to be sold abroad, together with a vigorous attempt to teach the peasants how better crops might be grown. While approving in principle of this proposal, the Government had hitherto failed to follow it up, mainly because they had lacked the funds and feared the conservatism of the people.

Re-reading these proposals, Freddy spotted a possible way of escape from present troubles. The low-grade, half-rotten stuff that was being offered for sale was poisoning the country's reputation and giving agents of the buying firms every excuse to pay rock-bottom prices. In the absence of a grading system, produce of better quality fetched no more than trash, and so the righteous grower suffered with the wicked and no one had any incentive to improve his methods or take trouble with his crops; and in other respects it was abundantly clear that the slow, expensive and inefficient chain linking peasant producer to distant European consumer could be tightened and improved.

Once Freddy had made up his mind that an improved market-ing system based on the grading of produce would be desirable— and this decision was not taken without a great deal of con-sultation and study—he lost no time in drawing up a concise and cogent memorandum proving his point. Being about to retire, and baffled by the troubles that beset him, Sir Harold Hampton was content to leave matters in the hands of his beaver-like and experienced Chief Secretary; but he did not endorse the scheme without some trepidation. On the one hand he feared native opposition, the whole idea of differences in quality being new, and therefore repugnant, to the peasant growers; and on the other a more correct and subtle resistance from the trading companies who, obliged to buy officially graded goods, would be deprived of their reason for paying such low overall prices.

These objections were clear and real to Freddy, but he knew—and his judgment in such matters was almost infallible—that a moment had arrived when action of some kind was imperative. One could postpone and consider for a certain length of time—indeed, a very considerable length of time—but not for ever. Authorities at home were expecting serious steps to be taken to avert complete financial collapse, and discontent among the native population was growing from day to day. The dangers of doing nothing had therefore become even greater than the dangers of taking action. Once this point had been reached (which, fortunately, was seldom) the wise administrator would grasp the nettle rather than wait to be set upon by bees.

Back to London, therefore, went his dispatch, and locally, a way was prepared. Reports were called for from every province on the state of native opinion and the repercussions that might be expected to follow the introduction of a grading plan. From these Freddy judged that the matter would be tricky and hard, but not impossible. To his surprise, one of the most dubious reports came from the emirate presided over by Commander Catchpole, where he had believed discipline to be effective and public opinion sound.

On this, Sir Harold Hampton had his own views.

"Frankly, the new Emir has been a disappointment," he said. "We thought he would change the whole outlook up there. He's amenable enough, but he doesn't seem able to stick to his guns. It's my belief that he's being blocked at every turn by the old Emir's party. And it's my belief also that we brought this on ourselves when we got cold feet half-way through the deportation and settled the old boy in what we hoped was an inaccessible part of the Protectorate. In fact, of course, no amount of precaution can prevent communications passing between him and his friends."

"Instructions from home?" Freddy hazarded.

"Of course. My own proposal was to have him shipped to the Cocos Islands or the Seychelles—anywhere right out of the way. But there was the usual outcry at home—high-handed treatment, freedom of the individual and all that. The Opposition took it up and thoroughly rattled the Secretary of State. So instead of letting us go through with the plan, he cancelled the deportation order. Asking for trouble, as I said at the time; and we've been getting it ever since."

"Most unfortunate," Freddy agreed, shaking his head, and experiencing afresh the irritation aroused at fairly frequent intervals in the breast of every colonial official by the vagaries of English party politics in which the affairs of his territory, universally disregarded and misunderstood, were liable to become suddenly involved—like a ball on a bagatelle table finding itself deflected from its path by an unsuspected pin, and rolling in an unintended direction towards a profitless end.

"Catchpole is due for leave pending retirement," Freddy added. "An immediate change might be a good thing."

The Governor looked dubious. "Yes, provided you can find a really first-rate man."

This was not easy. The men of Resident's rank available for transfer lacked the qualities that he had hoped to find. He was always reluctant to take the short cuts urged by those who so glibly, as he thought, talked of promotion by merit only, and picking the best men for the job. You were worse off rather than better if, to balance the best man promoted to one particular job, you had half-a-dozen passed-over and therefore disgruntled men in half-a-dozen perhaps equally important jobs. Seniority was the best guide. But on this occasion a man possessing first-hand experience of the emirate and the confidence of its people was clearly needed, more or less regardless of rank. Going carefully through the papers, Freddy decided that only one individual filled the bill.

He hesitated for a little, remembering Gresham's awkward and self-willed nature, and his tendency to follow his own notions rather than the policy he was employed to carry out. There would be no room for such luxuries now. Well, Gresham was four years older and had perhaps learnt better sense, and Freddy was always afraid, when the name was mentioned, that personal feelings might unwittingly colour his judgment. Without further ado he passed a recommendation to the Governor.

The transfer went through quickly, and Robert Gresham came down to take part in consultations held in the rambling wooden Secretariat, built round a courtyard like a very large stable with long rows of loose-boxes in which officials sat and mentally munched their dry and bulky diet of paper. Everyone greeted him cordially and with a hint of the sympathy accorded to those compelled to nurse a sick relative, for his particular emirate was known to be in a tacky sort of condition. Freddy was the soul of affability, and pressed him to dine at the commodious two-storey house—the second largest in the Protectorate, fitting his rank—into which he had just settled.

The party was neither too large nor too small—just right. Armorel had indeed become, through long practice and close observation, a most expert hostess, and Robert—now, as an acting Resident, paid the compliment of being seated next to her—could not but admire afresh her poise and her looks, so well preserved in a climate that had no mercy on women; her skin was still smooth, her dark eyes clear and brilliant, her hair glossy and well kept.

"Your island suited you," he remarked.

"A rest cure compared with this, my dear. A dinner once a week, an occasional garden party for the coloured people, tennis with the planters—a lotus-eater's existence. One had leisure, but not much ambition."

"You surely haven't left that behind?"

"Just the same Robert! Determined to dig your claws into me. But I know you too well to worry." She studied his face, shadowy in the candlelight. "You look older. Bachelor life doesn't suit you, I suppose. I'm sorry Priscilla has had to stay behind."

Robert made some perfunctory answer, knowing that his hostess was certainly delighted to see no more of Priscilla. Glancing at her, he caught a curious and fleeting expression: amusement, speculation, or even pity. It made him vaguely uneasy. There was something about Armorel that always frightened him a little—something cold-blooded, almost reptilian. Yet no woman of his acquaintance had been a better wife to her husband: how many times, he wondered, had the words been said of her 'She's been the making of Freddy'?

"I hope you're able to find distractions," she added. "You ride still, I suppose, and watch birds, and enjoy exchanging gossip over a nice cup of coffee with your polygamous old cronies? Why men should accuse us of scandal-mongering——"

"Or women claim to be the greater gossips—after all, we invented history and the newspapers. Talking of history, I've been writing one, about the emirates—or rather, trying to add a few scraps of tradition to the existing records."

Armorel smiled. "That's true to form. You've always been more interested in the past than the future. The trouble with

you, Robert, is that you're a reactionary. That's why you've
never got on as you should."

"Thank you. You recommend a seat on the glittering chariot
of the progressives, then, alongside you and Freddy?"

"Certainly. Chariots advance; at least you get somewhere in
them."

"They might advance downhill. Judged by their speed, the
Gadarene swine were extremely progressive."

"Don't be so gloomy, Robert! Let's enjoy planning our
rocket trips to the moon—we don't all want to welter with you
among smelly camel-drivers with their simple dignity and
internal parasites. Frankly, I prefer the chromium and plywood
age to crooked stairs and fumed oak."

"Ah, but you belong to it, and know how to manage it—or
think you do—hard and bright like one of your cocktail bars.
But what a mess next morning!"

"Dear Robert, you haven't changed after all! Do you notice
that we always insult each other when we meet? It's fun; you
must come and stay with us often. Now that you're a Resident
at last I'm sure Freddy will often want you to come down."

With one of her flashing smiles, Armorel turned to her other
neighbour and Robert to the lady on his right: who moved king's
pawn boldly forward two squares.

"Aren't we lucky to have the Beggs back again! Have you
been on leave lately? We're due for ours next month, I
hope. . . ."

Chapter Four

TWELVE gateways had once pierced the city's massive
wall, each with its guard-house and castellated parapet
offering protection to the bowmen. Each able-bodied man had
furnished his share of labour towards the upkeep of the wall;
since all lived in its shelter, none expected payment or thanks for
his part in its maintenance. But now the wall was crumbling
fast, grass roots were thrusting down to undermine it, and in
places you could scramble across the ramparts through weeds
and low bushes as if no boundary marked off the town. No days
came now when slaves and citizens alike would flock to clear the

ditch, to dig out the red earth and, forming a human chain to pass leather buckets from hand to hand, would lay on a plaster of clay to repair the corrosion of wind and rain. No songs rang out to lighten the labour and no smoke rose from fires roasting meat for the great feast marking the task's conclusion.

When Robert drove his car through the one gateway preserved as a vague gesture towards past glories, he noticed that the wall had crumbled a little more in the four years of his absence, and that vegetation grew thickly along the subsided ramparts. This natural decay was welcomed, indeed encouraged, by the administration, in the belief that the wall's obliteration would bring home to the citizens the full extent of their new safety—that for the first time in all their long and bloody history they could sleep at nights without fear of an invader.

True as this was, Robert wondered, as he drove through, whether his compatriots had been over-confident—not of the fact, but of the citizens' real desire to be free of a condition which, however stormy, brought its own delights of excitement and opportunities for valour. The fact was, he thought, we have made life dull. Under our ægis people have bread, but they lack circuses; we have done away with their own—the slave raids and pillages, the stirring return of the armies, the wild pagan or half-pagan ceremonies, the dances and sacrifices—without substituting new ones; even the Church no longer affords much in the way of pageantry or melodrama. Were we, he asked himself, too sure that our own values held for all peoples and places, that we could destroy selectively the evils of the primitive without also damaging its virtues? Sometimes it seemed to him that the death of the walls was letting in enemies more damaging, and certainly more subtle, than those which had come openly in ancient times to storm the city.

Once inside the walls he looked about him with pleasure; there had been little change. Indeed he found it hard to imagine that these streets winding between the courtyard walls could ever change, or the water-carrier's cry be silent, or the call to prayer be stilled; yet, he supposed, it would happen; seeds of disruption had germinated already. Here and there outward signs of progress intruded: the warehouses of trading firms just inside the walls; a big new hospital, halted now for lack of funds, that would one day have all the latest devices; poles for electric current; a long ugly building of concrete blocks, like a huge cowshed, housing the new offices of the Native Administration.

As he passed near the market, packed as always with chattering, sweating, bargaining humanity, he noticed a boy in a kind of uniform with a sheaf of newspapers under his arm hawking copies of the *Chanticleer*. The city's first home-grown newspaper: a sign of the times.

A different Emir, too, ruled the kingdom, a man of a new type: not only younger than his uncle and slighter in build, but less embedded, as it were, in a matrix of tradition conferring at once strength and rigidity, a supreme self-confidence and a quiet lustre. Although he had never visited Eurpoe he was more aware of the European mind and outlook than his uncle had been, and at once more attracted and more frightened by it.

Taken by Catchpole to pay his ceremonial call, Robert found the new Emir seated in the tall-backed chair that his uncle had installed, in deference to western taste, in the long, high-ceilinged audience chamber, with its filtered light and pargeted walls. Aboubakar talked with fluency and intelligence of his kingdom's affairs. These, he freely acknowledged, were not going smoothly. On the surface, all his troubles were due to the falling off of trade and the consequent poverty, stringency and shortfall in taxes. But behind these difficulties, in themselves formidable enough, a more subtle cause of embarrassment was at work. Aboubakar had known that he would have to deal with intrigues against him nurtured by his uncle's supporters, but he had counted on the removal of the old Emir and his sons to some distant inaccessible spot, and on his own ability to please the people by more vigorous and prosperous rule. He had been disappointed on both counts. Moreover one of the Emir's sons, the angry, fanatical and fearless young Abdulahai, but recently returned from the pilgrimage, had begun to rally round his own person his father's supporters and all who were discontented with his cousin's rule.

At first Aboubakar had dismissed his opponent as of small account, a wild young man without experience of politics or affairs; and, indeed, Abdulahai had lost adherents through his crude and tactless methods. But his sincerity and courage and his devotion to the faith were beginning to win supporters among a people in whose blood the fire and intransigence of Berber and Arab mingled with the torpid, easy-going Negro strain. In several underground trials of strength he had already won victories, and these were steadily adding to his prestige.

All this rankled with Aboubakar, but he did not wish to reveal to his European overlords these ominous cracks in the foundations of his authority. He discussed with them instead the crops, the shortfall in taxes, cuts in the salaries of his officials.

Robert found the moment opportune to propound the scheme he had been charged to launch for the grading of produce by inspectors vested with Government authority. The Emir listened attentively, his lean face immobile, shawls draped over bearded chin and heavy embroidered robes falling in folds at his feet. It was all as Robert remembered it so well: the high vaulted room with its geometrically decorated walls, the soft muted light, the space and quietness, and at the far end of the big chamber a bright arched doorway with a glimpse beyond of lounging guards and men squatting sleepily in the narrow shade of a young mango tree. All seemed so casually orderly, so half asleep, it was hard to believe in the existence of stormy undercurrents of violence and plotting.

"I understand," the Emir said, when Robert had finished. "Produce without blemish will be bought, and more money paid for it. And that which is rejected, what will become of it?"

"If it is quite worthless it will be destroyed, or the owner may take it away, if he wishes."

"A man who has paid to have a sack of groundnuts carried to market in a lorry will not be pleased if he must pay to have it carried back again."

"That is true; but if he is a sensible man, he will not send to market a sack of groundnuts so poor that it cannot be sold."

"The goodness of a crop is in the hands of God. Can a farmer help it if the rains are poor or if a plague strikes his fields?"

"We have a saying in England that God helps those who help themselves," Robert replied. "A man cannot prevent a bad season, but he can prevent his crops from becoming mildewed, for example, because they are carelessly dried or badly stored."

"Nevertheless a man who brings his crop a great distance and sees it rejected——"

"It would not all be rejected, only those parts which are rotten and worthless."

"Even so, he would not understand, and this would make him angry."

"To balance that, there will be skilful men who will receive much more for their produce, and they, I hope, will be pleased. Others will follow their example."

The Emir still seemed dubious. On his left sat two of his officials, his Vizier and his Treasurer, and opposite them, on his right hand, sat the Europeans. With an inclination of the head he invited the Vizier's opinion.

"All will appear just to those who receive more money, and unjust to those who receive less."

The Treasurer, speaking like the others in grave deliberate tones, asked:

"Will those receiving a higher price be fewer or more numerous than those receiving less?"

"At first," Robert said, "they are likely to be fewer; but when it is realized that more care and intelligence leads to higher rewards, we hope that those whose produce is sound and healthy will greatly outnumber those who offer what is inferior."

"At first, then, those who are displeased will outnumber those who are satisfied," the Treasurer said with finality.

There was a brief silence in the audience hall. Once again Robert was struck by the speed and acuteness with which the Emir and his officers cut through the rind of talk to the pith, seeing things as they would appear to the commonality. For all their privilege and riches, he had never known an occasion when they had not accurately reflected to their white overlords the thoughts and feelings of the subjects they ruled. And those feelings were always conservative. What the Government was trying to do was to introduce not merely a new method but a new principle: the principle of quality, which was, as a general rule, foreign to the ideas of these peasant farmers. They would get used to it in time (they could distinguish well enough, for instance, between a cheap flimsy cloth and a costly durable one) but it was time that was lacking. A flavour to which they should have been gradually introduced was being forced down their throats as medicine to relieve a sudden sickness. He sighed; it was an old story; and Catchpole, who had left this part of the talk to him, moved impatiently in his chair.

"They don't like it," he said in English, "but they'll have to lump it. You'd better get that into their heads and be done."

Robert made one more attempt. "It is surely agreed," he said, feeling the force of three pairs of eyes fixed on his face, "that the root of the trouble to-day is that the farmer receives so poor a price for the fruits of his labour. But it lies beyond our power to control the distant markets to which his produce goes. Only one thing can we do. The poorness of our produce is a poison that infects everything. In the distant markets of Europe merchants say: 'This is from a place that sends us only shrivelled nuts and weevily grain; we will not pay more than a few shillings.' And the buyer who is amongst us says: 'Much of what I buy will be too rotten to re-sell; therefore I can afford to pay only a little.' And that is why we receive a poor reward."

His listeners bowed their heads in silent agreement.

"There is only one way to put this right. It may be that it will not at first be liked by many. Often a man dislikes a medicine needed to cure his sickness. But without it, he dies. We must explain this fully to the people. That is a thing only you can do, Aboubakar. Let the word go out from you to the people in the most distant villages that this is being done to help them. In a little while they will get better prices, and then they will see that you were right, and they will call on God to bless you. There is no other way."

Catchpole added a few sentences of agreement and once again the Emir and his two officers were silent, studying the ground at their feet. How the office, Robert thought, absorbed the man; the fiery young Aboubakar had taken with the Emir's mantle a ruler's dignity and deliberation. He could hardly have been distinguished from his uncle by his manner. Yet there was a difference; he leant forward now and spoke with a frankness and volubility the older man would not have displayed.

"The Government's proposal," he said, "has merits, and I myself would be glad to see it carried out. But this kingdom has passed through a time of trouble and, like a market place after a disturbance, everything has not yet been swept away. There are men still in this city who, in the pay of the last Emir, stir up disloyalty to his successor. They make my path difficult and my way painful and slow. My grandfather would have known what to do! But to-day you stay the sword of the just executioner and allow such men to go freely about their dangerous business. Is not a weed best checked when it is young, or does the wise husbandman wait until it has grown and seeded? Well, that is your way, and I must bow to it; but do not then expect that either you or I can easily persuade the people to welcome your proposals, when you allow men to go among them whose business it is to inflame their minds against any measure which either you or I design."

The Emir was speaking now from the heart, with the ring of passion in his deep voice. Catchpole made a movement as if to

interrupt—no doubt he was only too familiar with the arguments
—but the Emir ignored him.

"You ask my support for this measure of the Government's.
Very well, I will give it, but only if the Government will support
a request I make of them. My uncle, the last Emir——"

Catchpole succeeded in breaking in. "You know that we
cannot discuss——"

"If you cannot discuss his proper treatment, neither can I
discuss the Government's plans!" The Emir's passions, exacer-
bated by the frustrations of his office, were gaining control. His
head was lifted, his eye flashing, his voice peremptory. "Do you
not see that the two are bound together like a donkey to his load?
Take away the Emir whom you deposed to a distant country
where he cannot whistle a tune that men dance to in this city, in
my very palace even—take away his sons and supporters who are
like a cloud of bees round my head—smoke them out, destroy
them, banish them—do what you like, so long as they cannot
stay here to pester and sting and await their time to set upon
their betters! Cut them off as you would a gangrenous hand!
Do this, and then we will talk of ways to improve the lot of the
people. Until that is completed, everything I do will be twisted
and reviled and everything you wish me to do will be
thwarted."

The Emir had lifted his arm and brought the other hand down
upon it to illustrate the motion of a chopper slicing off the rotted
member; with both arms raised, his eye sparkling, his closely-
trimmed beard seeming to bristle with anger, he was an impressive figure. After a pause the Treasurer, in more measured
tones, supported his master.

"You have heard Aboubakar; his words are true. This is a
thing we cannot understand: that the Government should allow
its enemy to live at ease within a week's journey and should leave
unmolested his sons and followers. There are people who say:
'Even a child would know better than to make so foolish a
blunder.' The men at the head of the Government are not
children, we are told that they have come here to teach us better
ways to govern. Can you explain——"

Catchpole again intervened. "I have spoken of this before;
why do you return to it? As to the treatment of the last Emir,
the Government has decided; it is useless to approach them.
And I have told you the reason. The decision was not taken by
the Governor; it was taken by those above him, the ministers of

the King. The Governor is the King's loyal servant, and must obey him; and you must obey also."

"Then I cannot believe that the King is fully acquainted——" the Treasurer began; but the Emir silenced him.

"He is right; the Government knows my views, and I have had my answer. So be it; but if you hobble a horse's legs, you must not expect him to win races."

He rose to his feet and clasped the hand of each visitor briefly but firmly in his own. In silence, but with courtesy, the Vizier conducted the two visitors to the outer courtyard and saw them into their waiting car.

"Of course, Aboubakar's perfectly right," Catchpole grumbled on the way back to the Residency, leaning against the cushions and wiping his face with a large handkerchief. "It's sheer lunacy to leave the old boy anywhere on the same continent, let alone a couple of hundred miles away. This son of his, Abdulahai, is at the bottom of all the trouble. A firebrand if ever there was one —and after the Emir's job for himself, of course. Can't stand the fellow! Or these endless intrigues. But there you are." He shrugged his shoulders. "Some damned M.P. kicked up a fuss at home—a lot of old women cackled about a thing they know less about than I do about axolotls—and no one has the guts to move him out of the country, for fear of a question in the House of Commons. That's the way the Empire's run nowadays! Absolute gutlessness! Well, I'm not sorry to be getting out."

Robert was surprised at the change in Commander Catchpole. The Resident he remembered had frowned severely on any suggestion that all was not for the best; loyalty to his superiors had closed his ears to criticisms. But now that his time was up and his pension due, he seemed to detect no longer an aura of wisdom about the heads of his masters. The last few years had, indeed, been hard ones for any man to live through and preserve undiminished his belief in upward progress and the virtue and wisdom of the western civilization be served. Even Catchpole must sometimes have been reminded that a primitive society lacked not only sanitation, machinery and popular literacy but also unemployment, depressions and the burning of surpluses while millions lacked for food and clothing.

Not that Catchpole had changed outwardly: still bluff, rubicund and hearty, but with his figure thickened, his dark stiff hair greying at the sides, he looked a picture of forcefulness and self-confidence. The differences that Robert noticed—a new sourness and asperity—came rather, he surmised, from private sources: from the prospect of years of hollow retirement in some gim-crack seaside villa (for Catchpole still missed the sea, his first love; and would there not be a flagpole in the garden above the rockery?) in the company of a wife who had always been peremptory and stentorian and was now, in late middle age, testy and given to recrimination; without a job of work to distract them and without the wine of high position to warm their ageing blood; worrying over the cost of domestic help and petrol, angering themselves by mistakes at bridge, clinging with an unacknowledged frenzy to old friends and striving by patronage to conceal their fears of boring or being bored by the new.

Depressed by this prospect, and by the dismantling of the Residency which was proceeding on all sides, Robert strolled off into the sun-parched garden and approached a small open-sided pavilion faintly (but very faintly) reminiscent of a little Greek temple, where tea or drinks were sometimes served. Bougainvilleas ramped up the columns, smothering the stone-work in their welter of violent bloom, and the flowerbeds round about were full of wilting petunias. At one side stood a wire cage containing sticks and foliage and part of the branch of a tree. Robert, recognizing the contraption, stepped up to it: and sure enough inside, only visible after a few moments' search, two chameleons crouched on the tree's limb, scaly and immobile.

Pyramus and Thisbe! Old friends: Priscilla had persuaded the Catchpoles to take them in when she went home on leave—for the last time, as it had turned out. And here they had remained ever since: neglected, probably, but apparently not starved. Short of going hungry, no doubt they preferred neglect; chameleons did not suffer from loving natures.

He peered at them through the wire netting. Strange, pre-historic-looking little beasts, like miniature dragons, with their sharp-ridged spines, their strong-clawed feet, their heavy-lidded eyes. It was fascinating to watch that immensely long tongue flash out, almost invisibly, to flick into its mouth an unsuspecting fly. Priscilla had loved to move them from a brown tree-trunk to a bed of green leaves and watch the surge of change creep over their skins, like a person very slowly blushing green. Animals had been her hobby; wherever he had been, the station had always acquired a floating population of deer, bush-babies, lizards, and small mammals of various kinds; generally the bathroom was full of cocoons in boxes and once a crocodile's egg had hatched against the kitchen wall.

But now it was painful to recall such things. By day, absorbed in his work, her image receded; but when he returned to a sad empty house, or awoke to a fine bright morning in a barren room —at such times his solitude was hard to bear. He lived with ghosts, but it was flesh and blood that he yearned for—the real Priscilla, warm, gay and unpredictable, not all these dreams and memories; often his longing for her became a physical ache, his solitude a torment. Sometimes he fled from his loneliness, but at other times (and they were becoming more frequent) he caught it out assuming the shape of a friend. He found himself shunning his colleagues making excuses to avoid company, settling down in his chair of an evening with a sigh of relief to be spared the effort of responding to company and to be left free to range over the past; and now and again he even intercepted a fleeting fear of the approach of his next leave, when Priscilla would be transformed from a taunting but delicious memory into an exacting reality.

How twisted and absurd were human emotions! His own, at any rate; and turning back to the chameleons, he surveyed them with a new respect. Perhaps that was why Priscilla enjoyed the company of animals so much: just because, not being human, they were simple in their needs, direct in their demands, honest in their intentions and consistent in their behaviour. If they had their faults, they did not pretend to be demi-gods while carrying on like demi-devils.

Feeling a desire to reward the chameleons for their natural virtue, he searched vainly for some acceptable insect, and opened the cage to insert instead a new branch with fresh green leaves. Pyramus—or was it Thisbe?—clung motionless to the trunk, and he put out a hand to touch it. But at that the chameleon came suddenly to life and slid down the trunk as fast as it could go, which was not very fast, with a curious motion something between a glide and a waddle.

Robert withdrew his hand ruefully and closed the cage. From humankind, even chameleons fled! Of all the thousands of species—hundreds of thousands, probably—that inhabited this planet, man was the only one abhorred by all its fellows, save those he had himself bred up as slaves. Robert recalled an incident described to him by a student of game: how one morning three lions, bloated from a night's feast, had walked slowly from their watering-place towards their shelter in the hills, passing within a dozen paces of a herd of zebra and antelope; and how those animals, who would have fled in terror in the night-time, barely interrupted their grazing to glance up at their enemies. Hunters were satisfied and hunted knew it, and between the two the instincts of preying and of fear were in abeyance. Had a man come down to that watering-place—full-fed, unarmed, with nothing but love in his heart—every animal would have fled precipitately, his very smell anathema. Sleeping or waking, peaceful or predatory, young or old, man was the enemy of all creation. The vigilance of those who feared him never relaxed. Not for a moment would the antelope stay to let him stroll among them, the fish in the river pause while he drank beside it, nor the bird share his supper.

But then only man of all creation in his staggering egotism regarded every other species as dedicated to his benefit and subservient to his will. Elephants did not make war on crocodiles, nor dung-beetles wish to do away with worms. All were satisfied to follow their bent as parts of a greater whole: all but man who, finding that the skins of some species or the secretions of others adorned his vanity, exterminated whole populations of beavers or koala bears, tempted musk-deer to their death with music, and combed oceans for whales. Man alone of all creation killed not merely for food and survival but for delight. Behind that fear which caused the chameleons to recede before Robert's hand, the bird to fly at his approach, lay, perhaps, the gathered force of the last agonies of a million bison, of all the Arctic's trapped and furry creatures, of cloud upon cloud of slaughtered wildfowl and of all those mighty herds of game that would graze no more over the plains of Africa.

Surely the pull of so much fear and hatred, Robert concluded, must raise in man a responsive tide of guilt; and this tide must carry him on to ever greater cruelties and excesses. A never-ending circle! Certainly the animals would laugh until their tails fell off could they comprehend man's vision of himself as an animal with a spark of the divine. An animal, regrettably, they would agree; but one with more than a spark, with a tall flame, not of the creative but of the destroyer.

Chapter Five

ROBERT tackled his new duties with a vigour disconcerting to those junior officers devoted to polo and sport, and even more so to the clerks and Native Administration scribes used to a decent moderation in office hours. Not that he was openly a hustler, but his presence engendered an uncomfortable feeling, to which the provincial office had long been a stranger, that an awkward question might suddenly be asked about a troublesome file that had been tucked away, or that an importunate complainant, kept at a safe distance by various minor officials, might gain his hearing by means of a direct approach.

To smooth a way for the Government's proposed reforms was clearly one of his first tasks. Although the excellence of its aim could not be doubted, he became convinced, the more he went into the matter, that the introduction of the scheme in its present form and at the present moment would be to ask for trouble. Nothing had been done to prepare the people for an innovation which would disturb the very roots of their life—their individual property. It was a matter of constant wonder to him that colonial Governments, renowned for their dilatory behaviour and accustomed to take months or even years to deal with the simple questions, would occasionally, in matters of major policy and great delicacy, suddenly and without warning take it into their heads—having left matters until the very last moment—to abandon all their traditional and ingrown caution and gallop forward at breakneck speed to enforce some ill-thought-out proposal. From all appearances such a mutation in official procedure was just about to occur on his own beat.

However much he might doubt the wisdom of these official proposals, the need remained to arrest the bleeding to death of the Protectorate through economic wounds. The question was, whether an alternative could be found.

Searching for some way out of the dilemma, Robert's mind turned to a half-forgotten experience of his own. In the early part of the war, after many vicissitudes and adventures, he had found himself, at the age of twenty-five, in charge of a large area of surrendered enemy territory, containing in it a port and many well-developed plantations. At first he was too busy trying to restore the rudiments of administration to pay any attention to these concerns, but after a little, when people began to drift back to their villages from hiding-places in the mountains hoping the British were not cannibals after all, he walked round some of the deserted plantations, starting already to lose their neat and tended look, and through some of the solidly built, well-furnished two-story houses, and into the factories with their idle but efficient-looking machinery, and began to worry about the waste of so much potential productivity. Clearly these plantations had cost tens of thousands and the toil of innumerable men to bring into being; it could benefit no one if the crops that marched in such neat rows up the valleys and along the contours of the hills were choked with weeds and ravaged by disease, if the waiting machinery rusted and fell apart, and if white ants triumphed over the houses.

While he was pondering all this, the submarine war increased in ferocity and soon there was talk of hunger and of a paralysing dearth of raw materials. In papers from home he read, in particular, of a famine in fats. Now fats had been one of the prime products of these factories. The nuts still grew, the natives were as anxious as ever for payment—in fact they were suffering because conquest had disrupted their trade; and the presses needed only fuel and direction to revolve again. Why not, he had reasoned, re-start the whole machine of production—gather the nuts, expel the oil, ship it to waiting and hungry consumers?

Like all those cut off at this time of crisis from their homes and fellows, he fretted at his own impotence and strained to join the fighting men of his own age and blood; but, try as he would —and he tried very hard—a short-handed Government would not release him. To one who had dreamt of glory, like other young men, the organization of a factory to expel vegetable oils scarcely presented itself as a St. Crispin's day boast for later years; still, it was better than nothing; vegetable oils, he told himself again, were sinews of war. And so, after a careful survey, he reckoned that the mills could be repaired and set in motion for the sum of five hundred pounds.

The military authorities were quite enthusiastic, but it was a civil matter, and both sanction and money, he was told, must come from London. His scheme was submitted with a strong endorsement from the C.-in-C., who saw in it a step towards the peaceful employment of rather disgruntled ex-enemy natives.

After a delay of several months, he was curtly informed that it had been turned down.

Incensed at the obvious absurdity of this at a time when a fat shortage was said to be holding up the very progress of the war, he left his district and hurried to the capital, intending to see the Governor himself. His efforts were quite unavailing. He was granted an interview, instead, with a young man at the Secretariat—a young man who, as Robert afterwards learnt, had but recently transferred to Government service from one of the trading firms and should, in his view, have transferred instead into one of the uniformed services. This young man was not sympathetic. On such a matter nothing could be done, he said, without sanction from London; and as the scheme had already been considered and rejected, there was no more to be gained from further palaver. After beating his head against this brick wall for some time Robert, still young enough to be rebellious and fiery, lost his temper, and said harsh and perhaps unfair things about those who sat in safe jobs and refused to risk even the esteem of their superiors in the interests of winning the war. He left in disgusted anger, conscious that he had achieved nothing but the making of an enemy. That was his first meeting with Freddy Begg.

Going straight to the bank, he drew out all his savings, which amounted to about half the needed sum. The rest he raised in small amounts borrowed from friends willing to do him a personal service, and returned to his distant station with the cash safely in his pocket.

Less than two months later, the first ship to carry produce from the captured enemy factories steamed out of harbour with a part-cargo of vegetable oil. Robert saw her go with jubilation. Although he had defied the orders of the Government, the little ship carried his personal quota of fuel for the machine of war. Watching the grubby tramp steam away he thought with pleasure that somewhere, at some time, guns would propel high explosives made from glycerine, or whatever it was, derived from this very cargo of oil; and he was naïve enough to believe that the success of his project would persuade the Government to admit its error. His satisfaction grew when a cheque came in for his first consignment. The sum received paid off all the borrowed capital and left him with a comfortable balance for working expenses.

Thereafter the factory flourished in the hands of an enemy-trained native staff and a skilled mechanic borrowed from the army. In the intervals of administration and further service with mobile columns, he kept the books and managed his little private business, which became a most satisfactory hobby. It was not until near the end of the war that the under-staffed and hard-pressed Secretariat got wind of what he had been doing. Peremptory dispatches arrived, beginning: 'It has come to the attention of Government that . . .' and in due course the illicit factory was closed down; but by that time the good had been done. Robert himself, while receiving a stiff reprimand, was saved from the more severe disciplinary action which would otherwise have been taken by the personal intervention of the Governor, who, getting to hear of the story, was rather tickled by the enterprise and business acumen shown by this unknown young man, and actually went so far as to say that he deserved an O.B.E. rather than a dressing down, a remark considered by his senior officials to be in poor taste. But the Governor was, of course, only joking.

By this time a large sum lay in the account which Robert had opened on behalf of his venture. An exchange of memoranda and minutes on the difficult question of its rightful ownership (clearly it belonged in the last resort to the Government; the question at issue was, which branch of which Government) was arbitrarily settled by the miscreant himself. Taking his first leave for over six years, he went straight to the lair of his masters and handed over a draft. It was they who had refused his request for five hundred pounds' worth of capital, and he could not resist the pleasure of presenting them with over ten thousand pounds' worth of profit. The individual whom he interviewed was startled and incredulous, and clearly most reluctant to accept the draft, which he looked at as if it had been some poisonous African reptile. Robert walked out of the office full of sardonic amusement, having had his first, but not his last, lesson in the workings of the machine of which he formed so minute a fragment.

All this came back to his mind as he pondered over his immediate, and quite different, problem. Yet was it so different after all? The staple crop of his province was valuable mainly as a source of vegetable oil. But the expressing of the oil was all done overseas, none of it in the region where the crops were grown. In the whole territory no simple mills, such as those he had operated with success in the war, had been erected. For this, he knew, there were several reasons, but the more he thought about them the flimsier they seemed. Why not get out of the dilemma by putting up small local mills, expressing the oil and paying over to the growers all the money that would be saved in freight on the bulky produce and made in the profits of the mills? The more he thought it over, the more convinced he became that his idea was sound—indeed, the only hopeful way out of the present impasse. Conversations with members of the emirate's technical staff confirmed his opinion and opened up promising ramifications, for instance the use of the residue for cattle cake to provide a much-needed dry-weather food.

There would be strong opposition—that he fully realized. In ordinary times he would have known better than to try to rush such entrenched positions. But times were not ordinary. Something had to be done; and if the Government could be convinced that their own scheme would lead to the kind of open trouble they most dreaded, whereas the alternative would be at once more effective and less dangerous, then it was possible that they might take a chance.

So, training and priming his guns, he fired the first broadside. Working far into the night, and gathering together all the facts and arguments he could muster, he drew up a clear, concise, and, as he thought, waterproof case. He knew better than to send this through the ordinary channels. All ordinary channels led to Freddy Begg. With his proposals in his pocket, he endured the long hot train journey to the coast and, securing an interview with the Governor through personal contacts and behind the Chief Secretary's back—he knew the ropes better this time—he presented it direct to the highest authority.

Sir Harold Hampton listened, as he always did, courteously and carefully. He heard his caller out, rubbing a stubby finger over a grey clipped moustache and staring over his imposing shiny desk into the sun-flooded garden. When Robert had finished he leant back in his chair, fiddled with a paper-knife and observed:

"I can see some merits in your scheme. In fact I've lost no opportunity, ever since I've been here, to persuade the home authorities that we should process some of our own crops as well as grow them. But I'm afraid that any such concrete proposals as yours would run up against very stiff opposition."

"I know that, sir. But with your backing——"

"You must remember that the Secretary of State is under

considerable pressure at home. Ours are not the only interests he must consider."

"You mean political pressure?"

"Partly—the general feeling against interference with business. And partly the influence wielded by commercial interests, who don't want to see a profitable sideline taken away. It's only natural, after all."

"Surely a few little mills out here would scarcely steal a crumb from the rich man's table!"

"Commercial firms naturally distrust the principle. To mix metaphors, they live with the thin edge of the wedge hanging over their heads like the sword of Damocles."

Robert was disappointed and at the same time angry at the Governor's defeatism.

"Then, sir, you think it's a waste of time——"

Sir Harold gestured with the paper-knife. "I didn't say that. I will give the scheme full and careful consideration, and consult with Begg and others——"

Robert rose abruptly to his feet. "In that case, sir, I'm afraid you'll waste your time. Begg won't support it, since he has a different scheme of his own, and unless something is done immediately it will be too late. The only hope lay in your personal and urgent intervention. I must apologize for intruding, and thank you for——"

"Just a minute, just a minute." Sir Harold looked startled rather than annoyed. "Sit down, and don't jump to conclusions. You can hardly expect a scheme involving the introduction of a new principle—a reversal of policy, as a matter of fact—to go through in the twinkling of an eye. "

Robert smiled grimly, at his most touchy and unyielding.

"I have learnt to expect very little, sir, in twenty years of service—if you'll forgive me for saying so—except delays and prevarications."

"Mr. Gresham, that is hardly——" Sir Harold checked the pompous rebuke that sprang to his lips. Of course his visitor had overstepped the mark, but he had a good deal of sympathy for such impatient feelings. He had suffered himself in just the same way. Even as Governor, there was always someone a step higher up the ladder who seemed to imagine it his business to delay decisions, modify proposals and reject anything a little out of the usual. In a month or two he would be finished with it all; no need now to add to a subordinate's sense of grievance—or even, now he came to think of it, to test every step lest he should bark someone's toes.

"So far as I am able to judge," he said, "your scheme seems to be sound, and to offer at least a chance of improving the economic situation. I tell you frankly, if the commercial interests get hold of it, they'll kill it. Your only hope is to persuade the authorities at home to agree before consulting them. I will forward it myself to the Secretary of State with a 'most urgent' slip, and a strong personal recommendation. I can do no more than that."

Robert, taken aback at the sudden crumbling of the first wall before his little trumpet-blast, thanked the Governor as best he could.

"At least the idea will have a run for its money."

Sir Harold smiled as he shook hands.

"Don't count on a win."

Chapter Six

THE Treasury official warmed the seat of his pin-striped trousers at the coal fire glowing in the grate of Sir Rosslyn Powers' room. Outside, wind and a grey drizzle beat on the window-panes in peevish flurries, but inside all was warm and snug. The tall, spectacled visitor looked round in quiet appreciation. Fools existed who spoke disparagingly of out-of-date Government offices, of the long grime-encrusted corridors, the dark tiny cubby-holes screened off by dirty frosted glass that served for waiting-rooms, the drab and cluttered offices with their worn rugs and leather arm-chairs, their stained brown walls and their fuggy air, lit all winter by bulbs dangling from the ceiling; such people yearned for expensive modern fads like desks in veneer, walls panelled in stripped pine, central heating and indirect lighting; but they were wrong.

Rooms such as Sir Rosslyn's had an atmosphere that subtly blended a little of the private study and the club smoking-room with the office, that spoke of dignity mixed with informality, repose with application; that brought the past, with all its wisdom and leisure, into the present's vulgar and restless span. Here, in this atmosphere, one could arrive at a cool, well-considered decision, mellowed like a good port, far from the environment of spurious efficiency, American hysteria and duodenal ulcers found in more up-to-date establishments. Above all such offices had an air of privacy quite lacking in modern ant-heap buildings; this was a gentleman's private room, where intruders would not be welcomed, if indeed any intruder should be so brass-fronted as to penetrate without due ceremony into this secluded labyrinth.

The Treasury man brought his wandering thoughts back to the matter in hand. He frowned slightly, recollecting the dispatch on which the views of his Department had been so urgently sought. That was the worst of these colonial Governors—wild fellows, hatching out in their swamps and jungles hair-brained ideas which were either quite ingenuous or else long since discredited, and writing home about them as if they had just made a great discovery—as if some child on its first walk in the park should claim to have discovered the Round Pond. This question of oil mills for West Africa, for instance—an old suggestion, first made perhaps twenty years ago, and turned down on several occasions for excellent reasons of finance and policy. Now this chestnut had been trotted out again by some enthusiast who saw in it a short cut to salvation. Fortunately, Powers was a level-headed fellow, even if his wild men from the jungles weren't, and this ill-judged proposal could be quietly and decently disposed of without much of a to-do.

Sir Rosslyn, blotting a note on the file, said: "Coming with such a strong recommendation, it will have to go to the Secretary of State. The proposal, of course, cuts right across the directive issued by his predecessor."

"Quite so, Sir Rosslyn. We should oppose it, you know. Since it contains financial provisions——"

"Oh, yes, you people would have your say. All the same there's something in the proposal, you know, even from your angle. These territories have run into pretty heavy weather. Unless they can get clear, you may have them coming down on you in earnest for a grant-in-aid."

The Treasury official, who had been examining his finger-nails with an expression of intense boredom, looked almost startled.

"Surely not! Your people must know that's quite out of the question."

Sir Rosslyn shrugged his shoulders very slightly—a mere twitch.

"There's a limit to economies. I think you'll find the present proposal symptomatic. Desperate times, desperate remedies."

The Treasury man, his ankles crossed and the edge of the mantel-shelf digging into his back below the shoulder-blades, raised his eyes from the threadbare carpet and looked sorrowfully at Sir Rosslyn. He, too, was becoming contaminated! In a weary and disillusioned voice he said:

"It's a matter of principle, you know. And of reversing a Cabinet decision. And of course if the combines got wind of it, they'd fight it tooth and nail. Whatever the merits of the proposal *qua se*—and of those I'm extremely sceptical—you haven't a chance of getting it over the hurdles. Frankly, Sir Rosslyn, it's a waste of time."

Sir Rosslyn smiled briefly: a wintry flicker of the firm lips, showing momentarily a row of excellent teeth. His close-clipped moustache, his flat leathery face and the big bat-ears looked as if they had been moulded from some indestructable and inorganic by-product of water, air and coal. The pipe in the brass ash-tray on his desk, the photographs of two children on the mantel-shelf, were human touches that seemed more like stage props than parts of the man.

"The combines have got to hear of it already. I wish our intelligence was half as good as theirs! This p.q. came in to-day."

He handed over a sheet of paper bearing the typewritten note: 'Mr. Pocklington to ask the Secretary of State for the Colonies:—Whether he is satisfied that the transfer to West Africa of a long-established branch of British industry, namely the processing of oil-bearing nuts, would be in the public interest; whether it would result in an increase of unemployment in an already acutely distressed area; and whether he will guarantee that the taxpayer is not called upon to finance measures which would lead to a further diminution of employment among British workmen.'

"Quite neat," the Treasury official said approvingly. "Pocklington. I seem to know the name."

"A director of the Coastal Trading Company, among other things."

"Ah!" He handed back the paper. "Your reply?"

"A matter for the Board of Trade, of course. But still . . ."

"Quite so." The Treasury man nodded understandingly, and resumed his inspection of his nails. Sir Rosslyn added:

"If it came to a showdown, the Opposition would support him. The only dispute between capital and labour is their relative share of the cake, and this is a question of giving away a slice to someone else, leaving less for both. There's a lot of cant on the Labour side, but they're no more willing than the bloated capitalist to give up some of their perks to the noble savage. They merely want other people to give up theirs."

"Don't we all?" said the visitor languidly, uncoiling himself from his position in front of the fire. "Well, that settles that, I think? Give me a ring if you need any clarification. It's hardly a matter on which I care to bother my master."

"I've made a note on the file. 'The Treasury view is that money could not be found from public funds, in present straightened circumstances, for an enterprise which would, on the short term, lead to a loss of taxable capacity and further unemployment, and which would certainly meet with determined opposition alike from vested interests and the Trade Unions.' That covers it, I think."

"Perfectly, Sir Rosslyn."

"I'm obliged to you for coming round."

"A pleasure, of course . . . I believe you're fond of the ballet, by the way?"

"I go when I can. My wife is an enthusiast."

"I recommend the new Viennese company—really quite impressive. The *Times* man this morning says it's the best choreography since Fokine. Well, I mustn't keep you; good afternoon."

Sir Rosslyn closed the file and laid it aside. Hampton really ought to have known better. Sir Rosslyn was momentarily sorry. As a conscientious official he always endeavoured to put the colonial case as convincingly as he could to other Departments, but through no fault of his own he generally failed to win their acceptance. Colonies, after all, were a long way off, and their denizens were not voters. It was only natural that the interests of the constituents who elected a Minister and put his party in, and who were liable at any moment to materialize on his very doorstep, should weigh with him a great deal more than the suggestions of a civil servant claiming to speak for remote and unseen black-skinned folk who were not in the least likely to send deputations to bother him, and, even if they did, could not possibly turn him out of office.

Sir Rosslyn was well used to seeing his representations brushed aside by more powerful Departments and knew that in the distant colonies he, or rather his office, was always blamed. It

was accused of incompetence, indifference, ignorance, reaction
and impractical idealism: but that was just something that had
to be endured. As for the Protectorate, if trouble arose they must
cope with it as best they could. They were not the only ones.
Hadn't we trouble enough here? Three million unemployed,
trade everywhere still shrinking, rumours of German rearma-
ment, further cuts called for in estimates already pared to the
bone. The telephone rang, a voice said: "The Secretary of
State can see you now, Sir Rosslyn," and he left the room.

His dispatch rejecting the proposals was short, regretful and
firm. Sir Harold Hampton was not in the least surprised. He
passed it without comment to his Chief Secretary, and Freddy
Begg's eyes gleamed when he read it through. Although he had
not for a moment feared that Whitehall would bungle, he felt a
certain sense of relief that the foolish notion had been so effectively scotched.

Now that the danger was over, he admitted to himself that
few events in his whole career had provoked him more than the
sending of this dispatch. He had not been consulted; he had
simply found a copy sitting on his desk one morning, and the
private secretary had informed him quite coolly that the original
had gone off by bag direct from the Governor's office. It was
monstrous: and when he read the dispatch, his anger was over-
powering. He, the Chief Secretary, had worked for weeks to
produce a workable remedy for the Protectorate's ills. That
scheme had been submitted to every possible authority, worked
on in the light of their suggestions, passed by the Council and even
provisionally approved at home, all at exceptional speed to meet
the urgency of the case. He himself had worked on it early and
late; and then, just as the scene was set for its introduction, the
Governor, without a word to anyone, had calmly proposed to
scrap the whole thing and experiment with some quite impractical
alternative! It was enough to strain beyond endurance the
loyalty of the most conscientious man.

Of course, he knew where to look for the source of all the
trouble, the nigger in the woodpile. Robert Gresham! It was
remarkable how often the man crossed his path, and how on
every occasion his actions were perverse, disloyal and irresponsible. Gresham had left his post and behind the back of his
chief, the head of the administration, he had sneaked into the
Governor's study and bamboozled him with half-baked notions,
persuading him, no doubt against his will, to send a wildcat

scheme back to Whitehall as his own proposal. And to think that he, Freddy Begg, had recommended Gresham's appointment as acting Resident! Well, this finally settled it; never again would he be so foolish as to allow a weak impulse of generosity to cloud his better judgment. Thank goodness, the underhand plot had failed. Trust the home authorities to keep their heads! No harm had been done; and Freddy, dwelling on this, regained his usual calm. He had, at least, a pleasurable duty in front of him. Pressing a buzzer, he summoned his stenographer and started to dictate, with his usual clarity, a formal letter to the acting Resident.

Robert was not in the least surprised at its contents. Since he had taken over the province he had become more than ever convinced that his own scheme would gain the support, even the enthusiasm, of most of the factions in the town and of all the growers; he was no less sure that the abrupt introduction of compulsory grading would arouse almost universal resentment, perhaps even disorder. But he was too old a hand to suppose that the mere merits of the two proposals would decide the issue. Freddy Begg, he knew, would oppose any scheme other than his own with gentlemanly ferocity; the big companies would act with equal vigour; and even if, by some miracle, his infant Hercules should slay those two dragons, beyond lay the hydra-headed monster of official inertia, timidity and fear of precedent —a monster that grew a dozen heads, rather than a mythical two, to cancel every decapitation.

Leaning back in his office chair, he began to plan the measures he must take to carry out his orders. The first thing was to explain it all with absolute clarity, and to see that his explanation was carried into the furthest market place and village. That was easy enough to say and possible to do, even, if you had the people on your side. But now the people were not on his side. Between him and the land-grubbing peasant stretched a long chain of native officials—the Emir, his councillors, district heads, village headmen and all the rest. That was where the weakness lay. They passed on not what you said but the words it suited their master to put into your mouth. It was like a game played at children's parties—Russian scandal: you whispered something and it passed from mouth to mouth round the circle of ears, until 'the boy stood on the burning deck' became 'Roy Stanning has a dirty neck'—funny enough at a children's party, but not when your message was deliberately distorted to stir into anger ignorant and gullible people who would be the first to suffer if their resentment flared up into violence.

With a reluctant hand, Robert scribbled a brief note asking for draft of police reinforcements. That would show them what he thought of things! But he derived no satisfaction from this. It had been his first senior, Pawley, who—even in those wild and golden days—had told him: "A political officer who asks for military aid signs his own certificate of incompetence." To-day a good Resident should reduce his police force and spend the money on schools; and now he was forced by circumstances he had opposed to take this distasteful precaution.

Robert's window looked out on to a lawn, at present as brown as the desert which lay so near to it. Dense and dark-leaved mango trees threw round pools of shade and offered shelter to drowsy birds; but others, indifferent to the fierce heat, flitted from shrub to tree in search of insects. He watched two sunbirds hovering with slim curved beaks over the scarlet bloom of a hibiscus; their outstretched wings, glittering with metallic colour, quivered like the heat-haze, beating against the air goodness knows how many hundred times a second. Except for these jewelled specks of motion everything was still and drowsy, as if enclosed in the very core of apathy; even the harsh straw-coloured grasses beyond the lawn did not bend their heads. Amid such drowsiness, such bludgeoned stillness, it was hard to imagine the possibility of turbulent events. Yet he knew this peace to be deceptive; beneath it lay the explosive elements of crude emotion and savage tradition; it was as if one rested on a bed of gun-cotton, soft and fluffy in appearance but impregnated with danger.

Knowing this, it was folly to play with matches. Yet that was what he had been ordered to do. Why must he serve as an instrument to carry out measures he believed to be mistaken? He saw himself as a spade pressed down by the foot of an authority quite indifferent to any protests or opinions of his own into the helpless sod, which was the close inter-locking life of native society; with a heave from unseen muscles he was forced to turn up a spadeful of earth, tearing roots, exposing all the balanced microscopic life that had established itself over the course of centuries. Neither spade nor sod could halt the motion; but if, in the downward thrust, a stone should be encountered, it was the spade that was dented or cracked. A dozen times he had been on the verge of resignation, but he knew that such a gesture would be hollow. Not by an inch would it deflect the intentions of the digger; the twisted spade would simply be replaced by a sharp new one. His belief in his own ability to act, to some extent, as a mediator between the native people and the impersonal authority over them kept him at his post.

Too restless to concentrate any longer on the pile of papers which, as usual, cluttered up his desk, he walked out of his office into the sunlight. The car stood in the shade, its little flag flopping over the radiator, its driver fast asleep over the wheel. He walked past it to a shed where his pony stood with drooping head, kept awake by flies. Nowadays he had all too little time for horses, but he still rode to his office in the early mornings, and now he resolved to go down to the town to acquaint the Emir and his officials with the Government's last word.

A midday languor lay over the town. The heat was heavy, the sky brassy, a fine dust blew about in puffs and eddies. The blue-robed men and black-swathed women going about their business seemed self-possessed and unperturbed as ever, yet beneath their poise they were tired and excitable; the fast of Ramadan was in progress and the cry of the water-carrier was silent, for all through the long hot day no liquid must pass the lips of the devout. Now was the time when people became jumpy and nerve-ridden, when at the slightest quarrel daggers might flash out of wide sleeves; the time when intrigues flourished over midnight repasts, and men grew restless, and the fiercer spirits of Islam could hear their God urging them on to deeds of devotion and valour worthy of their warrior forbears and the Prophet's exhortations.

Robert's pony picked its way between donkeys, children, beggars and the stream of passers-by, and those who recognized its rider curtsied to the dust, touching their forehead with the right hand. As he rode down the street of smiths those who stood in front of their booths at their hand forges, a small boy beside them to handle the bellows, tapped with their hammers three times on the anvil, rendering their craft's traditional salutation to the prince or noble. To each, Robert raised his hand in greeting; and, as he rode along, the sights and smell and gentle bustle of the city and the quiet respect of its inhabitants—his friends—spread like a soothing lotion over his blistered spirit, brightened his eye, and gave him back his self-esteem.

Chapter Seven

IT was more than two years since Benjamin Morris had dined in full panoply with Europeans, and he found that his manners had grown a little rusty. Not that he ate with his fingers at home, or anything so bush; it was just that the courses seemed endless and meal-time conversation laborious. He was used to a single plate—a very large plate—of stew, and perhaps some raw fruit, and of course his girl would never think of sitting with him at a meal—that would be a shameful piece of disrespect. Benjamin smiled to himself; these Europeans, clever as they were, all-powerful, still had much to learn from Africans about the really important things: the treatment of women, for instance. Imagine an African woman dictating to her husband as Englishwomen did, and getting away without a beating or a divorce! But then, he had always disliked European women; something about their angularity and the harshness of their voices confused him, and the hostile expression in their hard, pale, hyena-like eyes. He was glad that none were present to-night. Although this fact was in a sense an insult, he was relieved.

He knew very well the reason why no women were present, he told himself: because they did not care to mix with Africans. There was no colour bar, of course, in the Protectorate. Certainly not! Yet since he had returned to his native land he had scarcely ever been asked to share a meal in a European's house, except on official occasions—garden parties at the Residency, that sort of thing. At first he had wanted to live amongst them, in that quarter outside the walls, on high ground, where the spacious gardens and modern dwellings were set; but he had been told that these were all Government houses, that there was none for him. The Moslems would not have him in the town itself, so he had been forced to seek shelter—a kind of shelter far beneath his dignity and deserts—in the foreigners' quarter, near the Levantine canteens: a crowded, squalid, undignified place where his most congenial neighbours were clerks and schoolmasters, his least respectable bush-natives, sweepers and prostitutes.

Every evening the Europeans in their mansions dined off their gleaming tables with silver spoons and spotless napery at a groaning board, waited on by hosts of lackeys; every evening they told each other in their condescending voices of the poor African's laziness and dishonesty, and of their own superior virtues; yet he, who had read all the important books of science and philosophy, was not invited. There was no colour bar in the Protectorate, oh no! Now, it was true, the Resident had asked him to dinner, but he knew the reason: simply to curry favour, because the *Chanticleer* had become a power in the land. He was not so simple as to be taken in by that.

The small group round the dinner table—for in his wife's absence Robert did not go in for large-scale entertaining—was finding the going rather heavy. Benjamin was aloof, silent and antagonistic. The others did not like to chat away among themselves and leave him out of things, but he ignored every lead that was offered, refusing to be brought in. Shy, or contemptuous; diffident, or swollen with conceit? They did not know, and the evening was not a success. Silences kept fastening on to them and having to be shaken off with a conscious effort, they combed their minds for something to say. That was what put them off these mixed parties: not any foolish objection to sitting down to dinner with a black man—none of them had any prejudices about that—but because, after a long day's work in an exacting climate, they did not feel equal to the mental effort of a polite conversation, of continually making the running and watching their step.

At last, abandoning attempts to avoid shop, they talked about a current murder case. Most of the male population of a pagan village were under arrest for clubbing to death one of their number on the grounds that, while in the shape of a leopard, he had killed several young girls. Now they were standing trial for murder, although from their point of view they had merely carried out a routine security measure against a dangerous enemy of society.

One of the guests, the Government doctor, turned to Benjamin and said:

"I would like to ask you a question."

Benjamin, sitting very stiff and upright, inclined his head and muttered an assent.

"I read the report of this case in your paper. You reported the werewolf part of it all through as if it had really happened. I was so struck with the whole thing I cut it out—I have it here." He pulled a cutting from his pocket and started to read.

" 'Swift retribution was meted out by the people to a villain who assumed the guise of a leopard to claw to death two innocent girls. . . .' " He continued to read to the end. "You see—there isn't a word to suggest that the villagers were misled by superstition. Anyone reading it would think that the murdered man really *did* turn into a leopard. Now, you don't believe in all that nonsense. Isn't it your duty to help sweep away this mumbo-jumbo, not to encourage it? You could do much more than any of us, you know, in that direction."

Benjamin wriggled in his chair. So he was going to be lectured on his duty! Really, to be neglected was better than that. He looked down at his plate with judicial restraint.

"It isn't the duty of a newspaper to take sides."

They all laughed at that. "Duty or not, every newspaper does it. Don't you see that to report fantasy as fact *is* taking sides? The side of mumbo-jumbo and against reason. Considering your—well, your education—you've had a much better education than ninety-nine per cent of Europeans, you know—isn't that a bit irresponsible?"

The doctor had not meant to attack Benjamin, but he was genuinely puzzled by the *Chanticleer's* attitude, and he felt deeply on the subject, for he had come across some very unpleasant results of the more barbarous practices of magic. But Benjamin reacted as he always did even to a hint of criticism, feeling immediately offended and ill-used. These Europeans were so cocksure! How could they know that certain individuals weren't possessed of occult powers? Africa had its Merlins too! A small flat package suspended by a cord from his neck suddenly began to press into his flesh. They would laugh at him if they knew that he himself had paid a secret visit to an old greybeard to receive a charm which would turn the eyes of his veiled inamorata, the merchant's daughter, in his direction. They would laugh—his mind winced at the very thought of their laughter—and say that he was no better than a bush-native. But didn't they themselves fear broken mirrors and walking under ladders, and turn their money at the new moon? Didn't they, too, wear charms to bring them luck and carry foolish mascots? Pots calling the kettle black! He retorted:

"Are you quite certain that everything is really mumbo-jumbo? Can you rationalists explain all phenomena? It was your own poet who said: 'There are more things in heaven and earth, Horatio, than are dreamt of——' "

"But he wasn't thinking of men turning themselves into leopards, and spells to keep away infectious diseases."

"Perhaps not, but can you point the finger of scorn at us Africans? Is it more absurd to believe that a man can turn into a leopard than to say that wine turns into blood when a priest in his robes recites *his* mumbo-jumbo over it?"

There was a shocked silence; even the doctor, a scientific humanist, who in his callow student days might easily have made such a remark, felt that Benjamin had over-stepped the mark.

"To confuse superstition with symbolism merely shows——" he began, and stopped, not wishing to be rude. Robert intervened.

"What do you think should be done, then? Should the law uphold the accused men for ridding their village of a dangerous pest, or condemn them for taking a man's life without proof of his wrong-doing?"

But Benjamin never liked to be pinned down to a positive statement: that was a European manœuvre designed to trip him up. He shrugged his shoulders.

"As an editor, I am not allowed to tell the judges what they must do. But I must consider what my public wants. There is great interest in such cases, so I must report them. But I cannot say: 'Such-and-such a thing has happened. At least, people living in the village of so-and-so say it has happened, but the Europeans say that it has not, and that the people of so-and-so have made it up, because they are ignorant and stupid natives.' That would not bring me many readers, you must admit."

The doctor muttered something inaudible, biting off the end of a cigar with a savage little nip.

"So you believe in giving the public what it wants?"

"Of course. It is the public who must pay their pennies."

Someone else put in: "That was what Northcliffe did."

"Yes, and it created the gutter press," the doctor said vigorously. "If you give people tripe, naturally they'll want more of it. The human body can adapt itself to a diet of raw stinking fish or to one of milk and honey; so can the mind. Surely the job of a decent paper, even of a little local rag like this —excuse me, Morris, I don't want to belittle your paper, but you know what I mean—surely the editor's job is to guide and enlighten public opinion, not debase it."

"I deny that I debase public opinion!" Benjamin had at last been roused from his air of languid superiority. "I give people news of the things that interest them—what is debasing about that? Is it my fault if the things that interest them are not what you would like them to be? We are interested in different things, that's all. I'm not sure that even that is true. For many years I read your English papers and sometimes there was nothing in them but stories of murders, robberies, divorce and football matches. Is that debasing the public taste?"

"Yes, it is," the doctor answered. "I hoped you'd do better."

Benjamin smiled; he had been presented with the perfect rejoinder.

"How can you expect a pupil to do better than his teacher?"

Robert again intervened. "All teachers expect that of their pupils, just as all parents hope that their children will avoid the mistakes they made themselves. Unreasonable, of course, but human."

But the doctor would not be put off. "You're wriggling out of the point, Morris. I suggested that the attitude of your paper was irresponsible. Here's proof. You know that we launched an anti-yaws campaign a little while ago. You know that in one part of the country we met with complete non-co-operation, although the treatment was absolutely safe and effective. Why? Political agitation—anti-Government stuff—and someone who should have known better was spreading the old lie that the injections caused sterility."

"Surely you are not accusing me——"

"No, no, of course not. What I'm saying is that you reported this in your paper not as a lie, but as if it were really true. You said that the people of the district had fled into the bush to escape 'the bad needle' because they feared impotence. Anyone reading it would have thought that they were right. Well, you knew as well as I did that this was a malicious lie, and you must be at least as anxious as I am to see your people cured of yaws. Why didn't you come straight out and tell them that they were being cheated, and that the needle was their friend? That's what I can't understand."

The doctor had raised his voice, and his words drove like angry waves against Benjamin's mind, bludgeoning and soaking it. He could not bear to be so assaulted. Why had he accepted this invitation? Now he must sit among these hostile faces and be lectured to, abused, persecuted! They were jealous because he had made a success of his paper, because people believed the *Chanticleer* instead of the Government's proclamations. 'Have you seen what the *Chanticleer* says about it?' 'No, I must wait for the new copy before I make up my mind.' And so the Europeans abused and persecuted him, trying to drive him away. Looking more than ever aloof and contemptuous, he said:

"An editor cannot check everything personally. He must give his trusted staff a free hand."

"I see," the doctor said gruffly. "Well, that report of yours did us a great deal of harm."

Benjamin was elated. So they admitted his influence—what a tribute to his strength! All the more so for being reluctantly acknowledged. It had started, it was mounting, the tide of his power: slowly but irresistibly the minds of the people were beginning to come under his sway, as oceans felt the tug of the moon. One day that tide would carry all before it, a great cleansing sea, a flood of African might and power; and these white men who heckled him now, so sure of their righteousness, would be swept away like twigs before a torrent.

"Our trouble is that we expect too much," Robert said. "We try to make a new man in our own image, but better than we are, using the same old human stuff; and when our nice new model turns mean and vicious and tries to bite, then we despair. Benjamin, if he'll forgive me, is the new African Prometheus, half god and half man, stealing fire from heaven. And Prometheus, if you remember, grew cunning and cheated the gods of their burnt offering, much to their fury and disgust. Of course, he was the one who suffered most in the end, but that didn't stop him. It always happens, I'm afraid."

"Turning it all into mythology doesn't answer my question," the doctor said. "Nor did Morris—he evaded it. Why do the young men we've educated to become leaders—the *élite*—why don't they help to pull their own people out of the rut? Instead of that, most of them try to sabotage our efforts at every turn. After all, *we're* not getting anything out of things like education and dispensaries and hygiene campaigns—we're doing it all for them, not for ourselves. We get paid for it, admittedly, but not very much, and some of us give up a lot to come and live in this God-forsaken climate. Well, why don't they help? What are they really after?"

He glared at Benjamin, who did not answer; the thoughts in his mind were too big, too confused, for words. How could anyone explain what it felt like to be ruled by others? To be always lectured at, ordered about, jerked like a puppet on a string? To see others eating the kernel of authority and throwing you the empty husks?

Robert ventured to speak for him. "They're after what we're most of us after, in some degree. Few of them recognize it, but it's always there, dangling in front of their noses. They're after power."

"Our jobs, in other words. Well, they'll have them one day; but the sensible ones must know that they're not fit yet to govern without bringing injustice and sheer chaos——"

"Lucifer said the last word on that: 'Better to reign in hell, than serve in heaven.'"

"It would be merry hell, all right, if we left them to it—as it was before we came. Bloodshed, slavery, human sacrifice, tribal wars, filth, disease, malnutrition, famine—infant mortality sixty or seventy per cent—no security of life or limb—the tyranny of disgusting superstitions—that was Africa, that and a lot more, until we came, and if we packed up to-morrow morning it would be back to that before nightfall."

"I agree entirely," Robert said. "It takes generations to build up a tradition. But the fact that people always misuse power doesn't stop them wanting it. 'All power corrupts'—there, in three words, is the core of history. And the results were summed up by an experienced politician: 'Do you not know, my son, with what little wisdom the world is governed?' Benjamin might not agree with either of those statements, but sooner or later his people will have to discover their truth for themselves."

"I still don't think my question's been answered," said the doctor. "How about a rubber of bridge?"

Chapter Eight

BENJAMIN stopped the Resident's car a little way from his house and walked the last few hundred yards. He did not want the disdainful driver to approach any closer, perhaps to see into the squalid living-room with its fly-speckled walls and unscrubbed floor, its cheap cracked crockery and pictures always awry, the scraps of half-consumed food lying on the stained table.

To think that once he had been waited on by Englishmen who were glad enough to take his half-crown! And now even the road foreman and sanitary engineer passed him in the street. Not that he cared; he knew himself better educated than they; he had patience, and would live to see them grovel before him, or be swept away like chaff before the storm. It was really quite amusing to be patronized by such inferior persons, who could not have explained the differences between the Stoic and Epicurean schools, or outlined the quantum theory of mechanics, and probably knew no poetry at all, whereas he could quote reams of it, and understand the ringing words.

Climbing the steps on to his veranda, odd fragments danced in his mind. In rich resonant tones he declaimed aloud: "Resident incorporeal or stretched in vigilance of ecstasy among ethereal paths or the celestial maze." The rolling syllables affected him like wine; he felt elated, sparkling with wisdom and wit.

As he entered the house, some of his elation stayed behind in the shadows. How undignified it looked, how unfitted to his position! And yet this did not disturb him so much as it had done after his return. He had changed in other ways also. At first he had felt himself to be a European, sharing European interests, speaking their idiom and following their point of view. He had subscribed to the *Weekly Times* and the *New Statesman*, and for a while he had read them carefully every evening. But gradually his attention had wandered and his mind had found it harder to remember the details, week after week. Everything seemed so remote and far away—the coalfields of South Wales, factories at Yarrow, the Polish corridor, the American New Deal —as if it were taking place on another planet. Even the books on his shelves grew dusty. He did not renew his subscriptions to the English papers. The clerks and teachers among whom he lived could not discuss these topics, the Europeans held aloof; and so, from lack of nourishment, the plant of his culture had shrivelled and drooped.

Without family, without equals, with neighbours he despised, his solitary spirit had encased itself in a cocoon of dreams. Sometimes the Governor came to ask his advice, and sometimes he was seated in the Governor's chair; the Emir waited upon him and sent him costly presents, the Moslem nobles in the streets saluted him, clerks bowed their heads, and even in distant London clubs the members said to each other: "Have you heard about Benjamin Morris? He has become a great figure now, he is the man who counts in his own country, and the King is sending for him to consult him."

He could see a lamp burning in the sitting-room. Bessie again, extravagant slut! Why hadn't she gone to bed? He began to feel angry. To tell the truth, he was heartily sick of the girl. Her cooking was bad, she was slovenly, he knew that she cheated him, and she was always asking for money. While he was away in his office he suspected that she turned his house into a brothel, and whenever he corrected her she answered him cheekily. He had paid her father something but—thank goodness—he had not married her. As for marriage, he would wait until he found a girl who would not disgrace him. Unbidden, the bright eyes and cloth-swathed figure of the merchant's daughter filled his mind. There was a girl, now: beautiful, modest, quiet-voiced, meek, above all desirable! The Moslems knew how to bring up their daughters, that he must admit: but he cursed their stiff-necked arrogance. He, Benjamin Morris, would not be good enough for them, ignorant yokels that they were, because he did not bow down like a superstitious fool five times a day and regard as exalted any simple oaf who had travelled to an out-of-the-way Arabian town in order to run seven times round a meteorite.

And now not the lovely merchant's daughter but the cheeky slut awaited him. His anger rose as he mounted the steps. Very likely she had been entertaining some man there during his absence. Very well! Lately he had given her one or two good beatings, and for a while they had improved her manners. If that was how the land lay, he would repeat the medicine to-night.

He strode into the room, his face heavy with baleful intentions, and then halted abruptly. The figure seated in his one wicker armchair was not Bessie, but an elderly man with a short grizzled beard dressed in the robes and shawls of the Moslem. From the quality of the cloth and the discreet embroidery of the turban-end worn over neck and chin, and from the man's general bearing, Benjamin judged his unknown visitor to be a person of wealth and position. The stranger rose when he entered, and inclined his head.

"I have come to see you on important matters," he said, using the language of the emirate. "As your slave-girl informed me that your business would not keep you late, I waited. I hope that I have not unwittingly infringed any customs which you observe."

"You are welcome." Benjamin struggled to conceal his curiosity and surprise. "Visitors are always welcome here, I keep open house. Please resume your chair."

The visitor sat down a little uncertainly, in the manner of one unused to chairs.

"I see," he said, glancing round, "that you favour the European style of living. You must forgive me if I am clumsy; I do not find this upright furniture either comfortable or becoming."

Benjamin, a little nettled, replied: "And I prefer to sit than to squat like a bush-native. To each what they are used to. I crave your pardon for keeping you waiting; I have been eating dinner with the Resident."

The shadow of a smile flickered over the man's skinny features. His expression was one of alertness and self-possession, and he had a shrewd, keen look about him suggesting that a competitor would have to rise early to best him in a deal. Benjamin had by now turned over in his mind half a dozen explanations of this startling visit—it was almost unheard-of for a Moslem of standing to seek out an unbeliever in his own home—and by the time courtesies had been exchanged, and coffee heated up and served by a sleepy and sulky Bessie, he had a fair idea of the older man's purpose.

"I have a cousin, related by marriage," the guest said, at last coming to the point, "who is a good young man, very valiant, and not without wisdom when he is well advised. Unfortunately he is a little headstrong and hasty, and blunt in his methods; age and experience will remedy that. When he suffers from a wrong that bites into his spirit he is apt to blurt out what is in his mind without consideration for his listener's feelings. This young man has called upon you, and I fear offended you with crude and perhaps insulting suggestions. But although he was wrong in his estimate of your character, he was quite correct in his belief that your influence in helping to put right the evils from which we in this kingdom suffer would be as powerful and beneficial as a shower of rain falling on the sprouting corn."

Benjamin congratulated himself on his acumen: no doubt about it, his visitor had come as an agent of the party which was intriguing, with ever greater boldness, to oust the usurper (as they described him) and restore to power not the old Emir, but his son—that very Abdulahai who had attempted to buy Benjamin's support. Since his own impulsive refusal, Benjamin had thought about the matter a great deal. Certainly the present Emir had been a disappointment. Nothing had changed, save for the worse. It was sad—an anti-climax. Aboubakar had broken faith, and any obligations which he, Benjamin, might have had towards him were therefore liquidated. This young man, Abdulahai—he was vigorous, go-ahead, he had been educated, and he was no white man's milch-cow; he would know how to use his horns. He therefore listened with attention to his visitor, who, taking his time, bit by bit unfolded his proposition.

Benjamin learnt that a plot to dislodge the present ruler was already well advanced. Details were not revealed, but whereas the usurper Aboubakar had secured the downfall of his predecessor by guile, Abdulahai's party appeared to place its faith in direct action. Ramadan was almost over, soon the harvest would be in and men have strength and leisure for political affairs. At a signal, many would march to the capital and those within the walls would rise; the palace would be beseiged and the Emir and his entourage. forced to fly, and Abdulahai would be proclaimed in his stead.

"And the Europeans?" Benjamin asked. "What do you expect of them?"

"There will be no bloodshed," the older man replied. "Unless resistance is offered, that is, and I do not think there will be any fear of that. We have friends, naturally, within the palace as well as without. Unless there is fighting, the Europeans cannot interfere. In any case their police are so few that they will not dare to challenge us, who are many. The Europeans will simply find that they must deal with a new Emir, that is all."

Benjamin felt that this aspect of the affair had been rather lightly passed over, but he was in no mood to quibble. The idea of a plot stirred and excited him. At last something great was going to happen in this stagnant city! He saw himself at the head of an immense crowd of people flowing together towards the palace, shouting and cheering as he raised a banner and bore it forwards above their heads. He would liberate them from tyranny, their children would bless his name.

"But you have not explained what part you are anxious for me to play in this affair."

"Your part," his visitor said slowly, watching his face, "is first of all to arouse the people to a sense of their wrongs, and then to explain to them that these can only be put right if they act together and with boldness. A word printed in the *Chanticleer* to-day is known to-morrow even in the bush, for those who can read tell those who cannot by word of mouth. And so it has come about that your opinions are listened to with respect."

Benjamin, deeply flattered, nodded his head.

"When the *Chanticleer* crows, the bush-chickens cackle."

"That is well said. But now the *Chanticleer* crows only of Aboubakar's virtues, never of his shortcomings. People are beginning to say: 'Why does this fine bird lend its support to evil purposes? Can it be that it is not a cock at all, but only the Emir's tame canary?' "

Benjamin started forward in his chair with an indignant denial, but the other stopped him.

"I can only warn you what people are starting to say. There is still time to prove that the *Chanticleer* is indeed a bird of independence and spirit. You, with your great intelligence, have surely seen that people begin to grow weary of Aboubakar's misrule, of the high taxes, of the way they are cheated over the price of their crops. Has not God shown his displeasure by sending little rain and many locusts? The people grow weary and they turn away from Aboubakar and from all who support him—even from the *Chanticleer*. But if that cock would champion their just complaints, people would say: 'Here is a fine bird of courage that is not afraid to crow in the Emir's face; here is a bird we can trust'; and they would follow you. That will be your part: to command the support of the people for the rightful Emir."

Benjamin lit another cigarette—the ground at his feet was littered with flattened stubs—and considered. He saw it all now. His hand was to give the signal for a bloodless revolt. An important part in the vanguard of action! The idea appealed to him powerfully, but beneath all his visions and vanity he was a shrewd and careful young man. He saw that the revolutionary party had estimated too lightly some of the difficulties, and he was not at all sure how far their belief in Aboubakar's loss of prestige was correct. To make a blunder now would be an irreparable disaster. And while he knew that British laws of free speech would enable him to go as far as he liked in attacking the Emir and the Government that supported him (indeed the more he attacked them, the pleasanter the Europeans would probably become) he was by no means so certain of Aboubakar's acquiescence. He was in a land where barbarism and savage

practices lay only just beneath the surface, suppressed but far
from eradicated by the watchfulness of British-paid police. An
attack on his person, or at the least violence to his office, could not
be ruled out. He decided, therefore, to go slowly with this
emissary.

"I must have time to think over your proposal. Important
matters such as this cannot be settled in a moment."

The other nodded. "You are a man of discretion. This I am
glad to know, for I wish to mention another quite different
matter, of a personal kind."

"How can there be a personal matter between us, since we are
not acquaintances?"

"It is true we have not spoken, but, if I am not mistaken, your
wishes, if not your feet, have often crossed the threshold of my
house."

Benjamin was puzzled. "I do not understand."

"I have a daughter now of marriageable age. Friends have
told me of a young man, unfortunately not a believer, who has
followed her to the market place and sometimes waited by the
gate for a glimpse of her youthful form."

Benjamin was completely taken aback. "You are Sulieman
the merchant! I did not know—I have never addressed her—I
can assure you that nothing has occurred which you as a father
should object to——"

The merchant chuckled at these stammered protests.

"Of that I am quite aware. My daughters are well attended,
and good care is taken that no harm shall befall them. I know,
also, that a young man's desires may leap ahead of his discretion,
and that a young girl may throw her glances over the highest
barrier and through the thickest wall."

Benjamin was amazed at the merchant's good nature. For an
unbeliever to look at a rich Moslem's daughter was regarded as
an outrage, never to be mentioned except in terms of threats and
warnings. Could it be that this Sulieman, knowing the importance of the *Chanticleer's* proprietor, was prepared to consider
him as a son-in-law? Such a thing would be no less remarkable
than a flying donkey or a talking tree. It must be a trap. But
Sulieman went on:

"I must tell you that my daughter has taken a fancy to you
which nothing can cure. It is natural for her family to be distressed. Nevertheless this daughter, who appears to be possessed
of exceptional resolution as well as of great beauty, will not be

dissuaded. She wishes to marry you, Benjamin Morris. Although I do not deny that this is a bitter draught to swallow, I am an exceptionally indulgent father, and I am willing to agree, but on one condition—that absolute secrecy is maintained. Were it known that I had consented I should be openly reviled, and I should not dare to show myself again in the mosque. But if the girl can be secretly conveyed to your house and if you will swear to protect and cherish her, and never to breathe to anyone a word of her true identity, then—because of my love for her and my respect for you—I will consent."

Benjamin was wildly excited. Could it be that the dearest dream of his life, the most shining and unattainable vision, was about to become a reality? He could scarcely believe in such a miracle. Yet his sanguine nature would not listen to the nagging voice of doubt. Was not the girl's father, Sulieman the merchant, sitting here in front of him in his own house, telling him the truth? There was no illusion about that. After all, then, they had recognized his worth; they had not been able to stand out against his ability! And the girl—it had been no illusion when their looks had met, she had seen at a glance into his heart. Yes, it was certainly a miracle, but no more than he deserved.

His wonder became even greater when he learnt that payment of the bride-price, which would naturally be very heavy, would be postponed; since, as Sulieman pointed out, heavy payments of cattle and kola nuts would certainly be discovered by the gossips of the town.

"Your support for my cousin Abdulahai," Sulieman said, "will equip you with a fair claim to become the son-in-law of Sulieman the merchant, since by supporting a just cause, even an unbliever may serve the purpose of God. Later, when Abdulahai has been raised to his rightful position, we can come to an agreement on the sums to be paid."

Benjamin understood perfectly, and was quite content. Certainly it was only right to give his support to the cause of a man who behaved in such a gentlemanly fashion. With such a wife at his side he would dare anything, conquer all dangers, ride on to triumph and glory! The day would come when Sulieman the merchant, ashamed at present to give his daughter openly in marriage, would boast about his rich and famous son-in-law. And he would be a husband in a thousand; she should want for nothing. He would dress her in cloths of silk and velvet more costly than any in the city—if necessary he would send to

London for them. He would load her with jewels, they would sparkle like stars on her delicate fingers and soft arms. Beauty that all must envy she would display to an astonished world; he would teach her the manners of civilized people and she would go everywhere with him, to dine with Europeans, to Government House, to England; her grace, her poise, her wit would confound the proudest noblewoman and one day win the praises of the Queen.

He parted with Sulieman in a state almost of ecstasy, stammering his thanks. The merchant took his leave with dignity and rode off on his waiting donkey, preceded through the silent streets by a servant with a lighted torch.

Now Benjamin was all fire and impatience. To-morrow he would start to prepare everything for his bride. As he threw off his clothes he touched the charm dangling on his chest. He was electrified; and there rushed over him the conviction that the old greybeard's spell hid a potency no western scientific theory could explain. Beneath his fingers it seemed to swell and move as if animated, almost he could feel it throbbing like a heart. Europeans didn't know everything! And this old man, dwelling quietly with secrets inherited from his ancestors, had found a wisdom that eluded them. This charm had indeed drawn the eyes of the beautiful young girl towards him; how else could the miracle have been achieved? Awe-struck, he fell asleep in his tousled bed feeling that fate herself had stepped aside from her path among the stars to crown him with her favours.

Chapter Nine

THE end of Ramadan passed off quietly—that is, without disturbance, for the beating of drums and the shouting of the people kept the town anything but peaceful. The Emir paraded through the streets according to custom with his bodyguard on their prancing horses, ribbons and pennants flying from silver-plated bridles that glittered in the sun. The riders wore their traditional finery: some the old chain mail of the Crusades, some encased from head to foot in a curious quilted armour that gave them something of the appearance of mounted divers, brandishing spears. Their horses, also, wore this quilted armour, and with silver ornaments and ribbons fluttering from mane and tail presented an appearance altogether fantastic.

As the Emir advanced through the city on a charger even more fancifully caparisoned, the people who packed the narrow streets threw themselves to the ground and bowed their faces into the dust. Ahead of the ruler danced the court flatterers and heralds who kept up in high and urgent tones a continual stream of praise for their masters and exhortations to the people to show thanks for their immeasureable good fortune in having a ruler so noble, so mighty, and so merciful. The crowds shouted and cheered, in back streets fires were lit and feasts prepared. All was rejoicing, movement and colour, and memories of past triumphs and glories—the return of armies burdened with loot and hot with victories—were alive in the town.

Although excitement ran high there was no bloodshed, and all seemed loyal to the Emir, at least on the surface. A few days later the police reinforcements that Robert had asked for arrived. A senior officer came with them to take command of all the police stationed near (but not in) the town. He walked into the office, saluted, and reported his arrival, and the Resident looked up to see Maurice Cornforth standing by his desk. Robert welcomed him as an old friend, glad that someone he knew and could rely on was to take charge.

"I thought you were on leave," he said.

"I got back last week. I'd just got the curtains hung and the mottoes up over the mantelpiece when they told me to bring this draft up here. D'you really think there will be trouble?"

Robert shrugged his shoulders. "Who knows? They seem happy as sandboys at the moment. It's when we start chucking their produce on the fire that they may take umbrage."

"Shouldn't blame them," Maurice agreed. "When does the balloon go up?"

"Next week. How about accommodation?"

"The inspector has fixed me up in his bungalow."

"Well, come and dine to-night and tell me the latest news."

They dined alone, and it seemed to Robert that his companion had changed. Of course, it was natural—they had all changed, for that matter. They had grown older, probably not wiser and certainly sadder; nowadays life had become more earnest and more of a struggle. Maurice had lost the sparkle Robert remembered, even in appearance he was heavier and less lively. And he drank too much. That had always been a weakness, although he could not have been called, by local standards, a hardened drinker. But to-night he was drinking hard by any standards, and the flushed look on his face, the puffiness under the eyes, the unsteady hand suggested that this was no single aberration.

The table had been cleared of all but dessert plates and a bottle of brandy before Maurice, speaking thickly but plainly, startled his host with the words:

"I saw Priscilla just before I sailed."

"Oh? She didn't mention it in her letters."

Maurice laughed. "Hardly worth mentioning, was it? Priscilla's in a bad way." He shook his head.

"I hardly need your observations to tell me——"

Robert broke off, immediately regretting the harshness of his tone. It was only natural for Maurice to speak about her, and natural for him to see her, too; they had always been friends. He knew what people had said when they had all shared the same station: that he was a fool to let his wife be so much in the company of a man of Cornforth's reputation. He had never cared what people said nor had he wished to build his behaviour on a foundation of mistrust. He added, in less prickly tones:

"Of course I know only too well that Priscilla's health is rotten. That's the worst of being stuck out here—I can do nothing about it. But I'm afraid there's not much to be done."

Maurice shook his head mournfully over his brandy.

"You're dead right, old boy. Nothing to be done."

The glass, his host, his own voice, all seemed a long way off. He had not intended to speak at all of that visit; now he was afraid of saying too much. He had found her in a little house near the sea, within reach of her mother's, a place where there was plenty for Robin to do in the holidays—sailing, fishing, a pony to ride. She had lost her haggard fever-ridden look, but nevertheless he was disturbed by the way the veins stood out on her neck, and by an indefinable hint of frailty.

"You oughtn't to be living by yourself," he said.

Priscilla smiled. "Surely that's correct, in a grass widow?"

"But not someone whose health——"

"Please leave my health out of it!" He was startled by the sharpness of her tone. "I'm sorry, please don't pay any attention to my snaps; the thing is, I'm thoroughly sick of the subject. Nothing is more boring than to treat one's body like a kind of barometer: up this morning, we shall have fine weather; down this afternoon, we must put off the picnic and have indoor games. Much better just to do what one wants to do and forget about one's ups and downs."

She showed him round the place, a small farm house overlooking a green coombe, with a little garden and a large orchard. The farm buildings were used now for Robin's pony and for storing potatoes and fuel, but a few pigs and poultry had begun, as it were, to seep in, and in a paddock below the orchard two Guernseys munched the lush grass.

"You're turning yourself into a farmer?"

"Hardly that; but it seemed a pity to waste the buildings, and it's fun for Robin. A man comes from the village to milk the cows and feed the pigs."

"I've only got a month left. A place like this makes one realize that farm life's the best, when all's said and done. I wish I'd had the sense to have a crack at it myself."

She shook her head. "Then you'd have said: 'why sweat night and day to grow things that everyone wants but no one can afford to pay for? It's all muck and overdrafts; I wish I had a nice safe job in the colonial police.' All the same, it might have suited you."

They stood in the orchard near a little pond where ducks rummaged among water-weeds, sucking in food with a comfortable clabbering sound. It was late September, sunless but warm and muggy. Apples hung on the trees like lanterns, and above, in the garden, dahlias blazed in the borders as if they had gathered into their petals all the last of summer's violent colours. The grass under their feet was damp, the air heavy with a feeling of lethargy. Beneath this woollen cloak, silent and invisible activity proceeded: larvæ tunnelled away within apples, bees sucked at flowers, rooks and field-mice gathered the first acorns for secret storage, and from beyond the orchard came the sharp sound of a woodpecker tapping for grubs. The insect world was hard at work getting food in and the last eggs laid before the germ of life must needs be locked away in seed and egg, safe for spring's resurrection.

"Robin must like this place," Maurice said.

"Yes, he's blissfully happy. I hardly see him; he's made friends with the farmers and locals and is off all day. Social life at his age is terrific."

"And Robert? This must be a good place to come back to."

"No, Robert feels a stranger. It's not his place, you see, and when he comes back, it's like staying in someone else's house. Other people's books and other people's routine; he didn't plant the bulbs or dig the borders. Visitors come to the house who know more about my daily life than he does, and mystify him with small local jokes about the village. And Robin finds it easier to talk to them than to his own father. No, Robert hasn't been happy here."

"He expects too much, then," Maurice said unkindly. "And you? Are you happy, Priscilla?"

They were standing under an apple tree, a basket of windfalls at their feet. Without replying she stooped and began to pick up some of the fallen fruit. Her face was hidden but, as he watched her movements and the light on her hair—almost matched by the yellow jumper she was wearing—the old longing came back like an opening wound. He had never been free from it altogether. A hundred times, a thousand perhaps, she had invaded his thoughts, each time leaving a little bruise of frustration and sadness; and in defiance of his reason, hope had never quite died. Life without her was like music without rhythm or a ride without an object: all the parts were there, but no pattern; all the elements, but no satisfaction.

Turning to face him, she said:

"I owe you an explanation, I suppose. Dragging you down here——"

"You know I was glad of an excuse to come. If I can do anything——"

Priscilla began to polish absent-mindedly an apple which she held in her hand. He had the feeling that she was reluctant to say more, that in summoning him she had acted on an impulse which she now regretted.

"But if I can't," he added, "don't worry; the main thing is that I've seen you again. I shall remember this afternoon often —one does, you know, when one's alone, and not especially enthralled with the view from one's veranda and the umpteenth case of cattle theft. That's the worst of our sort of job; after a bit we live on memories of our last leave or plans for the next, and scramble through the in-between times in any sort of order."

"That's just the point—it's always the past or the future! Why can't we enjoy the present sometimes, as ordinary people do?"

"I'm an ordinary enough person, heaven knows!"

"Yes, and so am I. I wasn't made for a life of perpetual cold storage! Look at this apple—it rots if it isn't used. We all do, and that's been my trouble; for years I've been rotting, and now time's getting short. . . . But I didn't ask you here to listen to tirades of self-pity!" With a quick impatient flick of the wrist she tossed the apple into the long grass and before she could draw back her hand Maurice had captured it.

"What are you trying to tell me, Priscilla?"

"I wrote to you because I was lonely. Years ago you made me promise that if ever I wanted you——"

"Yes, I know. Have you changed your mind, then? Do you mean to leave Robert?"

She studied the damp grass at her feet, and answered, barely audibly: "Robert has left me, in a sense. I'm not a wife to him any longer, only an idea in his mind. Is it very silly to want a life of my own? I suppose it is, when one's middle-aged——"

"So you've seen it at last! That was what I tried to tell you the last time we met. You had no use for me then. It's no good, you know, unless you're sure that the two of us together——"

She had gone very pale, and at last raised her eyes to his face.

"Oh, Maurice, I've missed you so! I thought I should forget you, but I haven't, I've thought of you more and more. But all this is stupid—by now you've changed——"

He did not let her finish; and both found that their desire had only lain dormant to awake with greater force, as if during the long winter of parting it had gathered strength to thrust up with all the vigour of a March daffodil.

Yet something was wrong. As they walked back through the garden she leant on him heavily and he noticed a throbbing pulse in her neck, a little lump rising and falling. A sense of foreboding crept up like a morning wind, and strengthened when they reached the sitting-room with its big window opening on the garden to let in a smell of earth and wet flowers. Her breath was coming in shallow gasps. Noticing his distress, she brought out of a cupboard glasses and a bottle of brandy, saying with forced lightness:

"My secret vice! Only nothing's very secret here; it comes out on the bus and gets dropped off at the butcher's."

Sitting on a narrow seat under the window a strong light fell on to her face, and he was shocked by the change in her. It was something hard to define. Her eyes looked darker, and he could have sworn that she was in pain: her movements had a brittle, premeditated stiffness. Disturbed, he put down his glass and came to sit beside her on the window-seat, taking her hand. It was cold and dry.

"Priscilla, you're not well! Shall I call a doctor?"

She jerked her hand away as if he had stung her. "Can't you forget my everlasting health——" The hand went to her breast, and then back into his. "I'm sorry! We mustn't quarrel."

"We never shall."

"What do you mean?" She spoke sharply.

"Only that whatever you say is right, and I'm not the quarrelsome kind. Priscilla, what are we going to do?"

She looked away from him, out of the window.

"You once asked me to go away with you——"

"You'd be willing to face that?"

"Yes, if you would. But I won't fasten myself round your neck——"

"There's no question of that." But in his own ears his voice sounded leaden.

"If we can spend this last month of your leave together, at least life will have given us something for our money."

"You don't think I'm going to let you go now? Not this time, Priscilla! I shall cling like a leech. And neither of us wants a Grand-Hotel-for-the-week-end sort of business. We ought to explain things to Robert——"

"Robert! He has too much——"

Her voice broke off in a sort of choke. She was kneeling on the window-seat with her back towards him, and he could hear her breath coming in gasps, and then a half-formed groan escaped her. He put his hands out and touched her shoulders, but quickly withdrew, knowing that she did not want his help. Indeed, there was nothing he could do, and he turned away, not bearing to see her suffer. In a few minutes the rasp of her breathing quietened. Pouring more brandy he held the glass over her shoulder and without a word she took it with a shaking hand. When at last she turned her face was deathly white and the pulse in her neck was throbbing jerkily.

"All right?"

She smiled slowly and carefully, as if afraid that a twitch of the muscles might start again the wheels of pain.

"It's nothing. These—twinges are soon over. Sit down, Maurice. If you meant what you said, we must make plans."

He did not dare to meet her glance, but watched the pulse; it had a sort of double motion: long, short—too late, too late, it seemed to say, bobbing up urgently under the skin—too late, too late! He sat down beside her.

"You'd be better away from here—a complete change of scene. Abroad somewhere: France, don't you think? I've got an old car. We could get down to the south and the sunshine——" He talked on quickly, going into details. Priscilla agreed to everything with an exhausted calm that frightened him because it was so unnatural, but he could see that bit by bit his words were building up her confidence.

"Next week Robin goes back to school," she said. "It feels very empty and pointless here when he's gone. This time it won't matter, I'll join you in London, and then—Maurice, you aren't nervous about these stupid attacks? They're brought on by worry, I think, as much as anything. I'll promise not to land you with an invalid on your hands."

Maurice could not look at her. He had once seen a gazelle, shot through the heart, leap forward in a burst of gathered-up vitality, seeming barely to skim the ground until it fell stone-dead in its tracks. He remembered now that last spurt, that final flare-up of energy. With despair in his heart, he tried to force confidence into his tones.

"Of course you'll be all right—don't worry about that for a moment. All you need is a change of air. We can take things easy, and you'll be twice as fit once you get away. . . ."

But it was no good: he had over-done it, his voice had betrayed him—too loud, too bland, too hearty. Their eyes met, and he saw in hers recognition of failure. She knew then that they would never meet in London and drive together down the humped and tree-lined roads of France. But neither spoke.

Now, sitting at her husband's table and sweating slightly in the stuffy heat, her face was again before him, her voice in his ears. He tried to fix his wavering eyes on his dessert plate, but to his dismay the piece of china he had singled out (it had a vine-leaf pattern) began to move gently backwards and forwards, or rather up and down. It reminded him of something. Suddenly he saw that it was throbbing like a pulse, up and down, up and down, like the pulse he had watched in her neck, and he pushed back his chair, horror-struck, with a half-articulate cry. Then he realized that Robert was looking at him and, taking out his handkerchief, he flicked at the table, muttering something about a spider. He could see that Robert didn't believe him, but it didn't matter, he would only think his guest was drunk, as indeed he was. He had been drunk, off and on, for much of the time since he had left home, and there seemed no reason why he shouldn't be drunk a great deal more, as many better men than he had been before him in this part of the world.

But that did not keep Priscilla away. Maurice felt the need of speech, the silence was frightening him, and now that she had entered his mind he could not speak of anything else.

"I saw her once more," he said in a rambling way. "In a nursing home, by that time. Much the best plan—nursing home, I mean—properly looked after. She sent you a message—not allowed to write. Pale, the veins in her neck—I had to come back. That's what she said."

He was seeing her face, propped up on the pillows, and hearing her tell him that he must sail as he had planned and carry out his orders, and not stay, as he wanted, uselessly at her side. "I dare say I'll be up and about in a few weeks," she had told him, "so don't worry, and forgive me, if you can, for all the upset." "They'll put you right in here," he had said, looking round the bare hygienic room. "There'll be time yet——" "Time to repent, perhaps," she had answered, smiling; "but you mustn't fret, it's better this way. . . . Give my love to Robert, and tell him there's plenty of bramble jelly waiting (it's his favourite), and that Robin's in his school eleven this term—they won't let me write. And thank you for everything, Maurice, my dear."

He realized that Robert was talking: something about applying for special leave. He scarcely listened; it did not matter now.

"They won't release me until this business here is over. If things pass off quietly I'll get home next month. Everything depends on that: and that's where you come in, partly."

"Who'd be a policeman? Fools who rush in where administrating angels have trodden everything to hell!"

"We're hardly angels, unfortunately."

"Oh, I don't know. Look how you harp on your emoluments."

Under a cover of a random flippancy, he tried to control his feelings, but all the while his eyes dodged the patterned plate in front of him: it was throbbing up and down, up and down, swelling and shrinking with the unrelenting rhythm of a pulse.

Chapter Ten

A WEEK after Benjamin Morris had dined at the Residency —an event which Robert knew would be construed as a kind of bribe, but which had not been so intended, for he had simply invited Benjamin as soon as possible after his return—the very week after this, the *Chanticleer* elected to launch a stinging attack on the Government's new proposals. This attack was inaccurate, offensive and unfair. It suggested that produce rejected by the inspectors would be bought up for next to nothing by the Emir's agents, who would then re-sell it to the companies, and so enormously enrich themselves and their master. In fact the whole project was 'exposed' as a put-up job between the Emir and the companies, with the connivance of the Government, to fleece the innocent peasant.

Coming at such a moment, on the eve of the scheme's introduction, this report could do infinite damage, for Robert knew it to be a peculiarity of human nature, whether civilized or savage, to believe always the more complicated and less creditable explanation of human motives. He went straight down to the office of the *Chanticleer*.

Mr. Robbins was so startled at the Resident's advent that he stood tongue-tied, smiling and bowing with an almost Japanese effusiveness; and, before he could warn his employer, Robert had walked into the editor's office. Benjamin had borrowed Mr. Montgomery's typewriter to order from a London firm's catalogue some tastefully upholstered furniture worthy of his bride. He looked up angrily, having given orders that he was not to be disturbed, and was dismayed to find himself caught by the Resident at a task fit only for clerks, and beneath the dignity of editors. But he achieved an air of reserved welcome.

Robert carried a copy of the offending issue and, tapping the article with his finger, demanded:

"Whatever possessed you to publish this nonsense, Benjamin? You know as well as I do that it's a pack of lies!"

"Mr. Gresham, I do not print lies in the *Chanticleer*!" Benjamin sat up in his chair, genuinely indignant.

"Forgive me, but you do. There's not a word of truth in this story, and you know it. You know also that it's to the people's advantage to get this scheme running smoothly. You claim to protect their interests. Well, what about it?"

Benjamin felt more than ever injured at this hectoring attack. The intolerance of Europeans! Always bullying, trying to make people explain and justify, to twist things in their own favour.

"I have sources of information which, as an editor, I cannot disclose," he said in his most aloof tones. "They have revealed to me the secrets of this plot. Naturally, it is my duty to publish them. If the Government is behind-hand in finding out these nefarious activities, why blame me?"

"You seriously suggest that the Emir is planning to buy up the condemned produce and then re-sell it?"

"That is what I have heard."

"You must know that the companies would never connive at it nor the Government allow it! Come, come, Benjamin, that isn't worthy of you."

Benjamin shrugged his shoulders rather elaborately.

"How am I to know what is in the minds of the great men who control these great firms? They have not condescended to take a mere native into their confidence. My duty is to print what my agents find out, however unpleasant to the high and mighty."

"If you think it's your duty to invent sensational lies in order to put the people against measures taken to help them, I'm afraid you've got things quite wrong." Robert checked himself; he was losing his temper, and that would achieve no more than to provide Benjamin with free entertainment. More calmly, he added:

"Will you publish a denial?"

"A denial? How can I deny it, if it is true?"

Robert stood up and, taking his copy of the *Chanticleer*, tore it deliberately across and threw the pieces on to the floor.

"That is what every decent citizen will think of a newspaper that prints lies instead of truth in order to please the vanity of its editor! That is where such a paper belongs—underfoot. Benjamin, I warn you, you are going too far. The law makes it a crime to incite to disaffection or rebellion. You're running very close to the wind. If you persist—well, be careful. The penalties for that offence are heavy."

Turning on his heel, he walked out of the room, hoping that his bluff would take effect. For it was bluff, of course. Although Benjamin's article did in fact incite the people to resist the Government's measures, and although such resistance might lead even to rebellion, Robert knew that such accusations were almost impossible to prove and, in any case, could only be proved after the event. The British resolve to allow the fullest freedom of speech allowed also a degree of licence apparently impossible to limit.

The trouble, he thought, as his car hooted its way back to his office, was that under the British system society, in limiting its own powers, assumed that its self-denial would be matched by an equal moderation in the citizens. But moderation was a plant of slow growth, needing careful nurture in a highly civilized garden—not a wild plant, not a savage virtue. Ibrahim the court interpreter had once related how, as a child, before the British conquest, he had seen a man and a woman suffer the standard punishment for adultery committed during Ramadan—four hundred strokes laid on by slaves with a thonged whip of rhinoceros hide. Neither had survived the torture. Robert had himself seen evidence of the old penalty for theft: men whose hands had been so deeply slashed and then so tightly bound that fingers and palms had grown together into shapeless lumps of scarred and useless tissue.

What would have happened to Benjamin, only fifty years ago, had he ventured to oppose the Emir's policy? To begin with, fifty years ago there would have been no Benjamin. He was entirely a British creation. But had any individual shown even a fraction of his temerity, his fate would have been a certain and an agonizing death. To-day the only bogey that Robert could shake at him was a fine of a few pounds or the threat of legal action—in itself considered a highly diverting game—with, at the end, a slender chance of a mild period of safe and comfortable detention, carrying with it no stigma, but rather the reverse. (He remembered a sign he had seen outside a little carpenter's shop, bearing under the man's name the boasted qualification: 'Two years, H.M. Prisons.') No wonder the Benjamins of the country were out on the spree.

In other words, Robert thought, as his car drew up outside the provincial office, laws that did very well in our own temperate and tempered island were not always best for a raw and more than half-savage chunk of tropic. Why, indeed, should they be? We did not transplant the lilac and the rose to the land of date-palm and millet and.expect them to flourish; yet we assumed that laws and values—no less than plants the produce of long evolution—

would adapt themselves instantly to this alien soil. If the empire fell, he concluded, it would not be from abuses or oppression, but simply from lack of imagination.

Back at his desk, he drafted a telegram to the Chief Secretary. His proposal was twofold: to suspend publication of the *Chanticleer*, and to arrest Abdulahai. Suspension of the newspaper could only be temporary, and would doubtless both increase the editor's venom and advertise his wares; nevertheless, by the time the paper again appeared in the streets the grading scheme would be in operation, the Government's prestige upheld and Benjamin would have learnt that authority had claws and was sometimes not afraid to use them. As for Abdulahai, Robert believed him to be the ringleader, and his sudden disappearance might throw out the plans of his followers. Arrests on vague charges of inciting to disaffection were, he knew, looked on by authority with extreme disfavour, and scarcely ever made; he had no evidence against the young man; but if he could be got out of the way for the next ten days the crisis would be over and the bits and pieces could be tidied up afterwards.

Robert coded the telegram himself and handed it personally to the dispatch clerk, knowing all too well how many leaks were liable to spring up in the best regulated office. He smiled as he pictured its reception. Such decisive action—he would dub it 'high-handed'—would be anathema to Freddy Begg, and shades of parliamentary questions would close in on him. Yet, if he refused, and if the *Chanticleer* fermented trouble (as it surely would) and Abdulahai went about his nefarious business and trouble duly came, a Chief Secretary who had refused to the man on the spot the precautionary powers he had demanded would be forced to take a major share of the blame.

No reply came. By the end of a week the chance to stop the next and critical issue of the *Chanticleer* had passed by. Once again, Freddy Begg had sought a compromise: he had neither given authority nor denied it, he had simply ignored the request. Well, Robert told himself, that wasn't good enough; to withhold authority was tantamount to refusing it, and if trouble should come, he was resolved to place the blame squarely where it belonged.

The next *Chanticleer* came out two days late—the day before the grading centres were due to open. Robert's first impression was that Benjamin had paid some heed to his warning. The grading scheme was dealt with on an inner page, and with quite sober headlines. But as he read on, the inflammatory nature of the writing became more and more clear.

Benjamin started by describing, quite correctly, the main outlines of the Government's plan. He went on to repeat even more recklessly his previous falsehoods: that rejected produce would be seized and sold for their master's benefit by the Emir's officials. It was when he came to the action urged on his public that Robert smelt the real danger. This was simple: to burn all the produce openly in the market place.

'Let us build a mighty conflagration,' Benjamin declaimed, 'to protest to God against our enslavement under the heel of the tyrant! Let our crops ascend in flames to heaven rather than fill the coffers of the oppressor! Our clarion call goes forth to all patriots—rally to the city to pile upon the bellowing conflagrations the fruits of your labours, so the whole world shall know of the tyranny under which we groan!'

Robert threw the paper angrily on to his desk. He did not at all like this talk of fires and crowds. Once again he cursed the timidity and vacillation of the Chief Secretary. At the least, that article would draw unwanted and suspicious crowds to the city; at the worst it would incite them to carry out its suggestion with all the risk of over-excitement and explosion.

He was alone in the Residency that night—like a flea in a drum, he thought, for the place was much too pretentious for a solitary man. At such times he found it soothing to talk with his old friend Ibrahim and, summoned by a messenger, the court interpreter sat with him in the little open-sided pavilion where the chameleons had their cage. In his view, there was little popular feeling against the Emir Aboubakar, a just ruler honestly anxious to do his best for his people but gravely handicapped by events, and even more so by disloyalty in his own palace. Robert asked.

"His nephew Abdulahai—is his following strong?"

"He is known to be devout, he has made the pilgrimage, many respect him as a man of courage and strength. It is said that he would not consent to be a pack-ox for the Government, loaded down with burdens, over-meek. Yes, the young hot-heads follow him, and even a few of the merchants and older men who seek position for themselves. These nights, the Emir Aboubakar does not sleep soundly in his bed."

"To-morrow, a police guard will be set over the palace."

"Policemen without will not avail against traitors within,"

Ibrahim remarked; and added with relish: "It is said that Abdu-lahai's friends used a clever trick to win over the young nincompoop of the *Chanticleer*."

Robert picked up his ears. "Money, position, or women?"

"The last, lord. He desires a virgin, the daughter of a rich merchant. For the promise of this girl in marriage, he would proclaim in his newspaper that his own mother was a whore."

"Can an honourable merchant make a promise that he cannot keep?"

"Should the pack-ass bray at the purebred filly? Wits are a man's weapons; he must blame only himself if he does not keep them bright."

"Wiles and stratagems! There's nothing but trickery, Ibrahim, among your people."

Ibrahim chuckled. "You do not complain if the melon is full of pips. God who thus encumbered melons gave us teeth to spit out the pips. Trickery shows a ready mind, plain dealing a dull one."

"And all your history is of wars and massacres. A fine lot!"

"You hold it improper for young men to fight enemies and infidels?"

"Such is the teaching of the founder of our faith."

"It is not the teaching of the Prophet. Nor was it yours, when you came to us as conquerors. Now that you are masters, you tell us of the virtues of peace, which indeed are great, when it comes to the payment of taxes."

"Then you reject peace and order?"

"Not I, for I am old, and old men desire security. But the young men do not want to stay at home until they are fat like women. How can a man show his courage and hardihood except in battle? What is there to lift his heart now that the trumpets are silent? What pleasure can he take in a swift horse, save to pursue a flying foe? Life for the young men has lost its savour; they yearn for the delights of battle as the traveller for salt. We who are old remember the triumphs of our youth; but these young men, when they are old, what will they have to remember?"

"There are men in my own country," Robert said, "who think as you do; but the trouble is that it is no longer a matter of young men riding after each other—or after helpless flying slaves— with swords in their hands. The master of future wars will not be the youth with a sword but perhaps his father, short-sighted and weak-limbed, who sits among his books and instruments and invents devices to wipe out whole armies and cities, without himself seeing a single one of his foes."

"That may be your way; it is not ours."

"No, but it will become yours too; whatever else we fail to propagate, the gospel of scientific destruction never lacks missionaries, or those missionaries success. It seems now as if the Christian doctrine of universal brotherhood is more likely to be realized, if at all, through universal fear than through the universal love recommended by its founder."

"The brotherhood of man will come only when all men are of one faith," Ibrahim answered, "and that is why the man who spreads that faith by the sword (and how else can it be spread?) serves God and the cause of brotherhood."

They fell into a theological argument, such as all Moslems loved. Robert, well aware of his own frailty, would have liked to have confronted Ibrahim with Father Anselm, still toiling in the Lord's vineyard among his mountains, still hoping to be justified by the ripening of even one immaculate grape; but of course it would have got nowhere, for each, planted on his crag of doctrine, would have shouted into sealed ears. Between two faiths there could be no compromise—the world was flat or it was round, it could not be both at once; between the cypress and the date-palm no union could be fertile.

Chapter Eleven

MAURICE CORNFORTH watched events from the saddle of a grey pony, keeping on the move. As the produce came in it was carried to a fenced-off enclosure where native inspectors prodded and opened sacks, examined and weighed, and presented tags, coloured according to a rough estimate of quality, to the owners. The crowds grew thicker as the day wore on, the sun beat down with malignant intensity. His eyes were aching and his mouth dry, at times his head swam with the heat. He felt listless, and oppressed by the jostling busy crowds of dark-faced people. Listless, and indifferent; it mattered so little what labels they had on their sacks, or whether they had no labels at all, or whether they were pleased or angry. The whole scene appeared unreal, and slightly ridiculous. And now it began to look as though all this fuss and bother would be for nothing; everything was peaceful enough. If Robert Gresham had paid half the attention to his wife's feelings that he paid to the moods and foibles of the natives—but, with an effort, he switched his thoughts to other channels.

About noon, a man carrying away a load of rejected ground-nuts was stopped by an individual who engaged him in conversation. A few minutes later he gave a shout and turned to attract the attention of passers-by, saying that he had been offered a sum for his produce less than a quarter of its market value. A small group gathered and began to exclaim angrily that this was the Emir's doing and that things were turning out as had been prophesied: where was the trickster? Several men with sticks joined the crowd, crying that they would find him and teach him a lesson. At this point two policemen advanced on the group and dispersed it, and a scuffle followed in which one of them was knocked down. Maurice, seeing the start of a commotion, forced his pony to the scene, and the men with sticks fell back and vanished into the crowd. In a few moments no one remained but the policemen, who were only slightly bruised. The trouble-spot had dissolved, but Maurice was for the first time a little apprehensive.

Sure enough, he was attracted by shouts to the other side of the grading post where, in an open spot near a mosque, smoke was rising from the centre of a small gathering. By the time he reached the scene he found that he could not get his pony through. Over the heads of the spectators he could see billows of smoke rising. What had happened was clear enough: they had started to carry out the threat to burn rejected produce. From inside the now much larger and more excited circle he could hear voices raised above the tumult, haranguing the people.

Maurice extricated his nervous pony and made the best pace he could against a human tide towards the palace, where his reinforcements were standing by. He met a section of police coming towards him at the double, headed by his mounted subordinate. Giving this young man orders to take half the men and disperse the crowd at all costs but without the use of firearms, he himself led the rest of the section towards the palace, before whose doors lay one of the bare open spaces that were frequent in the town. Goats and donkeys, in normal times, roamed about here, looking for wisps of grass that poked up in corners not trampled into a smooth crust by sandalled feet. Along one side ran the high red wall of the palace with its crenellated top and single opening: a heavy double gate as a rule standing open to all who had business with the Emir; but to-day these gates turned blank nail-studded faces to the crowd.

People were gathering at the centre of this open space, but everything seemed quite orderly so far. An old man leaning on a stick, watching the scene with an interested but contemptuous expression, informed him that a pile of produce was to be burnt.

"Foolishness!" the old man exclaimed, spitting with force. "Wicked foolishness. Does God send us crops to be burnt? When I was young, men were not such idiots!" He hobbled indignantly away.

For the first time, Maurice felt uncertain. The police left on guard in front of the palace under a native sergeant had made a mistake in not dealing with the crowd before it had grown unmanageable; by now it was too large to disperse without a pitched battle. His own orders were to prevent the burning of produce, and a bonfire lit in the middle of this crowd would almost certainly start a blaze in more senses than one. He decided that, if he could not disperse the people, he must at least stop the fire. Taking a firm hold on his restless but well-trained pony, he rode slowly at the head of his men into the throng. As his mount picked its way forward, people stepped aside to make way.

The Resident was watching events from his car. He had gone first to the grading post, believing this to be the most likely centre of trouble, but had found it almost deserted. Seeing that all was peaceful and the crowds so far good-natured, he ordered his driver back to the office. His car rolled at unusual speed through empty streets. Only a few children scuttled out of the way and, at the doors of each house, cloth-swathed women stood chatting to each other in little groups, glad of this break in the monotony of their daily routine.

All at once he saw a familiar figure approaching on a bicycle. He called to the driver to stop; the car drew up in a flurry of dust and the figure jumped off its bicycle, fearing a collision. It was Benjamin Morris, spick and span in a dark London-made suit and a white topee. Without a word of explanation Robert seized him by the arm and propelled him into the back of the car, too startled to resist. As the door slammed and the car moved on again he came to and sat up indignantly.

"Sir, what is this? I demand to be set free! This is illegitimate —I am kidnapped! Let me go!"

Robert looked at him with a cold and hostile eye. "This is your show, isn't it, Benjamin? You worked the people up to this burning and mobbing and disgraceful behaviour. I hope you're satisfied!"

Benjamin glared angrily at his captor, but kept his temper. The Resident would pay for this—literally, for Benjamin had already resolved to sue him for assault, wrongful detention and the loss of his abandoned bicycle. But no amount of money could repay him for the ruin of one of the great moments of his life.

This, indeed, had promised to be a glorious occasion. To-day he had seen proof beyond question of the strength and depth of his power. He had only to tell people what to do, and crowds flocked from all corners of the emirate to do it. The fires had been his idea, and now they were raging everywhere. Such clear evidence of the force of suggestion gave him a new and quite extraordinary feeling, filling his mind with notions as bright and busy as flocks of small birds. Surely an editor was greater far than any king! When kings ordered, people obeyed reluctantly, but when he exhorted, people rushed with fire in their hearts to do his bidding. This was only a beginning, a curtain-raiser. One day he would try conclusions with the Governor himself, to see who controlled the hearts and ears of the people! Then all would know who was the real ruler. The thought of such a battle on Olympus was exhilarating, and enabled him to bear his present trial with Olympian calm. In fact, the situation rather amused him: this arrogant Englishman who thought himself governor of the province attempting to coerce the real and secret ruler. Sitting with folded arms in silence in the back of the car, Benjamin smiled. One day this high-handed member of the self-styled master-race would find out where the real mastery lay. The dogs barked, the caravan rolled on!

But his calm was sorely tried when, on arrival at the office, Robert again took his arm—so roughly this time that he almost cried out—and marched him to a little room near the door where messengers waited.

"There's enough trouble going on to-day," he said, "without your adding to it. You've gone too far this time, Benjamin; instigating riots and mixing in palace revolutions won't get you anywhere except into the local jail. You can stay in here till it's all over, and be thankful to be out of the way of the shooting, if it comes to that."

"I demand to know your authority——" Benjamin began, stung out of his aloofness; but it was no use, Robert was gone, and when he tried to follow a surly porter blocked his way. To crown all, he must submit to insults by common messengers, and share a menial's room! Swearing that the Resident should pay for this ten times over—certainly he would acquaint several Members of Parliament with the details—he retreated into a corner and sat down on a hard wooden bench with all the dignity he could muster.

In the office everything was peaceful, the town's excitement far away. Robert drafted a telegraphic report to headquarters. As he was finishing a clerk came in to say that the palace had just been on the telephone. He had not been able to make head or tail of the message; there had been a lot of pauses, and something about the Emir being taken away. Robert at once tried to get through, but nothing happened, and an operator at the exchange, who sounded rattled, reported that the palace did not reply.

This looked ominous. The car sped back through empty streets as it had come. In a sense, Robert was glad of the distraction. That morning he had received a letter he had long dreaded but which, when it came, was no less crushing for being expected: from Priscilla's mother, it told him that he must come immediately if he wished to see his wife again. At first his only wish had been to abandon the province with all its muddled affairs and jump on to the next train for the coast, ready to force himself on to the first home-going ship he could find. Twenty years ago he would have followed that impulse, but now a lifetime's discipline asserted itself. The crisis had at last been reached; there would not be long to wait.

The crowd was thicker than ever in front of the palace gates. He could see Maurice Cornforth on his grey pony above a field of turbaned heads, apparently directing operations in the centre. These activities were invisible, but evidently the police had succeeded in stopping the fire, for no smoke was rising. Everyone seemed calm enough, merely spectators, and so far there was nothing for them to see. In front of the gates perhaps a dozen policemen stood on guard.

Robert sat for a little watching events from the seat of his car. All at once his driver gave an exclamation and pointed towards the palace gates. Robert watched with astonishment: slowly, they were swinging open, pulled back by invisible hands within.

The police, taken by surprise, moved closer together in front of the gap at their rear. Then, all at once, as if impelled by some instinct, the crowd started to move towards the open gateway. A wave of people pressed up against the wall and poured in a narrow stream through the opening, as through a funnel, and the policemen simply vanished, swept aside. At the same time a sudden change seemed to come over the temper of the crowd. Before, it had been a collection of onlookers; now, presented with an object, it became all at once purposeful and menacing. It was as if a cold wind had blown suddenly across the open square.

The police detachment which had been grappling with the fire under Maurice Cornforth's direct orders now found itself left behind, and cut off from its colleagues on guard at the gates. Robert, watching anxiously from the outskirts and quite powerless to intervene, saw the mounted figure moving slowly through a solid human wall towards the palace, no doubt to the rescue of his vanished men.

And now he began to be seriously concerned for Aboubakar's safety. The crowd's respect for his almost God-like person would probably restrain them from violence, but the pressure of excitement was steadily mounting, and there was no knowing what the traitors evidently at work inside the palace were doing or had done.

The crowd in the open space seemed to be thinning, and Maurice Cornforth and his police had almost reached the gates. Then, from behind the palace walls, a dull shout went up like the thud of a wave breaking—an ugly, spine-chilling sound. Many of those who had poured through the open gates began to force their way back, creating a solid wedge of shoving and shouting humanity. The police were enveloped in a human blanket, invisible. Maurice Cornforth had either dismounted or—more likely—had been dragged from his horse, for his khaki-clad figure could no longer be seen over the people's heads. Then another dull muffled shout went up, louder and angrier than the first, and before it had died down Robert heard, with cold dismay, a ragged burst of rifle fire.

"Drive to the gates," he ordered. The driver hesitated for a moment and then, without a word, started the engine and let in the clutch. As soon as the car reached the thick core of the crowd it was forced almost to a standstill. The clamour of its horn rose above a cacophony of cries and distant shouting. The shots, Robert guessed, had come not from the police but from inside the palace. What he had feared had evidently happened: some of the Emir's supporters had lost their heads and, using perhaps old rifles dug out of hiding-places, had tried to drive the mob back from the inner doors.

He could feel the mood of the crowd change almost as if he had been an organic part of it. The excitement as it were solidified into a cold and primitive ferocity. Now the mob poured forward again through the gateway with a new and driving purpose, a lust for blood. The roar of their shouts became continuous, like the sound of heavy traffic on cobbled streets.

Robert's car moved forward a few feet at a time. Faces streamed past—black, excited, sweating, open-mouthed. Nothing could be seen of events inside the palace wall. The police had simply vanished. But a few moments later he knew that they must have managed to force their way through to the gates. A fresh commotion arose: the massive wooden doors began to move slowly together; boldly, the police were struggling to close them against the now purposeful invaders.

The tactics were right, but the action provocative. Robert was seized with a cold foreboding. Caught up in the bottleneck, the police could be attacked from front and rear. It was a brave attempt to regain control, but it came too late; the crowd was too large and now too angry.

"Drive faster," he said.

A few bruised rumps would be of small account; the driver kept his hand pressed down on the button of the horn; Robert's eyes were fixed on the brass-studded gates. Slowly, these converged, and for a moment it looked as if the police had pulled it off. There was a great shout, an almost ravenous shout; the gates swung wide open; a burst of rifle fire—this time a volley— sounded. A pause of confusion, almost of stillness, followed; then, breaking the unexpected hush, a high-pitched cry; then the crack of a second volley. And now the deep murmur that had filled the square ceased abruptly and a most uncanny sort of silence fell, broken again by screams and by the sound of high-pitched wailing.

Near the gates an open space suddenly appeared. People were pushing back on all sides, and Robert's car was forced to a standstill. Now he could sense in the air a different emotion: one which made the eyes stare and the blood run cold. It was panic. People began to stream past his car, pelting by with faces intent and sweating. They paid the car no attention. It crept forward again in bottom gear and almost immediately came to a stop within a few paces of the open gateway.

Robert got out of the car very slowly. The brilliant sunshine stung his eyes. It fell on bodies which lay in careless, awkward attitudes on the baked red clay, some motionless, others writhing, one crawling away in fits and starts like a crab, groaning horribly. Save for these prostrate figures and the upright policemen clasping their rifles, the whole square was suddenly and miraculously deserted.

Two policemen were bending over a khaki-clad body that lay stretched on the ground. They straightened up as Robert reached them; both looked dishevelled and shocked, the face of one of them was covered in blood. They had turned the khaki figure over on to its back and it lay quite still, blood everywhere, soaking the tunic and staining the dust-coated face.

"How did this happen?"

One of the policemen came to attention, bringing his heels together smartly.

"Men struck him with daggers, lord."

"Help me to lift him." He took the shoulders and, as a policeman sprang to seize the feet, he added: "Gently, there." But he knew the words wasted as he spoke them, for however roughly they lifted him, Maurice Cornforth would feel no more pain.

Chapter Twelve

O N the day after the riots, a nervous calm hung over the town. Prudent citizens kept to their houses and only a few children and beggars, and women going to fetch water or firewood, moved about the vacant streets. Drawing, perhaps, on long memories of bloodshed and rapine, they feared wholesale reprisals for the murder of a white man, or the indiscriminate revenge of the Emir. But the day passed off quietly. No one was summoned to the palace or seized by the police. Even at the funeral of the victims in the afternoon, no great crowds gathered at the mosque, or near the Christian cemetery outside the walls. People on that side of the town were startled by the sound of firing, but the beating of their hearts quietened when they recollected that to fire a volley over the grave of their dead was a European custom.

Next day the market started punctually and was no less packed than usual; but the grading centre was closed. The post office was doing business again, and the Native Administration offices; and when, in the middle of the morning, the gates of the palace swung open, it was understood that all would be normal within.

Benjamin, borrowing an old and miserably inferior bicycle, ventured down to his office, half-crazy with chagrin. He had seen all his hopes and plans brought to naught by the bungling of fools. He had seen, or rather heard about, the bright promise of the morning shattered by the crowd's cringing before the rifles of the police. And to crown it all he had himself been exposed to the grossest indignity, incarcerated with menials, only released long after the climax was over. His expectation of high office as right-hand man to a new ruler had once more been overthrown. This time he had broken openly with Aboubakar and must henceforth walk alone among a host of perils— a veritable minefield. The Resident, too, was now his sworn enemy. But he was not to be dashed down. With every man's hand against him, he would fight a solitary battle for justice and truth, and one day people would rise up and bless him, saying: "This man stood alone and defied the tyrant when all around him had faltered and failed; he rallied all good men and true to his banner, and has triumphed in the end."

That was all very well, he reflected, as he jumped off his bicycle in front of his office, but it did nothing to alleviate the bitterest blow of all: Sulieman, the merchant, had defalted on his promise. His lovely daughter was as far as ever out of reach— perhaps farther. Benjamin did not feel that he could endure much longer such frustration. The girl was becoming an obsession, he could think of little else, even his sleep was disturbed. It was not his fault that the plot had failed; its success had not been a condition of the bargain; at all costs, the merchant must be held to his word.

The *Chanticleer's* staff was engaged in a delightful exchange of reminiscence and rumour. Mr. Montgomery, according to his own account, had led a posse of cheated peasants into the fray, and only by throwing themselves on their faces and praying had they escaped the bullets. Mr. Fitzpatrick, also, had joined in the storming of the palace until he had seen the white man plucked from his pony by a group of over-excited young men; at this, he had extricated himself with dispatch. He had not actually seen the stabbing, but had heard from eye-witnesses that an evil spirit with the head of a toad had been seen to leave the mouth of the stricken European. Mr. Robbins alone expressed disapproval of the whole affair. He had stayed at home. This was a Moslem quarrel, he said, and others should have kept out of it, there was no knowing when heathens would not turn on good Christians and rend them, like martyrs, limb from limb.

As to the aftermath, everyone had heard a different story. Some said that a dozen men had been strangled in the palace and their bodies thrown into a pit; some that Abdulahai had fled in the disguise of a woman, or alternatively that he had turned into a large black bird and flown away; others that the old Emir was marching on the town at the head of an army of cannibals. It was rumoured also that the Emir Aboubakar had escaped by jumping into a latrine; that a great army was on its way from the Governor to blow up the town; that all who had been seen in the square were to be turned into eunuchs, and their women carried off in the train to be taken as slaves to America.

Benjamin's spirits revived a little as he listened to these exciting rumours. There was no doubt that the riots had been an historic affair. Sending two messengers to the post office to gather more information, he settled down with Mr. Montgomery and Mr. Fitzpatrick to write a report that would do justice to this momentous affray.

But first there was an even more important task to perform. No time must be lost in acquainting his friends in England of the truth, before they were taken in by lies invented by the Government. Borrowing Mr. Robbins' typewriter, he began:

"A peaceful demonstration of disenfranchized Africans against the despotism of reactionary and out-moded rulers requiring their subjects to grovel in the dust like slaves was ruthlessly crushed when British rifles fired point-blank into the innocent crowd and brutally slaughtered scores of defenceless victims, injuring hundreds more . . ."

The slender metal tongues of the typewriter chattered away like a roomful of gossips. This would be the most expensive cable he had ever sent to his friend the Member of Parliament who had close connections with the English newspapers; but it was his duty, and at such times he would not consider his own purse.

The day was busy, and when he set out for home it was long past siesta hour. Benjamin's head was aching from the heat and stuffiness of his office. As he approached the merchant's house he became infused with a new energy. Whatever happened, he was not to be put off and cheated. He would demand his rights, and if the merchant denied them he would expose the old man as a liar and a cheat. Even Sulieman the rich Moslem merchant, would find that he could not play fast and loose with the editor of the *Chanticleer*.

But when he reached Sulieman's house, the big doors were closed. This was unusual; as a rule they stood open and some kind of porter—perhaps a poor relative—sat just inside to discover the caller's business. To-day, repeated hammering on the door brought no answer. Benjamin stepped back to look into the windows above the street. He was rewarded by no flash of cloth or arm; the house had the look of a nest empty of fledgelings.

Cycling home, his feet were waterlogged with sorrow. So the fine Moslem had betrayed his promise like a common cheat! Europeans had a word for a man who ran away from his just commitments: a welsher. That was all Sulieman the magnificent, the merchant, had become: a common welsher, a wolf in sheep's clothing, a snake in the grass. Benjamin's heart grew blacker and more fiery as he sweated home through the dust. He was not to be treated in such a manner; he would follow Sulieman to the ends of the earth to claim his prize.

His house looked more than ever mean and shabby. He approached it in a raging temper, determined to teach a lesson once and for all to the slut Bessie; but then he noticed a robed and turbaned man seated on a mat in the veranda's shade. This man rose and saluted him, and without preliminaries said:

"I have a message from my master, Sulieman the merchant, who greets you, and says: the goods which are due to you shall be delivered to your house this night, when the moon is down, and he prays that you will be ready to receive them. That is all."

The messenger curtsied again and Benjamin, his black mood dispersed in a flash, rewarded him with a whole shilling, and bounded up the steps in a burst of jubilation. He had misjudged the merchant; and now there was no time to reflect or wonder, the house must be cleaned, food cooked, all preparations made for a fitting reception.

As night fell and wore on slowly, Benjamin strode a dozen times to his veranda to watch the progress of the splinter-moon that dropped by inches down a star-studded sky. In his excitement he waved to the moon and abjured it not to linger for a feast or a bargain, but to hurry like a bride to her waiting husband.

"The sky is too bright for you," he called. "Look at all the lanterns that shine in your path! You are a modest virgin, pale like a white woman, hurry down to your bed under the earth where all is warm and merry, leave the stars to leap and sparkle like fishes in the sea!"

At last the moon obeyed him, and in his house all was ready: the rooms scrubbed and tidied, pictures straightened, flowers in a jampot on the table, a stew simmering in the kitchen. Even a prayer-mat had been provided. And at last Benjamin's eyes discerned the shapes of a donkey with a rider and two tall men on foot striding by its side. The men halted and one of them lifted the rider down; in another moment the figure had glided quickly up the steps, the men had made obeisance and the darkness had swallowed them up.

So she had come at last, there was no deception! In the lamp-light her eyes gleamed like polished obsidian, the rims darkened with kohl, the lids blue with antimony. She was slender and tall —taller and more solid, as it were, than Benjamin had imagined her.

He stepped forward to greet her, but she eluded him and, with a low chuckle, ran like a frightened gazelle through the door; and at that moment Bessie, entering like a thundercloud, slapped down a dish of stew on the table.

"Careful, you fool!" he shouted at her. "Do you want to break all my dishes? Take a plate to the lady, who will think she has come among savages if you behave so!"

It was natural that she should be shy in his presence, but her shyness proved less than skin-deep. In the morning, awakened from a heavy slumber, sly doubts crept in like snakes. Lovely she was, loving and desirable, but a virgin——? He had slept late and she was astir before him, bundled up in her robes and busy with Bessie in the kitchen. He could hear their giggles and soft laughter.

He frowned, growing more uneasy. They had lost no time in making friends. He called loudly for his breakfast, and Bessie came in with a pot of tea.

"Where is my wife?" He spoke haughtily, and realized with surprise that he did not know her name.

Bessie, looking at him with a dreadful expression of contempt, amusement and lubricity, made an obscene reply.

Slapping her face with an open palm, he leapt from his chair and dashed into the kitchen. His bride was stirring a pot on a low brick oven. One look confirmed his ghastly suspicions. Her skin was black, she had the splayed nose and rubbery lips of the Negro, her expression was bold as brass. With a cry of anguish he rushed out of the kitchen and through his house into the street beyond.

It was late when he reached the office, hot and distraught. The expressions on the faces of his staff stripped him of his last shreds of hope. Already the joke had spread through the town. As he entered his inner room a snigger from Mr. Robbins seemed to strike into his back like the cut of a lash. He rushed on into his private office, slamming the door.

Behind him, half-suppressed giggles swelled into a burst of laughter. Mr. Montgomery rocked to and fro in his chair, tears trickling down his cheeks, gasping for breath; even the solemn Mr. Robbins was shaken by chuckles. The messengers, Mr. Montgomery's cousin and several callers joined in. The room resounded, for the joke was rich. The great Benjamin Morris, editor of fame and power, the equal of Europeans, taken in by the oldest trick in the world, bested by the sly merchant—his tender little Moslem virgin one of the town's horniest prostitutes—a battle of elephants indeed, the old and the new elephant, and the old one had come off victorious.

Chapter Thirteen

FREDDY BEGG, occupying a leather armchair in the Resident's office, was more disturbed than his outward manner suggested. He knew well enough that authority at home would turn a blind eye and a deaf ear to almost anything but an actual outbreak of violence. Riots were a kind of badge of shame in the cap of any colonial government, an openly proclaimed admission of failure. Publicity of the most undesirable kind followed—garbled stories in the home press and, of course, a crop of parliamentary questions. Already brusque cables had come in from the Secretary of State demanding an immediate explanation.

Although he strove at all times to be objective and impartial, he could not suppress a mounting sense of irritation as he listened to the acting Resident's words. An outbreak of violence was inevitably a reflection on the efficiency of the officer in charge, in this case Robert Gresham; such officers might be, and usually were, exonerated, but they had to admit the principle of being, as it were, on trial, and justifying their failure to maintain law and order, which was after all their basic duty. But Gresham seemed to be under the impression that the Government (by which he evidently meant the Chief Secretary) and not himself, was on trial. This monstrous attempt to reverse the true position angered Freddy a great deal. But he could see through it—an effort to shift the blame from Gresham's shoulders to those of his superiors. As such it could only increase suspicion that Gresham's own actions were hard to defend.

"I don't think you quite appreciate the position," Freddy observed, with an effort keeping his tone calm and his manner pleasant. "If I understand you correctly, you are saying that because the people's conservatism drove them to resist reforms, we should have taken no steps to overhaul their system of agricultural marketing. My dear fellow, you are surely putting the cart before the horse."

"I was saying nothing of the sort. I was saying that we were trying to bring in a policy which was quite certain to fail because of our own actions, or rather past inactions. Let me——"

"I am afraid you will only waste my time." Freddy's tone was sharp. "I have had occasion to remind you before that your task is to carry out policy, not to initiate it. If you do not agree with it, you have your remedy—to resign. So long as you elect to remain in the service it would be better to concentrate on the efficient carrying out of your orders rather than on continual criticism of them. In this case, let us keep to the point, which is not whether you approved of the Government's proposals—I am perfectly well aware that you did not—but of the steps which you took, or did not take, to carry them out."

Robert concentrated hard on two sunbirds fluttering over a shrub outside his window. He saw through Freddy's game perfectly. Freddy wanted to keep the whole inquiry within the narrow limits of what had been done or left undone to prevent or to control the outbreak of violence. If attention could be focused on whether or not enough police had been drafted into the town, on their disposition, on who had given the order to fire, and on a dozen insignificant and kindred points, the whole awkward matter would pass off without any hint of censure on the authorities. The police would be reproved or congratulated, as the case might be; his own conduct upheld or condemned (he had little doubt which), and everyone would be happy—until the next time. No one would think of questioning the actions of the Olympians at the Secretariat or even in Whitehall; of examining the basic attitude of governors to governed, the ignorance of native mentality, the hand-to-mouth behaviour which postponed decisions until the last possible moment—in fact the whole system of paper control by those out of touch with human realities that seemed to Robert to be the root of the trouble. To him this outbreak was merely a symptom—a sort of boil on the body politic whose irruption signified an unhealthy condition of the blood.

He himself was resolved to push the inquiry much farther back. This particular trouble had started, in his opinion, when Aboubakar had seized his uncle's title and the Government confirmed the coup. That Aboubakar would have been a more progressive and energetic ruler, had he been given the chance, Robert did not doubt, nor did he feel any special tenderness for the old Emir; but the fact remained that Aboubakar was a usurper and that the Government had allowed itself, largely through ignorance, to become embroiled in the intrigues of a cunning and unscrupulous clique. Having done this, it had lacked the courage to see the decision through. Short of funds, of staff and of political acumen, it had neglected to put together even a rudimentary intelligence service, and to inform itself closely about the feelings of the general or the machinations of the few. It had possessed no clear notion, therefore, of the extent of the plot against Aboubakar, and had disregarded every warning that its agent had sent.

Nor, in his opinion, had the Government proved any more adroit in handling a simple economic issue where the choice of weapons, so to say, was entirely its own. For twenty years it had 'considered' the need to improve the peasants' low-grade produce, and a dozen schemes had been put forward at different times by technical officers still young enough to be full of zest. For twenty years it had done exactly nothing, until a crisis came. Then, in a sudden panic, it had decided to act: and, having decided, had persisted in rushing matters forward according to the exact letter of its plans, in face of the clearest possible warning from the only one of its agents in a position to judge. Had time been given to preparation, had the project been allowed to ripen slowly like a reptile's egg in the sun, Robert had no doubt that it would have succeeded. The tragedy was that the Government had commanded time and to spare, and had squandered it; and then, down to its last minute, had gambled on a certain loser.

Behind all this lay something (Robert believed) hard to define and impossible to arraign: an attitude of mind, authority's belief that at all times it knew what was best for the people, its devotion to expediency—a devotion which at once inhibited it from thinking ahead and prevented it from making any clear-cut decision. And so it lagged always behind events, never shaping them; it became time's fool instead of destiny's master, like a man who, having missed his train, hires a car to catch it at the next stop, and arrives at one station after another only to see the train steaming away from the platform.

This ignoring of time, this bland neglect of human feeling, was something incurable, a quality of the machine. And yet its business was with time and humans. How could you change a machine? Come hell and high water, its wheels ground on, procrastination its rhythm, compromise its manufacture. Once in motion, its timing and purpose were set. Here, in this case before them, Robert had tried even at the last moment to avert the trouble, but his appeal to suspend the *Chanticleer* and to detain Abdulahai had gone unanswered—neither granted nor refused, but simply ignored.

His anger rose as he thought of these things. It was the Government he was accusing—amorphous, pervasive, incorporeal, aloof, all-powerful—like the Holy Ghost, but less beneficent and very much less wise. As hard to trap as a falling star, for once he had it cornered, here before him, in the person of Freddy Begg; and no amount of jinking and byplay with red herrings would, he resolved, prevent authority incarnate from standing face to face with its own responsibility and doing penance for its sins.

He became aware that Freddy Begg, in his dry, precise, level tones, was probing into his conduct in search of a tender spot.

"It seems unfortunate, to say the least, that the ringleaders were allowed to divert the farmers coming in with their produce from the grading centre to the palace, apparently without let or hindrance from the police."

"The police were fully occupied putting out fires."

"Reinforcements had been sent. Surely their numbers should have been sufficient to post pickets outside the town, as well as to deal with incidents inside."

"Have you ever tried to control a crowd of several thousands, stirred up by cunning and resolute leaders, with two Europeans and less than a company of police?"

"That is not my job. But I should——"

"Nor mine. You must ask the inspector about the disposition of the police. I'm satisfied that they did all they could in impossible circumstances."

"I'm afraid that I am less easy to satisfy. You mentioned ring-leaders. Are any of them under arrest?"

"We've arrested about a dozen men, but they're the small fry, as usual. The big fish are lying low until things calm down."

"That can't be allowed, of course. I take it that you will not rest until you've secured some at least of the ring-leaders."

Robert smiled without amusement. "Then I should have little rest. The prime mover is no doubt Abdulahai, and he's no doubt paying the visit of a dutiful son to his exiled father. We haven't a trace of solid evidence leading back to him; and you omitted, if you remember, to give me the authority which I asked for to detain him. That reminds me—I understand I'm being threatened with legal action for wrongful detention and assault by the editor of the *Chanticleer*."

"Yes, it's unfortunate that you had to take such—ah—drastic action. The fellow tells me that when you had him seized and dragged off his bicycle, he was on his way to dissuade the people from using violence and to send them home."

Robert's smile was now grim, his laugh theatrically hollow.

"As the Duke of Wellington is said to have remarked to a man who mistook him for a Mr. Smith—'Sir, if you believe that, you'll believe anything.'"

Freddy's reply was very stiff. "Naturally I do not believe everything he tells me, but it is my duty to give a hearing to complaints against your actions, just as it is your duty to justify them."

"Since we've brought up the subject of Benjamin Morris,"

Robert said, passing over to the attack, "I should like to put it on record that your refusal to give me the authority I needed to suspend his newspaper contributed quite a little—in my opinion —to our troubles. In fact it was a necessary precaution; but I wasn't allowed to take it."

"You could have taken action yourself without reference to headquarters."

"Not the kind of action that would have stopped the next issue of the *Chanticleer*. At any rate, I think I was entitled to an answer to my telegram."

From the slight flush that had risen to Freddy's pale cheeks, Robert judged that he was getting rattled.

"I really do not know what you mean."

"I thought I had made it quite clear. I mean that you did not even acknowledge my request for authority to suspend the paper."

"I do not remember having received any such request."

Robert, amazed, sat up straighter in his chair.

"You mean to say that an urgent telegram of such importance never reached you?"

"I have told you that I don't remember seeing it."

Robert could only shrug his shoulders. Either the Secretariat had been guilty of a blunder monumental even for that body, or Freddy was lying. Both alternatives seemed incredible.

"I must warn you that I shall lay the facts before the court of inquiry."

"The court of inquiry? Whatever do you mean?"

"The court of inquiry which I assume will investigate the causes of the riots."

Leaning back in his chair as if reassured, Freddy allowed himself a small and condescending smile.

"My dear fellow, you make the most extraordinary assumptions. This is the first I have heard of any court of inquiry."

"It will not be the last. I intend to demand one."

Freddy was not to be caught off his guard a second time. "Leaving aside the question of whether or no you have any right to demand such a thing, may I ask what good purpose you think would be served by securing a lot of undesirable publicity for an incident which I should have thought that you of all people, in your position, would not wish to see blazoned forth more than necessary?"

"Just what do you mean by that?"

"Simply that, as the officer responsible for maintaining law and order, an outbreak of violence is *prima facie* evidence that you have failed in your duty."

"If that's your opinion, then you can hardly refuse an independent inquiry. Since you accuse me of dereliction of duty, you must give me the right to defend my conduct."

"That's just what you seem unable or unwilling to do."

"To you, yes, because you are trying to be both prosecutor and judge. That won't do, you know. I've the right to demand an impartial tribunal."

Freddy leant back in his chair and pressed his finger-tips together, successfully concealing his annoyance. In a sense, the fellow had tricked him into a most unwelcome concession. If Gresham really insisted, it would be hard now to avoid an inquiry. Aloud he said:

"I'm sorry that you should take this attitude, which I fear will do you nothing but harm. Naturally, Government has nothing whatever to conceal, and would, indeed, welcome an inquiry. It's in your own interests to keep the whole matter out of the public eye. Government knows the difficulties and would no doubt be sympathetic rather than harsh. If you are satisfied that you did all in your power to avoid bloodshed, you need have nothing to fear. But, on the other hand, if you persist in washing dirty linen in public, you can scarcely count on Government support."

"I see. A combination of threats and bribery," Robert's voice was barbed with contempt; he was rewarded by seeing a faint flush once more creep up under Freddy's pallid skin. "I'm not to be silenced that way. For one thing the bribe isn't attractive enough, nor the threat sufficiently alarming. For another, there's the future to think of. This outbreak was no flash in the pan. There'll be bigger and better riots later on, if some altogether fundamental changes aren't made. A rap over the knuckles for an acting Resident, a censure for the police, a light sentence for half a dozen unlucky bystanders won't do anything to improve matters. In fact it will merely give you an excuse to turn over and go to sleep again."

"If you choose to be offensive and disloyal, I have nothing further to say." Freddy, now plainly flushed with anger, jumped to his feet. "There seems to be no point in my continuing this inquiry, so long as you are in your present mood. When you are ready to pay some attention to your duty, which is to furnish me with the information I need, perhaps you will be good enough to inform me."

With this parting shot the Chief Secretary stalked out of the room like a ruffled pigeon and Robert leant back in his chair with a sigh, feeling spent.

The trouble was that he no longer cared deeply, as he would have cared once, whether he was blamed or cleared, praised or reprimanded, promoted or sacked. With none now to share his pleasure or be hurt by his failure, it seemed to matter little which fell to his lot. Priscilla, always more eager than he himself to fight his own battles, would have urged him on, but Priscilla was past caring what became of him—if, indeed, she had cared at all for the last few years. It was only by thinking directly of Freddy Begg that he could keep alive a small flame of belligerence. Time and again he had found himself brought up against Freddy, as against a wall, bruising his head against the other's obduracy. At their first meeting, nearly twenty years ago, they had quarrelled, and their difference now was only a continuation of the same fight. And then there had been the matter of the tax-assessor murdered by the tribesmen of the hills: another fruit of one of Freddy's paper schemes. It seemed to Robert that quite enough blood had flowed to lubricate the Chief Secretary's onward march to higher spheres: like the savage chieftain, human sacrifice seemed to accompany the *rites de passage* of his career. This time he should not get away with it, at least without a struggle: Robert resolved to marshall all his strength behind his thrust so that a dent, at least, should mark the impact of his little lance on the triple-plated armour of the machine.

Chapter Fourteen

FREDDY drove away in an unaccustomed pother. Loss of temper always left him feeling dizzy and weak. And it was remarkable how infallibly Robert Gresham contrived to upset him; he was scarcely able to recall an occasion when they had not fallen out. Well, he had learnt his lesson, once and for all. In a very short time there would be a new Resident in this province, and he would be very much surprised if he were ever to be seriously troubled by Gresham again. In the meantime, there was this tiresome inquiry. Supposing he refused it, and Gresham resigned: by pulling strings at home, by meretricious employment of the devices of *suppressio veri* and *suggestio falsi*, the man might succeed in putting the Government into a very poor light. No, it was safer to allow the inquiry, distasteful as this might be.

And the more he thought about it, the more distasteful it became. The trouble was that he couldn't rely on the Chief Justice for discretion and common sense. Sir Michael Corrigan was an Irishman who, finding the English courts too slow and weighted by tradition, had sought relief in the colonies, and had risen to his present eminence at an unusually early age more because, in Freddy's belief, people were frightened of his cruel tongue and mordant wit than through any great wisdom or erudition. He was fond of declaring that only the Irish could understand Africans, since both had the mentality of subject races and a history of enslavement; his judgments were erratic, his private life by no means above reproach and he was unpopular both among junior officers, whose verdicts he often upset with cruel sarcasm because they had overlooked some minor point of legal procedure, and among seniors, whose dignity he signally failed to respect.

No, Sir Michael Corrigan was not at all the man to be entrusted with such a delicate matter. As for a gentle hint—if you dropped one in his path he would treat it like a football and kick it gleefully all round the market place. Out of sheer Irishness, he might listen to Gresham, a fellow malcontent, and push the inquiry in all sorts of quite irrelevant directions, in the malevolent hope of embarrassing the administration. Not that Freddy was in the least nervous of anything that an inquiry might reveal: nevertheless it was clearly in the public interest that an inquiry should be avoided.

How to do this was another matter. And in one direction he had perhaps been over-hasty. Gresham had so hustled and blustered that the matter of the telegram had quite gone out of Freddy's mind. Now that he had time to think things over, he remembered that some such telegram had appeared on his desk. In the press of more important business he had laid it aside, thinking it in any case a typical piece of Gresham hysteria. If he had not answered it, that was because it had answered itself. Imagine the howl that would have gone up at home had the Government arbitrarily suspended a newspaper for exercising its perfectly legal prerogative of freedom of speech! Even the best officers (and no one could put Gresham into that class) seemed to think that they lived on a desert island and could do what they liked, oblivious of the outside world. . . . All the same, it was a pity the telegram had for a moment slipped his mind. A small point, but Gresham would try to make capital out of it, no doubt, at an inquiry.

They were nearing the Residency, but Freddy did not feel quite ready yet to settle down to work. Instead, he ordered the driver to make a detour; he did not often get a chance to see the sights of this picturesque but squalid town. Besides, he might find in the market some small present for Armorel. He was pleased now that she had come with him—the change of air after a go of fever was sure to be beneficial. Besides, now that this stupid little trouble had cropped up, he would be glad of her advice. Stopping the car in the market he prowled among the shaded stalls, jostled by sweating and animated blacks, and selected a pair of leather moccasins embroidered in the strong primary colours which suited her nature and her taste.

He found her resting before lunch, after a strenuous morning inspecting the half-finished new Native Administration hospital and then the first nursery school to be started among purdah women. At such times, when her vitality was lowered like a flame, her face looked gaunt. She was pleased with the slippers, but noticed at once that Freddy had been upset.

He judged it best not to beat about the bush.

"Gresham intends to demand a judicial inquiry into the riots."

Armorel, stretched on the bed, looked at him through half-closed eyes, resting the back of her dark head on knotted fingers, her bent arms spread out like wings.

"Does it matter?"

Freddy was prowling round the high airy room, still unsettled by his morning's trouble. Green venetian blinds had been lowered over the windows, the room was restfully subdued. He sat down at the dressing-table on an imitation Empire chair and fiddled with a pot of face-cream.

"Not really, I suppose. But it's an awkward time. The new Governor will be coming and I shall be up to my eyes in work. And Gresham wants to rake up a lot of quite irrelevant matters, making it into a sort of inquest on past policy. And—well, it's tiresome, that's all."

He sniffed at a bottle of scent: delicious, cooling, faintly stirring. Even to Armorel, he did not want to explain all the awkwardness—that unanswered telegram, for instance. A leather-framed photograph of his two daughters caught his eye—small schoolgirls now; their faces had the pleading, sad, inscrutable look of sheep on a hillside.

"Who would do the inquiring?"

"The Chief Justice, I suppose."

"That virulent Irishman!"

"Yes, a most unsuitable man. He'd seize any stick to beat the Government with, I'm afraid."

"And what about Gresham? Can he shake any skeletons out of the cupboard?"

"Skeletons? Of course not!" Freddy put down the scent bottle irritably. "On our side, we've nothing whatever to hide. But you know what he is—eaten up with malice and spite. I've no doubt he'll try to shift the blame on to me, if he can."

Armorel lay back and watched him through listless eyes that felt like lumps of metal. Her temples were throbbing and her mouth bitter with quinine. The bout of fever was over, but the lassitude that followed had left her feeling half alive. And she did not deny to herself that the news of Maurice Cornforth's death had been a shock. Not that she had seen him for years: a dim lay figure from a long-forgotten past, she had told herself that he meant no more to her than a character she had read about in a book; yet, when she had heard of his murder, a dreadful depression had descended and she could not shake it off. Only then had she realized that she had never quite let go of a secret hope that one day he would return to renew in her, by some miracle, the magic of her youth.

Disengaging her locked fingers, she pushed her hair back once more from a damp forehead and her firm lips, edged now by little lines creasing the clear pale flesh, parted in a half-smile of contempt for her own folly. She brought her mind back to her husband's trouble. From his hesitant and distrait manner, she knew that the prospect of an inquest alarmed him. This could only be because of weak joints in his armour; and still smiling, she said:

"You'd better come clean, Freddy. Why are you so nervous about this inquiry?"

"Nervous! Of course I'm not nervous. I've explained once,

my dear.   An awkward time—unpleasantness all round—a quite unnecessary fuss."

Shooting at random, but not without shrewdness, Armorel added:

"Is Gresham going to accuse you of refusing him the powers he needed?"

Freddy, startled, put down a pot of skin-food with a small clatter.

"Then he's been talking already——"

"My dear Freddy, you do give yourself away.   Isn't that exactly what everyone has against the Secretariat, riots or no riots? What's the trouble, specifically?"

"I've told you, there's no trouble. Gresham wanted authority to do various quite illegal and provocative things—suspend the newspaper, for one thing, and arrest the Emir's nephew without a proper charge. His telegram, as a matter of fact, was—ah—overlooked, but that made no difference. Naturally I could not have given him the authority in any case."

"I see." Armorel stopped smiling and became thoughtful. Quite evidently Freddy had made one of his rare blunders. She could imagine how a disgruntled Gresham would press the point, a malicious Corrigan make play with it. Freddy would be paraded as a bumbling and cowardly bureacrat who had let down his subordinate. Even in the best of circumstances, an inquiry would do him no good at the present critical stage of his career. This was his first important Chief Secretaryship, and in the next year or two his whole future could be marred by any serious reflection on his ability or judgment.

"Gresham must be persuaded to drop the idea."

Freddy shook his head. "He won't. He's suffering from some imaginary grievance."

Armorel lay silent for a few minutes, thinking. Then she got up slowly and pushed her feet into the new slippers.

"They look gay." She wriggled her toes. "Every man has his price, they say."

"Gresham is out to make trouble."

"Two can play at that game."

"One doesn't want to compete. . . ."

Armorel laughed, stretched her arms, and walked over to the washing-stand.

"Don't worry, Freddy, I'll talk to him."

"My dear, I tell you it's useless——"

"Perhaps, but there's no harm in trying. I understand him better than you do."

Freddy polished his nails with the buffer, and said no more.

Chapter Fifteen

IT was evening before she found a chance to speak to Robert. She had lain in wait for him on the veranda when the daylight faded and he did not see her until she jumped up from her chair and barred his way. He carried a piece of paper in his hand and she thought that he looked extraordinarily white and haggard.

"Robert, I'd like a word with you, please."

He halted in front of her silently; a queer feeling came to her that she was speaking to a ghost and not a man.

"Is it a forlorn hope to ask you a favour?"

He was silent for so long that she thought he was going to refuse even to answer. When he spoke his tone was flat and abstracted, as though his thoughts were still far away.

"I'm hardly in a position to dispense favours."

"I want you to drop this inquiry. I know it's a lot to ask, and no affair of mine. Yet it is my affair, really, because it's such a worry to Freddy. He's convinced that an inquiry will only stir up mud and do harm to the country generally, and especially to you."

"It's kind of Freddy to put my welfare, not to mention the country's, before his own. Do sit down."

"Thank you. There's no need to be sarcastic."

They sat rather stiffly in two long armchairs while a servant materialized from the shadows with a flit-gun to spray their ankles and the whole veranda, and to switch on a reading-lamp standing on a low table between them: in its light they could see each other's faces as if cut out of white paper, all soot and white-wash. It was not quite dark, but nearly so; the primrose light had faded; outside the dusk was violet with the first bright silver stars breaking through, the earth a deep grey, the trees a solid black against the violet sky.

Armorel broke the silence. "Isn't it a little—well, egotistical—to insist on embarrassing everyone with this inquiry in order to defend your own actions?"

"Fancy being lectured by you on egotism!" Although his tone was light he was not smiling; the look on his face shocked her, it was so drawn, so tired and (she could only think) so forlorn.

"Why not? One gives the best lectures on the things one can speak about at first-hand."

"So you think I want this inquiry simply to justify myself?"

She shrugged her shoulders. "Why else?"

"If you knew how little I cared for that!" Robert's speech was often theatrical, yet this time it had the ring of a stripped sincerity. "You're far too intelligent not to know that this isn't just a piece of exhibitionism. You know as well as I do that there's something very wrong with things—with the country and with the way it's run. You're mistaken if you think I blame Freddy. Freddy's only a cog in the machine, as I am, and it's the machine that's wrong—the policy, the system."

"My dear Robert, *you're* far too intelligent to suppose that you can change the system merely by having an inquiry into a local riot."

"Of course you can't, but you can nail it down, you can show what it all boils down to in one particular instance, in one particular place and at one particular time. I know that what's just happened here isn't important—a mild little riot in an obscure town in an unknown country, a few dozen quite insignificant people injured or killed. We mustn't think we're important, but nor must we believe that we're unique. What's going on here is no doubt going on in dozens of other countries and places, all round the globe. And so what's happened here isn't entirely trivial, it's a portent and a warning. I tell you, this country, and other countries too, will run with blood if we go on as we're going now! Or worse, they'll sink into a welter of sterile bickering and simply drown. Is that the way it's all got to finish—just peter out in squabbles and intrigues and compromises, like a river that runs away into stinking pools and wastes of sand?"

Robert had jumped from his chair and was pacing the veranda, once more excited by his own ideas. "I can't believe that no one cares! There must be people at home who simply don't know what's going on; if they realize the facts, they'll put things right. For that's where the trouble starts, at home—the muddle-headedness, the slackness, the complacency, the fear! We've become an empire afraid of its own shadow—the shadow of strength. We can't have lost all our old genius and faith!"

"Of course if you put it all on the high moral plane of selfless patriotism——"

"I don't; and patriotism's seldom selfless. It's a kind of extended tribal loyalty, I suppose, and one day we shan't need it any more. But it has its points meanwhile."

"A convenient cloak in which to wrap one's less respectable emotions!"

"Perhaps; but surely it's a good plan to cover our indecencies? You lectured me on egotism just now. That's the alternative—one's own interests first, last and all the time."

Once again—it had happened so often in their relations—Armorel felt baffled and annoyed. Once more he had slid off the point at issue as smoothly as a seal to immerse himself in a sea of quite irrelevant generalities. Well, it was no good mincing matters. On the plane of patriotic purpose she felt helpless, but on the personal level she was better armed. Fitting a cigarette carefully into a holder, she lit a match and let it burn until it almost licked her fingers.

"I can only wish you luck, then. But sometimes these inquisitions drag out inconvenient things."

Robert smiled a little, though his face was weary.

"That's Freddy's worry."

"I wasn't thinking of Freddy."

"Of me, then? I've no buried secrets."

"Everyone has something to hide. For instance, King David, when he ordered Uriah to the forefront of the battle—although the roles are reversed in this case, of course: Uriah gives the order to David."

Robert, still clasping a paper in his hand, turned to look at her, startled out of his thoughts by her inconsequence. But she stared straight ahead.

"Uriah?"

"A thorough inquisitor might want to know the exact order you gave to Maurice Cornforth, that resulted in his being stabbed to death—the only European casualty."

There was a dead silence. Armorel, rigid in her chair, could not even catch the sound of breathing, but she could feel Robert's eyes on her in the darkness and hear the blood singing in her ears.

"Not that I suggest for a moment it was deliberate. These things happen, but you must admit that it looks a little odd."

Still Robert did not answer or move. She wanted to look

round, but dared not do so lest her movement release him from the paralysis of shock, a sort of rigor mortis of the mind.

"Not that everyone knows about Priscilla's affair with Cornforth. But Freddy does, of course; you know we ran into them once, in a hotel."

At last Robert got to his feet. She had prepared herself to face a furious outburst or a cold anger, but he was behaving like a tired old man.

"Your slanders have come too late. Priscilla——"

His voice tailed off; it was spent and without emotion, as a wrung cloth is dry. Armorel had not meant to say more, but she felt at sea in this inconclusive silence, and struck out as if for dry land.

"Funnily enough, it was the Angel Hotel. I thought at the time, how appropriate, in a sort of contrary way. . . ."

Robert, holding out to her the crumpled piece of paper in his hand, only answered:

"Read that, and cut out your tongue."

She spread the paper out under the lamp and read it slowly, and then again, and then a third time to postpone the moment of her own humiliation.

"I'm sorry, Robert, I didn't know——"

But when at last she mustered courage to raise her head he had vanished, leaving her to sit there immobile until the rustle of a gown and a soft footfall disturbed her and a houseboy came on to the veranda with a tray of drinks.

Seated at her dressing-table, sipping the whisky, she made excuses for herself. She hadn't known of Priscilla's death, Priscilla's affair couldn't have been news to Robert; her duty was to put Freddy's interests first. It was no good. Armorel was not as a rule introspective, but now some strong compulsion forced her to look into her own heart and to ask herself why she was ridden by this harsh and ruthless ambition. She knew well enough what it would lead to, if through the exacting years she made no false step: a handle to her name, a beflagged car, the obsequious respect of casual acquaintances. Beyond that, where she had never dared to look, wastes of emptiness lay: the village fête, the dummy hand, the fear of draughts, the weather forecast; obscurity feeding on past distinction, the slow withering of the body, the waiting grave.

Yet to-night even the bleak comfort of futility was lacking. All paths merged, all power dissolved, yet the conviction crept upon her that it did matter, and mattered above all, which path you chose. Hers, soft to the feet, had led her into a tunnel with walls of glass—smooth, shining and implacable; you could see through them fine views and sweet gardens but, try as you would, you could not break out, and your hands, beating against the sides towards light and air, met only an ice-like unyielding surface. Better the craggy path over the rocks than this, the biting wind and the bleeding feet, for it was the wind of freedom, and here in the tunnel was the calm not of death but of sterility, not the corruption of the flesh but the annulment of the soul.

As if a voice had spoken from a great distance, long-forgotten words drifted into her mind. Though I speak with the tongues of men and of angels, and have not charity, I am become as sounding brass, or a tinkling cymbal. The voice droned in her ears, into her nostrils crept a smell of damp and cold stone and wet coats drying in a cold fug, of mustiness and the ghost of scrubbing soap—the smell of childhood. She gazed again at the grimy marble bust of a toga-swathed notable opposite her pew and heard around her the snuffling and rustling and fidgeting children of the school she had detested; from the recesses of her mind crept memories of the home she had liked no better: a querulous hypochondriac father, a blowsy and complaining mother, the smell of cooking greens and tripe pouring up the narrow dirty stairs, the brown cold lavatory with broken chain and stubborn tank, the bedraggled tired garden squeezed between high walls and smelling of cats, her mother's cracked dirty finger-nails, the washing up at the greasy sink, the ugly feel of serge clothes.

Charity! There had been little enough of it there, or at the school where underpaid teachers had nagged and ill-bred children sneaked and bullied, or in a life where she had been forced to fight for every success and every pleasure. Charity—a word, a luxury. Could you be blamed for lacking something you had never received? She had done her duty to the best of her ability, and that had been better than most: a careful conscientious mother, a loyal wife. At this she smiled a little: who, knowing the two, would have expected her, and not Freddy, to be the faithful partner? Yet that was how it had turned out; and she had shown a generosity greater than society expected in never once reproaching him or forcing him to acknowledge his fault.

But none of these thoughts consoled her now. Somewhere, a

long way back perhaps, she had missed the path, and from the safety and warmth of her smooth glass tunnel she envied those who struggled over the crags in winter weather—even Robert Gresham, for whom she had so often felt a kind of pitying contempt. Unconsciously, perhaps, she had always envied him, the failure, as she rose on the wave of her own success: envied even his failure, for it was of his own seeking and in it she recognized, without being able to define, a knowledge that had eluded her— a knowledge not of happiness (for he was less happy than she) but of the paths by which it might be sought, of whose very existence she was unaware.

Leaning forward, she saw herself in the glass, haggard and old, and thought: that is the face of a murderer, whose crime is the greater because it was committed not against the body, corrupt and doomed, but against the faith which was the vital spark in a man's soul. And guilt and remorse, to which she had been a stranger, came creeping up to the walls of her heart.

But her husband entered, bringing respite, and inquiring with solicitude after her headache.

"I'm tired, Freddy. I shall have dinner on a tray."

"Yes, that's wise, my dear. I'm afraid Gresham has had bad news. There's a rumour, apparently, that Priscilla is dead."

"Yes, I know."

"You've seen him, then?"

"Yes."

"So it's true? Poor woman, so young, and so——'" He could not go on. The news had really upset him. He could see her face now: fresh, eager, soft, desirable; she had deserved a better husband; but pride had been her undoing. She had rejected disinterested offers of friendship and succumbed to the blandishments of a worthless loose-living bounder.

"I can't help wishing, now, that I could see some way to avoid this trouble with Gresham. Poor fellow, he was devoted to her, in spite of her—well, *de mortuis*, of course. . . ."

Armorel rose abruptly from her chair. It was as much as she could do to avoid crying out, even to dodge hysteria, Freddy's amiable bromides jarred so on her nerves; yet fear of solitude, and of the fanged thoughts lying in wait, held back the words of dismissal. Startled by her expression, he added:

"You should lie down, my dear, you look all in. For goodness' sake take care of yourself—*you* mustn't run any risks!"

Without replying, Armorel peeled off her neatly-tailored linen dress and lay down on the bed, her eyes closed. Freddy was shocked at the pallor of her face; her eye-sockets looked like caverns.

"Do you realize we've been married for nearly ten years? And that we're better friends than ever? I'm no good at making speeches, but you know that I admire you more with every year that goes by. All our happiness, all our little successes, have been due to you. . . . You mentioned that you'd seen Gresham to-night. I suppose he didn't say anything about that inquiry?"

"He won't go on with it now."

"You mean he's going to drop it?" Freddy was incredulous. "Armorel, that's your doing! Really, you know, you're a marvel —a worker of miracles. I won't deny that it's a relief. How did you manage to dissuade him?"

She did not answer. Making allowances for her fatigue, he planted a kiss on her forehead and, laying aside his spectacles, began to undress for his bath.

"By the way, I've got some news for you," he added, hanging his tie carefully over the edge of the mirror. "The name of the new Governor."

She put a hand to her damp, aching forehead, as if to ward off distractions; her eyes were closed.

"It's confidential, of course. I think you'll be pleased."

Like a maggot wriggling up from the rotting flesh, out of her shame and self-disgust a worm of interest emerged. A new Governor, a new world to conquer—her world, the only world she knew. Too late, now, to pine after others she could never find: too late for useless penitence and hollow remorse. Reaching for a cigarette on the bedside table, she said:

"Who is it, Freddy?" and awaited with attention his reply.

Chapter Sixteen

NIGHT lay thickly over the flat-roofed city when the camel-drivers herded their charges in from pasturage and began to hang the kneeling beasts about with loads of awkward shape and varied sizes.

A waning moon threw deep shadows under the walls and glinted on iron water-spouts set like canons on the battlements, and gave to the crouching long-necked camels a look of grey sea-serpents rearing their heads from a shadowy ocean. The cool night air was full of sounds: the munching of camels, the sharp commands of their veiled Tuareg drivers, the grunts of men tightening ropes and, in the distance, a low throaty pulsating chorus of frogs. The air was tautened by that sense of expectancy that precedes the start of any long journey, and men moved about quietly and with purpose, busy in the performance of tasks they understood. Behind them lay the comforts and luxuries of the city, the feasts and women, the songs and the market-place; before them the hardships and dangers of the desert road, the weariness and thirst, the steady shuffle towards ever-retreating horizons. For an instant they stood poised on the pivot of life's fluctuating motion: between travel and rest, safety and danger, the hard and the soft, hunger and its satisfaction.

By any ancient standard it was a puny caravan, for now the time-worn desert routes had fallen into desuetude. Motor-buses had worn new tracks, flagged by beer-bottles instead of bones, and many of the old wells were dry, the oases sanded over. Never again, perhaps, would the nomads of these regions watch like vultures for the stragglers of caravans that took weeks to trudge by, the camels roped nose to tail, their backs loaded with merchandise, twenty thousand camels to a single caravan. Never again would they see the magnificence of a pilgrim emperor riding a milk-white camel with a saddle-cloth of scarlet and gold, whose slaves drove flocks of sheep before them for his sustenance, whose architects built a mosque wherever he rested on a Friday, whose treasure was so great that on reaching Egypt his princely expenditure depressed the price of gold. All such splendour had faded; but at certain times of year camels still plodded north and east with corn and kola nuts for the desert settlements, and carried cloth and worked leather a thousand miles to Mediterranean cities, taking with them pilgrims who, at some sandy junction, would diverge and travel slowly towards the valley of the Nile.

These pilgrims, too, were astir early, rolling their few posses-sions into bundles and eating their simple breakfast under the stars. Years might pass before they would see again the doors of their own houses, and some were looking for the last time on these familiar things; hardships lay ahead of them, poverty, hunger and thirst; yet they were full of joy at the start of their adventure. For they knew themselves privileged above their fellows to earn a measure of holiness and to draw closer to their God. If fate decided that their bones must lie in a distant grave, so be it, for wherever they rested, their soul was God's, and they would die on a road leading to the springs of grace.

Ibrahim, lately the court interpreter, was among these pilgrims, dignified and venerable in his long gown and his draped head-cloth. Temperate living had left him spare and vigorous, and now, his post relinquished, his two wives provided for and his elder sons out in the world, he could devote his last years to his true interest: the worship of God and the preparation of his soul for immortality.

Before the last of the travellers had passed through the crumbling ramparts, the sky ahead was luminous and behind them the moon was going down. The stars, at the start so brilliant and so many, slowly withdrew their light; soon the horizon's dark perimeter could be seen against the sky. The crisp, cold, magical smell of dawn stung their nostrils. As the caravan wound along a dusty track with grass on either hand, object after object began to reveal itself in dim outline: first the swaying necks of the camels, then the covered heads of their drivers and the queer-shaped loads, finally the trees and grass beside the road, and long-horned cattle lifting their faces in gentle curiosity.

Soon the sky flushed a faint pink, and the whole earth busied itself with preparations for the sunrise. From the travellers, a voice rose in a high chant. The camels, waving like snakes their arrogant and foolish noses, came to a halt. Men dismounted, others on foot put down their bundles and, while the camels stood nose to tail, all turned their faces to a glowing sky. The same voice rose again, high and musical, leading the prayer, and all the men's voices joined in, chanting familiar verses in praise of God in unison, and in unison bending their foreheads to the ground. Praise be to God, the lord of all creatures, the most merciful, the king of the day of judgment! As they reached those words the first brilliance of the sun flooded over the horizon and everything—the tree-trunks and tall grasses, the patient camels, the red road—was suddenly suffused with gold.

Robert stood a little apart, his arms folded, watching the scene. Dressed now, like his companions, in the robes of a Moslem and the folded cloths that would shelter his head from the desert sun, his lips moved as he followed the familiar chant, but he did not take part in the prayers. Outwardly impassive, he was inwardly stirred, for now he was at the start of a journey he had hankered after for many years, a journey down trade routes that had been old when the Romans had used them, to oases where empires had stood when England was a war-torn island. There had thrived the lost pagan kings of buried Ghana who had tethered their chargers to a single nugget; the Berber kingdom of Audoghast, trading in gold and ambergris, famed for its cooks and its damsels; the empire of the Almoravids which spread into Spain and crushed the Christian kings; the Negro dominion of Songhai, so stuffed with riches that golden chains leashed the hounds of its rulers and the value of a civet cat was ten times greater than a slave. From these kingdoms and cities had come wave after wave of austere fanatics, their faith and belligerence fused by the desert's heat into a crystal harder than diamonds, to conquer and purge the softer lands of Mediterranean and tropic and to found new dynasties in place of those rotted by luxury and power.

Just after the sun rose he glanced back towards the city; its fallen walls lay blackly against a saffron sky. Beyond, he could see the dome of the mosque and the tower of the palace, surely for the last time. He would leave behind no monument, and in a year no one would remember his name. His hopes and fears and all the effort of his working days already lay as deeply buried in oblivion as the old imperial capitals that now slept under the sand. Yet he regretted neither the years he had spent there nor the fact of his departure. Since he had made his decision, he had known a peace to which he had long been a stranger, and had made his preparations with a calm detachment that had come to him unasked and taken him unawares. It was, perhaps, the resolution of conflict that brought him comfort: a life-long conflict between opposing impulses, the lift of the wing and the tug of the root. All his life the pilgrim had been bound to the bailiff, the nomad to the slave, and it had been the wanderer who had worn the chains. Now those chains had been struck off. Drawing a deep breath of the fresh morning air, he watched long shafts of golden light pick out the trunks of trees, the pale grasses and the shaggy camels, creeping upwards with a deft certainty. The very air tasted of freedom, and the taste was sweet.

Without haste, the caravan collected itself together and proceeded on its way. In the cool of the morning Robert preferred to go on foot. He trudged beside Ibrahim's camel, sometimes exchanging a few words with his companion, the caked dust soft under his sandalled feet and in his ears the music of creaking ropes, voices shouting to each other in good-natured banter, sometimes the squawk and flutter of a startled bird; but for the most part he walked in silence, his mind busy with the past. Looking back, it seemed to him that all his life had been spent in conflict with the machine to which he belonged, and that this conflict had been doomed from the start to absolute failure, since the direction of a machine cannot possibly be changed by one of its cogs or pinions; indeed, to prevent any such aberration is one of the principles of its construction. Slowly he came to accept the truth (an old truth, he knew, however frequently forgotten) that the faults must be corrected not in the structure of the machine, by making this or that adjustment, but in the human mind and heart that designed it. If men and women were base and selfish, if they put profit above virtue, expediency before justice and themselves over all; if, in brief, they sinned, it was not to be supposed that they could build a virtuous engine, with each part smoothly fitted and honestly contrived.

Nor (it seemed to him) could they start on that correction while, afraid to face their own unfitness, they turned themselves into gods. Narcissus-like, they saw reflected in the pool's water the face of humanity and worshipped it: believing, apparently, that a corrupt and self-seeking individual multiplied by many millions, and merged with the dead and the unborn (all equally corrupt and self-seeking) became mysteriously the ultimate good. They bowed down not to the sticks and stones of the heathen they despised but, with greater depravity, to flesh and blood, to their equals, to their own reflections, excusing their faults because they were human, and the human the source of the divine.

From this heresy he was seeking to escape, not because he was defeated but because the true fight had not begun. For if the wrongness of institutions sprang from the evil in the men who made them, the place to start was not at the end but at the source; and since the most a man could hope for was some measure of control over a single heart, and that his own, the field for the reformer lay very close at hand. And since the old path had led only to failure and humiliation he would explore a new one that led among strangers and through the beauty of the wilderness. For it could be no accident that from the desert's recesses and fringes had emerged those ascetics and mystics who had told of things beyond the lust for domination of which the world's history was made: of truth reached through simplicity, love through abnegation, strength through privation; of the lineaments of glory glimpsed through the spare rocks and buff soil and in the hard unclouded stars.

A shout passed from mouth to mouth along the line of travellers and all save the camel-drivers turned to look back. The flat low roofs of the city, illumined by a climbing sun, just showed above the flat horizon, and with another bend in the road would be lost to view. Ibrahim turned also, and said:

"God be with the men of the city, and with their children. Many months will pass before I shall see my wives and sons again."

"God keep them," Robert echoed.

"And you?" Ibrahim asked. "Will you return?"

"I shall travel for a while with the caravans, perhaps to Fezzan, to Tripoli, to Marrakech. And I shall search for the ruins of ancient kingdoms, for I am much interested—as you know, Ibrahim—in records of the past, and I have a mind to write, one day, a learned history. For the rest, I shall follow where fortune leads me, but to the city, I do not think that I shall ever return."

"I wonder that you go on foot, or on the lumbering camel, amid all the discomforts of the journey, when the aeroplanes of your brothers pass over the desert, I am told, in a single day's journey. Had I the wealth I would fly like a bird to Mecca, for the greater glory of God."

"You know your destination," Robert answered, "and I do not; that is the difference between us. And from the air men look like beetles—all alike, and all trivial; but from the ground a few seem to have the stature of giants, and that is how I prefer to see them."

"It is good for a man to travel," said Ibrahim. "It hardens the spirit as well as the muscles, but he needs a home and a woman to come to at the end."

Robert was silent, striding on with the caravan. He could think of Priscilla now without bitterness, but not yet without grief. She lived in his mind as she had been in her youth, gay and enthralled by her surroundings, loving and gentle; the later years had been expunged from his memory; but for the heart he had lost there could be no substitute. He thought that if love was a burden, then he travelled light. As water to the body, so love to the spirit; you could carry little with you but must find it or perish as you went along, and the route, like the tracks of caravans, was lined with the skeletons of the unsuccessful. But love rose from many springs, and as the dourest and most blistering desert concealed oases where birds sheltered in the shade of trees, so it was to be met with in the harshest places, and no journey need be without hope.

Already the sun was hot on their shoulders and the dust, churned by the feet of camels, rose up to sting their eyes and cake on their sweating faces. To their right lay the last spur of craggy terraced hills rolling away to the south, in front a vast tree-dotted plain that merged gradually into desert. Every day, as they approached it, the heat would grow stronger, until the long thin column of men and camels would enter that baked, bleached furnace that stretched between the Barbary coast and the Beled-es-Sudan.

Robert glanced back once more, but the walled city had disappeared and a cloud of red dust had risen up to obscure the horizon.

THE END